Of Dreams and Embers

PATTI E. JONES

To all those who believed and encouraged all my crazy adventures.
Especially, my incredible mother!

To all those who want to write, but don't believe they can.
Start and see where the adventure takes you!

Nadia knew she was asleep, but that didn't stop her from enjoying the wind as it sang through the sea of hundred-foot pine trees. She wandered down an animal path, brushing her fingertips over the scaly, brittle bark of the massive trees, feeling the life underneath almost aching to get out, to explore. She felt blissfully small as she wished, not for the first time, to not just commune with nature but to communicate as well. The wondrous stories the ancient trees could tell—

"Excuse me."

A strangled gasp moved up Nadia's throat as she spun to find a stuffy-looking middle-aged woman standing a few feet away. The woman was painfully out of place in the thick forested landscape.

"I am sorry for the scare," the woman said without a hint of sorry. She pushed a strand of hair into the tight bun on the back of her head and sniffed as a damp leaf stuck to her bare leg above her sensible flats. She flicked the leaf and straightened her black pencil skirt before looking down her nose. "Are you Nadia?"

Taking a step away from the woman, trickling fear still gripping her, Nadia nodded.

"Good," the woman checked her watch before pushing a pristine leather briefcase into Nadia's arms. "Hold this, please."

Nadia did, looking between the case and the

woman's face. The woman had deep-set frown lines around her thin, tightly pursed lips. *Does she ever smile?* Nadia thought even as her muscles remained tight with anticipation, all thoughts of a quiet forest walk gone. "Excuse me? Who are you?"

The woman snapped the case shut. "I am a gatekeeper of Baako, duty-bound to prepare you to travel."

"Travel? Travel where?"

The woman snatched her briefcase back, setting it propped against one leg. "Normally, you would travel on your eighteenth birthday and have more time for introductions during an extensive training period, but that's one of many luxuries not afforded to you." The woman whipped out a tape measure, jotting down Nadia's 5'5" height. "Your guardian has been assigned, is leaving training early, and will await your arrival."

"Guardian?" Nadia asked. "I don't understand. Are you selling something?"

"Please do not interrupt," the woman said, glancing around. Nervousness was etched all over her jerky movements, reminding Nadia of a tall, rail-thin bird. "I don't like being off-site, but I need a few answers before I can leave. Can I assume this outfit is fine for travel, and all the pieces exist outside of this place?"

"Exist?" Nadia looked down at her favorite jeans, oversized t-shirt, well-worn tennis shoes, and a paint-splattered sweatshirt tied around her waist. "Yeah."

"It says here you don't have any medical needs," the woman said.

"Right. But how—"

"Except you're clearly overweight."

"Hey." As self-consciousness flooded her mind, Nadia shrank in on herself like she always did when her weight was mentioned. But feeling small and becoming small were two different things.

"You've no real combat training?"

"Combat training?"

"Other than theatre combat? That's useless," the gatekeeper noted on her sheet.

"Is this a joke? Who'd you say you are?"

"A gatekeeper of Baako," she over-enunciated her words.

"Baako?"

"Who is your father?"

"My father?"

"Yes."

Nadia's face heated. "I don't know."

"Good, good."

"Good?" Nadia was a jumble of emotions, but anger was starting to overpower the rest.

The gatekeeper jotted a few more notes. "Please sign here." The woman handed Nadia a paper and pointed to a line on the bottom.

Nadia gripped it, seeing nothing through the gathering exasperated tears. The skinny, stuffy vulture called her fat and stupid without even trying, triggering other shame-filled memories like when Janelle, her grade school bully, used Nadia's weight to strip her of her humanity over and over.

"Hurry up, please. I'm extremely busy."

"No," Nadia said to both the gatekeeper and the memory of Janelle oinking at her.

"No?" The woman's eyebrows rose so high they were in danger of merging with her hairline. "What do you mean, no?"

"I'm not sure what I'm signing or where you intend me to travel."

"Really?" the woman asked.

"Also, you're kind of rude—"

"According to our records," the gatekeeper pulled a paper out of the briefcase with a flourish. "You're not satisfied with a normal life; you want adventure, and you have a hero's heart to a fault."

Nadia opened and closed her mouth several times. Whatever she had expected the woman to say, it wasn't that.

"You're a deft hand at growing things and find peace and kinship with nature," the woman gestured at the scene Nadia's subconscious had created. "You've shown an aptitude for gifts that should have been made dormant, and you have created and manipulated seer dreams. Correct?"

"My dreams are elaborate," Nadia said, looking around. "But seer?"

"Last, your mixed blood and potentially long heritage make you a target for evil and a candidate for the prophecy."

"Woah, what? Mixed blood? Prophecy?"

"Your ignorance is not my problem." The woman sniffed. "You'll learn more when you arrive. Now, will you sign it or not?"

Adventure? She thought. *I mean, this isn't real, so what harm can come from signing it?*

She did want to do more, to be more than average.

Action, adrenaline, and not boring were hard to find when taking college classes during her senior year of high school. Every day was work, study, sleep, and repeat. No time or desire to experience high school, but too awkward to enjoy college.

"Do you have a pen?" Nadia's hand extended as she glanced over the paper. She jerked her hand back as the tip of the woman's pen jammed into Nadia's finger.

"Owe," Nadia said. "Are you kidding me?"

The gatekeeper pressed Nadia's finger on the paper, leaving a single bloody dot before whisking it out of Nadia's hand.

"That's all I need at this time. Enjoy your, uh, walk."

Nadia stared at the rude, pushy woman's retreating back before dropping onto a stump with her back against a tree.

"You're clearly overweight," she mocked as tears sprang to her eyes again. "Yeah, well, you should eat more," she yelled over her shoulder, but the woman was gone.

Nadia punched her fisted hands onto her thighs before remembering the pen prick. She stuck her finger into her mouth. *I just signed something in blood.*

She took a few more deep breaths to calm her raging emotions and checked in with her sleeping body. *I'm still in this beautiful forest and probably have several hours before I need to wake up.* She pulled her brown wavy hair out of its ponytail before putting it in a messy bun. "And I'm not overweight. I'm just chubby."

The woman was right about a couple of things,

though. Nadia loved growing things. She grew most of her plants indoors since she lived in the hot desert of Phoenix, Arizona. She loved her plant babies of all sizes and had pots all over her room, her little oasis in a house filled with two dogs, obnoxious younger sisters, and her parents, not to mention the constant stream of friends and family stopping in to hang out.

Nadia placed both hands on the trunk of a massive pine, trying to find her calm again. Her palms itched at the power she felt within the tree, a power she had felt while awake too, a power just out of reach but ever present. Her sleeping body snuggled into her bed, using the too many blankets as body pillows and the too many pillows as something to kick while she slept. Thoughts of her half-finished essay and her untouched math assignment crept into her mind, almost causing her to wake.

"Well, this dream was kind of a drag." Nadia looked around. "Time for a new setting."

The forest faded to black before being replaced with the desert landscape of north Phoenix, her home for the last fifteen years. Everything glowed in the bright sunlight of midmorning. She breathed in with her whole chest, recognizing the sweet smell of fresh rain on water-starved plants. The anxieties of her waiting homework and the rude gatekeeper melted away until wings flapping in the distance overwhelmed her senses.

A massive bird blotted out the sun as it moved enormous wings up and down in a steady rhythm, getting closer and closer. The black feathers and white poof around the lower part of its long neck emphasized the scaly head of the vulture's oversized body as it sat forward, head pointing at Nadia. The size of the bird was three or four times that of a vulture of any kind, but the strangest part was the bird's resemblance to Janelle, the bully. Blonde hair and a constant sneer as if everything and everyone was beneath her and smelled horrible.

A smile crossed Nadia's face. *Fun,* she thought, thrilled to have a real dream with action and possible vengeance. *What superpower do I want tonight?*

Nadia's feet slowly left the ground as she began to fly up toward the villain of her new dream.

"Too fat to fly faster?" Janelle, the vulture, asked in the gatekeeper's voice. "I guess it's true; pigs do fly."

Nadia's sleeping body turned over in bed, throwing off her blankets as her body heated with rage. She clenched her hands into iron fists in her dream, swinging at the vulture's body as they collided mid-air.

"I." Punch. "Am." Punch. "Not." Punch. "Fat."

2

"Dimitri!" Lucian's voice boomed over breakfast, startling Dimitri to his feet.

"Sir?" Dimitri asked, fear creeping across his scalp.

"Come with me." Lucian left the multipurpose room.

Most of the day, it was a training room, but at dawn and 8:00 pm, it became a dining hall.

"What the hell'd you do this time, D?" Big Willis asked as Dimitri gathered his breakfast to throw most of it away.

"No clue," Dimitri said.

"Leave your tray. I'll take care of it."

"Earning your name again, Big Willis?" Dimitri tried to smile as Big Willis reached for the food Dimitri had left on his tray. "Wish me luck."

Being called to Lucian's office again could not be good. Dimitri wished he'd stretched. The last time he was asked to visit Lucian's office, Dimitri was made to run for twelve hours as a punishment for being too 'gentle' in a sparing match with a younger, smaller trainee.

"Hurry up and close the door." Lucian's voice rang out, and Dimitri ran the last few steps, shut the door, and stood straight with his arms bent and his hands at his lower back. "Why you, of all the guardians in training, I will never know."

"Sir?" Dimitri asked after a long, uncomfortable

pause.

"You have a charge arriving in sixty hours, about a five-day hard hike from here."

Dimitri would have laughed, but knew better, "So I need to run all the way there?"

"Yes."

I'm a guardian? Dimitri silently questioned. His body surged, and his stomach dropped as he stared just over the head of the man who said he would never get a charge, amount to anything, or leave the training camp. "Is there anything I need to know about this charge?"

"She's coming from Earth in a hurry, so her exact location is unknown. I've her general whereabouts."

"Why's she coming in a hurry?"

Lucian looked up slowly from the scribbled paper he held, and Dimitri clenched, having crossed some invisible line.

"Sorry, sir." Dimitri stood a little straighter. *Shut up or he'll never let you leave.*

"Information like that is not given to us. We show up. We guard. We try to survive."

"Yes, sir."

"You're not to bring her back here for training."

Dimitri's mouth fell open for less than a second before he locked a blank look back on his face. *No training,* he thought. *That's not normal. Do I have to train her?*

"Dimitri, are you listening?"

"Sorry, sir."

"You leave in thirty minutes. Pack powder, food, and a blanket for your charge. The rest is up to you."

"Thank you, sir." Dimitri turned to leave.

"Dimitri, try not to get your charge killed." Lucian shifted before standing. "You were one of the hardest, most irritating people I have ever had to train, and I'd hate for you to die before you learn I am right about everything. Now go."

Chapter

3

Beep. Beep. Beep.

"Dang it!"

Nadia reached out for her phone to turn off her 6:30 a.m. alarm.

I could have won. She smiled widely, remembering how vulture Janelle started to tailspin out of the sky right before Nadia woke up. She took a deep breath and pushed the dreams aside to run through what the day would hold.

Tuesday.

School.

English, math, and communication.

No work today.

Homework.

Knocking startled her out of her list.

"Nadia? You awake? You need to leave soon." Her mother spoke quietly through the door.

"I'm up, Mom. Thanks." Waking up to her mom's voice was an everyday occurrence and one she didn't mind.

Climbing over all her remaining pillows, she placed her feet on the soft, lavender, shag carpet she had added to her room. She sat on the edge of the bed, head in her hands. She was only three weeks into the fall semester. But she'd already rather sleep than get to class on time. *Mornings are dumb*, she thought.

Nadia was grateful that her dual-enrollment courses were all on the college campus and that she only had to go to the high school for graduation meetings and an occasional advisor visit. But mornings were still hard and always had been.

She wore a pair of blue jeans, a loose T-shirt, and tennis shoes, all well-worn and comfortable. After a quick look at her hair, she brushed through the frizz and ran some product through it before putting it up in a messy bun. She slapped on some mascara and half-jogged into the kitchen, backpack bouncing off one shoulder.

"Here." Nadia's mom handed her buttered toast with peanut butter.

"Thanks, Mom." Nadia took a big bite and gave her mom a one-armed hug.

A few minutes later, Nadia was pulling out of the driveway when her fourteen-year-old sister, Cassandra, ran toward her car with her ten-year-old sister, Hazel, hot on her heels.

"You forgot this, dork." Cassandra handed the phone through the window. "Try not to forget it somewhere random today."

"Shut up," Nadia said with a grin, though she often forgot her phone all over the place. "Try to earn your phone back today," Nadia yelled as Cassandra walked back toward the house. Cassandra waved with one finger.

"I saw that," Hazel said. "Mom!"

"You saw nothing." Cassandra chased Hazel toward the house as Nadia drove off laughing.

Air conditioning blasting, Nadia drove in silence, thinking through her day again. This time, she focused on how not to draw attention to herself. The other day, on the way to class, Nadia fell up the stairs at the feet of an older, much hotter student. He asked if she needed help, but Nadia only made a sort of grunting stammer before running up the stairs and into the bathroom. She could have cooked eggs on the heat coming off her face from the embarrassment. She considered dropping out of college, but then remembered how bad high school had been.

Plus, her English professor was great, super laid back, and kind. Nadia was a decent writer, but excelled in her college writing course.

"Write a small research paper based on something you like and has to do with your major," Nadia's English teacher announced a week ago.

Nadia had no major because she was a high school student, so the sky was the limit. She decided to study the psychology of dreaming. The research was interesting and overwhelming: houses represented self-image, teeth falling out meant someone toxic was around, pregnancy had nothing to do with babies, and everything to do with new beginnings. The subconscious fascinated Nadia just as much as nature called to her.

"Don't forget your first draft is due tonight at midnight," Nadia's English teacher announced ten minutes before class ended. "Enjoy the rest of your day."

As much as Nadia loved English class, she was equally afraid of her math class. Her math professor told them on day one that only idiots fail his class or even struggle with that level of college math. He was mean and almost cruel daily, showing nothing but disdain for all the students.

Nadia had never been bad at math, but was terrible at everything when someone told her it should be easy. She was convinced that a switch in her brain went off, causing her to be more stupid around intimidating people who judged the worth of others based on their intellect. Her fear of failure often caused her to push her physical and mental limits, or cause her body to freeze and her mind to turn to mush. It was always one or the other with no in between.

The moment her English class ended, she would start to sweat as heat rolled off her body. She never entered class first, but rushed to ensure she was not last. She walked to the middle of the old classroom, lowering herself into the chair-desk combo. She sucked in her tummy to make sure all of her would fit. She busied herself with getting her paper and pencil out, not making eye contact with anyone. The math teacher did not allow cell phones or computers to be out in class, so she tucked both away, still sweating profusely. The more she thought about the sweat on her hairline, upper lip, and rolling down her back, the harder she would sweat. She popped her bag on the desk and wiped her face on a napkin as discreetly as possible. She took slow breaths until the professor swept into the room and started writing on the old-school chalkboard. Scribbling math problems, breaking chalk, throwing the broken chalk, and grabbing a new piece to write three more problems.

"Do these," he barked. "Then we can discuss, or more likely, I'll talk, and you'll stare blankly like you are now... Go. Start."

After ten minutes of pencils scratching across paper, Nadia finished three of the six problems. The biggest issue was deciphering the numbers on the board. The professor's handwriting was awful, and his arm moved across the chalk, smudging most of the writing, but no one ever asked for clarification.

"Come on, people, this isn't hard," the professor said before he tapped, tapped, tapped on the chalkboard. "Two more minutes." Tap, tap, tap.

He worked through the problems at hyper speed for five minutes, scratching illegible numbers across the board before daring the class to ask questions. When no one raised their hands, he reminded them of the assignment due at midnight and swept from the room with thirty minutes remaining in the class. No one moved for an entire minute before a collective breath, chair scraping, and bag zipping were the only sounds.

Nadia had no idea what he had taught them, but was happy to leave early again and take her first full breath since entering the room.

After another boring communication class, she drove home, blasting classic rock.

"I love rock and roll," she sang as she entered the front door.

"Mom," Cassandra yelled. "Nadia is being weird again. Time to up her dose."

"Shut up, sweet sister," Nadia responded. "Or I'll sing for the rest of the night."

"Or, or, hear me out. You could stop singing now and forever, amen."

"Ha. Ha."

Cassandra bowed and walked up the stairs, bowing once more at the landing before disappearing up the last few steps.

"I love Rock and Roll too," Hazel yelled from the

family room.

"How was your day, sweet girl?" Nadia's mother asked the moment Nadia walked into the kitchen. Her mother was standing behind the kitchen island, putting away silverware.

The kitchen needed a makeover. The old countertop was chipped in several places around the edge, and one corner snagged on clothing if anyone walked too close to it. The cabinets had the typical wood grain, which clashed with the grey tile that had been put in a few years before. The kitchen table sat between the kitchen and the family room. The open floor plan allowed space to gather in both rooms and still feel together while they ate and hung out.

Nadia's youngest sister, Hazel, was sitting on the family room couch, watching a teenage vampire series while painting her toenails.

"Fine, but I have lots of homework." Nadia plopped into a kitchen table chair and pulled out her math homework. "And I don't understand any of it, but my teacher is such a jerk, so no one asks any questions."

"Well, I might be able to help while I make dinner."

"She's making grandma's spaghetti with pepperonis," Hazel said, bouncing up and down on the couch.

"Honey, can you turn that down a little so I can help Nadia study?"

Nadia loved her mother even though there was no chance her mother could help her with math. Since Nadia was little, everyone called her a clone of her mother: same hair, same eyes, same lack of understanding of math. For anything and everything else, Nadia went to her mother.

They were best friends, and Nadia could always talk to her mother no matter what.

"Okay, I need to figure out the answer or what math calls an answer to negative two X open parenthesis X plus three close parenthesis minus open parenthesis X plus one close parentheses times open parenthesis X minus two close parentheses."

"What?" Nadia's mom asked, still stirring the sauce.

"Is that math or English?" Hazel asked from the couch.

"Math," Nadia said, laughing.

"But there are letters." Hazel walked over to the table. "Why are there letters and parentheses?"

"Algebra, that's why." Nadia patted the chair next to her. "Sit. Let me show you what you have to look forward to."

"Show me too," Nadia's mom said, sitting on her other side.

For thirty minutes, Nadia tried to teach her mom and sister how to do algebra, even though Nadia wasn't sure she was doing it right. "So what do you do first?"

"The stuff in the parentheses."

"Right, and then?" Nadia asked.

"Ask why math would use letters instead of numbers," Hazel said, getting up. "Good luck." She went back to her show.

"Sorry, honey." Nadia's mom stood up, too. "I don't think I'll be any help, but you seem to understand it."

"Maybe. But when I get to class, I freeze." Nadia shuddered at the thought of going back.

"It sounds like your teacher is a bully." Nadia's

mom stirred the sauce. "Is he mean to you or everyone?"

"Everyone."

"And no one has done anything about it?"

No, Nadia thought. *No one. But someone should.*

Chapter

4

Fifteen minutes later, Nadia had not figured out the answer to her math or how to deal with her math teacher, but she had moved her stuff so they all could eat dinner.

"Daddy," Hazel yelled as her father and Nadia's stepfather walked in. Hazel and Cassandra were Nadia's half-sisters.

"Hello, little monkey," he said, picking up Hazel. "How was everyone's day?"

Hazel was tall for her age and all arms and legs. It was always funny to see her dangling from anyone's arms.

"Nadia tried to teach Mom and me math problems with letters in them. It's so dumb!"

"Math with letters?" Nadia's stepdad asked, the excitement clear on his face.

"Yeah, algebra," Nadia said, grabbing five plates. "Hazel, grab the silverware."

"I'll get the silverware," Nadia's mom said. "Hazel, go get Cassandra for dinner."

"Okay," Hazel half ran, half skipped out of the room. "CASSANDRA," she screamed from the bottom of the stairs.

"I could've done that," Nadia's mom mumbled, shaking her head.

"What?" Cassandra asked.

"DINNER!" Hazel skipped back into the room and sat at the end of the table.

"I can help with your math," Nadia's stepdad offered.

"No, no," Nadia said, waving him off. "It's pretty easy," she lied. "I was just teaching Mom and Hazel, that's all."

Nadia learned early on that her stepdad was a very frustrating teacher, trying to teach all the sides and angles of math without regard for understanding or comprehension. Basically, Nadia would get the answer right, and he would say, "Yes, but…" before launching into a different and beyond complicated way of getting the same answer. She always walked away far more confused than when she started.

After dinner, Nadia fought with her math but switched to her English essay anytime someone asked what homework she was working on. She spent far less time than she wanted on dream research, but after her family went to sleep, she focused on the unfinished math homework. She struggled to start and restart each problem over and over again, trying every formula she found online, watching tutorials, and using math cheats.

By the time she left the kitchen table, everyone else had gone to sleep. Even the dogs were curled up and snoring on the family room couch while Hazel's show still played on the TV.

Nadia watched a few minutes of the show. One hot vampire brother loved the girl of the other hot vampire brother, and she couldn't choose. It ended with her walking alone on the beach, torn between the two men.

Dumb, Nadia thought as she climbed into bed. *Though those vampires were hot.* Giggling, she rolled over, ready for a better dream than the night before. *I wouldn't mind a hot vampire dream.*

She woke up disappointed after not dreaming at all. Dreamless nights often left her feeling a little empty, but she had no time to think about it.

Wednesday.

History.

Math.

Work.

Homework.

Math was only fifty minutes, so she had it four days a week. Dread swept through her since Wednesday was the day he always went through the answers to the homework, and where Nadia found out how bad she had done. Thursday was the weekly math quiz, another painful class period. He liked to grade the quiz the moment it was put on his desk. He would laugh, scoff, and even throw things as people were leaving. But first, history.

When Nadia arrived at the history classroom, a note on the door said, "Class cancelled."

Great. Now, what do I do for the next hour and a half?

She found a table down the hall from her math classroom. She opened her next math homework on her computer but did nothing with it, opting to people-watch instead.

Nadia took college classes during her senior year of high school because they were free, she wanted to get ahead, and she was so sick of high school, especially the schedules, the lack of choice in assignments, the control everyone else had over her every move, and the people.

Janelle and her gang of popular girls had targeted Nadia since the third grade. In their opinion, Nadia was always too fat, frumpy, annoying, or a know-it-all. However, they were not smart enough to take college courses, so Nadia was safe from their taunts and stares.

But Nadia was awkward and had not made any college friends yet. She went to class, tried to learn something, and went home to study. Everything repeated, and everything was boring.

An hour before math class, Nadia decided to find an adventure or at least a new building she hadn't explored. She stumbled around campus until she found the library, but had to turn right back around the moment she found it. She walked into math class with a few minutes to spare, but the professor was already there.

He watched her cross from the door to her seat, take out her notebook, and try to discreetly dry the nervous sweat that had appeared the moment she entered the room. She glanced up as she took out a pencil, and he was still watching her.

"Are you finally ready?" he asked Nadia.

She glanced at the clock, and so did the professor. There were still a couple of minutes before class.

"The sooner we start, the sooner we end," he announced, sweeping up to the chalkboard. "So if you are settled and ready, we will begin."

Heat rose up Nadia's face, and the sweat poured down her back. *He's a bully,* she thought over and over, wanting to say something, but her tongue felt huge, and her mouth was completely dry.

Her rage was barely contained as the math professor

jumped into a lecture on how terrible everyone did on their homework and how they would all fail if they didn't study for at least three hours or more. The lecture continued so long that Nadia noticed a few people lower in their chairs or wiping their eyes. He was destroying everyone's self-esteem, and for what?

He turned back to the chalkboard, chalk raised, when a voice rang out in class for the first time.

"If we're all failing, doesn't that show it's a you issue rather than all of us?"

Nadia realized far too late that she had spoken.

"Excuse me?" the professor asked, turning toward the class.

Nadia shrugged as everything she felt about the teacher poured out. "You don't teach us anything. You write illegibly and wipe half of it away. You insult us but give us no help." She stood slowly, unsure if it was to emphasize her words or to get ready to flee. "You sweep in and out of the classroom like some villain in your own twisted story of power and privilege. You teach in a community college surrounded by, what, twenty other community colleges. You're no more impressive or important than anyone else. I came here to learn, but you came here to lord over a room of people. This isn't your kingdom." Nadia was trembling all over as she lost the nerve to keep talking, only half aware of what she had said.

Nadia had been bullied most of her life and often didn't fight back to help herself. But she could not stand by and watch others get bullied, no matter who the bully was. She always fought for others, often without thinking it through.

"How dare you?" the professor said.

"She's not wrong," a voice rang out behind Nadia.

"Yeah, I've never struggled in a math class before yours," someone else said.

"We have fifty minutes. Can we use all of it?" another voice asked.

"Enough," the professor said. Unblinking, he stared around the room as Nadia lowered herself back into her seat, weak-kneed. After a painfully slow head-turn, the professor said, "Fine. If you participate by asking questions, I will slow down and write more clearly. But in the future, speak with respect." He looked right at Nadia.

She looked right back. He had the smallest smirk, and was that respect in his eyes? Then he whipped back around to face the chalkboard.

Nadia slumped in her seat, all her adrenaline gone as she took the first understandable math notes of the semester. Forty-five minutes into the class, the professor asked, "Any more questions?"

Nadia shook her head like others in the room, and he swept out less dramatically than usual.

"Nice work," an older woman, a few rows away from Nadia, said. "This was the first time I understood his lesson."

"Oh," Nadia started, pride gently warming her. "My mouth started talking before I decided to say anything. So, ya know." Nadia smiled as she looked away.

"Well, you may have saved my grade," the woman said. "See you tomorrow."

Nadia stopped in the bathroom on the way to her car. She changed for work and threw water on her face.

Holy crap. I just told that dude off and then learned math. She wasn't sure which was more surprising. She leaned into the mirror, looking at her chubby face and bright eyes. "Now that felt like an adventure."

Chapter

5

An ocean dream, Nadia thought disdainfully as she became aware she was dreaming.

The vastness and unpredictability of the ocean and its inhabitants always overwhelmed her, and dreams set near water or, worse, in water, usually meant something in her waking world was making her feel small or anxious.

"Anxious," she said to the empty white sands and the occasional empty lifeguard stands.

Math is already stressful enough, and now I have to deal with sea creatures. I can't have a peaceful walk through the woods or a fun action scene? Nope, I get a freaking ocean dream.

White foam rode a wave to the shore, rolling and tumbling mindlessly, only to disappear on the sand.

"This is your dream," Nadia shuddered. "You're in control."

Nadia still loved to dream even though she didn't control every aspect of her dreams. Instead, she could adjust slightly in the moment by giving herself a little superpower or a weapon, but the plot, scenery, and emotions were rarely controlled and far less predictable. There were even times she was unaware she was dreaming. Regardless, all of her senses were engaged, and she often woke worn out and even a little beat up, though she never had any physical bruises or injuries. Those mornings made her fear that one day, she would lose control of a dream and get injured or die in real life.

The full moon illuminated the dark, choppy waters and white sandy beaches, throwing the empty world into sharp relief.

"Are we going to do this, or is this a walk around, doing nothing kind of dream?" She asked as she glanced out at the waters, starting to feel bored.

In the distance, a buoy showed for a moment, waving and splashing in the water before disappearing. Wait. Not a buoy. A boy?

His hands were thrashing until the waves swallowed him.

Nadia leaned forward, tension rising as she waited for him to reappear. Her breath caught as she internally debated entering the dark, foamy waters of the ocean to save the boy. When he reappeared for only moments, she tossed her sweatshirt and shoes, hesitating for seconds at the water's edge. "Ocean dreams," she scoffed, running into the warm waters before diving into the waves, breaking through the white caps and pushing past the weight of her wet clothing. Salt water stung her eyes and swirled in her mouth.

Her belief in the reality of the situation grew every time the boy dropped out of sight or a wave slowed her progress. *Come on,* she thought, the salt thick on her tongue.

After what felt like an eternity, she was only five feet away from the boy.

But he was not a boy, nor was he struggling.

He was a balding, middle-aged man and he was laughing.

Nadia gasped, taking in a mouthful of ocean brine. He had deep orange eyes.

"Sir?" she asked.

"Sir," he mocked.

"Are you okay?"

The laugh that exploded from him was cruel, floating across the water like a specter seeking a body.

Nadia bobbed in the water, kicking to stay afloat while indecision held her in place. "You looked like you needed help." Fear prickled in the back of her mind.

"You swam," he began, choking on his obvious glee. "You swam all the way out here to save me."

"I thought..." She was swimming backward to put distance between herself and the insane man, hyper-aware of how alone she was in the last place she ever wanted to be.

It's a dream, she told herself. *Not the ocean. It's only a dream.*

"As a thank you, let's play a game," he said, becoming serious. He stood still and straight, only half in the ever-moving water, but his clothing and skin were completely dry.

"How are you doing that?" Nadia asked, soaked and still treading water to stay afloat.

"Let's play 'what brushed your leg' or what I like to call 'what wants to eat me.'"

"It's only a dream. I'm in con—"

Nadia's head disappeared below the surface as something yanked her under. Reemerging, she spluttered and gagged, fear turning her mind to mush. Hooking her arms under her knees, she tried to pull her knees to her chest, but sank like a stone. Dropping her legs, she desperately tried to move the water aside to see the creature swimming around her. When that failed, she scrambled toward the shore. Dread overwhelmed her senses, making it hard to breathe, let alone swim.

Please, she thought as she imagined becoming dinner for a kraken or a great white, tearing her limb from limb, leaving this world screaming in pain. *I hate the ocean. I'll fight this dude anywhere else, just not here.*

No matter how hard she kicked, the beach never came any closer, the dream didn't change, and she gained no more control.

The sound of the man laughing was all Nadia heard as she was yanked under again.

Kicking as hard as the water would allow, her foot slid over something slimy, causing her body to recoil. Resurfacing only inches from the man's face sent her body into fight mode. She threw a startled punch, just missing his face, before kicking wildly for shore again, thinking of nothing but dry land and safety. But each stroke only brought her forward inch by excruciating inch.

"Nadia?" the man asked. "Leaving so soon?"

Glancing over her shoulder, she could see how little effort the man put into chasing her. He appeared to be gliding through the water without affecting it. Panic surged as she realized he would easily catch her.

"No," she mouthed between breaths. "I'm in control." Her real body ached with terror as her dream became more real for her. She felt like death was moments away, and there was nothing she could do about it. Her heart pounded in her throat. She imagined what drowning must feel like at the hands of this strange man, where no one would hear her cries for help.

"What was that? You want another game?"

"No," she sputtered as her mind clung to one idea: the shore was getting closer. It had to be or she wasn't going to make it.

"This one's called, you didn't know." He stretched out a hand to skim a finger over one of her bare feet while it kicked through the water.

Despite her almost overwhelming fear, his touch caused pure repulsion, which helped refocus her mind.

Live, she thought. *Fight.*

She glanced back, seeing a toothy, crooked smile spread across the man's pockmarked, aging baby face.

"It's simple," he continued. "I tell you what you don't know, and then you'll know. For example, you don't know how tired your arms are."

Nadia's arms suddenly ached as they sluggishly hit the water, trying to keep swimming, even as every movement cost her tremendous effort.

"What the? How?" She gasped out.

"You don't know your legs are so heavy in the water."

Slowing to a halfhearted doggie paddle as her legs stopped listening to her, Nadia screamed internally, willing her body to keep going.

"How are you doing this?" She asked through gulps of air.

The man reached his fat fingers toward her face, and she threw herself back out of his reach.

"Don't touch me," she said, panting.

"Such an attitude, Nadia. I like that." His toothy smile spread.

"Go to hell." She said through a mouth full of water as she barely remained afloat.

"Cute." His smile faltered. "But you don't know how hard it is to breathe."

He started to laugh again as Nadia leaned back, arms flung wide, willing her lungs to fill as a fire erupted in each of them, burning her from the inside out. Her head slipped below the surface for moments that felt like lifetimes.

The evil, pudgy man wrapped his arms around her chest, fingers skimming her body as he did before pulling her above the surface and pressing her body to his.

"Stop fighting," he said. "I'll save you." His crooked teeth glistened, and his moist, rancid breath was wet on her cheek.

Nadia's fist balled even as she filled her burning lungs with salty air. She twisted, throwing her arm back.

Shock flashed in his eyes just before her fist made contact with his face, but he didn't let go. One arm tightened as the other dragged her face closer to his.

"Stop, you wretched little girl," he growled. "You will learn to obey."

No more, she thought, barely listening to his ranting. She wound her hand through his remaining hair, yanking his head back.

He released her, fury written all over his purpling face.

"Don't touch me, creep!" she said, mustering as much disgust into her raspy voice as possible, trying to mask the almost overwhelming pain every breath caused in her chest.

"Really?" the man was, still dry except where her fist made contact. "You didn't know how heavy your waterlogged clothing is."

She desperately gulped burning breaths of air before her head slipped beneath the water again, her favorite jeans and T-shirt dragging her down. Her throat and chest constricted as she tried to resurface. Thoughts scrambled in her mind. The punch, the danger, her pending death, her desire to wake.

Fight, damn it, she thought, trying to get her legs to work, give herself superpowers, or a weapon. Anything to win, to survive.

Her feet hit sand and rocks only seven feet below the surface, and she realized, with a crushing blow, how close she had come to the shore. Her lungs screamed in agony. Her eyes burned as she searched through the salt water for some help, some rescue, but all she saw were the orange eyes of the man glowing softly and the moon over his shoulder, still, full, and bright, watching as Nadia gave up her life.

Can you die in your dreams? She wondered again as a sense of calm fell over her.

Not this one, she thought, as something inside of her, some unattainable power, twitched and jumped. *I'm in a dream. Only a dream. My dream.* She kicked hard for the surface. The fight back in her. The manipulation broken. "No," she said into the face of the startled man spraying water over his dry clothing. "No more games. Who the hell are you?"

"Is this not the adventure you asked for?" He rose out of the water before slamming all his weight down onto Nadia's shoulders, holding her under the water. "Is this not the adventure you wanted?"

Chapter

6

Nadia's arms shot up involuntarily as she squinted against the assaulting rays of the sun.

That dream was intense, she thought, closing her eyes. She took a few deep, steadying breaths, thinking about her latest villain. *Where in my subconscious did that guy come from?* She rubbed her eyes, surprised to find tears on her cheeks.

"It was only a dream," she said aloud. "You're safe, and you're being ridiculous. You dream all the time." She took another deep breath, breathing out all the fear still coursing through her body. "What's on today's list?" She glanced at her alarm clock. "What the…"

Where her clock should have been was a mossy boulder. Cocking her head to the side, she touched the foreign object in her bedroom, confused.

No, not in her bedroom.

She was not in her bedroom. Her safe bedroom on the ground floor of her mom and stepdad's house. Their annoying yappy dogs running around. Her two sisters being loud. Her plants. Her bed. Gone.

"What the hell!" She jumped up with scenario after scenario running through her head.

Kidnapped.

Tricked.

Sleepwalked.

Dead.

Still Dreaming.

She pinched the top of her thigh. "Ouch. Okay. Not dead, but that doesn't rule out kidnapping or dreaming."

She bit her lip and wrapped her arms around her chest to hold back the panic that was never far from the surface. Her pulse quickened as she turned and kept turning until her t-shirt snagged on a bush with bright pink berries.

"What the actual hell?" She was wearing her favorite blue jeans, a t-shirt, and tennis shoes, with her paint-splattered sweatshirt tied around her waist. All of which showed signs of her having slept on the forest floor.

She mindlessly brushed off the nature from her clothing as she took in the trees, bushes, underbrush, and wetness of an unfamiliar forest.

"I live in a desert." She brushed her fingers over the damp rock again.

If I'm not dreaming, where am I? She started to run through all the possibilities. *Not Phoenix. It's too wet and cold. More north? Midwest? Am I even in America?*

Teetering on the edge of a panic attack, she closed her eyes and started her quick grounding exercises. She tensed both of her arms. *Fine,* she thought, releasing them. Then, both her legs. *Fine.* Her back and chest. *Not awesome, but I apparently slept on a forest floor.* Her breathing sped up again, and dread stuck in her throat. *No, pick something and focus.* She opened her eyes, stared at the purple pine cones littering the ground, and traveled up the ancient pines around her. *Purple pine cones?* For only moments, her mind wrapped around that thought before fear turned her mind to emotional mush once more.

She tried to focus on the vibrant, almost glowing

green leaves on another massive tree. Then, the rocks and moss-covered boulders that were strewn throughout like a giant had dropped them wherever as he'd walked. She crossed to a small clearing covered in tiny wildflowers and tall grasses. The sugary-sweet scent of flowers filled her senses when a light breeze blew through the unfamiliar area.

More movement caught her attention, causing her body to freeze.

Squinting into the distance, she saw a massive black-blue panther run into the clearing fifty feet away before slowing to a walk as it stalked toward her. It panted as its chest pushed aside the wildflowers and grasses. With head held high and mouth open wide, all his sharp, menacing teeth could be seen from a distance. Its eyes were locked on Nadia.

Nadia stumbled back, tripped over her own feet, and landed hard on her left side. Lying in the dirt and flowers, she tried to see the giant cat without moving. Her heart pounded in her ears as she got into a crouch, popping out of the flowers like a whack-a-mole to see where the predator was.

Nothing.

Stand, she thought. *Stand, or he's gonna eat you where you fell. Don't be an easy meal.*

She stood, trembling all over with barely contained dread, scanning the entire field for movement.

Still nothing. The panther was gone.

A new sensation pushed past the fear.

Pain.

Pain from the fall washed through her, culminating

in her left hand. She moved to the nearest fallen tree. Her adrenaline speed out of her, replaced by shock and exhaustion. "Panthers don't live in forests, right? It was probably a house cat, and I'm an idiot. Or I'm still dreaming. Right, it's just a dream."

She sat on the damp log, pressing her palms into her thighs, willing herself to calm down and think. A blossom of blood appeared on the left thigh of her jeans, and she was immediately ten years old again, riding her brand-new ten-speed bicycle.

She had loved it. The speed and freedom as the wind had thrown her hair back. She had ridden for hours before taking a corner too fast, dragging her right hand and knee on the ground as she had crashed. Brushing off the pebbles and dirt had caused her injuries to throb, but it had been no big deal until she had noticed the blood.

Her head had swum, her vision had blurred, and she had woken up in a hospital bed. The cuts and tiny bit of road rash weren't bad. The concussion she had gotten from passing out and hitting her head on the curb was what had sent her to the hospital.

Her eyes focused on her current injury. *It's just blood.* She slid off the log so that it was pressed against her back, and she was sitting on the ground as she lifted her left hand. Her heart was beating in her palm, causing stabbing pain.

Beat, stab, beat, stab.

Blood started to pool around a one-inch thorn that was embedded in her palm.

Her stomach churned, threatening to empty as she reached for the thorn. She was almost grateful as tears blurred her vision.

"She's never going to be a nurse," her stepdad had said after the bike incident, and it became a long-running joke in her family. He was not wrong.

She ripped out the thorn, gripping it in her right hand as blood, dirt, and tears mixed together on her left palm.

"Stupid," she said before snapping her lips shut to prevent herself from vomiting. Her vision came in waves as she turned the bloody thorn in her uninjured palm. The slow but steady drip, drip, drip of her blood hitting dead leaves brought her back to the immediate issue and reminded her of the intense pain in her palm that she had only begun to feel. *I have no idea what to do. No phone. No idea where I am. No hospital.*

"I'm going to die," she said aloud. "I'm going to die in the middle of some stupid forest because of a stupid thorn and my own… my own… stupidity." She was furious at her clumsiness and ignorance. *I want to go home*, she thought. *I want boring. I want uneventful. I want anything but this.*

Movement cut her pity party short. The panther was back and much closer.

"Shoo, cat!" Nadia said, nausea still rolling through her body as pain blurred her vision. "Please." Fear saturated her voice even as embarrassment rose to her cheeks. *Who says please to a giant wild animal about to eat them?* She ran through every memory that might help, landing on a hunting documentary her stepdad used to watch.

Appear big, she thought. She threw her hands up,

flinging tiny droplets of blood as she waved her arms. "Shoo, cat!"

Her throat tightened as the panther weaved in and out of the trees on the edge of the clearing, getting closer and closer. She felt her spine tingle with the need to do something, anything. "Damn it, go away!"

He kept walking.

"Ya know what, fine! Eat me. I don't care. If you don't kill me, my hand will."

The panther cocked its head before walking behind a massive tree. A tall man with black, almost blue shoulder-length hair and deep brown skin stepped out from behind the tree. "Sorry for the fright. I needed speed, and my panther form is far faster, but I don't eat people." A smile danced on his round lips. "Do panthers eat people on Earth?"

"You're—" Nadia started.

"Late," he cut in. "Yeah, sorry about that. I got the notice kind of late, so I basically had to run for two days straight…" His smile faded as he looked her over. "You're hurt." He set down the bundle he had been carrying before crossing to Nadia.

"Wait," she said, swatting at him as her mind grew fuzzy. "You were a panther."

"Yes," he stopped a few feet from Nadia, concern edging his sharp features.

"How?" She shook her head, and the man, who was a giant cat, started to fade in and out of focus. Pain made her grip her bloody hand to her chest. "How's any of this possible?" She stumbled back, slurring her words. "Dreaming. That's it. Yeah, I'm still dreaming. Men can't be giant murder kitties."

"You're Nadia of Earth, right?"

"Of Earth?" The ground swayed as she gripped her pounding hand.

"You traveled—" he began, but Nadia cut in.

"What's happening?" She collapsed into the panther man's arms even as she fought him weakly, slurring her words. "Let go. I don't know you."

"Nadia," his voice sounded far away as he picked up her left hand, sniffing her palm. He searched her face in slow motion while his mouth moved.

"What?" She heard nothing but her blood roaring.

Chapter

7

Fear rose in Dimitri's chest as he half held Nadia's slumped, unconscious form.

Think, idiot, Dimitri thought. *What did you learn in training?*

"Not to leave the charge alone or let them get hurt immediately," he said aloud. "Perfect start."

Then Lucian's voice boomed in Dimitri's mind.

"Great Guardians forbid your charge gets hurt in your care, but if you fail them in some way, you need to know some basics. 1: warm, dry spot. Shelter is better, but you work with what you have. Cold can be deadly."

Dimitri laid Nadia on the ground before unloading the bag he carried.

He grew up with a healer and knew more than the basics Lucian had taught. Dimitri gently picked up Nadia's hand and sniffed it again. He immediately knew a datura plant had poisoned her. Most people from the area develop an immunity to the plant very early on, but having never been exposed to it, he knew Nadia was in for a rough time. He bathed her hand using her unconsciousness to poke around in the wound, making sure nothing of the thorn was left before rewashing it. Then he wrapped her hand tightly and laid it back down on her chest.

He pulled two blankets off his pack. One of the perks of the shifter gift was that everything he wore shifted with him, so he could carry more than most people. That never helped him during guardian training, though, because, as Lucian had repeatedly said, "Gifts are used as crutches and therefore will not be used here. Train without them or die using them."

Dimitri laid a blanket on a flat, smooth, grassy area, hoping the grass would make Nadia's temporary bed more comfortable.

He knew Lucian would have rolled his eyes or worse because he did not believe in comfort, and Dimitri had the scars to prove it.

He bent down and grabbed Nadia's arms, pulling her to a standing position before allowing her to fall over his right shoulder. He walked her to the grassy blanket area and gently lowered her back to the ground with a slight grunt. He must have been tired after his long run because Big Willis or BW had at least a hundred pounds on Nadia, and Dimitri had to carry BW all the time during training without a sound or complaint.

Dimitri knelt next to Nadia.

She's so unlike the women of Baako. Fierce almost. He smiled before silently chastising himself. *She's my charge, an asset, maybe even a weapon, that's it.*

He moved her hair, watching the contours of her face change slightly, wishing he could see what she saw. After a few minutes, he remembered his job was far more than healing or watching her sleep. He also needed to protect her. He walked several perimeters, scattering dried sticks to ensure he would hear anyone approaching. After a few minutes of internal debate, Dimitri cleared an area for a small fire pit in the most defensible location in the area.

No one should know she's here, he thought. *At least*

not yet. We'll be safe tonight.

When the fire was built up enough not to smoke, and Dimitri had a small pot of herbs and meat cooking over the open flames, he moved Nadia closer to the fire without allowing a sound to escape his lips this time.

"You'll be glad you did this when you have to carry your charge out of harm's way," his trainers had yelled. "Now move, or I'll know why." Dimitri had carried BW, a shorter, thick guardian-in-training, over one shoulder like a grain sack for three miles on one miserable, rainy day. The whole group had to stop when BW suddenly threw up all over Dimitri.

"What did Dimitri do wrong?" the trainer had asked while forcing Dimitri to stand at attention in front of everyone despite being covered in what Dimitri assumed was the partially digested slop they called morning breakfast.

"He bounces when he runs," BW had said between dry heaves. "He kept hitting my guts, and I just couldn't hang on anymore."

"You run like a sissy, little girl, Dimitri," the trainer had yelled in Dimitri's face. "How many times have I told you to run straighter and flatter, save your energy. You don't know when you'll need it." The trainer waited, but Dimitri knew better than to answer. "Now go clean up. You stink."

Dimitri shook the memory from his mind, opting to watch Nadia's eyes race behind her lids. *He can't pull her into the dream world,* he thought, stomach contracting painfully. *There's no way he knows she's here.* He covered Nadia with the blanket he brought for himself and waited, meditating over what their next move should be.

Nadia suddenly whimpered without opening her eyes. Then her body tensed before aggressively collapsing into fetal position.

"No. Dang it! Nadia, don't get pulled in. Time to wake up."

Chapter

8

Nadia woke at dusk, stiff, alone, and very cold. The clearing was silent and shrouded in mist, or was it her eyes unwilling to focus? She knew this dream, this place, but couldn't place it, couldn't remember.

Rolling onto her knees, she gently shook her head. A breeze licked at her clammy skin as it pushed through the dying flowers. *Wildflowers?* Her mind was a dark cloud of shifting images, each as far-fetched as the last: panther, thorn, orange-eyed creeps.

She brought her trembling left hand up, trying to focus on the damage, but it was wrapped in a thick, rough fabric. With her anxiety growing on the outer edge of her mind, she began to wander, easily ignoring how wrong the place felt.

There were no signs of life in the thinning forest. Her aching eyes squinted, trying to take in her surroundings, but nothing came into focus. Nothing made sense. She stumbled half-blind through the woods, stopping only when her growing headache became too much. Placing her fists against her eyes, she rubbed the pain, breathing slowly through her nose and out through her mouth for several long minutes.

Nadia thought about how her mom would rub her head and sing quietly off-key when she got horrible headaches as a kid. She would fall asleep with her head on her mom's lap.

Her mom back home.

Home, on Earth, the man said.

Man?

No, cat.

Big cat.

Where am I?

She opened her eyes, blinking several times. A room had appeared around her, but it had no visible doors and only a single window that took up almost one entire wall.

Nadia's mind felt like mush while it remained disconnected from her body. The growing fear in her gut didn't register, didn't tell her to run. Instead, her mind flooded with confusion and indecision.

The room was a dusty office with a gaudy, oversized antique desk, a threadbare carpet, and bookshelves. Nadia focused on a massive, throne-like chair beside the desk. It was an out-of-place, ornate, redwood mahogany monstrosity polished to a high shine. The back of the throne was four feet wide, covered in a thick, red velvet with intricate scales sewn into the cushion and pressed into the wood almost to the top of all seven feet. As her eyes traveled up the chair and over the delicately carved life-like cat eyes near the top, the prickle of fear became a steady stream. She imagined the eyes blinking and quickly looked away.

Inanimate objects don't blink, she told herself with a slight shudder.

Chairs also don't have lizard legs and massive, sharpened claws resting on two softball-size starlight rubies that topped staves, but this one did. The rest of the chair was painted or carved to look engulfed in dancing flames. The large arched window just behind the desk and chair had dusty, gray velvet curtains that looked like billowing smoke. Nadia could just make out a graveyard through the slits in the curtains. It was overgrown and unkempt, like the rest of the room.

"Time to wake up," she said, confident she was dreaming again, because she couldn't shake the feeling that everything was wrong, foreign, fake.

A hissing giggle rolled through the doorless room.

Nadia's stomach dropped as she spun slowly, searching the room for possible hiding spots where the giggling person could be. "Hello?"

No answer.

She looked at the chair again.

The chair's eyes blinked.

Chairs don't blink, she reminded herself, still staring.

It blinked again.

She stumbled back, hitting the far wall of the small room.

"Oh, child," the chair spoke in a deep, raspy voice, though it had no visible mouth. The male-sounding voice reverberated off Nadia's chest like too much bass at a rock concert. "Don't be afraid."

What the actual hell, she thought. "This isn't real," she said aloud. "This is a dream. This isn't real."

"Come. Sit."

"Chairs don't talk. Chairs don't giggle. You aren't real." She turned, feeling the wall for a secret door or some other way to escape, to wake.

"Rest your weary body."

"Nope. Wake up. Wake up." She reached the corner of the room, refusing to turn toward the chair.

"I'll take away your pain." The chair held the 'n' longer than necessary, drawing on Nadia's exhaustion and forcing her to look at him again.

"Pain?" she questioned, alarm bells ringing in her head. Looking down, she saw that the wrap on her hand was blood-soaked. "Am I dying?"

"You don't have to," the chair said.

"Am I already dead?"

"Not yet. Sit. I'll save you."

"No." She shook her head, making the room spin. "I'm good over here."

"Why do you fear me, child?" The chair's right-clawed hand was slowly rubbing the starlight ruby like a pet. "Just a few more steps."

Nadia realized she was walking forward like a marionette controlled by a puppet master. She mumbled over and over under her breath with each jarring step.

"What, child?" the chair asked.

"I said no."

"What?" the eyes closed slightly.

"I'm leaving." Anxiety urged her out.

"Wait. You can't. No one is ever this difficult."

"I'm not arguing with a chair. You're a figment of my subconscious."

"Are you sure?" The chair simpered, and Nadia paused.

"Yeah," Nadia said. "This is a dream."

"Stay. You're tired." The voice grew impatient, and

the edges of the chair started to blur.

"I can't be tired. I'm dreaming." Nadia moved to the desk.

"You don't understand. You have to obey."

"This is my dream." Lifting one of the large volumes off the bookshelf, Nadia stepped toward the window. "I control it. Not some chair."

The giant lizard arms swiped at Nadia, ripping her sweatshirt and slicing into her right arm. Nadia stared at her new, throbbing wound with confusion.

"You will come to me," the chair began to diminish. It reached for Nadia again, gripping her wounded right arm. "You'll stay for as long as I like. I control this place and you."

"Let go!" She fought through the pain with everything she had left. The claws didn't loosen as they pulled Nadia toward the chair. Inch by painful inch, she slid closer until she would have no choice but to sit. Her entire being told her sitting would be bad, really bad. She threw the large book at the chair with her damaged left hand and dug her fingers into the lizard's hand until she drew blood.

The chair screamed, releasing her.

Nadia scrambled back frantically, rubbing the blood from her fingers. She grabbed another book and chucked it at the window. The crack of the glass silenced the chair's raging before the next book flew through the window.

"I'll have you," the chair screamed, fading from view as the orange-eyed man from her ocean nightmare appeared in its place.

"You, again?" She hesitated for only a moment before scrambling onto the desk, kicking out the remaining glass, climbing slowly out of the window to prevent more injuries, and running through the hundreds of headstones as fast as her body would take her. She only stopped when she reached the edge of a cliff.

"Of course," she said as rain began to fall. "Only rain could make this better."

She didn't know why she couldn't wake up. She didn't know why the orange-eyed dude showed up in another dream. She was miserable, alone, and ached all over. Tears mixed with rain as they fell down her face.

I'm such a baby, she thought.

"Nadia," a man called from far off.

She glanced around startled, finding a cloaked figure behind her.

"Who are you?" Nadia asked.

He threw his hood back to reveal deep orange eyes.

"Nadia. Time to wake," a man called again from far off.

"Ignore him," the orange-eyed man said.

"What could you possibly want?" she asked the irritating orange-eyed jerk.

"It's what I can give you that matters. Come with me, and I'll show you."

"No thanks." Nadia felt a pull to wakefulness.

"Stay." He grabbed for her injured arm.

Without thinking, she stepped aside and watched as the man stumbled to the cliff's edge. He slipped, groping for anything that would keep him from falling.

"Help me!" He grabbed onto the wet foliage, sliding closer to his death.

Nadia didn't hesitate. "Hang on." She reached for

him with her bruised and bloody right arm.

The orange-eyed man clasped her arm before throwing himself at her with inhuman speed.

"Trying to save me again?" He laughed, knocking her onto her back. Swinging wildly at her face, he made contact with her forearms as she protected her head. "You can't win, you foolish little girl. You'll obey like all the others, or I'll kill you painfully. I don't care who wants you to live or what was foretold. I will end you."

Her anger rose as she rolled to the side, throwing him off balance but not dislodging him. Nadia threw a couple of wild punches, connecting with his ear and cheek. He whimpered, falling off her.

"That hurt," he said.

Nadia got to her feet, watching him in disbelief, knowing her punches were weak at best.

"I…" she started. "I have to go."

"You'll lose," he called from the ground. "And then I'll kill everyone you care about back on Earth before killing you."

Fear ran up Nadia's scalp as she turned to look at the stupid, little man still on the ground.

"You aren't real," she said, fighting the pull to wakefulness.

"I most certainly am. And I'm looking forward to when we meet again."

Chapter
9

Nadia's attempt to roll over in bed caused her to groan in pain.

"I'm seventeen," she said to no one, her eyes squeezed shut against the sun. "Why am I always in pain?"

She wiggled around, trying to find a comfortable position on the ground.

The ground?

Pushing herself up, she immediately gripped the wrist of her throbbing left hand as the memories of her most recent dream washed through her.

She took stock of the pains in her body. The blood-soaked wrap on her left hand didn't surprise her, but the three slices through her sweatshirt did. She pulled the sleeve up, revealing cuts and puncture marks on her forearm where the chair clawed her. Not the chair. The orange-eyed dream stalker.

"Freaking psycho." *Dream psycho.* She looked at her cuts again. Lowering her sleeve, she tried to ignore her growing anxiety that never seemed to go away.

"Who?" a man said, causing her to jump to her feet, raising her arms into a weak fighter's stance she had learned in her stage combat class.

"Dominant foot slightly back," her theater teacher had said repeatedly. "Both arms pulled up to protect your face. Squat a little, loose knees. Good."

"What are you going to do?" a small voice in her

head interrupted. "Pretend to hit him?"

"That's useless," the gatekeeper's voice also rang in Nadia's mind.

Nadia stiffened as the tall man she almost recognized walked toward her. *I've gotten in a few decent punches over the last couple of dreams*, she told the small voice and rude gatekeeper.

"Nadia, you're safe," the man said, his arms held up in a non-threatening way as his eyes traveled over the rip in her sleeve. "That's new."

"Wait, you're real?" Nadia's mind finally connected him to the panther man from the day before. Taking in his wavy, shoulder-length, black hair, chiseled chin, and deep tan skin, Nadia searched his features for the panther he had been. *I mean, the cat had been giant,* she thought, gawking at him. *But this man is like 6'5". Look at those arms. Nadia, stop it. You don't know this guy, and he can change into a murder kitty at any moment. Focus.*

"What do you mean?" he asked.

"You were a panther and became a man."

"Yes."

"And that wasn't a dream?"

"No. Shapeshifting is my gift." He lowered his arms, visibly relaxing a bit.

"Gift?" Nadia's arms dropped a few inches, exhaustion creeping up both.

"You should sit. You've been through a lot." The man turned his back on Nadia before bending over to restart a fire.

I guess his chin is not the only thing that's chiseled, she thought, immediately feeling the heat of embarrassment climb up her face.

"Please." He gestured to the scattered blankets.

Nadia remained standing despite feeling woozy and tense like a rubber band pulled too tight. "Who are you?" she asked, needing to know more.

Her body was exhausted while her anxiety created scenarios and fears from every noise and pain, even as her rational mind tried to write off the whole experience as a dream or a small, harmless mental break.

"I'm your guardian." He stood and gave her a small, formal bow. His slightly rounded cheeks showed youth, but his rigid jaw and shadowed eyes gave the impression of being much older than Nadia.

"Guardian? The rude, stuffy lady from one of my dreams talked about a guardian. But that was a dream for sure." *Even if I'm not quite sure about this one.*

"You must be referring to a gatekeeper."

"Yeah. What a jerk."

"Jerk?"

"Yes. Awful, and she ruined my peaceful dream."

"Oh, well, Gatekeepers are the only people from Baako who can travel between the two worlds through dreams. It happens so rarely I wasn't even sure gatekeepers were used or if the deal was struck some other way."

"Baako?"

"This world. Didn't the gatekeeper tell you?"

"No, she didn't say much."

"But you knew you were traveling?"

"No."

"No?"

"No, not really." Nadia finally sat, too tired to stay

standing. She pulled one of the blankets onto her lap and hugged it. "I thought she was just part of my insane dream."

"Did you choose to come?"

"How could I choose? I didn't know this place existed!" She gripped her hands tighter into the blanket, but regretted the decision as her left palm throbbed. "She said something like they usually wait until I'm eighteen, but couldn't because I'm needed. Pricked my finger and pressed it to some sheet." The pounding in her head grew. "Oh, and she said my guardian would also be called up early."

"Hardly early," the guardian said in a pouty voice with furrowed brows. "That doesn't matter." He waved his hand dismissively. "You know so little and weren't at all prepared—"

"Who are you?" Nadia cut into his grumbling. "What's your name, and how do I know this isn't a dream?"

"My name is Dimitri," he said.

Nadia took in his beautiful face again before noticing his gray, almond-shaped eyes surrounded by thick lashes. *Could this man be more gorgeous?* She blinked a couple of times before looking away.

"And I assure you, this is real. I'm real. Plus, look around, this place is way too elaborate to be a dream."

Nadia had been looking around, and it was gorgeous, but it was not more or less elaborate than her other dreams. "Actually, it can be, though my dreams usually have much more action."

"Well, you're on Baako in the Forest of Bagrach."

"Baako? But what or where is it?"

"Baako means first. It's the older sister to Earth." Dimitri pulled out a small pot and placed it near the fire as he spoke. He filled it with water, dried meat and vegetables, and a packet of herbs. "But, as I'm sure you have noticed, this planet is very different now. The ancestral people of Baako chose gifts and peace over technology and war."

"Planet? You mean, a totally different world?" Nadia's mouth fell open as she looked around again. "But it looks so, so normal. Just like a forest on Earth."

"Yes, the two planets are made of the same stuff. Earth people used to have gifts and everything."

Nadia immediately thought about the witch trial when primarily women were killed for alleged gifts. The fear and panic. The torture and destruction.

"How long ago?" she asked.

"Most of the gifts on Earth faded almost a thousand years ago. But according to Earth lore, some gifts were passed down through families. Even now, people may have touches of gifts, tiny specks of magic."

For half a second, Nadia thought about what it would be like to have a gift. Her prim and proper mother worked so hard to give Nadia and her sisters everything they needed and most of what they wanted. *A gift would've—*

"Wait." She snapped back to Dimitri. "If I really am on a different planet, what does my family think happened to me? When will I get back? I have classes tomorrow and just chewed out my math teacher. I can't miss his class. He can't win, and I'm just starting to understand the homework." She clutched the blanket. "College professors don't give extensions. I mean, maybe my high school teachers would've, but neither would accept 'kidnapped to another planet' as an excuse."

"Kidnapped?" Dimitri sounded insulted. "You were hardly kidnapped."

"I also have to pick up my younger sisters from school on Friday. My sisters! What do they think happened? Oh, and then I wake up with freaking cuts on my arm, from a dream! How does that happen? I'm a missing person. My family, my mom, is going to lose it. This can't be real. You're not real. This world isn't real. These cuts aren't real."

She gripped her arm, willing the pain to not be real until it became too much. *I feel that. But…but… this can't be real.* She took in short breaths, forgetting how to breathe properly. The need to act coursed through her entire being, even though it felt locked out of reach.

"Woah, calm down." Dimitri stood. "Don't you think you're overreacting a bit? I mean, if you sit, I can explain—"

"Overreacting? I'm on a different planet!" Nadia was starting to hyperventilate. "Planet! I fell asleep in my own room, on my own freaking world, and woke here, being stalked by a giant cat that turned into, well, you, and you have the nerve to tell me I'm overreacting?"

"Sure, alright. Poor choice of words. I can see how this could all be a bit shocking, but the gatekeeper did say—"

"In a dream." Nadia stood and began to pace. "She said I would travel while I was dreaming. You know, not real, made up, subconscious style stories, imaginary!"

Nadia was swaying and trembling all over. She thought about what her mom would do when she found her bed empty. "How do I get home?"

Dimitri ran his hand through his wavy hair, clearly uncomfortable.

"What?" Nadia asked when he didn't respond. "Tell me."

"It's just," he began. "You don't go home."

Chapter

10

Tears sprang to Nadia's eyes as she stumbled back, unable to catch her breath.

"No, I mean," Dimitri said. "I don't know if, when, I don't know when or how you get home. That's all."

"That's all?" Nadia mouthed. She took a few deep breaths, determined not to fall into a panic attack. Her head was pounding. "Okay." She closed her eyes and rubbed her temples.

"Okay?" Dimitri asked.

"Yeah. Tell me why I'm here and who brought me. Once I do whatever they need, I'll go home." Nadia's heart still wanted to beat out of her chest, but she knew being an emotional puddle would not get her home.

Dimitri just stared at her, frozen with what Nadia assumed was indecision. His slack-jawed, open mouth would have been comical if Nadia weren't trying to rein in her panic.

"Go on. I'm not some fragile little woman who needs a big, strong man to hug me and tell me everything will be okay." *At least I hope I'm not,* Nadia thought as she wrapped her hands in the blanket so Dimitri wouldn't see them trembling.

"Maybe you should sit down."

"No, thank you. I need answers first."

"Please. Your wound. The thorn was poisonous," he pointed at his palm since her hands were hidden in the blanket. "So I really must insist you sit before you get another injury."

He insists? She thought as anger calmed her anxiety. "I get that you're my guardian or whatever, but I must *insist* you allow me to make my own decisions for me. You've known me for all of what, twenty minutes? I think I know what I need more than you do."

There was a long, tense, silent stare-off that only ended when Dimitri looked away, crossed to the fire, and stirred the bubbling food. The aroma of the meat and herbs filled the small clearing, chipping away at Nadia's resolve.

"Now," Nadia started slowly. "Will you answer some more of my questions?"

"Are you willing or able to eat while we talk?" Dimitri asked. "It's a bit of a peace offering because you're right. I don't know you and shouldn't assume. But the food will help you feel better or at least more human while your body fights the poison."

"Maybe." Nadia's anger was the only thing keeping her on her feet. Without it, she was lightheaded and dizzy. She slowly lowered herself. "Let's start with that. What does it mean to be poisoned in this place? Like, do you have nurses and doctors or medicine? What are the expected side effects, and when will they go away?"

"You were poisoned by a plant that is quite common on Baako, but there is no immediate cure. Don't worry," he said quickly when Nadia opened her mouth. "It only takes a few hours to a few days for it to leave your body. Food, sleep, and not getting worked up will help you heal more quickly."

Dimitri handed Nadia a wooden bowl about the size

of her face and a wooden spoon that was closer to being a shovel. The bowl was half-filled with steaming stew that smelled so good that Nadia wanted to dump it in her mouth.

"Wait a couple of minutes to eat that," Dimitri said, getting some for himself. "It's hot."

Nadia felt sheepish. She had been nothing but worked up the entire time she'd been on Baako. "How can I not get worked up? Between this place, you, and the orange-eyed stalker, I'll be—"

"Orange-eyed who?" Dimitri said, forgetting the bite of food he had lifted to his mouth.

His sudden seriousness startled Nadia. "Just some villain in my latest dreams, though…" She looked down at her torn sweatshirt. "I told you. I woke up with these."

Dimitri abruptly stood and crossed to Nadia. He pushed up her sleeve without even noticing her protests. "How did you get these?"

"The orange-eyed guy was a giant lizard chair and then an irritating little man, but it was a dream…" Nadia said, leaning away from Dimitri as he held her arm tightly. "Right?"

He lifted her cuts to sniff them.

"Woah," Nadia said, and Dimitri released her arm. "What the heck?"

Dimitri returned to his spot by the fire, picked up his bowl and resumed blowing on his food.

"What was that about?" Nadia asked while Dimitri looked anywhere but at her.

"I wanted to make sure you weren't poisoned again," Dimitri said, still not meeting her eyes.

"Who is the orange-eyed dude?"

"Dude?"

"Guy. Who was that guy? Do you know him? I mean, I thought he was just a made-up villain from my subconscious in both of the dreams."

"He has been in other dreams? Before you got to Baako?"

"Yes," Nadia said, still on edge. "But only one, and it was right before I got here. I mean, it's possible I was already here. It was a couple of days after the Gatekeeper dream."

"Interesting," Dimitri said. "You must worry him."

"But why and how? Who is he, and why is he after me?"

Dimitri searched Nadia's face, making her squirm under the intensity of his stare. She focused on the bowl of food that had been forgotten when Dimitri sniffed her arm.

Sniffed it, she thought. *I get shapeshifting is cool and all, but so is modern medicine, not sniffing cuts for poison. Also, it would be great if he answered one freaking question completely.*

She took a big bite, forgetting Dimitri's warning.

It was hot.

She opened her mouth, trying to cool the bite by breathing around it. She covered her mouth with her wrapped hand, but embarrassment still rose to her cheeks. She glanced up at Dimitri and was relieved he was no longer staring at her, but there was a distinct smirk on his face as he blew on his spoonful of stew.

When she could swallow, she almost hummed at the vibrant, delicious food. The meat was not beef but something richer and leaner, while the herbs had earthy undertones like they were freshly picked from wet soil. Chewing caused bursts of flavor as the food danced over her taste buds despite half of them being burned. It was one of the best bites of food Nadia had ever had. She blew on another spoonful, careful not to burn herself a second time. She hadn't realized she was tensing her arms, afraid the second bite wouldn't be as good. She immediately relaxed as the food hit her tongue.

Her mom had always made stew in a slow cooker, which resulted in chewy meat, soggy onions, and overcooked carrots. Dimitri's stew was perfect: melt-in-your-mouth meat, a starchy potato-like vegetable that was a pleasure to bite through with a welcome texture, herbs that enhanced all other flavors, and a sweet yet savory carrot. She could feel her body warming from the inside, and the tremors in her hands stopped.

"Who's the orange-eyed man?" she asked after another bite. "And can he really travel to Earth?"

"He said that?" Dimitri asked through clenched teeth.

"Yes. He said he'd travel to Earth and kill everyone I love if I didn't do what he wanted."

"Threatening you, interesting." Dimitri ate another spoonful of stew.

"Yes, but that didn't answer my question."

Dimitri chewed for a few moments. "I'm not sure if he can travel off Baako, though I wouldn't put much thought into it. He's a liar and a killer. Scum who should be wiped off of all worlds."

"Yeah, but who is he?"

"A villain, an evil this world has had to deal with

for a long time."

Nadia could see Dimitri's hand clench around his spoon until his knuckles were white. She wanted to ask the thousand or so questions swirling through her, but the irritating little man from her dreams would have to wait. She needed other answers first. "What does my family think happened to me?"

Dimitri sighed, "I don't know."

"How can you not know?" Nadia felt her temper rising again.

"Guardians are given very specific training to protect our charges. We're taught how to keep ourselves alive, how to defend, and even how to kill, but very little about our charges and never why the charges come or how they return. We know nothing of your family, your lives, nothing before you get here, and learn only from what the charge chooses to share."

"So you're literally just my bodyguard. Brawn, but no brains. No knowledge, no bigger picture, nothing?"

"Owe. That's a bit harsh, but yes."

"Great." She wanted to throw something, but she only had the stew and definitely wasn't throwing that. "Great! I'm stuck on this planet with a bodyguard—"

"Guardian."

"Guardian." She rolled her eyes. "And his amazing stew, but no way to get home, no idea why I'm here, and I feel like crap. My arm hurts because I got attacked by a chair in a freaking dream, and my hand is bleeding through its wrap. I'm going to die on this damn rock, and my family'll never know why I abandoned them."

"Nadia," Dimitri said, suddenly right in front of her.

She looked up and up and up, not realizing how tall he was until he was inches away. "I'm not just a bodyguard. I was also taught basic healing and can help, but only if you calm down." He took her bowl, setting it next to the blankets. Then he helped her stand. "Please, let me rewrap your hand." He was so gentle with her despite having large, calloused hands.

Nadia looked into his gray eyes, seeing earnest worry. "Okay," she said, a little unsure.

He rewrapped her hand while she looked anywhere other than the injury. She didn't want to throw up on him or pass out. The intimacy of the gorgeous stranger gently washing her wounded hand confused and surprised her enough to take her mind off the wound itself. She realized how much she did want to be 'that girl' who needed the large stranger to hug her and tell her it would be okay.

Wow, he even smells good, she thought. *Like worked leather and soft pine.* His hair looked so soft that she wanted to touch it. She followed the contours of his cheeks with her eyes until she realized he was looking at her.

"Am I hurting you?"

"Uh, no. Not at all." Heat rose to her face again. *Get it together, girl*, she told herself silently. *You never mooned over boys back home.* Of course, Dimitri was no boy.

When he was done and Nadia pulled her thoughts together, she took another bite of stew, chewing the tender meat slowly. The flavors were just as rich as the first bite, with hints of the woods around her: pine bark, grasses, and breezes dancing through the field of wildflowers. She almost sighed aloud as she swallowed, feeling the warmth spread through her again. She wanted to finish every morsel, but exhaustion crept through her limbs and mind, making even small movements difficult. She watched her spectacular guardian finish eating and rinse his bowl while her thoughts jumbled and ran together.

Don't be taken in by his pretty face, she thought, glancing at his sculpted figure again.

She had a bad habit of trusting handsome men. She chalked it up to never meeting or knowing anything about her dad, though that probably wasn't entirely the reason why. Her mom had her; a few years later, she was engaged to her stepdad. Her stepdad was great, and her mother loved him, but Nadia always wondered what man could leave a pregnant woman behind.

Did he ever think about me? Did he even know I existed? She shook her head, trying to focus.

"What are you thinking about?" Dimitri asked, interrupting her thoughts.

"Hm? Oh, nothing," she lied, not wanting to tell this delicious stranger her daddy issues.

All Nadia wanted was to lie down and sleep, but she eyed the ground resentfully. She desperately missed her room, with her queen-sized mattress, too many blankets and pillows, plants all around her, and a door that locked.

"Am I in danger?" Nadia asked.

"Why do you ask?"

"The orange-eyed man threatened a lot of terrible things."

"We call him the Dream Killer."

Nadia laughed.

Dimitri did not.

"Sorry," she said. "Dream Killer seems so

dramatic."

"He kills people by entering their dreams and never releasing them," Dimitri said.

"Oh my god."

"They often die slowly of starvation. Some are lucky enough to die quickly of some mortal injury they received upon entering the Dreamworld."

"That's brutal." She gently touched her injury.

"Yes. But you escaped him. Twice, it seems." He stared at her again.

Nadia looked away quickly. Dying in a dream was one of her biggest fears, but someone else stealing her into a dream and then killing her was terrifying.

"So I'm in danger?"

"Yes," Dimitri answered with only a slight hesitation. "There are no safe places for you on Baako." His straightforward tone made Nadia nervous. She set her bowl down, unable to eat anymore.

"Done?" Dimitri asked.

She nodded before an embarrassingly large yawn escaped her. Despite her fear and pain, her exhaustion was winning.

"You should rest," Dimitri said, reaching for his bag.

"You just told me people get kidnapped in their sleep," Nadia fought another yawn. "How does anyone sleep here?"

"Some of us have the training to close our minds." He pulled out a bag of red powder. "Others take this." He shook the bag. "This is dreamless sleep powder. I'll mix it into some water for you."

"The powder prevents dreaming, I assume?"

"Not entirely." He poured the powder into a small wooden cup. He added water and mixed it. "It'll prevent you from entering the Dreamworld, but you may still dream."

"Okay."

"I must warn you; it tastes pretty awful and has side effects if taken too often."

"Side effects?" Nadia eyed the liquid as she swirled it around the cup. It was thick and powdery.

"Headaches," Dimitri said, watching her closely.

"You said I'm in danger." She looked up at him without drinking. "Is it safe for me to take this stuff? What if someone comes?"

"I'll keep watch."

She looked at him for a long moment. *I don't know if I trust this extremely hot man.* She let her eyes wander down his broad shoulders, thinking about who this guardian really was. *All brawn?*

"Drink quickly, and it won't taste as bad." Dimitri waited for her to finish.

What choice do I have?

Nadia knew from the smell that it was going to be awful. She gulped the mix down quickly, but it was still the most disgusting thing she had ever tasted, like fresh-cut grass mixed with cough medicine and an old penny. Dimitri took the cup. Nadia watched him, thinking about his graceful movements before lying back.

Brawn and beauty, but can he protect me?

Chapter

11

Nadia knew she was dreaming the moment the dream started. Water breaking on the soft sandy beach, the sun warming her skin, it was all too perfect, too generically beautiful. The tropical scene had clear, blue waters and palm trees swaying gently in a rhythmic pattern.

"What is this place?" she asked aloud.

"My home," an old, raspy voice answered.

Nadia spun to see a very small, very old woman standing too close, her wrinkled face displaying a mischievous grin.

"Well, my created oasis."

The ancient woman was hunched over an old, knobby walking stick. Her salt and pepper hair, braided loosely, was pulled by the breeze as it fell to her waist. She was shoeless, wearing a dress that looked more like a nightgown and a large quilt, made into a coat, that was faded and worn by time.

Nadia was fascinated by how old the woman looked, but she was no longer foolish enough to trust anyone in a dream place. She tensed and took a step away.

"Smart," the stranger said. "You're not what I expected. Shorter and fatter."

"I'm not fat," Nadia bristled. "I'm average. Well, on Earth and in my country." Nadia almost rolled her eyes at how pathetic she sounded. "And 5'5" is not short. Whatever you are is short."

There was a long, uncomfortable silence. Nadia's chin jutted forward slightly, daring the older woman to argue. Then, the woman's harsh glare broke, and she cackled.

"Feisty," the woman finally said. "I like that. Come." She began to walk toward the thick vegetation of the island.

Nadia bit her lip, staying exactly where she was. "Actually," Nadia said. The woman turned around several feet away. "I'd like to ask you a few questions. Out here. In the open. If you don't mind." Adding internally, *where I can run if needed.*

The woman cackled again, startling Nadia. "Of course." She hobbled back before resting her time-worn hands on her knobby stick. "Ask your questions."

"Thank you."

"No thanks needed," the woman cut in. "I'm just glad you're not a complete dimwit. Maybe there's hope for you to live through this after all."

Nadia shifted. "Who are you? Is this another dream? And how do you know me?"

"All good questions," the old woman said. "I am Gaia of Baako. What you see is only one of my many forms," Gaia continued with a knowing grin. "I come to you as the crone today, though I prefer the name grandmother. I find most feel more comfortable seeing me this way when we meet for the first time. I won't tell you my other forms because I don't want to give the game away."

Gaia winked and laughed at an inside joke, pausing for so long that Nadia started to say, "So, um," but Gaia held up a hand to stop her.

"I'm one of the Great Guardians of Baako, the Goddess of Death and Rebirth, the keeper of prophecies, and your humble servant." She gave a stiff, one-armed bow. "Today, I'll be your teacher, but in time, I may be counted as your friend." She started to walk, Nadia trailing a few steps behind, still processing all the titles.

"This," Gaia gestured with one gnarled hand. "Is my home. I have created it to look this way because this is where I'm most comfortable for now. I change my land often. This is a dream-like world. It's more accurate to say you are visiting my mind rather than a dream. Now, your final question: how do I know you? This may be heartening or frightening." Gaia spun around far too agilely for her age. "We've been watching you for most of your life." Nadia's mouth dropped open. "Long before your birth, a prophecy was discovered about how to end the war that has raged in Baako for a generation. We believe you may be the girl-child of that prophecy."

"Prophecy? War?" Nadia mouthed.

"You also have innate abilities that shouldn't have worked on Earth with the guards placed on them..."

"Abilities? Guards?"

"Abilities, powers, gifts," Gaia brushed away the words. "Much of the prophecy has been lost, but it spoke about manipulating the elements."

"What?" Nadia laughed. "You must've gotten the wrong girl."

"We shall see," Gaia winked. "But I hope, for your sake, you're wrong." Nadia's laughter died on her lips. "Before we go into my home. I want you to go to the well, drink, and bathe your face and hands. I think you'll find the healing waters… illuminating."

Gaia pointed the end of her knobby walking stick at an ancient-looking well beside a beach shack. The shack didn't look like it could withstand a light breeze, leaning to one side with shutters unable to close. The well looked straight out of an old western, with a rusted hand crank and leaky bucket.

Nadia didn't think the request was unreasonable, but she found it odd and the whole situation a bit alarming. *Is she who she says she is? Is this a trick?* She dropped the bucket into the well. The water was only a yard or so down. *Can I even get this stupid bucket up?* She winced and hissed each time one of her many injuries twinged or burned with every crank of the handle. *There's no way I'm in their stupid prophecy.* By the time the bucket was on the side of the well, Nadia was panting and didn't care if it was a trick. She was thirsty and exhausted.

She drank deeply.

It tasted unbelievable. Both clean and crisp, with a hint of springtime just under the frosty surface. She dipped her hands in the bucket and splashed water over her snarled, dirty hair and down her blood-stained clothing. The water cleaned her almost immediately. Delighted, Nadia dipped her hands in again, scrubbing the wrap right off her left hand, revealing only a tiny scar to remind her of her injury. Amazed, she put her arms in the bucket up to her elbows, and her pain melted away.

"What is this stuff?" Nadia asked. A quick sweep of the area told her Gaia was no longer nearby. "Well, it's incredible and should be bottled."

She picked up the bucket and poured all its contents on her head, soaking her hair, back, legs, and chest. Standing next to the well, she snaked her hands in and out of her wavy hair as the tropical sun and ocean breeze dried her. She leaned over the well to see that her hair was clean and untangled. A large smile spread across her face until an image flashed across the surface.

She froze.

Her mother, with her telltale short, curly hair, spoke calmly to someone on the phone. Her younger sister was in the kitchen cutting vegetables, and her youngest sister bounced a basketball, taunting the dogs running around her. Nadia leaned closer, watching the scene as if the well's surface was a TV.

"I know, Nadia," Nadia's mom said into the phone.

"Mom?" Nadia asked, as close to the water as she could get.

"We miss you, too," her mother said. "But it's for the best, honey. You have to get better before they can send you home." There was a pause.

"Mom," Nadia's voice rose. "You're not talking to me." The image played on without stopping, even when Nadia started screaming, "Mom! Please."

"I love you, too. We'll talk soon." Nadia's mom hung up the phone with a sigh.

Nadia almost fell into the well when the scene suddenly changed. She watched her entire family gather around a small urn. Some were crying; others were staring off.

"How did this happen?" Nadia's mother cried out. "She was so young." Her voice broke as tears streamed down her face.

Nadia watched helplessly, her heart breaking at her mother's pain.

"This can't, she was getting better." Nadia's mother's voice rose. "Please… Why?" Then she collapsed into tears. "No mother should outlive their child." Nadia's sisters held their mother, sobs shaking their young bodies. "My sweet Nadia. Why?"

"Mom," Nadia whispered. A tear fell into the water, blurring the image. "This isn't real. I'm not dead. I'm just stuck here." Nadia's throat burned with overwhelming emotion. "Please, Mom." The vision started to fade. "No, wait. She needs to know." When the water was still again, Nadia slid down the well's wall, holding her head in her hands. Sobs wracked her body as her mom's tear-stained face swam in her mind.

"I'm not dead," she said aloud over and over. *It's another trick, another strange dream, no matter how real it felt.*

When Nadia stood, her clothes were dry and her tears had stopped.

"I know where you are." A familiar, oily voice came from the well. Nadia brushed away her tears. "I'll find you, and you'll be just as dead as your family thinks you are." He laughed.

Nadia wiped the tears from her cheeks, rolling her eyes.

"You're awfully melodramatic for a short, sweaty dude who lost… how many times now?" She refused to show how upset the images had made her.

"Lost! It's you—"

Nadia dropped the bucket back into the water, cutting him off. She lifted it, relishing in the painless movements, and splashed a final handful of cool, healing water across her tear-stained face. Brushing dirt off her back, Nadia walked toward Gaia's shack, heartsick.

A woman in gleaming body armor intercepted her a few steps from the door.

"You must go," the woman said, grabbing Nadia's arm and moving her away from the rickety house.

"What?" Nadia asked. "Who are you?"

"You know me in another form. I have very little time, so listen well."

"Gaia?"

"Yes," Gaia said from the body of a forty-year-old warrior woman. Her eyes were blazing as brightly as her polished armor. "You need to start training the moment I release your gifts and send you back to your guardian."

"Dimitri?" Nadia's anxiety grew with each word Gaia said, as ferocity and bloodlust rolled off the woman.

"Dimitri," Gaia repeated with a noticeable softness. "Trust him and learn. You're not safe anywhere in Baako. Not even here. Tell him…" She grabbed Nadia's shoulder and bending closer to her face. "Tell him he must train you immediately."

"But I don't understand. What's wrong?"

"He's tracking you."

"Who? The orange-eyed freak or Dream Killer or whatever?"

"Start moving when you wake, and give this to Dimitri. Tell him to guard it with his life just short of dying." She shoved a small book into Nadia's chest. "He'll understand. Now, hold still. This is going to hurt." With one hand on the back of Nadia's head and another on her forehead, Gaia said, "Deep breath."

Before Nadia finished breathing in, pain ripped through her head. She jerked, but Gaia held her.

"Steady," Gaia said, all joy and gentleness of the grandmother figure was gone.

Nadia's body was rigid with shock. The pain grew until she was sure her head would explode.

"Tricky," Gaia breathed. "But your wards can't stop this."

Nadia whimpered before the intense pain popped like a water balloon seeping through her body. She could feel Gaia's hands trembling as one, then the other were removed.

The pressure and agony were replaced by the flowing of something vital, something unpredictable, something that had always been just out of reach. It was euphoric and terrifying, foreign and familiar. Then it settled, and for the slightest moment, everything felt calm, and Nadia felt whole.

"Are you okay?" Gaia asked, gruffness saturated her raspy voice.

"Yes. Are you?"

Gaia was panting slightly and sweating profusely. "Fine."

"What just happened?"

"Stop asking so many questions. You need to learn your place."

"But what just—" Nadia tried again.

"I see you'll need more than one lesson in

manners," warrior Gaia leaned in threateningly. "But that will have to wait. Right now, you need to wake." Gaia shoved Nadia forcefully.

Chapter

12

Nadia was falling, almost flying from Gaia's island, before violently smashing into her own body on the forest floor. Her back ached, and her sense of calm was gone just as quickly as she had been ripped from Gaia's dream world. Sitting up, Nadia still held the book.

"What did she do to me?" Her head had a dull buzz vibrating through it while she tried to understand her new sense of self. *I'm not different, but...*

She knew she was still Nadia, clumsy and average, but something felt new and unaverage. She felt she belonged with, no, to nature. She closed her eyes to breathe in the pungent wildflowers, smelling each variety momentarily before another fought to her senses. A breeze whipped through the clearing, and Nadia almost jumped up to dance with it.

She giggled, internally chiding herself for such a ridiculous notion even as the urge to soar was almost overwhelming.

"Nadia?" Dimitri's cautious-sounding voice broke through her imaginings.

Opening her eyes, she saw Dimitri standing just past the wildflowers and tall grasses growing up all around her.

"Did we move camp?" Nadia gently ran her hand through the flowers. They shifted toward her as she passed over them. No, it must have been the breeze shifting them.

"We did not."

"Well, your plants grow much faster here than on Earth."

"Not usually. Are you okay?"

"Yeah, I'm supposed to give this to you." She stood slowly before handing Dimitri Gaia's book.

"What? Where did you get this?"

"Gaia."

Dimitri almost dropped the book. "Gaia?"

"Yeah. Do you know her?"

"Everyone knows her—well, everyone knows of her. Very few know her as I do. She's my mother."

"What?" Nadia's jaw would've hit the ground if it were capable. "Your mother? The Great Goddess of Prophecies or something?"

"Or something." Dimitri laughed, though it did not reach his eyes. "She's a Great Guardian and the Goddess of Death and Rebirth."

"Yeah, and something about prophecies."

"It's said she carries the book of prophecies…" Dimitri looked down at the book again. "Unless." He tried to open it, and his face went slack. "Is this the book of prophecies?"

"Beats me." Nadia shrugged, watching Dimitri's black hair blowing slightly in the breeze. "Gaia said something like," she cleared her throat, adopting her best warrior Gaia voice. "Guard it with your life just short of death."

"She was the warrior?"

"Yes, after she was the grandmother. Have you ever drank from her well? It was nuts."

"Oh, that explains how you're healed and clean."

"Yeah, but there were also images… Is your mom or the well or whatever trustworthy?"

"She's a Great Goddess and above questions like that."

Is he also telling me to learn my place? Nadia wondered. "So is that a yes?"

Dimitri nodded in a sanctimonious way.

Nadia's throat suddenly burned, and her eyes filled with tears, remembering her younger sister gripping her mom's hand as they both sobbed over the urn. "They think I'm dead."

"What? Who?"

"In the well." Nadia angrily swiped at her tears. "There were images of my family, and they think I died of some disease. They had my ashes, Dimitri. Were they real, the images? Do they think I'm dead?"

"I don't know."

"How can you not know? You just said your mom is trustworthy, so is her well real, or not?" Nadia's anger gave way to grief before Dimitri could respond. She turned away, embarrassed and ashamed of her unchecked emotions. Her arms wrapped tightly around her chest, only slightly constricting the deep breaths she took to calm down. *In and out*, she thought, breathing in through her nose and out her mouth. Humidity rose around her, and the smell of rain became more pronounced, which helped to calm her grief and the buzzing in her head. The whole forest felt like it held its breath.

"Nadia?" Dimitri asked. His long fingers wrapped around her arm, he gently turning her, and slowly pulled

Nadia to him. When she didn't object, he wrapped his arms around her tightly, pressing her into his chest.

She stood for a few seconds, feeling his breath on her head. *I guess I get that hug after all.* She breathed in his scent, further calming down.

"Thanks," she started, pulling away. "I'm okay. I guess it's just overwhelming to attend your own funeral. Sorry about that big mood swing. That's not really like me." She collected her bedding, coming to terms with her new reality: new worlds, hot guardians, dream killers.

"Don't be sorry. I can only imagine how this experience has been."

"Yeah, but no rest for the wicked and all that, because Gaia said we can't stay put. I'm being tracked or something."

"I figured as much," Dimitri said, and Nadia noticed for the first time their camp was packed and the fire pit was gone. "Also, you're not wicked, are you?"

"No, it's a phrase we use back on Earth, super cliché."

"Cliché?" He asked with genuine interest in his eyes.

"Never mind. Where to?"

"The Forest of Bagrach is large and expansive, covering great distances in all directions. We'll be traveling north for most of today, but it probably won't feel like we get very far. It all looks much the same."

"And we're traveling on foot?"

"Of course."

"No cars or even a bicycle?"

"Gifts and peace over technology and war," Dimitri

tossed over his shoulder as he took off at a brisk pace.

"Bikes are hardly technology," Nadia grumbled. "Just some wheels and speed." Jogging to keep up, she tripped over her second tree root in only a few minutes. "You need to slow down. I'm clumsy at the best of times." She was panting slightly and mumbled, "And fat, according to your mother."

"Fat?" he asked, glancing over his shoulder at her. "No, but you'll get leaner as we walk and train." He slowed down. "But not fat. I once met a man who was so fat he could devour an entire large chicken, a loaf of bread, and a pie and still be hungry. He got too fat to walk and was dragged on a bedroll by the village children. He was amusing." He chuckled.

Nadia's anxiety over her weight lessened, but her hunger grew. She had only had a few bites of his amazing stew since arriving. She imagined how great an entire chicken would taste, and her stomach growled embarrassingly loudly.

"You're hungry," Dimitri stopped abruptly.

"Yeah. Sorry."

"That was dumb of me." He dug through his bag as he spoke. "I ate before you woke. Here." He gave her a large jerky strip.

Nadia ripped off a small piece and let it melt on her tongue. It had been soaked in a sweet honey sauce before drying, and it was good, as good as the stew. She reached her fingers up to her mouth, fully intending to lick the sauce off, but she caught Dimitri looking at her. Her cheeks grew hot as embarrassment crept up her face.

"So," She said. "Gaia's your mother?" She took

another, even bigger bite. The second was even better than the first. Savory and sweet. Melt in your mouth delicious.

"Yeah." Dimitri fell silent again.

"And?"

"And I haven't seen her for many years. She has many responsibilities and never remains in one place long." Dimitri's voice had a deep sadness that Nadia couldn't miss.

"Do her different appearances also come with different personalities?"

Dimitri smiled. "Yes, but only slightly."

"And you're the son of one of the Great Guardians?"

"Yeah." Dimitri looked at her sideways.

"And stuck being my guardian?"

"Yes, but where are you going with this?"

"I don't know." *You're beautiful and connected. How'd you get stuck with me?* The silence stretched as Nadia searched for a subject to lift Dimitri's dark mood. "Can you do more than shapeshift?"

"Not that I'm aware," Dimitri said. "But gifts can grow and change as you train and use them. Some gifts only appear after you train in a certain skill or have great use of them. I once heard of a man who fell into a frozen lake and suddenly grew gills as his blood cooled to keep him alive."

"What happened to him?"

"He's still in the lake," Dimitri shrugged. "Once the gills grew in, he couldn't get rid of them."

"Well, that's awful."

"It is, and it isn't. Gifts are not good or bad. It's

how you use them that matters."

"Oh yeah, Gaia said she released the wards on my gifts so I can use them properly."

"Use them properly?" Dimitri asked as casually as his apparent curiosity allowed.

"Yeah." Nadia grimaced after stepping on a rock with her trainers, wishing she were wearing hiking boots for the hundredth time. "I supposedly used them a little on Earth."

"You what?" Dimitri's nonchalance gone. "How's that possible if you had wards on them?"

"Hey, I don't remember using any gifts. I'm as average as they come. I sucked at sports and was only okay at theater stuff. Never shifting into anything or doing anything cool. No gifts here."

"Oh, you have them." Dimitri wore a knowing smile Nadia found annoying. "I've never seen plants grow or clouds form like they have since you've been here."

"Yeah, okay." She rolled her eyes. "What are wards, and why'd I have them?"

Dimitri frowned. "Wards are controls or locks placed on a person to prevent them from using their gifts. It's complicated to place wards on people, but putting them on a place or building is a little easier. It affects everyone who enters, but the wards have to be replaced often. Do you remember someone placing wards on you?"

"No," Nadia said. "I don't have gifts, so what would they ward against?"

"Or maybe you were too young to remember?"

Nadia rolled her eyes again, wishing for more jerky but not brave enough to ask for it.

After a few minutes, Dimitri asked, "Did my mother say what gifts you might have?"

"Uh, no. I mean, maybe the elements." Nadia lifted her shoulders in an apologetic shrug. "She took off the wards or whatever and kicked me out of her dream world."

"Really? Hmmm. Let's test you." He slung his bag on a low branch.

"Now?"

"Yes." He dropped, smoothly turning into the panther before leaping at Nadia.

Nadia dropped into a frightened squat. As the need to act overwhelmed her, her eyes closed, her arms flew forward, and she braced for impact. Half squatted, half dropped uncomfortably, she stayed for a few seconds before cracking open an eyelid.

Dimitri, the man and the panther, was gone.

Chapter

13

"Dimitri?" Nadia's heart pounded in her throat, making her voice sound choked. She took a deep breath. "Dimitri!"

"Here," he said from far off in the woods. She heard his slow strides before she saw him. He was holding his left arm and had leaves in his hair.

"What happened?" Nadia ran over to him. Blood was seeping gently through his fingers. "You're hurt?"

"Yes." He sounded both amused and annoyed. "You threw me." Nadia giggled nervously, and his eyebrows shot up. "No, really, you threw me twenty yards or so. Through the trees."

"No. I couldn't. I didn't."

He showed her his superficial but painful-looking wound. "Then how did this happen?"

Nadia swayed a little.

Dimitri clamped his arm again. "Not a fan of blood?"

She shook her head, willing herself not to throw up.

"Well, you'll need to get past that. With a gift like yours, you'll likely see a lot of blood."

Dimitri wrapped his arm in silence, allowing Nadia to replay her reaction. She stood on the path. He dropped, changed, and ran at her. She dropped like a child with her eyes closed, and a surge blew through her. Surge? No. Despite a tingle running up her spine, she couldn't remember using any gift.

But she knew that tingle. She had felt it back on Earth when she was afraid or upset, especially around plants. Her mom used to call her the plant whisperer because Nadia had dozens of plants growing in her room, and every plant her mom touched seemed to die.

She thought about her favorite tree in the backyard of her parents' house. When she was five or six, the tree seemed to be dying, and Nadia was devastated. She sat with the tree every day for a week, telling it to grow strong, because they were friends and friends grow strong, or some other dumb little kid thought process. That tree was still there and Nadia's favorite place to sit in the cool evenings. *But I didn't do anything. It just grew. Trees do that. They survive.*

She opened her eyes to Dimitri's crooked smile.

"That was impressive," he said. "Do you know how you did it?"

"Are you sure I did it?" Nadia was both curious and unconvinced.

"Yes. I know you did it, and I have the wound to prove it."

"I'm sorry about that. I just don't see how I could've possibly thrown you without deciding to. It makes no sense."

"You didn't actually throw me. It was more of a massive wind. One second, I was running at you, expecting, well, not that. The next, I hurtled through the air, hitting several trees in the process." He rubbed his arm, laughing.

They walked in comfortable silence while Nadia

replayed the moment over and over before asking, "Where do gifts come from?"

"Bloodlines usually."

"How is that possible? My mom was just as plain as me."

"And your dad?" Dimitri asked.

"I don't know." Nadia tried to hide her shame. "He wasn't around."

"Oh, I'm sorry."

"Don't be. My mom was great. I mean, she was no Great Guardian of Death and Rebirth or anything, but she was always there at all our school events and big moments, ya know."

"Not really." Dimitri looked away.

"What do you mean?"

"Gaia, my mother, being a Great Guardian, made her pretty busy. My dad used to say, 'feel lucky, boys. She chose me, and therefore, she chose you. She'll be back when she's done doing great things.' He was right, but it was still hard."

"I bet. What about your dad? He sounds lovely."

"He's dead." Dimitri's demeanor changed, and he walked faster.

"I'm sorry. I shouldn't have pried."

"No, it's fine."

Say something before he goes back into cold shoulder guardian mode, Nadia thought. "But where do gifts come from?"

"I told you."

"No, you told me how they are passed down. Supposedly, I can wield the elements, or at least wind, but you change into a giant murder kitty."

"Murder kitty?" Dimitri smiled.

"Those are very different gifts. So why do you have one type and I have another?"

"Well, ironically, I know more about your gifts than mine. According to a handful of our myths, elementals once roamed the world."

"Elementals?" Nadia imagined a campfire with legs. "Like people made of elements?"

"Yeah, kind of. The myth was that they appeared in the shape of people, but could only interact with a very select few. But, like so many gifts used in the myths, the elementals are either just old stories with no truth, or they are lost to us now."

"So, I might be part elemental? Ha! Okay…"

"You still don't believe me, do you?"

Nadia shrugged.

"Do you remember the grass and flowers all around you this morning?"

She shrugged again.

"They weren't there when you fell asleep."

"Okay?"

"You did that."

Nadia snorted. "Now I know you're messing with me."

"The weather change?" He asked. "The water clinging to the air as you wept?"

"No, and I didn't weep." Nadia tried to keep the pout from her voice. "Not really."

"I told you Earth and Baako were once similar," he began. "They're twin planets, worlds apart, both magical, beautiful, and uncorrupted. Then your industrial revolution, religious upheavals, and unquenchable appetites for more, bigger, now happened, and the magic faded. One generation after another lost more and more of their abilities. Well, I told you some have specks of gifts left, drops of magic that help them know, see, heal, whatever. Maybe you have more, a lot more, and Earth has built-in wards? I mean, I guess it's possible. I don't know. What I do know is you have gifts. Specifically elemental, I think."

"That would be cool if I believed you, but it doesn't make any sense. None of this does."

"I'll prove it to you."

Chapter

14

Dimitri glanced up at the sun's position as his trainer's voice ran through his head, "Do not get comfortable with your charge, or you'll let down your guard and get both of you killed."

"Dimitri," the head trainer, Lucian, had yelled. "What are the key things you need to survive?" Lucian was not a big man, but what he lacked in size, he made up for with venom and viciousness. "Dimitri! Are you deaf or just stupid?"

"Sorry, sir." Dimitri was not sorry at all. *Give me a chance to answer, and I will,* he had thought, but would never have had the guts to say. "Shelter, food, and water." Someone had snickered, and Dimitri knew he had said something wrong.

"You're not playing house, baby guardian," Lucian had barked. "Water and a defensible space. Shelter is nice if it's defensible. Food you can do without if needed, and some of you, Big Willis, could do without it more often."

"Watcha thinking about?" Nadia asked, interrupting his thoughts.

"Uh," Dimitri said, still hearing 'don't get too comfortable.' "Training. It's not important. We'll walk until sunset, which is still several hours off. There are several hunters' huts on the path we travel, and there's one not too far from here I'd like to get to before dark."

"Goodie," Nadia said under her breath.

Dimitri ignored her obvious dislike of his plan. "Then, we'll train for a few hours before sleep. Hopefully, you don't destroy the hut." He winked at her and picked up his pace, but internally kicked himself. *Joking and winking are comfortable. Don't get too comfortable. You already held her. Mistake after mistake.*

"Wait," Nadia said, and he let his thoughts fade. "Why am I here? You never did tell me."

Dimitri took a deep breath and held it momentarily, unsure how to answer. "It's kind of a hard conversation."

"It seems like we have the time, so let me have it."

"When I was a boy." Dimitri disconnected himself from the memories that always occupied the story. "A great war started that continues still."

"So much for the peace Baako was supposed to have."

"Yeah." He took another deep breath, pushing down the creeping grief in his chest. "It was prophesied that the war would produce an unnatural tyrant no one could kill. The tyrant would feel no fear and have no limits or weaknesses except for the other. The other will have the power to end the tyrant."

"Whoa," Nadia stopped. "That one's not about me, right?"

Dimitri turned to her, "That prophecy has no names attached to it, or maybe this war would have ended long before now."

"That's why I'm here?"

"Your name had to have been thrown around for a handful of years now," Dimitri said. "I'm not sure if you're in a prophecy or if you're a strong contender to be the other of the prophecy. Either way, someone knew you'd be special."

He looked at Nadia, really looked at her. She was an Earth girl with potentially remarkable gifts, no understanding of Baako, a target painted on her back, and the most intriguing eyes. He had his work cut out for him. *Why me?* He thought for the thousandth time since getting called up for Guardian duties.

"Special?" Nadia interrupted Dimitri's memories again before she rolled her eyes. "I damn near killed you on my first try at this gift thing."

"Yep." He bumped into her. "And it was special."

Chapter

15

By the time Nadia saw the hunter's hut, her thighs and butt were tingling and numb, but her feet were screaming. Even her chest hurt from the long walk. She wanted nothing more than to collapse onto her queen-size mattress covered in a five-inch foam topper, six pillows, and four blankets. But one look at the hut told her it would be another dirt bed night.

"Nadia," Dimitri said, drawing her attention away from her pity party. "I need you to light the fire to make food."

"Okay." Nadia practically collapsed next to the well-stocked fire pit. "Do you have matches or a lighter?"

"Yes." Dimitri tried to hide a smile. "You."

"What?"

"You're the lighter," he said with a small throaty chuckle. "This is test number two. There are four elements, and you've only shown flashes of them. Fire is next. Try not to blow up the surrounding area."

"You're joking, right?"

Dimitri shook his head. "I'll stand over here just in case."

"Ha. Ha." Nadia frowned, eyeing the pile of wood.

"Aren't you hungry?" Dimitri asked after a few minutes of silence. "Without fire, we have no food."

She *was* hungry. She tried to feel some gift inside her. Nothing. Nadia pushed a couple of logs over and laid her hands on others. She stood slowly, wincing at the pain in her legs and feet, and took off her sweatshirt, tossing it away before she sat back down. She threw her hands forward, feeling ridiculous again—still nothing.

"This is stupid." She turned on Dimitri. "I can't do this. I've no control over the elements. I'm not some savior from some prophecy." Even as she spoke, she felt the pull she was beginning to recognize, the urge to act, to use a new part of herself she could only vaguely remember feeling before coming to Baako.

"Just as I thought," Dimitri said, wide-eyed.

"I'm sorry. I just can't."

"But you did." He pointed at the blazing fire.

"That wasn't me." Nadia stamped her foot like an angry toddler, exhaustion and fear making her unreasonable. The fire shot up, licking the sky.

"Woah." Dimitri's hands raised toward her. "It's reacting to your anger. I'm pretty sure your gifts are directly tied to your emotions."

"Great," Nadia threw her hands up, and the fire exploded. Dimitri threw himself to the ground, but Nadia froze, finally accepting the obvious. The fire calmed as Nadia cocked her head to the side. "I did that?" She felt her gift flex as she giggled. "Cool." She wasn't just some chubby, uninteresting teenager anymore.

"Well, that changes things." Dimitri brushed himself off.

"What do you mean?"

"Gifts tied to emotions are often only as stable as the person."

"I'm stable," Nadia said, hurt evident in her voice.

"Most of the time."

"I'm not saying you aren't." Dimitri ran his hand through his wavy hair. "Most in Baako find out they have gifts as children and then master them or at least learn control over years. You don't have time to do that. Your gifts are strong. One burst of rage and you could start a forest fire or burn through your essence, killing yourself." He was silent for a long moment.

"Killing myself?" Nadia questioned, breaking the silence.

"Meditation," he announced. "That'll help, so let's do that."

"Now?"

"Yep, the sooner you train, the better."

"Cool…"

Nadia's exhausted body protested every position Dimitri told her to try. She removed her shoes so her swollen feet could breathe and found a position that hurt the least—then fidgeted, sighing.

She knew she was a no-go at sitting still and emptying her mind. She needed a focus, something more, or the thoughts poured in, and her hurting body got all her attention.

"Okay, fine," Dimitri didn't hide his irritation. "What do you suggest?"

"Don't ask me." She tossed a small stick into the fire, then pine needles, then some rogue grass she plucked.

"Stop that." He adjusted his position. "Try just staring into the fire and do what I say. Breathe in. Watch the fire devour each log."

Nadia did as he said, taking a deep breath, watching

the small stick she had just tossed disappear into flame.

"Breathe out and see the flames dancing. Breathe in…"

Dimitri's voice softened as Nadia stared into the heart of the fire, embers of wood scorched and maimed by relentless hunger. She was so involved in the drama of the fire that she stopped listening to Dimitri, allowing her exhausted body time to relax and her mind to melt into the flames. Nadia imagined walking among the blaze, holding the heat in her arms, cradling the warmth. She smiled at the idea of bathing in the flame until…

An explosion ripped through the air, forcefully pushing Nadia back.

Standing in the fire pit was a being made of pure red-yellow flames.

Equal parts awe and a frigid emptiness she didn't understand filled Nadia.

"Who are you?" She asked as her teeth chattered and her body convulsed with all-consuming shivers.

"I am all the fire that burns within you and without."

"What?" Nadia asked as the fire beings' breath burned her eyes.

"I'm an Elemental."

"You're real?"

He nodded, "But I've never been brought to being by one so young and untested."

"But I didn't." Nadia struggled to form words through her chattering teeth. "Why am I so cold?"

"You gave me life by sacrificing your own heat."

"That wasn't part of the myth. At least not the part

Dimitri told me."

"Do you want to feel warm again?"

"Yes, please."

"You have a choice," the fire elemental said. "You can have your heat back if I blend with you. It's dangerous. Most who attempt a blending perish."

"Why would I attempt it then?"

"Those that do not attempt it remain cold, unable to retain or feel heat for the rest of their short lives. Those who blend successfully have the gift of my powers until they die, and I am released back into this world until another proves worthy."

"Oh." Nadia would rather be cold than hot, but not an all-consuming winter. "I'm new to my gifts, like brand new." Nadia felt sure she would fail and die.

"Take heart, Nadia of Earth. If you were unworthy, you could not have called me forth. To blend, you must understand fire, both physical and emotional. Mortals feel differently than we elementals; therefore, I can give no more understanding than that."

Nadia looked at Dimitri for the first time since the fire elemental appeared. He was ten feet away and sprawled out on his back.

"Dimitri?" Nadia asked, rising as quickly as her frozen joints would allow.

The fire elemental turned. "The guardian will be fine. Elementals are often brought forth through violence that incapacitates all but the chosen. He'll soon wake."

Even as the tower of fire spoke, Dimitri began to stir.

"Make your choice, young one."

Nadia tried to think about the importance of fire, but found it difficult as her teeth chattered loudly and her mind went completely blank. *When have I experienced fire?* She looked at the burning heart of the fire being. *Think.*

Simple memories around the campfire with her family or candles lit on the kitchen counter surfaced first. Then, the time a house burned down in her neighborhood, and when she watched transfixed as forest fires devastated a neighboring state. Nadia was hit by the memories of her family in the well, and fiery rage boiled up in her chest. Valentine's Day, when one of her classmates gave her the Valentine back because she was too "ugly" for him. Burning shame intertwined with her rage and mixed with hot embarrassment. Her math teacher, Janelle, the bully, the gatekeeper, all enraged her further. Her fiery side was part of who she was. It drove her. Calm came over her as she thought about embracing the elemental and dancing among his flames. She knew her choice.

"Blend," she said, resolutely. "There is no other choice."

"Are you sure, Nadia of Earth? Your life is yours to lose."

She looked at Dimitri for a long moment. He was getting to his feet. His mouth was open, and his eyes were huge as he watched the elemental.

Nadia was shaking from the cold but felt very little fear. The blending had to work, or it didn't matter anyway. She smiled at Dimitri, and realization crossed his face. He started to drop, and Nadia knew.

"Yes. Before my guardian does something stupid."

The elemental smiled, bowed to her, and sprang.

Chapter

16

Heat built inside Nadia's body, throwing her arms wide until the pressure of a bomb exploded and consumed her very being. Flames erupted across her skin, and a smoke-filled scream ripped from her very soul. She fell to the dirt, thrashing, slapping at herself, mindlessly trying to stop the torment as the fire hungrily ate another limb. She barely felt her clothing drop away as her insides boiled and popped. Every thought and emotion was replaced by scolding, parching misery. She was disappearing into ash, into nothingness like the small stick had within the fire pit. Her edges melted, and her life neared its brutal end.

"Make it stop," she mouthed. "Please." She could feel nothing but flames gorging on her flesh.

"Accept me," a voice spoke from inside her.

"I can't." Her tears were unable to fall even as she openly wept at the agony of her death. "I don't know how."

"I am you," the elemental said inside and outside her.

"I am you," she repeated.

"You must believe," the fading voice said.

Nadia lay in suffering stillness, moments from her last breath. "I am you," she whispered, using the last of her coherent mind to convince the rest of her of the truth in her words.

Immediately, the pain stopped, and Nadia's body released all tension. She panted and sobbed without tears.

Thank you, she thought.

We are one was the whispered mental reply before his consciousness faded, leaving only Nadia.

Nadia felt cracked like an ancient desert floor. She still trembled, but not from cold. She wasn't even sure she could feel cold. She trembled from the phantom pain still in control of her mind and pure exhaustion radiating through her body.

"Nadia?" Dimitri asked from several feet away. "Are you okay?"

She stared at him for a long moment. "I don't know."

He stepped toward her, never taking his eyes from her face.

"Wait." Her voice was harsh and gravelly. She held up a hand that instantly ignited into flame. She stared at it as she sat up. "That's new." She closed her fist, and the flame went out. She put up the other hand, and with barely a thought, it, too, lit up. "Wow," she mouthed and tossed the fire between her hands. She sighed as the warmth went from palm to palm before it flickered and died. She was too tired to play with her enhanced elemental gift, but knew her gift was even more dangerous than before. If Dimitri was right and her gifts were tied directly to her emotions… one bad day could result in her scorching Baako. *I need to train.*

A light breeze nipped at her skin, reminding her…

Her whole body burst into dancing flames, proving her point. She had not intended to cover herself in fire, but her nakedness triggered burning embarrassment, which triggered burning.

"Nadia!" Dimitri jumped back from the sudden heat.

The fire felt like a soft, warm blanket draped over her body. She quickly crossed her legs and folded her arms over her chest, and any chub she could cover before the fire went out. She was still nude but a little more covered and a lot more exhausted.

"Sorry." Embarrassment coloring her voice and skin. "Can you hand me a blanket?"

"Will it burn up?"

Nadia shook her head but couldn't look into his eyes, afraid she would see fear or, worse, disgust.

Dimitri wrapped the blanket around her shoulders. "You're not giving off any heat." He crossed to the other side of the scorched fire pit and sat hard, staring at Nadia. "What just happened?"

"Elemental," Nadia began, but her throat felt burned and raw. Dimitri tossed her his water, and she downed half of it. "That was a fire elemental, and we blended." She rubbed her face and eyes before tightening the blanket around herself again. "Do you, by any chance, have any extra clothing with you?"

Dimitri was staring at her open-mouthed.

"What?" she asked, struggling to keep her embarrassment and fire in check. Their blanket stock was limited, and she didn't want to show any more nudity.

"You blended with an elemental?"

"Yeah, and it was pretty rough."

"I heard." Dimitri had an edge in his voice. "But you survived."

"Seems like it. Also, you didn't mention any of that

when telling me the myths. That fire guy was created from my heat. It was blend or freeze."

"Do you even understand what just happened or what it means?"

"Yeah, I took my heat back and, I mean, my gift of fire does seem a pinch stronger."

"I saw, but that is not what I meant." Dimitri stood and started pacing. "You lived through a blending with a creature I more than half believed was a myth, a legend, not real."

Nadia's mind flashed back to the intense, almost life-quenching pain. "I almost didn't," she whispered, lost in her nightmare.

"Blend?"

"No, live, I mean. The pain almost ended me. It was—" Her eyes burned with phantom tears.

Dimitri crossed to her, dropping to a knee. "Are you okay?"

Startled by his sudden closeness, her gift surged inside of her. She clenched down hard.

"I'm fine," she began. "However, I've a favor to ask."

"Clothing," he said, glancing at her blanket. "Yes, sorry."

"No," she smiled. "I mean, yes, but that wasn't what I was going to ask for. Wait. What are you doing?"

"I packed light." Dimitri pulled his shirt over his head. "I don't have extra clothing, but you can have my shirt, and I'll just wear my jacket."

Nadia stared open-mouthed at his lean, muscular back and almost lit on fire when he turned toward her with his shirt in his hand. He was even more beautiful without clothing. His chest was sculpted under his gorgeous tan skin. She snapped her eyes shut, struggling to keep control. Breathing deeply, she smelled burning and clenched her hands shut, too. When she felt completely in control, she opened her eyes and saw the fist-sized holes in her blanket.

"I don't have another shirt," Dimitri said, holding his shirt out to her with a big grin. "So if you burn this one, you'll only have blankets to wear or what's left of them."

"That's kind of what I wanted to talk to you about." She grabbed the shirt without looking at Dimitri's perfect body again. "You can't do anything unexpected or sudden because my supercharged gift is a little volatile, and I don't want to burn up my clothing or you or the forest. Now turn around so I can put this on."

Dimitri smiled widely at her for another moment before turning. "If you do, one or both of us will be traveling naked."

Even as visions of his incredible body flashed through her mind, she still wanted to slap the arrogance off his face. "Well, no one wants to see that."

"Are you sure?"

"Stop it, guardian."

"If you wish, charge."

Nadia rolled her eyes as she dropped the shirt over her head and stood, allowing the blanket to fall. Dimitri's shirt was only form-fitting across her chest and hips. Otherwise, it was long, soft, and thick, falling to her knees. It was also still warm from Dimitri's body. Nadia glanced around, debating what to wear on her feet when she saw her sweatshirt and shoes.

"Oh, good, you survived." She hugged the last things she brought from Earth to her chest.

"My shirt suits you," Dimitri said, all arrogance gone. "Really," he glanced at her again before looking away quickly.

Was that embarrassment? Nadia wondered as Dimitri ran his hand through his wavy hair and pulled his jacket closed.

"Do you think you can travel tonight?" he asked, not quite looking at her.

"Um, yeah, sure," she lied. "If I had to, but we'll have to go slow."

"So no," he laughed. "It wasn't even fair of me to ask. It's just, I'm worried your elemental blending was seen and heard from far off. But it's probably paranoia." He paused, looking at the hunter's cabin. "If we sleep in that wooden hut, will we live?"

"Ha. Ha." Nadia said dryly, unsure if sleeping in a combustible hut was a good idea. But she grabbed her blanket and crossed to it anyway. *Another dirt mattress*, she thought, curling up in a corner and falling asleep before she stopped grumbling.

Nadia rose, what felt like moments later, disoriented. Dimitri was nowhere to be seen, and she couldn't call out. Stepping out of the hut, she was surprised to see snow on the ground.

Something's wrong, she thought with growing dread.

Then she heard it.

The low groan of a man in pain. Her heart started racing, but she couldn't make her feet go any faster. She

entered a clearing and knew immediately he was dying.
Nadia screamed.

Chapter

17

"Nadia!" Dimitri shook her. "You're dreaming and smoking. Nadia!"

Looking at Dimitri's shocked face, she took in his disheveled hair and bare chest. She touched him, trying to see past the deadly wounds on his abdomen the nightmare had shown her. His real body was warm and clean, with no blood, no gore. Tears spilled down her cheeks. It had felt so real, his injuries and her deep love for him. Both had been so real, unshakably real.

"Nadia, what is it?"

"A nightmare," she said, her voice breaking. "You had, there was so much blood. I knew you'd die." She touched his chest again and felt all the muscles ripple before leaning into him, desperate to make sure he was okay. She felt his arms wrap around her, holding her tightly.

"You're awake," he said softly in a deep, gravelly voice. "And you only scorched the blanket a little. Win, win." He laughed lightly, and she heard it rumble through his perfect, unmarked chest, relaxing immediately.

The dead don't laugh, she thought. *He's alive. And I'm hugging him and he's half naked.*

"Sorry." She pushed away from him, trying to hide her embarrassment. "I'm sorry I woke you up like this." She was trembling slightly from waking up so abruptly. "And for basically groping you and scaring you and anything else I already did this super embarrassing morning," She dropped her head into her hands, mortified. She had just met this man; he had seen her naked, bawling like a child more than once, and she caressed his chest. *But in the dream*, she thought as the all-encompassing emotions lingered. If he had died, she would have lost everything. It felt like she would break and burn the world down. *Why? I just met him. It was just a nightmare. He's just my guardian. Nothing more.*

"No apology needed," he said, and she could hear the smile in his voice.

She glanced up to make sure he wasn't mocking her.

"Besides, it wasn't an unpleasant way to wake up." He touched his chest where her head had been, then abruptly turned away, color rising to his face just as it rose to Nadia's. They stood in awkward silence before he said, "We should eat and get going anyway."

They walked most of the day, stopping to eat and remove small stones from Nadia's shoes. She hated wearing shoes without socks. By the time they reached the next and even smaller hunter's hut, Nadia's feet felt slimy and battered.

"Nadia, we're almost out of water." Dimitri shook his animal skin water pouch. "And this area has seen very little rain for far too long."

"Yeah." She dropped next to the hut and leaning against it. "I could feel that as we walked."

"Well, can you water the land or at least fill this pot?"

"What?" Nadia untied her shoes to let her feet air out. "How?"

"That's not for me to say. It's your gift, not mine."

Nadia yawned widely behind her half-clenched hand.

"I can only start dinner after you fill this." He held his small pot to her.

She took it and felt it start to get hot. *Wrong element*, she thought, reaching for the source of her gift. She couldn't sense a difference. She growled under her breath, straining to feel something, anything. Then she heard noises outside and inside herself. "Did you hear that?"

"Hear what?" Dimitri jumped up, tension in his entire body.

"It sounded like…" Nadia stopped, unsure.

"Like what?"

"But…" She paused, listening. "But that can't be, right?"

"Nadia, what are you talking about?"

Nadia could hear the anxiety in Dimitri's voice. "Nothing bad." She walked toward the nearest tree, hand outstretched. "I think…"

Dimitri appeared in front of her. "Where are you going?"

"Wait, please." She walked around him and touched the ancient giant. Foreign yet familiar energy coursed through her bones, and she heard them again. The weight of the voices almost knocked her back. It was like a waterfall rushing under her skin, trying to wash Nadia away and refill her with hundreds of voices. She gasped, unable to pull away.

"Nadia?" Dimitri laid a hand on her shoulder.

"What is it?"

"I'm okay." She gritted her teeth, closing her eyes to keep them from rolling into her head. "I just have to—"

Her head yanked back as her gift surged, mixing with the ancient tree. All the voices calmed, and the connection became a tremor rather than a quake. Panting slightly, Nadia realized Dimitri was holding her up and calling her name.

"Nadia? What's happening?"

"The trees…"

"What?" He hovered around her.

"I can hear the trees, and they're chatty." She laughed, and her body relaxed. She pressed both hands against the tree, and her gift flowed freely without her control, mixing with the ancient magic.

"Nadia, can you let go?" Dimitri asked.

She tried to pull away but felt rather than heard, "Wait."

"No, not yet," she told Dimitri. She gasped in awe. Dimitri put his hands on her forearms.

"Dimitri," Nadia mouthed. "It's incredible."

The trees showed her her gift, how to feel its depth and see it dancing in and out of her skin. It was hers and not hers. Ancient patience and childlike wonder pulsed through it and, therefore, her.

Why help me? She asked through the connection.

"We help all saplings," the tree responded. "No matter how strange."

She started to understand what the entire community of trees wanted, even as the individual trees still tried to talk with her.

"They do want rain." Her voice showing the awe she felt. "I don't…" Nadia was embarrassed. "I don't know how to make it rain."

"May I?" The tree asked, sounding almost human.

"Please." Nadia was unsure of what she agreed to.

Thunder rolled, causing Nadia to jump as the ancient tree pushed the knowledge of rain into Nadia while pulling her gift from her. Nadia's eyes widened as she looked at the gathering clouds. Then the drops started to fall, soaking Nadia and the trees in seconds.

Nadia laughed at how overjoyed the trees were as they sang up to the rain.

Then she felt it. It felt like a dull ache in a muscle she had overworked, but the pain was growing.

"Something's wrong," she said to Dimitri. She blinked sluggishly, her mind screaming to let go of the tree. "I think it's my gift." The pain was growing. She tried to double over but was stuck by her hands to the tree.

"You're using too much." Dimitri's alarm written all over his face. "You have to stop." He yanked on her hands. "Let go."

"I can't. The tree is controlling it." Her knees gave out.

Chapter

18

Nadia collapsed, half lying in Dimitri's arms, and the rain stopped.

"Are you okay?" he asked, trying hard to keep his voice steady.

She nodded, "I will be in a couple of minutes, I think."

"You spoke to the trees." Dimitri stared at her, emotion after emotion coursed through him.

"Yeah, sort of. I mean, I didn't have a choice." She slowly sat up.

"You did, though." Dimitri's anger flared even as amusement danced through his mind. "Nature has rules. They couldn't have used your gift without your permission."

"Okay." She sat up. "Wait, can everyone talk to trees here, and I was just foolish enough to allow them to use my gift?"

"No. I know of no one who can commune with nature that way. Grow things, understand dirt, roots, plants, sure. But it's said…." He stopped, frowning as stories his father used to tell him before bed crept into his mind. "It's said the gift of communicating with nature with pure understanding was lost to us long ago." *What are you?* He thought, searching Nadia's face for the answers he needed. *Who are your people?*

Nadia shifted and slowly stood, moving a few steps

toward the fire pit to dry off.

Dimitri moved through the camp, touching the dirt and the hunter's cabin before he continued. "You made it rain, but not in camp."

"I didn't do that." Nadia shrugged. "The tree did it with my gift." She yawned openly. "It felt like a freight train slamming through me, but it slowed and calmed."

She has no idea. So few people could have… She needs real training. Dimitri crossed to the fire finding the cooking pot half full of water. *Training I can't provide.*

"How's your gift now?" He asked after taking the simmering stew off the fire. "Can you feel it?"

"Yeah," Nadia said. "I feel like an empty box that got chucked down a couple of flights of stairs. I guess that means my gift is pretty worn out. Kind of like my feet. I'm not very used to long walks and making rainstorms." She chuckled.

Dimitri tried to smile. "You're a marvel, Nadia of Earth." He handed her a bowl of steaming hot stew. "But I have seen people burn up their gift doing far less than what you just did, and it killed them. They tapped into their essence and grayed before dropping dead."

Only after the guardian-in-training had burned up did Lucian enforce the no gift rule. It was horrible to watch. He was just a cocky kid trying to show off.

Dimitri shook off the memory. "Never give anyone or anything permission to use your gift ever again."

"Okay," Nadia said through a yawn.

"Promise me." Dimitri leaned toward her.

"I promise."

"Do you want to sleep inside tonight?" Dimitri took

her already empty bowl.

"No. Right here by the fire suits me."

"Okay." Dimitri handed Nadia her blankets, scanning her face, trying to figure out her level of tiredness. He knew she had to be exhausted.

"Will I feel this empty every time I use my gift?"

"No." Dimitri tossed the rest of the wood on the fire, giving him time to rearrange his expression. He refused to diminish her with lectures or put-downs like his trainers did, but also didn't want to show fear. She could've died, and he would've been powerless to stop it.

"Always show strength to your charges, or they won't have confidence in you or your leadership," Lucian had repeatedly told the guardians-in-training.

Dimitri gave Nadia a weak smile. "Your gift will grow with use and training, and you'll learn your limits." He mixed the red dreamless sleep powder into a small glass before adding water from his almost empty canteen. "Here."

"Why do I need to take this tonight? I didn't take it last night and was fine."

"I dusted you." Dimitri laid out his blanket only a few feet from Nadia.

"You what?"

"I blew some over you. It's not as effective and wastes a lot of the powder, but it works if needed. Drink. I need to gather wood."

Dimitri smiled at her grumbling but knew she was sound asleep before he left the circle of the fire.

"No emotions are better than showing any," Lucian had yelled into the face of a guardian-in-training who laughed within earshot of him. "You're not their friend. You're not their mommy. You are there to guard them after we've taught them to use their gifts and sent them out into our world. Without you, they would die faster. With you, maybe they live long enough to see their home again, but that's not likely."

As Dimitri had carefully but quickly packed before he left training to find Nadia, Big Willis had found him in their shared twenty-bunk room.

"So today starts my walk towards death?" Dimitri had asked jokingly, but he couldn't keep the worry off his face.

"No," BW had said. "I know what Lucian said, but look at your brother. His charge has been here for five years, and they're both alive."

"As far as we know," Dimitri had said as an ache filled him.

"How long has it been?"

"Four years."

Dimitri had followed his brother into guardian training at a young age. They were inseparable for years until Dimitri's brother was called up, and his charge arrived at the camp. Six weeks later, they had left, and Dimitri had not heard from his brother in four years.

"Just remember," BW had said. "Kill or be killed." He had tried to use his most Lucian voice. They both had laughed as quietly as they could. "No, really. Be true to you, and you'll do alright. Oh, and don't forget us while you're out there saving the world."

"What would you have done that day?" Dimitri had asked, almost afraid to hear the answer.

"Honestly?"

"Yeah, would you have killed them?"

"I don't know, and I hate that I don't know."

"What? Why?"

"Because you knew. At that moment, you knew you wouldn't kill a couple of unarmed kids who were forced into service." BW had looked at his own hands. "I don't know. Lucian taught us, really drilled into us, that everyone is out to kill us and our charge. I hate that I may have… I'm just glad it was you."

"Yeah, me too," Dimitri had rolled his eyes.

"No, really," BW had said. "You showed all of us there is another choice."

Chapter

19

Nadia was annoyed when something pulled her from a sound sleep.

Voices.

She lay perfectly still, grateful that she felt more of her gift.

"He said to take her unharmed," one deep male voice said.

"Yeah, but how?" asked another man.

"Never had to hunt a girl like this," the first man said. "Feels wrong."

"Yeah," the second said. "But we gotta do what we's told. Don't want to get on the bad side of the monks."

Nadia was frozen with fear and uncertainty until she heard a thump nearby.

"What do we do with the shifter?" a third whiny voice asked. "He's heavy, and I don't want to drag him all the way to the big house."

"Kill the guardian," an older, commanding voice responded. "Take the girl."

Nadia was standing before any thought was given to the action. The men were startled, giving her precious seconds to take in the scene. Dimitri, in his human form, was thrown near the dying fire. He had a cut across his cheek and a bruise spreading across his jaw. There was dirt and blood caked on the side of his head.

The embers in the fire exploded to life, dancing

around Dimitri, free of the fire pit. Despite her physical exhaustion and overuse of her gift, fire was easy. The drain of the magic was only a trickle, rather than a flood the rain had taken.

Her gift felt like a willing weapon, cocked and ready. She jumped into action like she always did.

No plan.

No flight.

Just fight, half ready but all willing.

"Child," the commanding voice said. Nadia walked through the fire pit to stand beside Dimitri's prone form, smiling as the fire licked her like a loving puppy. "Child," the man said again. Nadia turned, anger rolling off of her. "We have come to bring you to him."

Nadia had no idea what she expected, but this man was not it. He was dressed in a medieval monk's brown robes with a large orange eye on his chest. His hands were spread out to her, calling her into an embrace.

Nadia felt her face twist first with confusion and then with amused disbelief. She looked into his deep brown eyes, and that's when something shifted inside her.

Her gift? Was he pulling it? Searching it?

Nadia tried to look away, tear away, cover her eyes, but her body did not respond.

"That's right," the man purred as cold trickled through her body like icy fingers searching for something. "You'll make a perfect vessel. The power." He sighed deeply, sliding his hand up his chest. "The power in you is intoxicating. You are as they said. You are needed, and you will come with me."

The small clearing got darker as each of her dancing

flames popped from existence.

"No," she said, still stuck. Her knees started to wobble, and her head began to spin. "I'm not going anywhere."

The monk breathed in, and Nadia felt the pull of his magic against hers. He was tasting her gift, wafting it to him like a fine wine. Nadia's skin crawled, and her body lurched. She took a step toward him.

"Yes, girl-child." The monk held both his arms out to her. "He calls you even now. You know your destiny."

"What the hell?" Nadia planted her feet, fear threatening to overwhelm her. "The orange-eyed freak?" She swallowed, forcing as much snark into her voice as she could. "You can't be serious."

The monk laughed, and Nadia's stomach rolled at the feeling of his gift caressing hers.

"He's but a pawn. Come." He took a deep breath, allowing his chest to expand, and Nadia's legs betrayed her—first, one step, then another, toward the monk.

"Nadia?"

She stopped. Dimitri's voice sounded worlds away, even as she was drawn to it.

"Dimitri, I can't…He's holding…" Panic was rising in her mind as her eyes were still linked to the monk's.

"Take him down." The monk never broke eye contact. "Now, you fools."

"Nadia," Dimitri's face came into view, blocking the monk from her sight. Nadia partially collapsed into Dimitri's arms when the connection broke. "Don't let him do that again." He protectively pushed Nadia behind him once she found her feet again. "Don't look into his eyes."

"How did he—"

"Later," Dimitri said, glancing around at the armed unmoving soldiers. "Are you okay?"

"Sure." She felt her gift and knew the monk's connection was truly gone. "It was so weird. I was, I don't know, stuck." She shook off the need to shower.

"Get me the girl," the monk commanded. "Kill the guardian."

Nadia and Dimitri were both unarmed and hopelessly outnumbered.

"Can you run?" Dimitri asked. "You need to run the moment you see an opening."

"I don't run if I can help it," Nadia said with a crooked smile. "Especially not from a fight. It's one of my charms." Nadia's voice cracked with fear despite her goal to sound endearing. She had no intention of leaving Dimitri to die while she ran off into some unknown woods.

"You are stubborn." Dimitri lunged for the first man.

"Yes," Nadia danced from side to side to keep her mind from turning into fear-induced mush. "It's another one of my charms." She was trembling with terror and anticipation, but didn't stop moving. "I have many charms."

"Stop talking, little girl," the next man said, grinning widely and unsheathing his sword. "Give up, so your cute little head stays on your plump little shoulders."

The man swung his sword at Nadia before being picked up off his feet and set back down right where he had been. The look of confusion on his face could've been comical if he weren't trying to kill her.

"Dang it." Fear prickled Nadia's scalp. "That's not what was supposed to happen."

The man ran at her and was actually picked up and tossed into the woods by Nadia's gift of wind.

"That's what was supposed to happen," she swayed on her feet, stumbling against one of the nearby trees. "And I'm not plump." Her breath came in harsh waves, and she knew she was in trouble.

Chapter

20

"Take from us," someone said.

Nadia looked up, confused. Three more soldiers were walking toward her.

"Take from us," the voice said again, and she felt her hand vibrate ever so slightly. "You gave us rain. We'll give back."

"How?" she asked the tree.

"She nuts," the man closest to her said. "Who's she talking to?"

"May I?" the tree asked.

"Please," Nadia said just as she had the last time before she realized she probably should have thought it through. She felt the ancient magic of the trees pour into her. Her head flung back once again, and a shocked scream ripped from her lips. Then, it was over, and she stood before a small group of stunned men, her gift buzzing.

"What's wrong with you?" One asked, his sword hanging in his slackened hand.

"Nothing," she said and meant it. She felt incredible. "I cannot say the same for you three."

"What?" One of them asked.

"Well, it seems your pants are on fire." She flicked both hands at the men, sending a quick stream of fire onto their military pants.

They lit up almost at once. The men dropped their swords, frantically patting their pants. One ripped off his entirely, throwing them down and stomping on them.

"Nice dance moves." She half laughed, flicking the men with sparks. "Maybe you could teach them to me when we aren't, you know, fighting each other." She knew she sounded silly, but the banter helped her keep her head. Her jokes and wit often saved her from panic attacks and tears. "Who's next?"

"Child," the monk called again.

"Nope," Nadia said. "Not ready for you. Who else?" A boy not much older than Nadia stumbled into the clearing. She turned her attention to him, trying to remember how she threw the first guy. "Come at me!"

She reached for her supercharged gift as the whoosh of an arrow zinged past her ear. She turned to see it embedded in the hunter's hut at an angle before she was slammed to the ground. Pain shot through her side, and her head spun as it smacked the dense dirt. The boy soldier flipped her onto her back, allowing her a deep breath before pressing his sword to her throat. He had both knees pushed on her forearms and into the ground, but the rest of his weight pressed down on her hips and upper legs.

"Don't move," he said in a small voice. "I don't want to hurt you."

The boy's face swam in and out of focus as her head pounded, but she could see he meant what he said. She lay back, staring into the trees, breathing shallowly as the boy pressed a hand into her sternum. Nadia struggled to make sense of the noises all around her and to focus on her gift.

"I've got her," the young soldier said barely above a whisper, his excitement too great. He turned to call again, and Nadia saw movement in the trees. A soldier pulled his bow back, aiming at Dimitri. Her mind screamed, and the tree answered with a jolt. The man released, dropping from one branch to the next until his body crunched on the forest floor. The boy's sword slipped sideways, cutting a fine line into Nadia's neck. He fell forward onto Nadia, the arrow sticking out of his chest, digging into Nadia. She pushed her hands into his shoulders, staring into his startled, wide eyes. Death took him instantly, but his boyish face still had color and life even as his eyes drained, and his body became nothing more than an empty vessel. Nadia pushed him off of her, getting to her knees.

"No," she said. "No, no, no. He was only a boy." Her hands grazed his face, chest, arms, the arrow, and back to his face. He was already growing cold as Nadia was growing hot with fury.

"More will die," she heard the monk say only a few feet behind her. "More will die because of you. You can end this war if you come."

"What was his name?" Nadia asked, trembling with barely controlled rage.

"What?" the monk asked.

"His name." Nadia rose. "What was his name?" She pointed at the body.

The monk turned to the men around him, and Nadia knew he had no idea what the boy's name was. Her rage broke free. She dangled the monk 20 feet in the air.

"You don't know his name!" She lifted her hands, and the monk rose further. She wasn't sure how to throw him, but she knew she could hold him for now. "You commanded a boy. A boy who is now dead."

"Because of you," the monk said.

"I didn't ask to be attacked," Nadia countered. The monk wobbled in the air thirty feet above the ground. "I didn't ask to come to this world."

"It's your destiny."

"I don't believe in destiny," Nadia spat back. The monk started to spin slowly, which Nadia had not intended.

"Nadia?" Dimitri asked, moving toward her.

"Yes, guardian," the monk said. "Talk sense to your girl-child."

"Shut up," Dimitri said. "Nadia, he's lost. He's not worth the power you're expending."

"Archers," the monk called. The word was still on his lips as he flew through the forest as far as the wind could carry him. Branches snapped as his body mercilessly hit one and another and another. Nadia released the power and knew he had fallen to the forest floor too far to be heard.

The twang of several bows rang in Nadia's ears as Dimitri threw her to the ground, landing on her, and holding her head protectively.

Heat rose around them as arrowheads and ash rained down, leaving small, thin cuts across Dimitri's cheek and Nadia's wrist. Silence rang through the area for only seconds before they could hear men running through the woods, fleeing Nadia's final display of power.

"You burned the arrows," Dimitri said, reaching for an arrowhead with all his weight still pressed against her. He turned the arrowhead over and over, whispering words of awe.

Nadia's head turned, looking at the face of the boy soldier. "Did I…" She couldn't finish the question as her voice broke, physical exhaustion and grief flooded her. Dimitri pushed himself off Nadia, and she curled into a ball, openly weeping. "He said I killed… I didn't want—" Her voice quaked.

"You didn't kill him," Dimitri said. "The archer did."

"Oh god." Nadia tried to rise. "Did I kill him too?" She ran to the forest's edge, but the man was gone. Digging her hands into the ground, moving underbrush, she was looking for a sign of life, but there was none to be found. No body, no blood.

Dimitri's large hand gently grasped her arm. She pulled hard, still searching, but Dimitri tightened his grip, pulling her up.

"Nadia," he said gently but firmly. "No one's there."

She struggled, unaware of what she was doing. She just knew she had to keep moving. She had to see if she had killed the archer. She had to know, or the pain would overwhelm her, and she'd be lost.

"Nadia. Stop." Dimitri wrapped both his arms around her, pinning her to his chest.

She fought half-heartedly, burning up the remainder of her rage and collapsing in his arms. He scooped her up like a child and laid her on the singed blankets. She lay wide-eyed, replaying the boy's death even as Dimitri left the clearing and returned with wood.

"Nadia," Dimitri startled her from her spiraling misery. "Nothing I say will console you tonight. But sleep may help. Drink this."

Her hands raised automatically, grasping the warm

cup he held out. As the drink crossed her lips, she knew it was dreamless sleep powder again, but she welcomed the nothingness. She stared at the boy's dead eyes as she fell into darkness.

Chapter
21

Dimitri followed the tear stains across Nadia's cheeks. Why had she reacted like that? The boy would have gotten her killed or gladly turned her over for a bit of praise. She didn't even kill him. Why care so deeply about an unknown enemy? Then Lucian's voice rang through his head like it had weeks before.

"Dimitri," Lucian had yelled. "You don't let the enemy live! Why didn't you kill that bastard?" Lucian had screamed in Dimitri's face. "It is kill or be killed, boy. Your brother understood that. Learn it or die." Lucian had looked Dimitri up and down before he had mumbled, "What a waste."

The trainees had been taken out on a reconnaissance mission to scout the hills and woods fifty miles south of their usual training grounds. All the trainees were excited about it because it meant camping, fishing, and hiking through green woods. Their regular training camp consisted of tan barracks, a tan mess hall, and a tan training field filled with dead grass and dirt. A change of scenery sounded downright fun despite having to run with forty-five-pound packs on their backs. After a quick setup of camp and their individual tents, they set out to explore. That's when the drifter got the jump on a trainee.

A yell had ripped through the quiet of the forest, startling everyone except the trainers. "Get down," they had hissed. "You and you, that way. Weapons out. You three, go."

Dimitri, Big Willis, and a tiny new trainee had been sent higher up and toward the yell. Dimitri had led with his bow out and arrow nocked. He had held up a fist to stop the other two and pointed toward a small clearing and a trainee on the ground gripping his leg. It was caught in a metal trap, bleeding, and possibly crushed. One drifter was rummaging through the medical kit all trainees wore at all times, and another looked off into the trees. Neither seemed armed. A third sauntered through the trees with a bow and homemade arrow.

"Look at the size of that rabbit," he had said, laughing as he pointed the bow toward the trainee. "Bet that's poor eating."

"We shouldn't stay," the smaller one had said, still looking at the trees. "Where there's one, there's always more. Always. And they don't hesitate. They just kill us dead."

Dimitri had already pulled his bow back to hit the man, still pocketing things from the med kit, when a voice whispered, "Shoot."

"They aren't armed," Dimitri had whispered back without pulling his focus.

"What do you call that?" the smaller trainee had said, pointing at the drifter with the bow.

"That arrow is only for looks," Dimitri had said. "It would shatter if shot. Draw your swords, and let's go." Dimitri had traveled silently through the trees for a few yards when he noticed only Big Willis was behind him. The young trainee was frozen near where they had stopped. BW looked back, but Dimitri had hissed, "Leave him."

When they had been within five feet of the drifters, Dimitri had gestured for BW to take the bowman first. They both burst from the trees and made quick work of the drifters. The small, nervous one had immediately fallen to his knees with his overly thin arms in the air. The medical kit guy had thrown his hands up, still gripping the bag. The bowman kept muttering, "It's only for show, it's only for show," as he lay face down on the ground, his bow and arrow forgotten.

"Nice work," Big Willis had mouthed as the trainers and other trainees entered the clearing. Dimitri smiled back before turning to see Lucian's beet-red face. Lucian was dragging the tiny trainee Dimitri had left behind.

"Why are these assholes still alive?" Lucian had yelled, filling every inch of the clearing with pure rage.

Nadia whimpered softly in her sleep, pulling Dimitri from the memory and a creeping feeling of shame.

Dimitri had never killed and would never kill if he could help it, no matter what Lucian had taught him, no matter how many times Lucian had made him run for cowardice, no matter how many meals he had to miss due to being 'unworthy' of food.

He had the shot, but he would've killed a kid that day. A kid who had been recruited by a fanatic, just like the boy soldier. Would either fighter have killed him? Yeah, probably, but Dimitri knew he would never forgive himself if he had killed without knowing for sure.

He covered the face of the boy soldier with a small rag and watched tears roll down Nadia's cheeks even as she remained asleep. *How can I help you heal and move past this?*

Chapter

22

"We should bury him," Nadia said, clearly startling Dimitri as he bent over the fire. The sun was still low in the sky, and the morning was cool and dry.

"Are you okay?" he asked.

"Yeah. I mean, no, not entirely, but this world doesn't allow for rest." She shivered to her core at the thought of the dead soldier boy and the light fading from his eyes. *I didn't kill him,* she reminded herself. He was excited to turn her over to the psycho monk. *But why? What the hell do they want with me?*

Dimitri was watching her, worry written all over his face.

"Sorry if I woke you last night." Nadia made sure her voice was calm and steady, even if her emotions felt ragged.

As she gathered her bed things, she felt her muscles groan in protest, but her gift hummed with power. Rubbing her eyes, she then dragged her hands down her face to her neck, abruptly stopping on the thin knife cut, reaching almost from ear to ear. Her eyes filled with tears, and her chest tightened, thinking about how close to death she had come on some random planet, far from her own family.

Of course, they already think I'm dead... She shook the thought away and blinked her tears back.

"I must confess," Dimitri started, sitting back on his legs. "I'm amazed that you're even up and moving."

"Why?" Nadia glanced at the body of the soldier boy before putting on her shoes and tying her sweatshirt around her waist.

"Between the amount of power you used and anguish you were in after… I just expected you to be, I don't know—"

"A puddle?" Nadia asked with a slight smile, she knew didn't reach her eyes. She pulled Dimitri's shirt further down her legs. "I'm sorry for my freak out. I'll try not to break down like that again. At least, not for a couple of minutes." She tried to laugh, but it died on her lips when she saw the worry on Dimitri's face. "I still don't think I have some destiny like that a-hole monk said, and I'm definitely not some kind of savior the prophecy talks about. But I'm stuck here, people want me dead, and I apparently have some cool, new gifts that desperately need to be trained up. So, I choose to fight. I choose to train. I choose to live. Not to kill if I can help it. But I choose me." She paused, trying desperately to believe her own words. She pointed at the body, "I know I didn't kill him, but through my choices and his, he's dead."

"You didn't—" Dimitri began.

"No. You don't have to try to make me feel better. I'm okay-ish. No pep talk needed."

Dimitri looked at her for a long moment. "We don't have time to bury him"

"We can't just—"

"However, and if you're up to it, we can burn him."

"Burn him?" Nadia's stomach flipped at the idea. "I don't know if I can."

"Fire should be easy." Dimitri moved the extra

wood closer to the soldier. "It'll cause a lot of smoke, so we'll have to move fast, but if you burn him hot and fast like you did when you were nak… I mean, burned up your clothing…" Dimitri's face reddened. "Are you up to it?"

"No, I don't think I can burn a body." Nadia stared wide-eyed at the soldier boy. *I can't. That's still a person or a shell. What about the smell?*

"I understand. It was wrong of me to ask."

"We can't bury him?"

"No." Dimitri gathered all their belongings. "We've already stayed too long, and I'm guessing only their fear of your unknown gifts and the way the monk flew kept them away after the first attack last night."

"We can't just leave him," Nadia said in a strangled voice as her throat tightened and tears gathered in her eyes again.

Dimitri stepped between her and the body. "Nadia, he doesn't deserve your pity."

"No one deserves to be left to the elements." Nadia blinked back her tears. "Animals will—"

"But we need to leave to protect ourselves." Dimitri tossed the bag over his shoulder.

"Fine, I'll do it." Nadia crossed to the body.

"Burn him?"

"Yes, he cannot just be left out to be picked apart. If I die on this rock, I hope someone will do the same for me."

"Are you sure you can do this?"

"Not at all." Nadia pulled Dimitri's shirt sleeves up to protect them from her gift. "Please step back." *Can I do this?* She stood next to the body and put both her trembling hands out. Closing her eyes tightly, she thought about how the boy soldier was so excited to hand her off to the crazy monk who didn't even know the soldier's name.

A gasp laced with rage escaped her chest as her gift rejoiced.

"Nadia." Dimitri touched her shoulder. "Nadia, he's gone. It's done."

Nadia looked down at a pile that looked nothing like a human form. It was ash, burned dirt, and twisted metal from the soldier's weapons.

Nadia turned to Dimitri, emptiness ringing through her body even as her gift still hummed.

"You did it." He gently wiped her tears Nadia hadn't know she had been crying. Then it all crashed in on her. She stared at the ground as sobs began to roll through her.

Dimitri appeared in front of her without touching her for a few moments. When he did reach for her, Nadia could feel his hesitation and doubt. Then, he held her tight, and she leaned into his chest.

Dimitri held her tight and let her cry herself out. "I've got you. You're safe. You did what you had to. It's okay, or it will be."

She breathed in his scent, warming and calming her. "Thank you," she said as she pulled away. She knew she was an ugly crier, so she tried to rub the ugly off her face. She also knew she had cried for the last time over the boy soldier's death.

Dimitri and Nadia walked in silence for a while.

"How do you feel physically?" Dimitri asked in a stilted voice, breaking the silence.

"I'm sore everywhere."

"What about your gift?"

"Good. I'm still getting used to it and don't really have a grip on the wind-tossing trick yet."

"We can work on that during training."

Then they fell back into silence.

Nadia was deep in thought about all the craziness the monk said: destiny, power, and some other villain who was not the orange-eyed menace. "Hey," she said, breaking another long silence. "How did that monk dude cause me to get stuck like he did?"

"His gift," Dimitri said. "His gift is a type of manipulation while he tests your abilities. It's a rare gift and hard to break."

"Great." *Add that to the swimming pool of new and terrible things inside my mind.* "Why do all these bad guys want me? He talked about destiny, but never mentioned the prophecy. What was he talking about?"

"I don't know," Dimitri said too fast.

"Try again."

He sighed deeply. "I'm truly not sure. It could be the prophecy, but they would just kill you if that were true. So why try to take you?"

"Great…"

Nadia's head was pounding by midafternoon, and she was still trying to ignore the sideways glances Dimitri gave every twenty yards or so.

"If you have something to ask," Nadia said when she caught Dimitri looking at her again. "Just ask me."

"Okay." Dimitri handed her a large strip of jerky.

"Why did you care so deeply about the soldier dying?"

"He was young," she began, trying to understand herself. "I don't want to be responsible for anyone's death, even indirectly, especially someone only a year or two older than me."

"He would've killed you," Dimitri's voice was low and even. "If you gave him a reason, he would've cut us both down."

"Maybe."

"No. There is no maybe. That boy would've slit my throat and yours in our sleep if those were his orders. You'll always be ready to fight when you know all soldiers will kill. You'll always be ready to live even if others cannot."

"Nope. I told you I won't kill if I can help it. And if I think like that," Nadia's temper rose. "I'll lose myself, and then what would it matter?"

"If you hesitate in a fight because you're too afraid or soft-hearted to kill, you'll be killed instead."

She stopped in her tracks. "I noticed only one body on the ground last night."

"Yeah," Dimitri crossed to her.

"You fought last night, too." Nadia squared up to him despite their height differences, anger causing her voice to deepen. "And yet you didn't kill those you fought."

"I had no sword." Dimitri walked down the path without her.

"At first." Nadia watched a blade bounce off his back. He must've taken it from one of the soldiers. "Not the big killer you want me to be, are you?"

He stopped and dropped his head.

Nadia had won the argument, but also knew Dimitri was not entirely wrong. Still, 'kill or be killed' did not sit well with her.

"You're right," Dimitri said quietly after a long silence. "I won't kill unless I have no other choice."

"Why did you push me so hard then?"

"My trainers were furious when I didn't kill when I had the shot. They said I showed weakness, and I'd get my charge killed. I, honestly, didn't think they'd allow me to become a full guardian after that."

"Well, they did." Nadia bumped into him casually, all anger for Dimitri forgotten. "I'm your charge, and you're my guardian. We both believe the same when it comes to life; maybe we'll die because of it. But not today, so let's talk about something, I don't know, less heavy."

"My trainers also said not to become too close to our charges by getting to know them too well."

Nadia's mouth dropped open before she frowned and rolled her eyes. "No offense, but your trainers sound like complete dumbasses."

Chapter
23

A moment of silence passed during which Nadia thought she'd gone too far until Dimitri laughed.

"You're right. Not talking all day would be excruciating."

For the next few hours, they talked about Baako versus Earth, starting with favorite foods. After hearing how the food on Baako was cooked, Nadia immediately missed a real kitchen with prep space and a convection oven.

"First, there is the planting," Dimitri started. "Then the food has to be treated to last all year. For our stew, I hunt the deer, skin it, and spend more than a day smoking it. Some meat is turned into jerky or placed into my stew balls with smoked vegetables. I create a dozen stew balls and a large sack of jerky from one animal. Then all the ingredients must cook in the water for at least a half hour to become tender again."

"Wow." Nadia thought about her ten-minute trip to the grocery store and twenty minutes of prep. "That's a lot. What about restaurants or pizza?"

"Pizza?"

Nadia explained pizza in minute detail, from the types of sauces to all the possible toppings.

"And you can buy this at one of your restaurants?" Dimitri asked.

"Yeah. We call them pizza joints, but you can also

buy frozen pizza and cook it at home."

"Over a fire?"

"Well, yeah. There are wood fire ovens, but I'm not sure if you can cook them over an open fire."

She explained the different types of ovens before moving into more complex conversations about electricity and nuclear power. Nadia knew so little that she had to change the subject.

They discussed their similar histories and where they diverged. Baako never took to the idea of monarchs and presidents. No kings or queens and no religious leaders ruled over the serfs. All people were equals and lived to survive. They worked to better their villages or their own families if they didn't live among others, and they honored the Great Guardians. Honored, not worshiped, because the Great Guardians were not gods ruling over all. They were long-lived mortals with immense gifts, walking and even living among the people. They changed over the millennia when a Great Guardian chose to retire or die, usually of ancient age or in battle. Then, another takes their place within the temples and sanctuaries throughout Baako. Some, like Gaia, have children living among the people, known and unknown.

Evil men rising and killing was one thing Earth and Baako shared fully. Earth had manufactured weapons, and Baako had gifts of power corrupted and used to kill, maim, and control.

They talked until the sun was low in the sky, and Nadia's mood was much improved.

"We're not far from the cave I plan to stay at for a day or two," Dimitri said. "We should get there just after nightfall.

"Sleeping on the ground, again," Nadia grumbled. "So fun."

Dimitri laughed. "But, as you can probably hear, there's a river not far off, we can fill our water skins and bathe if you want."

The smell emanating from Nadia was not pleasant, and her hair was a tangled mess of oil, sweat, and dirt. She was grateful for her one hair tie, but there was no masking the yuck caked all over her body. "Yes, please."

"The water will be cold, and we need to stay close to the river's edge."

Nadia's mouth dropped at the size of the river. It was massive compared to any river she had ever seen in Arizona.

"So, how does this work?" She watched the water bubble and swirl at the edges, but it raced past in the middle.

"Something like this." Dimitri stripped out of his jacket and popped off his boots before running into the river. He dipped his body before popping out of the water and running his hands through his wet, wavy hair. Nadia watched open-mouthed. The water cascading off his chest caused her body to start to heat. She popped her shoes off and tossed her sweatshirt on top of them before getting in the water to prevent herself from lighting on fire. The water was clear and swift, but oh so cold. She shivered for only a few seconds before her fire gift kicked in to regulate her temperature without her doing anything.

"Don't stay in too long." Dimitri swam closer to her. "It's too cold."

"Actually." Nadia smiled while scrubbing her hair with her hands. "My gift is warming me."

"Without you asking?"

"Yeah, I guess."

"Hmm, that could be a problem. Add turning off your gift to our training needs."

He dipped his head once more, rising out of the water with a sputter and shake before crossing back to the shore.

Nadia stayed low in the water, knowing her borrowed shirt would leave little to the imagination. She watched Dimitri walk awy. Water clung and rolled down his muscled back. His pants clung tightly to his lower body, showing how toned he was as he walked onto the rocky shore.

The pull of the river caused Nadia to stop gawking at Dimitri's perfect form and start swimming back.

Glancing up, she screamed, "Dimitri!" as an arrow flew past his shoulder and straight for her. Throwing herself backward, she scrambled further into the river and out of danger. Treading water, she desperately searched for Dimitri and any more potential danger, but he was gone. Their stuff was gone. The shore was gone, replaced with thick trees and a crumbling bank, and it was moving fast. No. She was moving fast.

Oh, shit, she thought, her stomach dropping as she looked where the river was sending her.

Rapids.

Large boulders and broken tree trunks came in and out of view as the water rose and fell over the land below. Nadia's brain immediately turned to mush. No thoughts other than the painful death she was facing. *I am going to die on this planet.*

Immense sorrow swallowed her before rage burned everything else away. "Fight," the buzzing of her gift seemed to say.

The rapids were yards away when she tried to use her gifts to lift her out of danger. At first, nothing happened. Panic rising, she tried again, but only lifted inches before arriving at the first white tipped waters.

She gulped down a mouthful of river, trying to take a deep breath. The swirling water swung her around, disorienting her before slamming her against a low, large rock. The current dragged her under, pinning her to the front of the jagged stone, bending her back. Her scream of pain was only a muffled sound and bubbles. Just as her desperate need to breathe caused stars to dance before her eyes, the water and rock released her, and she surfaced. Her back still arched as relief was quickly replaced by pain as she was violently shoved hip first over another jagged stone, slamming her ankle into the next unforgiving surface.

Think, dammit, she thought after hitting another rock that ripped into her shoulder, tearing her shirt. The river mercilessly tossed her like a rag doll in the washing machine. She couldn't see past the white waters all around her and only moved forward because the river was in complete control.

It has to end, she thought. *Just survive. It has to end.* Her body was turned the wrong way and pushed over a smaller rock before her head made violent contact with something unmovable and unforgiving.

Chapter

24

If she dies, he dies, Althea thought for the hundredth time since watching Nadia throw herself into the center of the river and get swept away. *She's clearly from some large city on Earth. Most from Baako wouldn't have been startled into the center of a rushing river.* Althea kicked herself internally again for how close her arrow had come to hitting Nadia. *Moron. I was supposed to save her, not kill her. Now I have to contend with her idiot guardian.*

"Althea," Dimitri interrupted her internal chastising. "Are you listening to me?"

"What guardian?" Althea spat back, hiding any fear she had.

"You're bouncing her too much," Dimitri said. "Keep her steady."

"You're lucky I showed up when I did," Althea shot back over her shoulder.

Nadia was on top of a blanket that Althea and Dimitri kept as stretched and straight as possible. Althea was carrying Nadia near her feet while Dimitri held the blanket near Nadia's head.

"You're little girlfriend here would be dead, drowned in the river back there." *If she dies, he dies.*

"She's my charge, and I already thanked you for saving her."

"As it is, she'll probably die anyway." Althea's stomach twisted painfully. *If she dies, he dies.*

"She'll be fine," Dimitri said with clenched teeth as they ran through the forest toward the nearest shelter.

"She'll be fine," Althea had said to herself over and over as she watched her mother's body being devoured by cancer. Althea had only just turned six when her mother had called her into the hospital room.

"Listen, Thea," her mother had said in little more than a whisper. "I need you to be strong, my girl. I need you to protect yourself first and always because I won't be around to do it for you." Althea's mother wrapped Althea's small brown hands with her dark, soft ones. Althea always felt safe in those hands. "Baby girl, I need you to live even when I'm gone. You're special. Use your special to change this world."

Althea didn't know then, but that would be the last time she would hear her mother's voice. Her mother had stopped all treatments for the cancer she knew she wouldn't beat. Two days later, Althea entered the foster care system in Detroit, Michigan, and immediately had to learn what it meant to be strong, to protect herself. She went through dozens of placements, some worse than others, but each had their unredeemable issues. The older she got, the more beautiful she got, and the more problems she seemed to attract. At almost six feet tall, her flawless light brown skin, bright green eyes, and long lashes turned every head when she walked into the room. But she knew that girls from the projects and then foster care didn't make it as models or afford to be good girls.

"Protect yourself," her mother had said. So, as everyone was looking at Althea, she was looking for the exits. Her IQ was off the charts, but that didn't stop her from dropping out of school at sixteen and running cars for a local gang to pay the bills. Then, some random gatekeeper entered one of the only dreams Althea had ever remembered.

"Althea, what in the hell is wrong with you?" Dimitri asked, startling her.

"I was just thinking about every rock your girlfriend hit in that river and what kind of damage she probably has." *If she dies, he dies.* "And how damn heavy she is."

"Well," Dimitri cleared his throat. "There's the cave."

"Great," she said aloud as her mother's voice rang in her ears, "protect yourself."

Chapter

25

"I appreciate the help, but I'm sure there are other things we're keeping you from." Dimitri's usually level voice sounded pinched and rude to Nadia's semi-conscious mind.

"Nah," a husky female voice responded, causing Nadia to surface from the darkness.

She slowly opened her eyes as pain raked her body with no start or finish. Staring straight up, too afraid to move her head, she could see a jagged rock ceiling and hear a gentle drip, drip, drip. The memory of the river washed over her one rock at a time.

Arms? The right shoulder was throbbing and wrapped. Pain surged when she attempted to lift her left arm.

Legs? She wiggled her toes with a painful but happy sigh. Not paralyzed, but not in good shape. Just the toe wiggle exhausted her.

There was no need to check her back and chest. They were screaming every time she took a shallow breath.

"We made it to the cave?" Nadia's voice sounded harsh.

Dimitri swam into her view; signs of fear and exhaustion were written across his furrowed brow. He reached for her but stopped, hovering just out of reach.

"How are you feeling?" he whispered.

His behavior reminded Nadia of how her mother

cradled Nadia's grandmother in her final hours.

"Why are you acting like I'm dying?" Nadia tried to turn toward him, but pain burned through her body.

Breathing slowly and shallowly, she watched Dimitri's face twisted into a painful-looking smile.

When her pain subsided enough for her mind to work again, she asked, "Am I dying?"

"As far as I can tell, no," Dimitri said, through gritted teeth. "You're one giant bruise. I'm unsure if you have broken bones, but your breathing has been shallow and your pulse erratic for the last two days."

"Two days?" Nadia glanced around using only her eyes, trying to find the time she had lost.

"You also cried out every time you were touched or moved." He looked away. "But didn't wake."

"I'm sorry. That must have been awful for you. I didn't realize—"

"Awful for me?" He cut in. "I thought you were dead. I saw you after… You were on the riverbank. After you, I mean the arrow caused you, I ran next to the river, but you were going too fast. I saw you hit... I should've been there. I should've gotten you out, not..." He paused, looking over his shoulder.

"Um," the female voice said. "I'll go get some more firewood."

"I should've— I'm your guardian, not..." He trailed off again.

Shame flared in Nadia's chest. How did he get saddled with her? Clumsy, chubby, and untrained. She clenched her eyes. *They never should've brought me here.*

"Nadia? What hurts?"

"I'm so sorry," she rasped through her clenched teeth, emotion and pain filling her eyes with tears. "I'm so stupid. There was that arrow, and I got pulled away. The water was so fast, so strong. There were rocks. A lot of rocks. And I think I hit every one of them, but I swear I tried not to. I mean, I tried to get to the shore. I tried to use my gifts, but nothing happened. I'm, I'm, I'm just so, I tried." She was close to hyperventilating when she stopped talking.

"You're unbelievable," Dimitri's voice was almost unrecognizable, causing Nadia to open her eyes. He wore a forced smile. "You're in so much pain, you cannot even take a deep breath, and yet you're apologizing to me, the person who should've prevented all this." He shook his head slowly. "Nadia of Earth, I'm your guardian. That means I guard you even from yourself when needed, especially from yourself. Don't take this blame onto your already damaged shoulders. It's mine, and I'll carry it and you when needed."

"Stop it," her voice was louder than she had expected. "No one could've prepared you for me and my epic clumsiness. Seriously, I might be cursed."

Dimitri's face was set in stubborn lines.

"Fine," she said. "We can carry the blame together. No." She raised her left arm with painful effort when he opened his mouth to protest. Setting it on his bare chest. "You may be my guardian, but I've known myself for much longer." She felt exhausted and heard the slur in her speech. "Help me sit up. I don't want to sleep."

"You need to," Dimitri said.

She felt a sprinkle of powder hit her face and knew

he had dosed her with dreamless sleep powder.

She fell into an uneasy dream where the trees had a secret and wanted to tell her, but someone would cut the tree down whenever she got close. "Don't trust," they would start. Then one axe swing from an unseen assailant. Each tree screamed as it died, falling silent only after it hit the ground.

Nadia woke in the darkened cave. The fire had burned low, and she felt utterly alone and emotionally shattered.

"Dimitri." Her voice sounded little used.

"I'm here." He sounded some way off.

Nadia's relief drove away the screams of the nightmares. She flicked her gift at the fire, and it flared to life. She sighed with relief before rolling onto her side and pushing her protesting body up.

"Nadia." Dimitri appeared at her side. "What are you doing?"

She ground her teeth against her aching, well, everything. She was making a poor decision, but wanted to see the extent of her injuries and couldn't stomach the thought of going back to sleep to watch and hear more trees die.

"You shouldn't move." Dimitri gently slid his arm around her.

She leaned on him gratefully and a little embarrassed. "I need to. Plus, lying down is just as painful, and I don't want to go back to sleep, at least, not yet." She put more weight on her legs, feeling out her pain tolerance.

"Okay. But be honest, how do you feel?"

"Um." She thought about lying, but it was easier to

be honest when she was already focused on not passing out and throwing up. "Terrible." She tried to smile at him and realized even her face hurt. She twisted slightly to look in his direction, causing pain to roll through her chest and back. She gripped Dimitri's arm. "Sorry. I promise I'll be okay in a second or two." She was clenching her eyes and teeth, trying to ride out the pain.

"What hurts?"

"Everything." Nadia didn't open her eyes. Panic bubbled up through the pain. "I can't breathe."

"What?" Dimitri shifted, and pain shot up Nadia's right leg. "You can't… Nadia, focus on my voice. Slow even—"

"What's the matter?" the female voice said.

Nadia opened her eyes and rotated her hips toward the voice. She had just enough time to see a tall woman in her mid-twenties standing at the mouth of the cave. The woman was heavily armed and very beautiful. Then, Nadia's eyes rolled, and her body convulsed in Dimitri's arms.

"Nadia!"

26

Dimitri's scream rattled around in Nadia's head even as she opened her eyes in a new, strange place. She stood at the bottom of a large staircase, looking at a highly polished, black granite building.

"How am I…" She took a deep, pain-free breath, slowly twisting her body this way and that before jumping up and down. She giggled at how ridiculous she must look. But no one was around except the granite building. "Maybe I'm dead?" She climbed the stairs, thinking about what she knew of the afterlife, and this didn't quite feel right.

The building had two ornate wooden doors delicately carved with motifs of people gathered around a central figure; sometimes the figure was a man, other times it was a woman. She pulled open one door to reveal eight-foot-tall painted portraits on every wall, with gigantic, closed wooden doors between each. Nadia's eyes were drawn up the grand marble staircase to the second level. Like everything else, the staircase was absurdly oversized, like she was in a place of extreme wealth. The inside was also spotless and uncluttered, almost sterile and uninviting.

"Hello," her voice echoed oddly around the room.

"Who's there?" Another familiar voice called back. "Oh dear, dear, dear." A woman appeared at the top of the stairs, and Nadia immediately knew her.

"You," she called up to the gatekeeper she had only

met in a dream.

"Nadia of Earth?" the vulture-like gatekeeper asked. "Why are you here uninvited?"

"Uninvited? I didn't seem to have a choice. Kind of like my trip to Baako."

"No," the gatekeeper started. "No, no. You had a choice, and you signed off."

"Did I?" Nadia began, anger saturating her voice, but the gatekeeper cut her off.

"Now, hurry and tell me what you are doing here. I have much to do, schedules to keep."

"Go then," an ethereal female voice responded. "I'll take care of our guest."

"Yes, my lady." The keeper turned and immediately disappeared.

"But," Nadia called with so many more questions. She turned to the new woman, and her mouth fell open. The woman was painfully beautiful. She seemed ageless, with a soft glow to her flawless skin and symmetrical features. Her hourglass figure moved gracefully down the stairs. Everything in the room lost some of its shine as she approached.

"What brings you here, Nadia?" The woman's voice was soft and delicate, with edges that could cut. "Have you learned your place yet?"

"Gaia?" Nadia asked.

The woman inclined her head ever so slightly. "This is the maiden." Gaia had a slight smile that made her ridiculously beautiful face look haughty. "I prefer this." She ran her hands delicately down her silken dress. "When I am working in the office, this form is less intimidating."

"Less intimidating?" Nadia mumbled, feeling like a hairy wart next to such unrealistic beauty.

"Nadia, look at me," Gaia said, cutting off Nadia's self-pity. "Last we met, you were injured, but now it seems you are beyond mere injury. You'll die very soon if you do not see a powerful healer. My son is discovering the truth of the situation even as we speak, I think."

"You don't happen to have a magic well nearby?"

"No."

"So I'm dying." Nadia glanced around the room, wondering again about a possible afterlife.

"Why so laxidazical about your own death? Does life mean so little?"

"No. I plan to fight, especially now." Though, she shuddered at the thought of all the pain.

"Why now?"

"Well," Nadia felt uncomfortable at the intensity of Gaia's stare.

"Go on."

"I'm here, I mean, on Baako and this adventure with Dimitri."

"You feel deeply for him, don't you?" It was not a question, nor did she sound kind or understanding.

Nadia shook her head even as the emotions she felt in the nightmare about Dimitri pushed to the surface. "I, uh, I just met him." Gaia's beautiful face looked sternly at Nadia. "And he's my guardian."

"And an unremarkable girl-child from Earth is unworthy of a Great Guardian's son." Gaia turned to climb the stairs in a clear dismissal. "But he's your guardian, so call his name and go."

"What?" Nadia felt like she had been slapped.

"Call his name and go." She overenunciated each word.

"Dimitri," Nadia said, feeling diminished and pissed. *Maybe haughty jerk is just part of being the maiden,* Nadia thought. "Dimitri?"

"Nadia?" Dimitri said as an almost overwhelming sense of pain flooded her body and mind.

Then it stopped.

The pain, her ability to move, even her sense of self, were just gone.

"I, I can't move," Nadia stared at Dimitri, panic rising in her throat.

"Did you?" Dimitri addressed the other woman in the room.

She nodded, walking up, "My name's Althea. I'm using my gift to hold your body in place and to tell your mind you're not in pain." She winced. "Please stop fighting me. If you break through, your pain'll flood your brain and send you spiraling."

Nadia searched Dimitri's eyes.

He nodded gently and tried to smile. "I asked her to help you." His voice was little more than a whisper.

Althea sighed. "I'll hold you in this state as long as I can."

"Thank you," Nadia said.

"You're welcome." Althea gave a little bow before walking to the mouth of the cave.

"How do you feel?" Dimitri asked, his eyes overly bright.

"I feel nothing."

"I'm sorry I didn't ask you before Althea—"

"No. I understand. Thank you." She paused memorizing his perfect face. "Your mother said I'm dying."

"No." Dimitri jumped to his feet, startling Nadia. "No. I won't. You can't." He grabbed his bag.

"Dimitri, please listen." He paused. His face was a mask of determination. "She said if I don't get to a healer, a strong healer—"

"Stop," Dimitri started moving again.

"Listen," Nadia tried to get his attention. "None of this is your fault. If I—"

"No, not now."

"You need to hear—"

"No, I have to pack. We have to go."

"Where?"

"There's a village two or three days from here and a town, a big town not far from there." He abruptly left her line of sight, leaving her in frozen silence. It was unnerving and panic-inducing, so when she saw Althea, she felt a surge of gratitude.

"Dimitri asked me to put you into a dreamless sleep because he is out of powder."

"Wait," Nadia said, still trying to see Dimitri. "I can tell you two aren't, well, you don't seem to like each other.

"We have a bit of a history. Why?"

"I've a favor to ask you."

"What?" Althea looked skeptically at Nadia.

"He's stubborn."

"That's a bit of an understatement." Althea laughed to herself.

"Will you make sure he doesn't kill himself or you

or anyone else to save me?" Nadia kept her voice low.

"I'll do my best. But I really must…"

Nadia sighed, wanting to stay awake, but hated being frozen more and more every second that passed. "Go ahead."

Chapter

27

"What do you mean?" Dimitri growled between breaths. He struggled to keep Nadia from bouncing on the quickly-made stretcher. "From what I've heard," Dimitri said, "You can incapacitate a small army, but the mind of one girl is giving you trouble?"

"First off, guardian, don't believe everything you've heard," Althea shot back as she panted. "Second, the physical labor of carrying her on this crappy stretcher is a lot. And I've never encountered anything like this. Something outside of this girl is fighting me."

Dimitri scoffed, ready with another quip.

"And," Althea cut in. "Nadia is fighting me from within."

"She's fighting your gift while unconscious?" Dimitri was both impressed with Nadia and skeptical of Althea.

"You need to make a choice, Dimitri. Either I keep her in a dreamless sleep, becoming too exhausted to keep walking, or I release her mind, and she's on her own with whatever is fighting me. Either way, she's probably gonna die no matter what we do."

"No," Dimitri said.

"No what?"

"She isn't going to die. Stop saying that!"

"Fine, neat, whatever," Althea said, annoyance clear in her voice. "Make your choice, or I'll stop right here."

"Release her mind," Dimitri said after a long silence of labored breathing. "But we move faster."

Chapter

28

Pain flooded through Nadia's body, causing her to almost wake before being dragged further into unconsciousness.

The pain abruptly stopped, replaced just as quickly with motion sickness.

"Hello, my dear," a voice Nadia could never forget spoke from the edges of her consciousness.

Damnit, why him?

Nadia was on her back, staring at an iron chandelier covered in dripping wax and low-burning candles. The chandelier spun slightly over a hazy, poorly lit room that smelled strongly of rust, smoke, and blood. Looking for something more stationary caused her to realize she was the one spinning, not the chandelier. She was lying on a medieval t-shaped wooden table with her ankles and wrists shackled by thick leather straps. Dimitri's shirt fit great when standing, but rode precariously high while strapped to the table. Everything was covered, but just barely, and the shirt clung and pulled everywhere she didn't want it to. But she could do very little if the shirt crept up with her arms straight out to her sides. She was grateful for her sweatshirt and the extra layer it provided, but the blood smell and extreme vulnerability of her position made her queasy and terrified.

"If you want your charming torture chamber to be covered in vomit, by all means, keep spinning me," Nadia

159

said, trying to cover her fear with snark. *It's a dream. It's only a dream,* she said on repeat in her head.

The spinning stopped so abruptly that the restraints gouged Nadia's left wrist and ankle. She knew her face betrayed her pain, but she worked hard to school her features.

"Cute." She shifted slightly, righting herself on the table.

"Oh, you're so brave, aren't you?" The orange-eyed man mocked. "Little Nadia, come to save the day from wicked ol' me? I guess I should give up now and save myself the trouble."

"That's the first good idea you've had." Nadia had to stop herself from shuddering when the man laughed. "Gah," she gagged. "Laugh in a different direction. Your breath is toxic."

The orange-eyed man snarled within an inch of Nadia's face.

She didn't flinch, sizing him up. His eyes were bloodshot, and entirely too much hair stuck out from his bulbous nose.

"May I ask you a question?" Nadia asked with as much sweetness as she could.

The man's chins and neck wobbled in unison with surprise as he stood up and gave a slight nod, curiosity painted across his unfortunate features.

"Baako is different from Earth, but do you all have breath mints or toothbrushes? And are they nearby? Seriously, bro, you could use one."

Anger flashed in his eyes before manic laughter escaped his chapped lips. "You do possess bravery, or maybe no one told you who I am?" He drew himself up to his unimpressive height. "The peasants fear talking about me and my gifts, believing I'll steal their children in their sleep." With his sweat-soaked brow and barely recognizable chin, he looked like an old man boy, but Nadia could feel the power surrounding him. Power that didn't feel like it was coming from him, more like the place itself, much like Gaia's beach world.

"Oh, sorry," She simulated sorrow for him when she realized he had asked her something. "Your voice is so irritating, I stopped listening."

He snapped his fingers, and Nadia was punched across the face by a much more impressive and stealthy man. His six-and-a-half-foot bulk didn't stop him from blending into the shadowy corner like a man who had lived in the shadows his entire life.

Her eyes instantly filled with tears as half her head rang from the impact. She moved her jaw a little, hoping it wasn't broken. It hurt like hell, but seemed alright."Thanks for the love tap, um, you," she tried to point with her restrained hand, blinking back tears. Her face ached as it began to swell from her jaw to her left.

"Oh, how rude of me." The orange-eyed man gave a mock bow, his eyes never leaving Nadia's face. "I forgot to introduce myself and my friends."

Friends? She glanced around the room for the first time. A man with a similar build to the man who punched Nadia occupied every corner of the grimy room except one. The corner near the door had a man seated in a chair. His wrinkled, worn hands and shabby grey robes were the only things Nadia could see, but there was a clear feeling of power radiating from him. He was not introduced. The other three men were not named but instead given numbers.

"Interesting names you give the help," Nadia said sarcastically. "And what is your name?" She asked him, as if talking to a small child about to throw a fit.

The orange-eyed man's sneer melted into a toothy smile as he slowly spun Nadia, tracing his hand around the table's edge, looking at every inch of her body like she was a feast, and he was deciding what to eat first. "You're feisty," he stared at Nadia's somewhat ample chest. "You'll be more fun to break than the others. My name is Sergei, but you may call me master, sir, or Your Highness. Someday, you may even call me to your bed."

Nadia's perfectly constructed façade broke for a mere moment as alarm rolled through her.

Sergei clapped with joy. "Ah, you do fear. There'll be other ways you'll fear before this is over."

"You're right." Nadia's need to act, to take back control, was overwhelming. "I fear your blood getting on my clothing when I kick the crap out of you."

Sergei laughed again, and the gray-robed man leaned forward momentarily, holding Nadia's gaze. His face was a stoic mask even as interest gleamed from his eyes. She knew he had no intention of helping her.

"Oh, I'm not done." Nadia turned back to Sergei, hiding a shudder.

"Then, by all means," Sergei gestured for her to continue.

"Thank you, your royalness. I fear your receding hairline. Sunlight may hit it and blind me." His smile faltered as she continued. "I fear the oversized child you are kicking and screaming for your mommy when you don't get your way." Sergei's fists balled up. "I fear you may someday hit puberty, and your voice will no longer be the sweet-sounding five-year-old little girl's voice it is now."

"Enough," he growled as one of his men stifled a giggle.

"No. I'm just getting started. I fear you'll breathe on me again with your tooth decay and dragon's breath." Her table started to spin more aggressively than before, but she knew panic would debilitate her if she stopped talking. "I fear your tiny man syndrome will continue to grow, and we'll all be crushed under the weight of your ego."

Nadia gasped in the sudden darkness, no longer rotating. Discovering her arms and feet were free, she flexed her hands and rubbed her wrists until she hit a wooden surface directly above her body. Kicking out, she hit the walls of the structure. Her breath caught as she groped in the dark of a coffin.

Claustrophobia rose in her chest. Panic cutting off her air.

"A dream," she gasped, closing her eyes tightly. "I'm free of this box." She could feel the hysteria mere inches from the surface and spoke faster. "I'm only dreaming. I'm in my bed, safe and sound. No coffin." A knock shattered her concentration.

"Nadia?" Sergei asked. "Are you comfortable, my dear?"

"Go to hell!" Nadia tried to sound fierce but fell short.

"So much animosity," Sergei said with obvious delight. "What's wrong, deary? Are the walls closing in on you?"

Nadia's breathing picked up again.

"Maybe you can feel the air thinning around you, stealing your breath."

Nadia was nearing hyperventilation at his words, pressing her limbs against the walls.

"You know, I'll let you out if you want me to. All you have to do is ask nicely."

She had the uncontrollable urge to slap the smirk off his stupid face, which gave her a small amount of hope. If she could still think of violence, she hadn't lost the battle, yet.

Consider your options, she thought, eyes still closed.

Ask to be released. Never.

Kick your way out. Maybe.

Feign death. If needed.

Sergei wanted to play with her, and dying would take away his favorite new toy.

Nadia took a deep breath and hoped she had learned more than just stage combat in all her theater classes. She started kicking and pounding on the walls and lid of the coffin, growling and groaning to punctuate the performance. It took only moments to realize she wouldn't be able to kick her way out, so she played up her loud breathing and frantic movements, rocking from side to side, pounding her fists on the sides of the coffin over and over, using all of the real panic she felt to sell the performance.

She heard Sergei say, "It won't work, my love, but

by all means, keep trying." He laughed as she kept up the noise for another minute.

She cut her knuckles and could feel blood running down her hand as she gasped with effort. Her claustrophobia would only be held back another few moments before her act dissolved into a full-blown panic attack, uncontrolled and undeniable.

"I," Nadia gasped, scratching at the lid and feeling the wood splinter under her nails. She cringed in pain, tears falling down her cheeks. "Can't breathe." She scratched feebly and kicked lightly before stopping altogether. She held her breath with difficulty while she counted to five before taking a silent, deep breath for another count of five, focusing entirely on breathing until it wouldn't be heard outside the coffin. *He better hurry up.* Tiny lights danced in front of her eyes, her chest tight, and unconsciousness threatening to overwhelm her.

"Nadia, honey? No more outbursts or sarcastic comments?" Sergei sounded victorious, but Nadia didn't answer. "Nadia?" His voice was colored with concern. Nadia felt a smile spread across her face, pushing the panic further away. "Damn it. I told you to leave enough air for her to breathe. I swear, if she's dead, you must answer to Mother."

Nadia draped one arm across her face and the other over her chest, smearing her bloody knuckles on both. She stayed perfectly still as someone lifted the lid, allowing light to flood in. She didn't flinch when Sergei touched her neck to feel for her pulse, nor sigh with relief when he pulled away.

"You're so lucky she's not dead. Take her to her

room." A few drops of Sergei's spittle landed on Nadia's arm, making her stomach churn.

She allowed her body to swing uncontrolled when one of the numbered men tossed her over their shoulder. Her arms bounced around on his back with every bounding step the giant of a man took. She brushed the man's double swords in sheaths strapped to his back twice before realizing he had a small dagger between them. A desperate plan slowly formed in Nadia's mind.

"Put her there and leave us. I will not need you anymore tonight."

As the large brute lifted Nadia, she grabbed the dagger, swinging the pointed end toward her elbow and hoping for a soft landing. Luck was with her. She didn't impale herself. She was dropped onto her stomach, sinking into an overly fluffy bed. Opening her eyes ever so slightly, she could see Sergei's back as he leaned out of the bedroom door. Nadia inched her arm with the dagger under a pillow, stopping when the door shut. Sergei took a deep breath from one side of the room while light poured in from what must have been a window on the other side.

Dawn or dusk? She risked opening her eyes ever so slightly. Sergei locked the door, pocketing the key, and gliding a stubby finger down the side of his scabbarded short sword. He walked toward the window and out of her eyesight, but she felt him watching her in silence that made her want to squirm. She almost broke until she heard him drop what must have been his belt and sword before kicking off his shoes. Then, the bed shook as he grunted onto it, grumbling about things being too tall in this world for him.

Fingers lightly ran through Nadia's hair before she felt him sniff the back of her neck, drawing a deep breath. Still on her stomach, faced away from him, she gripped the dagger under the pillow, focusing on keeping her breathing even and not slapping him for his audacity.

Walking his fingers across her arm, he gripped her shoulder and abruptly rolled her toward him and onto her back. She kept her left arm and dagger under the pillow but allowed her right arm to flop across her face. He wriggled closer to Nadia, moving the entire bed in the process, before pressing his stomach against her body. He gently lifted her arm from her face and placed it on her chest.

"Mother thinks you'll never submit." His stubby fingers brushed against her neck. "But she's wrong, my dear. I always get what I want and I want you."

Nadia's skin crawled. The repulsion of Sergei touching her, lying in bed with her, was fogging her mind. She didn't know what to do.

"You're so beautiful," he whispered so close to Nadia's cheek she could feel his chapped lips moving against it. "You're plump and delicious like one of Cook's perfect little dumplings."

Sergei licked her cheek, and her body reacted before any decision was made. Sergei's eyes were closed as she shoved him onto his back, pressing the dagger into his throat.

"You devious, little pretender," he said, lying perfectly still. "I'll kill you slowly for this."

"Try it," Nadia challenged before pain racked her living body, pulling her mind in a dozen directions.

Chapter

29

"Althea," Dimitri said, anger saturating his tone. "Be careful with her."

"I can't keep up this pace." Althea's voice was barely a whisper. "Where are we going?"

"We only need to travel a few more miles tonight," Dimitri said, glancing into the dark sky. He knew the moon would rise soon, but traveling at night was always a risk. "There is an old village there, with a temple that should still be standing."

"Wait. The Village of Bedros?" Althea said, stopping abruptly. "That place is haunted."

"Rumors."

"Weren't all the villagers burned or something?"

"Let's take a short break."

"Subject change?" She asked through labored breathing.

"No," he said more aggressively than he meant to. "The moon will be out soon."

They gently placed Nadia on a patch of grass. Dimitri slipped his bag off with an internal sigh. His arms and back were starting to ache. "Here." He handed Althea one of the two remaining jerky strips.

"Thanks." She nodded, ripping off half with her teeth and chewing loudly. After a few minutes of silence, Althea asked, "Why would you want to sleep among the dead?"

Dimitri smiled as sarcastically as he could muster through his exhaustion and fear. "Is big, bad Althea afraid?"

"Shut up." Althea stood, rolling her shoulders before moving toward Nadia. "Let's just go. The sooner we get there, the sooner I can get away from the two of you."

Chapter

30

Nadia's pain was replaced by claustrophobia. It was pitch black and silent. She was back in the coffin.

Wait. No. She couldn't be. She was standing.

Her eyes slowly adjusted to the dark of the small bedroom.

"She's back," she heard Sergei say, not too far from her. "I can feel her. Find her, you idiots."

Damn it. How could he—

"Keep looking, moron!" Sergei was closer and sounded on the edge of a child-like fit.

She was still deciding what to do when the door flew open. She dropped and belly crawled under the four-poster bed, surprisingly pain-free. She could just see the large black boots and thick legs of one of the numbered men walking around the bed to where she had just been. He stood silently near the window for so long that Nadia had to force herself not to move. Then he dropped to the floor and looked right at her.

"Hi," Nadia said. The man said nothing, just stared. "Not much of a talker, are you?" The large man lay flat and reached under the bed for her leg. "No, please."

The bed had been barely tall enough for Nadia to shimmy under it. The large man lifted it slightly with his girth as he wrapped his hand around her ankle. He tugged Nadia toward him while trying to unstick himself from the bed.

Nadia flung her arms at him in hopes her gift would kick in, but it didn't. She couldn't even feel it.

"Uh," she said stupidly before kicking the man's face. Through the bottom of her bare foot, she felt his nose break. Releasing her ankle, the large man grabbed his nose, still stuck.

Nadia scrambled out, ripping out a chunk of her hair that got stuck to the wooden slats of the bed. She stumbled through the open door, away from the silent ogre, giving no thought to where she was going. She just ran away, away from the feeling of helplessness Sergei caused and any bedrooms in the damnable place. Her bare feet were loud on the stone flooring, causing her to slow to a quick walk until she hid behind a gaudy statue in an alcove. Her entire body shook as she took deep, raspy breaths as quietly as possible.

I was caught again, she thought, on the edge of tears. *Fire is easy.* Searching for her gift, she found she could just barely feel it, but couldn't reach it. *Damnit. Is this place warded?* She dropped her head into her hands.

"She's near," a small female voice said quietly from inside the hall, causing Nadia to shrink as small as her fluffy body allowed.

"Shut your mouths," a man answered. "Prisoners are silent, or they get punished."

"Sir," the same small voice said. "She will release us."

"That dream again?" The man laughed harshly. "You ain't never going to leave this world alive."

Nadia stood, slowly looking out from her hiding spot right into what looked like a medieval dungeon.

"What you looking at, putrid dolt," the man said before Nadia heard a slap and cry.

Nadia entered the torchlight, her feet carrying her right up to the man's back before he stopped laughing. He leaned against the stone wall near the first cell. A girl of about twelve was lying on the floor, cradled by an older woman. Nadia's rage flared as she grabbed the flickering torch and cracked it over the man's head. He dropped without ever turning around. Nadia searched for his keys. The large key ring slid smoothly off the man's belt even as Nadia's rage was subsiding and realization was kicking in. She had knocked the guy out, like, out cold. She watched his chest rise and fall to reassure herself he was still alive.

"I tried to warn him," the young girl said, interrupting Nadia's thoughts. "I knew you would come, Nadia of Earth."

"How—" Nadia began.

"My gift. It's that key," the girl pointed to the large metal keys, singling out a sizable two-toothed key. Nadia unlocked the cage, and the girl ran out to hug her. "I must go," the girl said. "But I know we'll meet again."

The girl took Nadia aback, but Nadia was downright floored when the girl disappeared. The older woman followed her after giving Nadia a slight bow.

Whispers from the other cells made the room sound like a beehive.

"Shhh." Nadia pressed a finger to her lips. "Please, stay quiet, and I'll get you out."

She had to hurry. If Sergei could feel her entering the Dreamworld, he had to feel people leaving.

The next cell held a man in his mid-thirties dressed

in simple clothing made of sturdy materials and animal skins. After several tries, she found the right key and swung open the door. The man disappeared the moment he walked over the threshold. She opened one cell door after another so the people inside could step out and disappear. Many of them thanked her by name or gave a slight bow. She didn't understand how any of this was happening, but was consumed by allowing more of Sergei's toys to leave his twisted fun house before she got caught.

Then she heard them. Footsteps.

"Quickly," a woman in her early seventies said. "Quickly, Nadia, before they come for us." The woman gripped the hands of two younger women, and all three were trembling.

Nadia silently tried one key after another before letting the women out. Nadia hoped, not for the first time, that they were waking up somewhere safe. She swung open one more cell before the footsteps stopped at the mouth of the dungeon two dozen yards away.

"Nadia?" Sergei's voice was saturated with malice. "I know you're here, Nadia, and you are stealing from me."

She tiptoed to the next door, gripping all the keys tightly.

"I also know you're injured," Sergei said. "Your leg…"

Nadia's right leg buckled under her. The man in the cell caught her through the bars.

"Damnit," Nadia mouthed. She had not thought about her injuries while in the Dreamworld.

"You don't have to free us," the man in the cell whispered.

"Yes, I do," Nadia whispered as she regained her footing. *Not like some kind of savior,* she thought, as if the universe was arguing with her. *Short, clumsy me is no savior. These people just deserve better.* She pulled open the cell door, but the man hesitated.

"Go," she mouthed. She gripped the next cage door, the pain growing as it rose up her leg.

"How dare you release what is mine!"

Nadia felt a surge of energy as she watched Sergei's shadow jumping up and down like a toddler throwing a fit. Pain or no pain, she felt like she was winning against the oversized infant.

"You're far more trouble than you're worth, no matter what anyone says," Sergei said before a slap echoed through the dungeon. "Wake up, you idiot." Grumbling came from the man Nadia had knocked out. "How could you let an injured little girl get the best of you?" There was a long pause full of shuffling before Sergei spit, "Never mind, you moron! Go and get her."

"What?" Nadia said, pain coloring her voice. "Too afraid to come get me yourself?" Four more cells were shrouded in darkness, and Nadia intended to release all the captives she could. She knew she couldn't open the cells that were lit, and the occupants seemed to understand. They were all huddled in the back of their cells, with their eyes averted.

"Don't tempt me, little girl," Sergei struggled to keep his voice even. "You're a small challenge, what with your shoulder ripped open."

Nadia unlocked another cage door as her shirt ripped open, allowing warm blood to drip down her back.

She hissed through her teeth. Her left arm hung uselessly as she swung open the cage door with her right. The hinges squeaked as Nadia said, "Go," no longer caring if Sergei heard her. Pain raked her body. *How's he doing that?* Nadia barely stopped a groan of agony while opening the next cage.

"Nadia of Earth, please let me help you," an older man said before leaving the cage.

"When you wake up," she said. "Find Dimitri, the guardian. He's traveling north in the Forest of Bagrach, I think. Find him and bring a healer." He nodded once and disappeared. Raising her voice, Nadia said, "Hey, Serg. Can I call you Serg?"

"No. Stop letting out my prisoners."

Nadia crossed to the next cage. "Okay, Serg. How do you know about my injuries?"

"This is my world, little brat." Serg's voice was getting closer. Nadia flung open the next cage. "I know everything about my victims."

"Strange," Nadia scrambled to the next cell. "It took you a while to find me. Do you know if I'm armed or not?"

Sergei's footsteps faltered.

"It doesn't matter," he said after a few moments of silence. "You're too damaged to fight back."

"Nah," Nadia wrapped her useless arm around her aching chest to relieve some of the pull on her bleeding shoulder, swinging open the cell with the other. "You don't know me well if you think a little pain can bring me down." She nodded to the two teenage boys as they left the cell.

"Oh, Nadia," Sergei sounded amused. "It's not a

little pain. You really got the hell beat out of you, didn't you, my little dumpling? A broken rib and internal bleeding."

Gasping, she fell onto the cage door she was unlocking. Sergei chuckled as he walked toward the sound of her labored breathing. She jammed the key into the next cage.

"Open it," she mouthed to what she thought must be an entire family of five. They pushed it open.

"We'll find you," the woman said before she disappeared with her family.

"Stop letting people out, you stupid, little whore!" Sergei's childish whine made his nasal voice more annoying.

"Whore?" Nadia said, swallowing down blood. "What happened to dumpling?"

"Clearly, you need to be reminded of your head injury. Did you know it's now infected?"

"I'm sorry," she said to the next cell, sliding down and laying her head on the cool ground.

"Do not be, Nadia of Earth." An elderly woman smiled down at her through tears. "Take heart in those you have saved as we do."

As Sergei approached, the cell's occupants faded to the back of their cages. He pulled Nadia's head up by her now bloody hair. She hardly reacted. Pain overwhelmed her senses.

"Don't forget the internal bleeding in your lower back, too," he said directly into her ear. "And your damaged lung." He started to laugh as Nadia gasped for breath. He let go of her hair, letting her head bounce off the stone floor.

"Dimitri," she mouthed.

"What, my dear?" Sergei said.

Nadia looked at Sergei's face as it swam in and out of focus. Dimitri's panicked face also swam in and out. She smiled as she called to Dimitri again.

She saw Sergei's fat face turn puce and contort with rage before the Dreamworld dissolved, and only Dimitri could be seen.

"I'm here," he said, laying Nadia flat. "Stay awake."

Nadia blinked at Dimitri rapidly as she choked on her blood. "Dimitri?" She didn't understand how, but was grateful to be awake even as the pain rolled through her with every breath.

"Stay awake," Dimitri lifted her head to place a blanket underneath it. He pulled his hand away, bloody. "Your head?" he questioned.

Nadia gripped his arm, opening and closing her mouth like a fish out of water. She couldn't breathe, and the panic rising rapidly in her chest didn't help. She heard Althea walk into the room before Nadia's breathing stopped altogether.

Chapter

31

A voice. No, a presence flooded Nadia's mind and body.

"Don't be afraid," the presence said. It felt wispy and sad.

"I'm not breathing," Nadia observed.

"You're dying."

"Then why am I standing?"

"I'm doing that."

Nadia couldn't tell if the presence was female or male.

"I'm borrowing your body, but I will return it," the presence said.

"But then I'll die?"

"Perhaps."

"Who are you?"

"I'm one of hundreds trapped in this place. One of many waiting for him to come back. We are waiting to be released from this plane."

"Who are you waiting for?"

The presence used Nadia's arm to point at Dimitri.

Nadia watched as the presence spoke aloud. It was a strange sensation to feel her mouth and body moving without any control over the movement. But she welcomed the temporary relief from the pain.

"Stop."

Althea dropped into a fighter's stance, but her

178

mouth fell open.

The presence was looking at Althea, "If the unbelieving and unworthy disturb the dead, they will not hesitate to disturb you back. Are you prepared for that, Althea of Earth?"

Of Earth? Nadia thought.

"How?" Althea mouthed. "How could you know that?"

The laugh that left Nadia was harsh, nothing like her own.

Nadia watched realization cross Dimitri's face before he said, "Who are you?"

"Dimitri of Bedros, Gaia and Benicio's son." The presence slowly looked over at him.

"What's going on?" Althea asked, clearly freaked out and still half crouched.

I'm with Althea, Nadia thought. *Why is Dimitri so calm? I'm literally being possessed.*

"His relationship with death is different than most," the presence said in Nadia's mind.

"No, that's who I am," Dimitri said to the presence. "Who are you?"

"I saw you many times when you were a boy," the voice said. "You came here and stayed for weeks at a time. Did you ever find what you were looking for?"

"No," Dimitri said.

"Dimitri," Althea stepped between him and Nadia. "Is Nadia—"

"Just wait," Dimitri stepped to the side.

"You were looking for answers as to why someone would do this," the voice said.

Nadia watched her arms move. She saw the cuts on her knuckles from the Dreamworld and the colorful bruises she had received in the river, but she felt nothing.

"How those who followed orders could look away when the screaming started, or walk away when they knew the death they had caused. How they could sleep at night when you could not for fear of hearing the screams of those you could do nothing to save."

"Yes," he whispered, his voice heavy with deep sadness.

"He sacrificed himself to give you and your brother time to escape," the voice sounded less and less like Nadia's with each word it spoke through her. "He was brave, and his actions saved many future lives. You were a mere child, yet you carry the burden of those dead so long ago. Why?"

"He was my father, and everyone who died in this damnable village were my friends and neighbors. My father was tortured," his voice broke. He looked at her with unshed tears. "And for what? Why did the soldiers come to this village, my village? What were they looking for?"

"You." The voice began sounding more distant, and Nadia could feel the first trickles of pain on the edge of her awareness. "The enemy tortured your father to find you and your brother because of what he was told. If you had died that day, how many more would have died in all the years you have lived? This girl, for one." Nadia's hands touched her chest, and her legs started shaking. The presence was leaving. "Let the pain in your heart go. Learn to accept, and you will be able to heal her and so many more."

The voice was a whisper by the end. Nadia's eyes

widened, and her legs gave way when the presence left.

"Dimitri," Nadia said through gasps. She was looking past him at the man beside him.

"Don't talk." Dimitri laid her on her blankets.

Nadia clawed at her neck, trying to breathe. Her shallow breaths were wet and bubbling with blood. Her panic rose as pinpricks of light appeared in her vision.

"Calm," the man said. He reached out to touch Nadia, but his hand went right through her shoulder.

"Dead?" she asked the ghost man.

"No," Dimitri said. "You're not dying."

"I am," the man said. "He was always so stubborn, even as a little boy." The man smiled, and Nadia knew. She could see the similarities: same shape to his eyes and nose, same defined chin.

"Dad?" Nadia mouthed.

"Yes," Benicio said. "Can you get him to listen?"

"Dimitri," Nadia said through painful gulps of air. "Stop."

"No," Dimitri was bandaging her shoulder. "You'll be fine," he said over and over.

"Stop!" she hissed more than spoke, causing her to choke.

He stopped, defeat written all over his face.

Nadia looked at Benicio.

"He's my son. He has my gift."

"Your father's gift," she said.

"He's always been taught to fight, but my gift comes from surrender."

"I don't have his gift," Dimitri said. "I've never been able to heal."

"Surrender," Nadia said. "Gift from surrender." Nadia's words were broken, but she could see understanding cross Dimitri's face.

"Surrender? How?"

Pain overwhelmed Nadia, and her eyes rolled in her head. Her body convulsed, and her head bounced painfully off the blanket Dimitri had put under it.

Shit. I really am dying this time.

"No," Dimitri screamed, and Nadia could feel his weight pushing her convulsing body into the ground. "Surrender. How?" He screamed. "I don't understand."

Nadia felt the convulsions slow, and her breathing hitched in her chest. She looked up at Dimitri and tried to smile, but was suddenly looking down on herself. She watched the smile melt off her own pale face as her eyes dimmed.

"It's not your time." Benicio was standing beside her.

Nadia looked down at her ghostly self and back at her broken body.

"I look pretty dead," she said, surprised at how bitter she sounded.

"My son may yet save you if you're the one."

"Is this more prophecy crap?"

Benicio only nodded, watching his son.

Moments that felt like hours passed as they both watched Dimitri's efforts. He tried CPR before shaking Nadia's body, screaming at her to fight. He collapsed onto her chest, choking on his sobs and pounding one fist into the ground.

"Stop," Althea said from across the room. "She's

gone, Dimitri. Let her go."

"No," he said and started compressions again.

"Dimitri," Althea crossed to him. "You know what death looks like." She reached for his hands, and he shoved her hard, causing her to fall.

"I cannot lose you too," Dimitri's voice was muffled as he lay back on Nadia's chest and sobbed. "Not here, not in this place."

"He's ready," Benicio said. "Go back. He can heal you."

"What?" Nadia said, ghostly tears streaming down her face. "He's so defeated."

"Go now, or it'll be too late."

Nadia didn't understand. One moment, she stood over her body; the next, she was filled with pain and heat. Heat that was coming from Dimitri's hands.

"Dimitri," Nadia said, though she wasn't sure any sound came out.

"What the actual hell?" Althea said, still sprawled on the floor.

"Why are you still here?" Dimitri lifted his head slightly to look at Althea, clearly unaware Nadia had said anything.

"Dimitri." Nadia touched his face with a shaky hand. Breathing still hurt. Everything still hurt, but she was no longer drowning. "You did it." Nadia smiled through her swollen face, another gift from the river and Sergei.

"He did it," Benicio said. "He surrendered his external strength and control. My gift has always been a different, quiet strength neither of my boys appeared to have until now. Until you." Benicio looked at Nadia, and she was surprised she could still see him. He was wispy and translucent, but he was still there.

"Nadia? But how?" Dimitri touched her swollen lip and eye ever so gently. "You're still very broken."

"I'm sad that my face makes you think broken," she smiled through the pain, grimacing through a deep breath. "But I'll live. Right?" Nadia turned to look at Benicio, but he was gone.

"You were dead," Althea said, her mouth and eyes wide.

"Yeah, I was. I imagine I'll have thoughts on that when I don't feel like a semi has slammed into me."

"Semi?" Dimitri asked.

"It's a, no, it doesn't matter."

"I still don't understand. How are you not dead?" Dimitri said.

"You have your father's gift of healing," Nadia tried to hold back another wince. "He said you had to surrender to be able to use it. I don't understand, but you did something."

"I, um," Althea interrupted. "I'll take the first watch." She ran down the stairs.

"Okay," Dimitri watched Althea leave before turning to Nadia. "But you were—"

"Let's figure it out in the morning."

"Are you, I mean," Dimitri stammered. "Did I heal enough for you to rest? Do you need, uh," he glanced around the room.

Nadia followed his gaze.

It was not a room, more like a landing in an abandoned building overrun by animals.

"Are you hungry, or do you want me to try to heal you more?"

Nadia knew he was rambling. "I'm okay for tonight." She touched his arm. He looked at her, and his eyes were filled with tears. "I promise. You did it. You saved me from me."

He suddenly laughed, wiping at his tears. "I thought you were…" he couldn't finish.

"I was," she said, and he took a shuddering breath. "But I'm not now." They looked at each other for a long moment. Nadia touched the dark circles under his eyes. "You're exhausted. Can you sleep?"

"I don't know," he said, looking at the stairs.

"Althea has the first watch. Please try." She patted the blanket next to her. "Platonic sleepover for warmth?"

Dimitri stayed on his knees, indecision written across his face.

"I promise no funny business," Nadia said with a painful smile. "I just have awful dreams, and it'll make me feel better knowing you're there."

She shifted, sending a bolt of pain through her back and chest. Dimitri wrapped Nadia in her blankets and lay beside her, gently placing his arm around her.

"Thank you." She intertwined their fingers without thinking and listened to his breathing. She tried to think about anything but her pain as she slowly fell asleep in her guardian's arms.

They both woke up at the same moment, still holding hands, and stood in a stone hallway.

Chapter

32

"Dimitri?" Nadia asked. "Why are you..." She yanked his hand.

"Nadia," he smiled down at her. "Why do you fear? This is only a dream." His voice carried, and Nadia tensed.

She tugged his hand, flattening them both against the wall. "This isn't a dream," she said. "Well, it's kind of, but even if it was, how often do you dream with other people?" She paused, listening. "We're in the Dreamworld, and he'll already know we're here. Let's go."

"Dreamworld?" Dimitri said, looking around slowly. "Wait, the Dreamworld?"

"Yes," Nadia said. "And you shouldn't be here."

"We shouldn't be here."

"Right," Nadia said. "No, you're right." She thought about her broken body sleeping next to Dimitri. But she knew she had left people behind on her last Dreamworld visit. People Sergei could hurt or even kill. "But we have to take this chance to find the others."

Dimitri stopped Nadia, forcing her to look at him. "Others?"

"It's a long story." She tried to pull him down the corridor with their still linked hands.

"Nadia, how are you not injured?" he began, but was silenced when Nadia placed her finger to his lips. She pulled Dimitri into an outcropping behind a suit of armor.

"Listen," she mouthed. "There's a dungeon somewhere in this damn castle, and I need to release the people Sergei is keeping there."

"The Dream Killer?"

"What?" Nadia's mouth fell open. "It's true? You all don't say his name? That's dumb."

"If you say his name—"

"He appears," Sergei said.

"Shit." Panic flooded Nadia's mind.

"You," Dimitri said. Nadia felt him try to release their hands to step toward Sergei, but she tightened her grip.

"Me," Sergei had a spreading grin. "What a great catch. A thief and her guardian. Goody!"

"Oh, Sergei," Nadia said, thinking hard about how she left last time. "We both know you can't catch—not a ball, not a break, and definitely not me."

She closed her eyes and thought hard about her body.

"Watcha doing?" Sergei asked. Footsteps were heard running toward them. "Trying to leave so soon?"

Nadia's hand, still gripping Dimitri's, started to shake as fear threatened to overwhelm her.

I got us caught. Dimitri caught.

She thought about Dimitri's peaceful, sleeping form and how their hands were clasped in the Dreamworld and the waking world. She thought about the tears and joy he had when he saved her. She looked into his face and gasped in pain.

They were out and awake.

"It worked," Nadia breathed deep, steady, painful

breaths. Between jumping out of the Dreamworld and her injuries, she felt like she had been pushed down several flights of stairs.

"Do you not have an ounce of self-preservation?" Dimitri asked, his voice pitched into a low growl. He stood abruptly, releasing her hand, and paced the landing. "You willingly went back there, didn't you?"

"Listen," she said.

"And why weren't you injured in there?"

"I can, kind of, explain if you—"

"How many times have you been there?"

"Dimitri," Nadia said. "Please sit. You're making me nauseous."

"I would douse you with sleepless dream powder right now if I had any left." He sat with a plop on his blankets. "You're something, something crazy, something maddening, but something."

She raised an eyebrow at him, and he gestured for her to start.

"Are you sure you're ready to hear this story?"

"Yes," he grumbled.

Nadia could see he was not by his face, but she told her story anyway. "I figured I would get pulled into the Dreamworld, but I hoped to drop into an unused room. And, well, I kind of did."

"How did I end up there?" Dimitri asked. "I have trained all my life to keep my mind closed to attacks like that."

"Actually, I think it was our linked hands. I was pulled in by, uh, him, and I pulled you in. Maybe I pulled us both in. I'm not sure."

"Well, then," Dimitri immediately intertwined their fingers. He shrugged, "I'm not taking any chances."

"Okay." Nadia tried to get comfortable through the exhaustion and pain that were quickly becoming her constant companions. She almost missed the Dreamworld, where she was healthy and uninjured, at least until Sergei told her otherwise.

She told Dimitri how she had woken in the Dreamworld, strapped to a table, and explained the coffin and bedroom scenes. It made her skin crawl, and shame colored her cheeks, but she felt he needed to know precisely what Serg was capable of in that place.

"When he found me, he, I don't know, told me I was injured, so I was, I guess. It was debilitating. I was a puddle of pain, and then I thought of you." Her cheeks colored again, but this time with embarrassment. "And I popped out of there and into this mess." She tried to gesture to her own body while hiding a yawn. "Of course, I died, and you saved me, so happy endings all around."

A laugh came out of Dimitri, even he hadn't expected, given the surprise on his face. Then he broke into genuine laughter, wrapping his other hand around their held hands. "You, Nadia of Earth, are incredible."

She felt warmth spread from his hands into her body, and her pain eased ever so slightly.

He looked down at their hands. "I'm starting to understand this new gift, and it's telling me you're very injured and beyond tired. Can you sleep?"

"Yes." She tried to pull their hands apart.

"Not a chance. You won't be going back without me."

"Okay. But be quieter next time." She was awake long enough to feel Dimitri get comfortable at her back without loosening their fingers.

They didn't go back.

Nadia woke somewhat rested, disappointed, and like she had fought and lost against ten angry bears. Gently rolling on her back, she winced when her wounded shoulder made contact with the floor, growling under her breath about pain and clumsiness until she saw Dimitri watching her.

"You didn't go back."

"How'd you know?" she asked.

He held up their still-intertwined fingers.

"You also stayed almost perfectly still all night," he said. "There were a couple of times I had to check to see if you were still alive. This new gift is handy even if I can only do a little healing at a time."

"If you keep using it, it will grow," a woman's voice said as she climbed the stairs.

Dimitri was on his feet and armed before Nadia's freed hand hit the ground.

"Stop." Dimitri was low in a fighter's stance, ready to drop if he needed his other gift. "Who are you, and why are you here?"

"She asked us to come." The woman looked at Nadia. "After she saved more than half my people from the Dream Killer."

"Is this true?" Dimitri asked without looking away from the newcomer.

"Yes." Nadia was trying to rise. "She was in a cell with four others."

"My family." The woman smiled. "You saved every member of my family, and now we have come to help you and your guardian."

"Just as you said you would," Nadia finally got to her feet. "Oh." Her head swam, and her left leg ached. She would've hit the floor if Dimitri had not caught her.

"Please," the woman gestured to her blankets. "May I help Nadia while we speak?"

"But who are you?" Dimitri still held Nadia while in a half-fighter's stance.

"Forgive me," the woman said with a slight head nod. "I'm Astrid, leader of the Prestarians. All my people have traveled through the night to help and support Nadia of Earth. You saved us, and we repay our debts."

"No debt." Nadia's eyes teared up from the pain. "I just got lucky. Dimitri, will you put me down? This hurts."

"All of your people?" Dimitri asked, ignoring Nadia. Astrid nodded. "How did you know where to find us?"

"Nadia," Astrid said. Astrid set the large bag she was carrying on the floor and began unwrapping bottle after bottle of herbs and salves.

"How did you know where we were?" Dimitri asked Nadia.

"I heard you and Althea talking."

"Althea?" Astrid asked. "Is she still here?"

"Probably not." Dimitri finally set Nadia back on her bedroll. "She was supposed to be on watch. Why do you ask?"

"She came to my people the day before the sleeping sickness spread," Astrid said. "She left just as quickly. I don't know if she was involved, but I would love to ask her."

"If you can find her, feel free to ask her whatever you want."

"My people will remain on watch while we are here. Nadia of Earth, you've done something no others have by escaping the Dreamworld. He'll hunt you through your waking and your sleep. He'll not want others to hear."

"Then we should tell them," Nadia said. Both Dimitri and Astrid looked at her. "Too many people fear him. Let's give them something else to think about. Do you have people you trust to spread the word?"

"Yes." Astrid smiled as she ground herbs in a mortar. "I can send out a couple of people today if you wish. How far do you want your tale to spread?"

"As far as they are willing to take it."

Chapter

33

"You must be starving," Dimitri said, setting an overflowing tray of food on a cot the Prestarians gave Nadia.

Despite her near-constant pain, Nadia was starving and bored as she sat on the end of the uncomfortable bed, looking out her second-floor window at all the Prestarians working in the clearing below.

"Yes," she said, ripping off a large piece of the warm bread and forcing herself to chew the oversized bite a couple of times before swallowing.

Dimitri smiled as he ripped off a piece for himself. "You can eat more slowly. No one will take away your food. I promise."

"You would know," Nadia said with her mouth full.

Since the Prestarians arrived, Dimitri had been making all of the decisions for Nadia and her care. He wouldn't let her explore the building, let the Prestarians visit, or even let her stand on her own while he was around.

"I'm not sorry." Dimitri smiled. "You've no self-preservation. My job is to protect you."

"Meh." Nadia tried to stay annoyed but hadn't had bread since she arrived in Baako and was shocked by its flavor. It had a smoky, buttery taste with a crusty outer layer that ripped apart with a satisfying crunch. It was still warm and melted on her tongue as she chewed another oversized piece. She grabbed a chunk of yellow cheese, wrapped it in the bread, and took a large bite. She closed her eyes and sighed at the nutty flavor of the cheese mixed with the smokiness of the bread. She did not open her eyes until she swallowed. Then, she noticed Dimitri watching her from the other small cot he insisted on placing in her room.

The Prestarians were a conservative bunch, but when Dimitri explained the jump to the Dreamworld, Astrid agreed to allow him to stay in the same room as Nadia.

"Good?" he asked, trying to hide a smile.

"Mmm hmm." She took a smaller bite out of embarrassment. She moved more slowly through the rest of the food, and Dimitri ate what Nadia couldn't while urging her to eat more. By the time the plate was cleared, Nadia was stuffed and content despite her constant pain. "Why am I the only person in the Temple? It's big enough for everyone."

"The others are afraid," Astrid said from the open doorway. "They call this place the City of Whispers and feel much more comfortable sleeping among the stars."

"Oh." Nadia lay back on her lumpy bed, watching Astrid and Dimitri work with and talk about herbs, absentmindedly petting her new deerskin pants. *They were so soft,* she thought as she drifted off to sleep. She felt Dimitri grab her hand, but didn't open her eyes.

"Should we give her dreamless sleep?" Astrid asked.

If Dimitri answered, Nadia didn't hear him.

She woke alone in the well-lit grand hall of the

Dreamworld castle. She looked down at her hand, knowing Dimitri was holding it outside the Dreamworld, but he had not traveled with her.

Did I choose to come here this time? She was trying to figure out the strangeness of straddling both worlds.

"Move!" she said to herself, leaving behind the waking world as she ran as quietly as she could across the hall and into the first open door she could find. The room reeked of blood and sweat. A dark cell was on one side, and a well-used bench was on the other. Whoever was kept in the cell often had visitors. Nadia heard movement. *Whoever is in the cell,* she corrected mentally. "Hello?"

"You shouldn't be here," a voice said with effort. It sounded like their voice was little used, or they were starved for water, or both.

"Why?" Nadia got closer. "Who are you?"

"This place is evil and dangerous," he said so quietly Nadia had to lean closer to the cage.

"I know. This isn't my first visit."

"How is that possible?" the voice asked from the dark.

"I'm not entirely sure," was Nadia's vague response. "Can I see you?"

"Why?"

She wasn't sure.

Changing tactics, she asked, "Where is the key to this cell?" She searched the metal door, but she found no keyhole.

"There isn't one. It's inescapable."

"Nah. Nothing is inescapable. I've left the Dreamworld a few times, on my own, and isn't this place supposed to be inescapable?"

"You should leave, then." The man was suddenly pressed against the bars. He was tall and built like Dimitri, with the same stubborn chin. The rest of his face was gaunt and aged from starvation. He looked like he was wasting away.

"I can't yet," Nadia said, startled. "There are people trapped here. I... They're... I need to get them out. I need to get you out."

"You can't." He disappeared to the back of his cage. "Leave us here to die. It's better than being out there when he unleashes that thing."

"What thing?"

"It doesn't matter."

"Listen…man." Nadia was unsure what to call him.

"I'm Godric. And you're from Earth."

"Yeah, I'm Nadia. The more you despair, the longer you'll be stuck here."

"I've been stuck here a long time, useless… forgotten." His voice was little more than a whisper. "Go, please."

"No," Nadia said a little too loudly before she heard it: running, getting closer.

"Go!"

"I can't leave the castle." Nadia shut her eyes, thinking hard about the room she had woken up in within the castle. "Not yet." She opened her eyes, still looking at the cage. "Shit."

Godric came closer. "Why are you waiting?"

"Shhh," she closed her eyes again. "I'm trying something." She heard the door slam open, but felt the tug.

"You did come back to this damn place." Dimitri's whispered anger carried.

Opening her eyes, Nadia was shocked to see Dimitri standing in the castle with her. She glanced at their held hands as exhaustion made her sway on her feet.

"Are you okay?"

"Yeah." She looked around the castle bedroom she had visited before. "It worked."

"What worked?"

"I jumped or traveled or whatever within the castle walls!" Her voice was little more than a whisper, but her glee poured into it. "I wasn't sure it would work, but it did."

"How?"

"I'm not sure. If I can leave and come back, why not jump around? Like inside the castle? Does that make sense?"

"Not really. Maybe it's part of your gift?"

"No. I can't seem to use my gift in here. Can you?"

Dimitri dropped a little, looking at her. "No, and I don't like that. I feel naked."

An image of his bare chest flashed before Nadia's eyes. Slight heat rose to her face. "How are you here?"

"I fell asleep, and I think you dragged me in." Dimitri wiggled their held hands.

"Do you feel your waking self?"

"What? Like my body back in the temple?

"Yeah."

"No, not at all. Do you?"

"Yes." She knew she was lying, slightly propped up on her lumpy cot. "Wait, are our hands tied together?"

"How do you know that?"

"I can feel it, but we need to move." Nadia inched toward the door, almost dragging Dimitri with her.

"I know you're anxious to get the Prestarians out of the Dreamworld," Dimitri started. "But is it smart to come back here so soon?"

"I'm useless awake but healed in here."

"Nadia."

"Plus, the longer the Prestarians stay, the more chances they have to get hurt or die. I also want to stick it to that nasty, spoiled little man." He looked at her with disbelief. "But that's my vendetta. I can try to get you out of here first if you want."

"I leave when you leave," Dimitri answered. "I almost lost you once, and I'd rather stay here forever than awake without you." Dimitri's statement surprised even him based on the shock on his face. Then he set his face into a stubborn frown. "Are we doing this or not?"

"Uh," Nadia said, her stomach flipping in giddy surprise as she tried to regain her focus. "Yeah, we have a couple of choices. I can do another dream jump, or whatever I did, right into the dungeon area, or we can just try to find it."

"Let's try to find it. If we get caught, then jump."

Nadia nodded and inched the door open. Hearing and seeing no one, they crept into the hallway the same way Nadia had traveled the last time.

"This way," she mouthed.

Her footsteps quickened as more and more of the castle looked familiar. Dimitri pulled her hard into a side hall, pushed her against a wall, and covered her mouth before she could protest. He held a finger to his lips, then pointed at his ear and back at the hallway. Finally, she heard it. The footsteps were so quiet Nadia didn't know their direction. But she knew when they were passing their hiding spot. Holding her breath, she could just make out the shape of one of the large men with numbers for names. Even Dimitri seemed small compared to the silent monsters that surrounded Sergei. The numbered men had arms the size of Nadia's thighs and thighs the size of her torso.

She snaked her hands around Dimitri, mouthing, "Don't let go."

Chapter
34

Eyes closed, she locked an image of the dungeon in her mind, and after two deep breaths, she felt the pull. "Whoa." Nadia celebrated and braced herself. The jumps took a toll on her energy, and her legs shook while the edges of her vision remained unfocused.

"That was insane," Dimitri said. He was wide-eyed, glancing from side to side. "The world sort of melted away to be replaced by this room."

"Next time, I'll keep my eyes open." Smiling even as she stumbled sideways into Dimitri. "Sorry. That jump took a lot out of me."

"Let's not try that again, then."

"Damn it." She released Dimitri's hand as she ran into the dungeon's darkness. When she turned to run back, she ran into Dimitri.

"They're empty," he said, having seen what she saw.

"That slimy piece of—"

Dimitri placed his hand over her mouth, pulling her against him.

"Was that Nadia's ever-so-sweetness?" Sergei's irritating words scurried in from the entrance of the dungeon. "Did you think I would let you steal more of my property?"

Her rage flared past her exhaustion at the sound of his simpering voice. She wanted to beat the location of the rest of the Prestarians out of him.

Dimitri tightened his grip on her.

"Only to find that they aren't where you left them? Are they dead, or did he just move them?" Sergei said. "That's what you're thinking, isn't it, Nadia?"

She wasn't.

She would've known if he had killed them because she knew where their bodies were. She smiled beneath Dimitri's hand. For once, she knew something the pompous, bulbous Dream Killer didn't. She could just see him, stopped on the edge of the darkness. He was flanked by two of his giant bodyguards. Nadia slid Dimitri's hand off her mouth, gripping it tightly.

"Come out, come out wherever you are, and I'll bring you right to them. I'm sure they're more than willing to share their cell with you."

"Don't," Dimitri mouthed.

"I have to try."

There was no way they could take on the two giants, and she had no intention of getting Dimitri killed or stuck in that damnable place.

"What was that, my dear?" Sergei was stupidly trying to see through the darkness. "I grow tired of this." His voice shifted from passive-aggressive to just aggressive. "Go get her."

Nadia gripped Dimitri's hand, imagining the temple at Bedros. Dimitri wrapped his arm around her, and when the room stopped moving, he held most of her weight.

"Crap." Nadia closed her eyes.

"What?"

"I tried to get us out." Exhaustion seeped through

her words. "I couldn't."

The corridor they popped into was spotless, well-lit, and probably inhabited by several of Sergei's people.

"We need to move," Dimitri said. "Can you walk?"

"Yeah." She took a shaky step forward. "I think so." Her fear and exhaustion grew with every moment. Why couldn't she get out this time? She ran through every scenario before she landed on pure exhaustion. *I must be too tired.*

She stumbled as her mind wandered. To help her focus, she watched the muscles of Dimitri's arms bulging and rigid with a hunter's intensity as he pulled her down one hall and then the next. He slowed, listening, turning his head from side to side, and Nadia watched his perfect jaw flex and release before he pulled her again. She wrapped her other hand around their held hands, giggling softly like an idiot.

Pull yourself together. You're running for your life, not holding hands with a new beau. Her mind was crumbling. She felt drunk or like the drunk people shown in movies since she had never had alcohol.

"Nadia." Dimitri shook their held hands. She slowly looked up at him. "You're trembling. Are you okay?"

"I'm not sure," she said with a slur. She desperately wanted to lie down.

"Here." He practically dragged Nadia to an outcropping in the stone wall, housing a small column holding a gaudy-looking vase. "Stay here tucked away. I'll find somewhere safe for you to rest."

Nadia slid down the wall, hitting each large stone on her way down. She didn't care. She couldn't care. She had no idea how much energy she'd burned making the jumps, and time seemed to slow. Had a minute or an hour passed when she heard Dimitri's footsteps? No, that's not right. Dimitri's walk was always silent.

"Hello, my pet," Sergei said, looking around the ugly vase.

Nadia kicked out, hitting the column and smashing the vase on the floor. She tried to crawl away even as Sergei was growling about priceless reproductions. He grabbed her hair and pulled her onto her knees before wrapping his arm around her throat and pulling her up against his chest. He dragged her into the hallway before slamming her face first into the wall and pressing his body against her back, pinning her in place. "You gave me quite the chase, my little mare. Now it is time for a whipping."

Nadia fought with the last of her energy, stomping on his foot and throwing her elbow toward his head, but only hitting air. She pushed off the wall, spinning both of them slightly even as Sergei tightened around her throat. She saw Dimitri running back toward her as she threw her head back, breaking Sergei's nose and almost knocking herself out. She landed on all fours. Dimitri dove for her, but he was too late; a booted foot kicked her in the back, flattening her.

"Don't," Sergei said, pressing his foot into Nadia's injured rib cage.

Dimitri slowly raised both hands.

"So you are Dimitri, the guardian. You were a hard boy to kill. I wonder what it will be like to kill the man."

She saw Dimitri's perfect hunter's mask slip momentarily, only to be replaced with something else, maybe pure hate. If he were looking at Nadia like he was at Sergei, she would've run, screaming, as fast and far away as possible.

"Where's that not-so-healed rib? Oh, yes." He lifted his boot before slamming it down again. "This one, I think."

Nadia clawed at the ground, coughing a spray of red droplets.

"No, no, no guardian. Don't take another step." Sergei pushed her onto her back, leaving his booted foot on the right side of her rib cage.

"You scum-sucking, piece of—" Dimitri's voice was a growl, but Sergei cut him off.

"Now, now, what harsh language and with a woman present." Sergei pressed his boot onto Nadia's rib cage, and she cried out. He lifted his leg, allowing Nadia to take a deep breath before stomping her rib cage again.

She screamed as another rib shattered. She opened her tear-filled eyes in time to see Dimitri slam Sergei into the wall. By the shock on Sergei's face, Nadia knew he had no idea how fast or strong Dimitri was.

Sergei let out a choked scream before Dimitri pressed his forearm against Sergei's windpipe. Dimitri punched Sergei hard in the stomach with his other hand, and the whole room faded, or maybe Nadia was losing consciousness.

Three large guards arrived just as Dimitri pulled Sergei's own knife, placing it against Sergei's fat, wobbly neck.

"If you come any closer, I will not hesitate to end this despicable creature," Dimitri said.

"Uh oh," Sergei said as Nadia started coughing up blood. "I must have punctured a lung."

"Send us back. Or I will cut off your head. Do you think you could control this place then?"

Nadia retched blood. Gripping her chest, she fell on her left side. She could see Sergei smile even though Dimitri was a good foot taller than him.

"Go ahead. Unlike you, I can't die in this world. I control it completely."

"Really?" Dimitri asked. "Nadia has stopped you three times in this world, and my guess is, if you could have escaped from me, you would've."

Nadia watched, only dimly aware of what was happening, but she knew Dimitri was winning as a thin line of blood appeared on Sergei's neck from the knife.

"Ah," Dimitri pressed a little harder, moving Sergei forward. He reached for Nadia's hand, pulling Sergei down with him. "You aren't really in control, are you?" Dimitri pressed the knife into Sergei's throat. "Send us back now."

Chapter

35

Dimitri woke in Nadia's room on the temple's second floor, his hands still tied to hers. He immediately untied them while searching Nadia's wide-open eyes. He could tell she was in pain. Rage and fear coursed through him. *I will kill that son of a bitch.*

"Astrid," Dimitri called, but there was no need.

"Heal what you can," Astrid said, walking in. "But go slow. Healing too fast or all at once will weaken her in the long run."

"Okay," Dimitri's rage intensified with each injury his gift told him Nadia had. "Slow breaths." He told Nadia, trying to keep his face calm even as his heart rate increased. He closed his eyes, searching for his gift, finding it deep inside before coaxing it through his fingers and into Nadia. He followed the progress of his gift with his mind's eye as it spread, looking for the most dangerous damage first. He had to move some of his gifts away from superficial wounds to repair her punctured lung and infected head wound. He laid one hand on her ribs and another on her head to urge his gifts there. *Slowly*, he thought, breathing evenly to help Nadia do the same.

Nadia sighed, causing Dimitri to open his eyes.

"Why are you so, I don't know, happy?" Dimitri asked.

"Am I?"

"You have a crooked smile."

"Oh. Well, why shouldn't I be?"

"You just got beat to hell again."

"I guess, but you beat him too," Nadia yawned. "Literally and figuratively."

"Nothing worth smiling over." But Dimitri's mouth twitched at the corners. Her praise broke through his rage.

"So it's true?" Astrid asked. "You both reentered the Dreamworld and left again?"

"Yes." Dimitri still looked at Nadia. "How do you feel?"

"Sore," Nadia said. "But we're both safe, right?"

"For now." Dimitri's tone caused Nadia to raise an eyebrow on her bruised face. "We're safe enough for you to sleep dreamlessly."

"Are you sure?"

Dimitri was surprised by the fear in her eyes. Since arriving in Baako, she had been so strong, almost too fearless. What changed?

"Yes," Dimitri reached for the mug Astrid offered, but Astrid hesitated. "I know there are side effects, but I'd rather have her wobbly than beat to hell by that, that…" The cup shook with Dimitri's anger, threatening to spill the contents. He took another steadying breath and handed it to Nadia.

Nadia eyed it suspiciously. "Wait. Astrid, do you have any idea why every bad guy in this world is stalking me?"

"Every bad guy?" Astrid had a smile tugging at her lips.

"That's what it feels like."

Dimitri watched Nadia fight and fail at stopping a

huge yawn before she grimaced.

"We did not hear or see much while in there." All laughter gone from Astrid's face. She took a deep breath, trembling slightly. "Dark moments should not be talked about before sleep. However, I don't know why he hunts you so fervently."

"Oh, I'm sorry, Astrid," Nadia said. "I didn't mean to have you talk about your time there."

"Soon, it will be inevitable to speak of as we'll all need to compare stories to better equip your visits there."

"Maybe, but still." Nadia eyed the cup again. "Is it wise to sleep now, even with this terrible drink?"

"Yes," Dimitri leaned into her, taking her free hand. "You're safe and need sleep to aid in healing."

Nadia threw her head back to swallow the drink in one gulp. "Still horrible." She yawned widely before snuggling into the pillow and falling fast asleep.

"She's already been through so much," Astrid said as Dimitri stood.

"She has, and she'll go through a lot more before this is all over." Dimitri glanced at Nadia's peaceful face, awed by her. He wanted to stay near her, protect her, and… *And what,* he thought. His stomach flipped, and he caught himself grinning like an idiot. He shook off the sudden need to embrace Nadia. "I need to create a more complete medic kit. With a charge like mine, it needs to be well stocked. Will any of these herbs work for that?"

"Yes," Astrid pulled out a small bag. "I also made you more dreamless sleep powder."

A scream ripped out of Nadia, causing Dimitri to jump into a fighter's stance. He was ready to shift as he frantically searched their surroundings.

"Sorry." Nadia was sitting up, searching the room. "I thought..."

A nightmare. Dimitri breathed a sigh of relief, crossing to Nadia.

"I thought he…" she looked around the room as if searching for something. "I felt...I saw the gray man. He just let it happen, just watched…"

"Nadia," Dimitri took her hand, and the small bed groaned as he sat beside her. "You're safe."

She looked at Dimitri and then into each corner of the room again. "Why?" She began and then leaned into Dimitri to whisper. "All the people, why are they here? Who are they?" She buried her face in Dimitri's chest.

Dimitri hugged her tightly, feeling her body trembling.

"Astrid," Dimitri asked in a soft voice. "What did you give her?"

"Dreamless sleep and herbs to aid in healing," Astrid gently sat on the end of the bed. "She's fighting sleep, which can cause vivid, waking nightmares and confusion..." She gently placed a hand on the blankets covering Nadia's legs. "Sleep, Nadia of Earth. You're safe and well protected."

"Yes," Dimitri tried to lay Nadia back down.

Nadia wrapped her hands into Dimitri's shirt. "No, please stay with me until they all leave."

"And longer if you need me to." Dimitri was confused and concerned. He saw only Astrid, but he'd never experienced the side effects of sleepless dream powder. Dimitri lay back beside her, and Nadia wrapped her body around him, placing her head on his chest. He could see her eyes were closed, and her trembling immediately began to slow. A knot somewhere deep inside him began to unravel, and he relaxed as his charge used him as a pillow. "You're safe, Nadia of Earth." He said with emotions he'd never named bubbling up in his throat. "You're safe."

Chapter
36

"Dimitri?" Nadia asked without moving. Her head had cleared, and her fear was only a tiny buzzing in the back of her mind.

"I'm here," he said. His voice, rough with sleep, tickled Nadia's ear as it vibrated through his chest.

She stiffened, eyes wide.

Am I lying on Dimitri? When...

She remembered her freak-out after drinking the nasty drink Astrid had given her, but she felt like her memory was broken into pieces. Like it was hers and not hers.

"Are you okay?" Amusement laced Dimitri's voice.

She raised her head to look at his face, "I'm, yes, it's just, ha." The most awkward, embarrassed giggle escaped her lips, and she put her head back down, forehead first on Dimitri's chest. She took two steadying breaths, wondering why she was suddenly this foolish schoolgirl around her delicious, no, um, older guardian.

He's supposed to be your protector, not your eye candy. Pull it together.

He was still smiling when she gingerly sat up. Her body protested, but her embarrassment won.

"Thank you." She was proud of how even her voice sounded.

"For what?" He also sat up.

"For staying with me."

"You gave me no choice. Every time I moved, you would wrap yourself around me despite your injuries."

Nadia's face felt as hot as a cooking iron.

"Don't be embarrassed. You've gone through a lot since arriving here. You just needed to feel safe, and I was more than happy to oblige." Dimitri's face went a little red before getting very serious. "Nadia." He grabbed both her hands. "You're an incredible woman, and I, you see, I mean, I shouldn't because there are unspoken rules about fraternizing, not that we're fraternizing..."

Nadia snorted in a very unladylike way.

"What I meant is, I'm your guardian and your friend, but I feel closer to you, more protective than anyone—"

"Like a brother?" Nadia teased, relieved he was just as awkward as she was.

"No." Dimitri took his hands back to run one through his black, wavy hair. "I just want to be near you."

"Where I go, you go, kind of thing?"

"Yes." Dimitri didn't hear the unmistakable smile in Nadia's voice.

She laughed at the cheesiness of the situation, even as her stomach flipped with the beginnings of what, love? Infatuation? Lust? Holding Dimitri's hands and lying on his chest, even if a freakout caused it, were the most romantic and intimate gestures she had ever had. Her smile faltered. "Are you sure this is not a duty thing because you're my guardian?"

He retook both of her hands, searching her eyes. "I am sure." He gently pushed her matted hair out of her face, making Nadia more self-conscious.

"I bet I'm a disastrous mess." She pulled one hand out of his and tried to run her fingers through her filthy, tangled hair. She noticed the blood, tears, and dirt all over her sweatshirt and the shirt she borrowed from Dimitri. She felt her swollen lip and the blood caked on her neck and cheek.

If he can say all that when I look like this... She smiled the biggest, most painful smile at Dimitri, and he smiled back.

"May I?" he asked, bringing his hand to her face.

She nodded, and he set his hand against her cheek. Warmth spread through her face, and the pain in her smile eased.

"I wonder how much other damage you have." He closed his eyes with his hand still on Nadia's face.

She watched his eyes moving under his lids and traced his jawline and high cheekbones with her eyes. Dimitri was the perfect specimen of a man, and Nadia was average at best, with fuzzy hair, a chubby tummy, and thick thighs. How could he even look at her twice?

He opened his eyes. "Well, all in all, it's not awful. Your ribs are healing. Your ankle is still shattered, but it's a little better. You've bruised most of your body, with the worst bruises on your back and hips. Maybe you'll be about half healed after another week in bed."

"A week." Nadia shot up, forgetting all the injuries he had just rattled off. "No way." She tried to keep the pain off her face. She failed.

"Woah." Dimitri stood to keep her in bed. "I was kidding. Let me start healing your ankle, and we can take a short, slow walk."

He took over a half hour of small bursts of warmth to heal her ankle.

She felt rather than heard her ankle pop into place with a sudden burst of pain, then warmth wrapped her foot like she had stepped into a hot bath. She slowly ran her fingers through her hair until she could put it back up. She also took in every inch of Dimitri while he worked. The fear she had felt earlier returned, but it was different. It was laced with doubt.

When he was done, Nadia stood on both legs with all her weight, marveling at how good she felt for the first time in weeks. She still couldn't twist, bend, or bump anything, but could breathe and walk. She crossed to the bowl of clean water and scrubbed her face, neck, and hands before she felt ready.

They walked down the staircase of the temple and out into the morning light.

Shock rolled through Nadia. Few houses remained in the village, most destroyed by fire and overtaken by nature. The Prestarian camp was northwest of the temple on the outskirts of town. Rings of tents surrounded individual fire pits, with one large pit in the middle. Dimitri immediately turned away from the camp and walked through the village instead.

"The Prestarians are a passionate people," Dimitri said at Nadia's quizzical look. "You freed them even while being tortured by the Dream Killer." Dimitri gave Nadia a sideways glance. "They told me, in detail, all about it. But more than freeing them, you've given them hope and thousands of others due to Astrid's people spreading the word of your doings. Hope is a powerful weapon and tool.

They want to thank you, touch you, praise you, and I don't know if you're ready for that."

"Praise me?" Nadia glanced back. People were gathering on the edge of the encampment, but not leaving it. "I just did what anyone else would do. I simply opened the door and let them out."

"No one else could have, though. Now they see you as some kind of, well, savior."

"Gah. I'm no savior. I'm not in some dumb prophecy. I'm just a clumsy nobody." Nadia hated being put on a pedestal, preferring to remain average so she could never fall off. "The first time they see me trip over my own feet, they'll learn the truth. I'm a clumsy, awkward, average human." Dimitri tried to protest. "And I'm totally good with that." She looked back again. Her unease grew as more and more Prestarians watched them. "Why don't they come over here?"

"The dead."

"I'm sorry." She felt thoughtless. "This was your village?"

"Yes," Dimitri said at the same time as his father.

Jumping slightly at Benicio's sudden appearance, Nadia asked, "Will you tell me about your life here?"

"Oh, no. The story is not a happy one. At least it doesn't end happily, as you can see."

"Please," Nadia reached for Dimitri's hand without thinking.

He looked down at their held hands, smiled slightly, and sighed. "I don't even know where to start."

"Start with your mom. I cannot imagine her living in a place like this when she's so, well, so her."

Dimitri laughed softly. "My father used to tell my brother and me the story of their meeting. Do you want to start there?"

"Please."

"My father told it in a somber voice, acting out parts of it for emphasis. I think he wanted us to see it as a cautionary tale, but he always failed to stay serious. I'll try to tell it like he did." He let go of Nadia's hand, pausing on the path. "He said," Dimitri began dropping into a serious tone. "As a young man, my father traveled from village to village to administer medicine to the sick and heal them with his gift." Dimitri laid his hands on imaginary people, then Nadia, before removing them with a flourish. "My father was a handsome man with a soft, comforting voice."

Nadia could see what Dimitri meant as she looked at Benicio again. He followed in step with them, smiling at his son in his sad, wispy way. Nadia could see other ghosts milling about, but they didn't pay much attention to them, and Nadia pretended not to see them.

"He came upon a village." Dimitri used exaggerated gestures, looking around for something. "There were many ill people due to contaminated water. He healed as many as possible until he could no longer stand." Dimitri pretended to collapse, startling Nadia and causing dust to rise from the path. "He continued to heal from a seat, but he still lost many, including a young boy who begged for his life. This is where my father would always take one of our hands and become still and serious. By the time the villagers had found the boy and brought him to my father, the boy was delirious with sickness, and my father had used up his healing gift on others. The boy was fourteen, and the boy's mother had already lost her husband. She was desperate not to lose her only son, taking her own life after the boy died. 'Grief is a powerful weapon,' he would say. 'Do not let it overtake you, or you may never escape its blinding grasp.'" He paused, and Nadia nodded, wrapped up in the story. "Dozens more were found too late, and my father left the village that night, weak and tormented. Consumed by his own dangerous grief, he did not see the coming storm, nor did he care. He thought his death was a proper punishment for the loss of so many."

Dimitri sat abruptly, softly dragging Nadia down with him right in the middle of the dirt path. "He built a small fire," Dimitri mimed the fire and food. "Ate a small dinner and prepared to sleep." Dimitri lay down shivering. "As the black of night descended, his shivers slowed, and he waited for death." Dimitri lay still, slowly closing his eyes. He was still so long that Nadia started reaching out to him when he suddenly popped up. "Of course, he would not die that night." Dimitri reached for her hand, smiling widely, and helped her to her feet. "My mother appeared to him in her warrior form and healed him with a sip of her water before yelling at him until morning." Nadia and Dimitri started walking again. "He said by sunrise, he was so much in love with my mother he would've gone to the ends of this world and any other for her. She also told him he would never see her again. My father was very headstrong and decided Gaia, the Great Guardian of Death and Rebirth, was wrong. He told her they would not only see each other again but also love each other until his heart stopped beating or until she found someone more important to save. It took one year and dozens of foolish, life-threatening acts on my father's part, but he was right. Against all the rules and the odds, he made her fall in love with him, and they stayed side by side until…" Dimitri trailed off as they entered a burnt-down structure at the edge of the village.

"Until when?" Nadia asked, afraid of the answer.

"Until I was called away," Gaia said, appearing in her maiden form. Her stunning beauty made the destruction around them more prominent.

"Mother." Dimitri had shock, respect, and love saturating his voice as he gave her a slight bow.

"I'm so sorry it has been so long, my son," she said, embracing him. "Even now, I'm breaking the rules coming here, but that story and this place, our old home called to me." She glanced at the blackened ground, sighing deeply as a tear rolled down her beautiful cheek. Dimitri stepped back and took Nadia's hand as he beamed at her. "Hello, Nadia." Gaia turned, glancing down at their hands ever so briefly.

"Hello, Gaia," Nadia said, feeling strangely embarrassed.

"I'm glad to see you up." Gaia was straight-faced and cold. She immediately turned back to her son. "Dimitri, as your charge, it's your responsibility to protect her, but she must be trained, and you must keep your distance to be successful."

Dimitri immediately released Nadia's hand and followed his mother, like a good soldier, as she left the remains of their family home.

Nadia flexed her hand, looking at Dimitri's back.

Benecio stood next to Nadia, watching his wife and

son. "It's good to see them together," Benicio said in his wispy voice.

Nadia stayed silent, uncomfortable with the entire experience, and listened intently.

"Mother, I know my responsibilities."

"That girl is an asset to us only when she's trained and taught our ways. Do not delay, my boy."

"I'm not. Nadia's learning control, and we're on track for other training to begin when she is healed."

Gaia suddenly turned to Nadia. "Come here."

Nadia's urge to defy authority almost prevented her from doing anything, but she ambled toward Gaia, milking her injuries.

"Have you been to the Dreamworld?" Gaia asked.

"Why do you ask?" Dimitri's eyes narrowed.

"We cannot pierce the Dreamworld no matter how hard we try individually or collectively. It concerns us." Gaia stared at Nadia, "We need you to report all you've seen and done within that world."

"Who are we?" Nadia was still fighting the urge to defy the tone Gaia continued to use.

"The other Great Guardians," Dimitri said quickly. "Right?"

Gaia nodded, "Have you been to the Dreamworld?"

"We have." Dimitri broke the silence.

"We?"

"Yes, I've been as well." Pride saturated his voice.

"How were you able to leave again?" Gaia leaned toward her son.

Dimitri glanced at Nadia quickly, saying, "I persuaded the Dream Killer to let us out."

"Do not go back, my boy."

"What?" Dimitri deflated. "Why?"

"Because your task is to protect the girl child from Earth. If you're inside, who will protect her sleeping form?"

"Yes, Mother," Dimitri said with only slight hesitation.

"Wait," Nadia said. "I get that he's meant to guard me, but what if I don't come out of the Dreamworld? He'd be guarding a corpse, and then what?"

Gaia slowly looked at Nadia with what could only be disdain. "You look tired and should rest."

Nadia could feel the prickle of heat at her fingertips before she slammed her hands into a fist. Losing control of her gifts wouldn't help her case, and Nadia wouldn't let this Great Guardian or whatever know she was pissed.

Gaia turned back to Dimitri. "I must go."

"So soon?" He asked, his shoulder drooping.

"Yes, but I'll be back, sweet boy." She embraced him. "Do as I ask. Train her and protect her on the outside." she turned back to Nadia. "Next time, you will be expected to report all your trips into the Dreamworld, so do not delay your task. This isn't a vacation from your Earthly duties." With that, Gaia was gone.

"Vacation?" Nadia was furious. "She's kidding, right?"

Dimitri looked deep in thought and did not answer.

"Are you okay?"

"I haven't seen my mother in more than five years. It was good to see her, even if the meeting was short."

It took everything in Nadia not to huff. Instead, she

tried to smile at him.

"And." He turned to her. "She was right, at least in part."

Nadia frowned, puckering her lips.

"You do seem tired and need to be trained, as do I."

"You?" Nadia asked. "What do you need training in?"

"The Dreamworld. Healing. Herbs. You. But lunch first, I think."

"Who all is coming? Why are they coming?" Nadia asked, pushing her food away, suddenly nauseated.

"It's only Astrid and her youngest, Kieran. It's not a formal meeting." Dimitri moved the almost empty lunch plates. "Well, and Waylon."

"Waylon?"

"Yeah, and it's just, I mean, Waylon is the eldest and quite conservative. His opinions matter to many Prestarians."

"Wait. So if this meeting goes bad—"

"It won't," Dimitri cut in.

"How long before—"

"I think that's them."

"My hair…" Nadia tried in vain to flatten her hair. "My clothing is covered in blood still."

Dimitri took her hands. "They aren't coming to judge your hair or clothing."

"Still. You gave me literally no warning."

"I'm sorry." Dimitri stood up. "They asked when I got the lunch plates, and I sort of forgot."

"Sort of forgot?" Nadia pouted.

"You'll do fine." Dimitri helped Nadia to stand.

She felt stiff and had a dull ache in her hips and back. Moving felt better than standing still, but she did her best to greet her guest without showing her discomfort.

Dimitri bowed slightly to Waylon and ruffled

Kieran's hair before he moved closer to Nadia.

Kieran smiled as he looked between Nadia and Dimitri with a knowing look that no nine-year-old Nadia had ever met had used before.

"You must be Kieran." Nadia held her hand out to him, but he only looked at it. "You all don't shake here in Baako?" Dimitri shook his head, trying to hide a smile. "Well, it's very nice to meet you, Kieran, and you, Waylon."

"And you," Waylon replied with a raspy voice and a critical eye. "But please do not tax yourself just to be formal. We know you're still healing."

"Oh." Nadia looked at Dimitri. "I'm doing okay."

Kieran laughed at this, and Dimitri smiled down at him, sharing a joke Nadia didn't understand.

"What's so funny?" Nadia gently placed her hands on her hips.

"Kieran is gifted, very gifted," Astrid said. "He can see when someone is tainted or evil by looking at their auras since he was very young. He can also tell what someone is feeling most of the time."

"Most impressively," Dimitri said. "He can see when someone is lying, and he knows, as I do, you're a bad liar."

"Good to know." Heat rose to Nadia's face. "I don't feel awful." Kieran raised an eyebrow. "Okay. Not super awful. But I feel good enough for this meeting. Please make yourself comfortable." She gestured to Dimitri's unused bed, pressed against the far wall.

Kieran smiled and nodded slightly before jumping onto the bed next to his mother. "That is no lie," Kieran said in a soft voice. "I'm honored to meet you, Nadia of Earth."

"We should get started," Waylon said after a moment.

"Yes," Astrid said. "We're here to talk about the Dreamworld, our experiences, and yours."

"Then we're hoping to try a little experiment." Dimitri sat on Nadia's bed, leaving a respectful foot between them.

"I'll begin." Astrid launched into how most of her people ended up in the Dreamworld.

The Prestarians were camped not far from the Village of Bedros when the sleeping sickness hit them. The first to become ill was Kieran. He fell asleep one night and did not wake until Nadia let him out of the cell. It didn't go unnoticed that the first to fall ill was the only one with the gift to see darkness and deception.

"It caused discourse," Astrid said, her voice serious. "Among a usually welcoming people, the suspicions ran deeper with each person who fell ill."

They had tried every remedy. Some of the sleeping Prestarians would receive an injury or convulse with pain, but there was nothing anyone could do but watch and wait. Until there was no one left awake to watch over the others. It happened over only a few days.

"If Nadia had not found us," she continued. "We'd have been doomed to walk the Dreamworld for all eternity. Our bodies would have truly died in the winter snows."

Nadia was stunned. "No one could wake themselves or fight back in the Dreamworld?"

"No," Astrid said. "We woke in cells and remained

there unless the Dream Killer or one of his men came for us. That was rare. We never ate or drank. Nor did we feel hunger or thirst. We just existed. Except on those days when one or two of us were removed from the rest. Every time someone was returned, they were covered in bruises but would not speak of their ordeal." Kieran wrapped his arms around his mother, burying his head in her side. "It's okay, Kieran, the story must be told." Astrid looked past Dimitri and Nadia, clearly seeing something they could not. "When the doctor, or the man who called himself a doctor, arrived at our cell, we knew it was our turn. But only my daughter, Zarin, and I were taken. They put me in an empty room with nothing but a chair and walked my daughter to the room next door." Astrid shuddered, and Kieran tightened his arms around her. "They asked me about my gift, but I said nothing. The doctor marked something on some papers and then nodded. I was hit across the face and tasted blood. It was the first thing I had tasted in what felt like months. They asked me what gifts my family had been given. I stayed silent. Again, I was hit. Every time I did not answer, I was hit somewhere new. After a dozen or so questions, the doctor held up a hand and said, 'If you will not answer, maybe your beautiful daughter will instead.' They left my room but did not shut the door. I heard them ask her the first question, and my heart sank as no reply came. I heard them hit her seventeen times. Seventeen times, I heard my baby girl get asked a meaningless question, remain silent, and get struck. It was the hardest thing I've ever been put through, and it was my proudest moment. Then, we were returned to our cell. We were told nothing, and we had said nothing. It took Zarin days to be able to sit up, and what I think was a week or two before she could stand. But we were the lucky ones. Since waking, we found the broken bodies of those who were taken and not returned to their cells. They died violently and alone. Every moment we were in there, I feared the doctor would return for more of my people or family, but the next person we saw was you."

Nadia was appalled and horrified. "How many died?" She asked, afraid to hear the answer.

"Twenty three men, women, and children."

He's a child killer? I knew he was sadistic, but children?

After a few moments of silence, Waylon said, "Now you."

"Um," Nadia said. "I have been there at least three times since I have been in Baako."

She told them about her time in the Dreamworld, and they listened politely, interrupting only with questions. By the time they were done talking, the sun was setting.

"We have much to think about and discuss," Astrid said, rising. "For now, dinner and rest. After dinner, should we try our experiment?"

"Yes." Dimitri looked at Nadia. "I think we'll both be up to the challenge." All three left, and Nadia rounded on Dimitri.

"Up for what challenge?"

"A little trip," Dimitri said. Nadia's face lit up. "Into the Dreamworld." Nadia's face fell. "Unless you are not up to it." Dimitri took her hands, searching her eyes.

"What about what your mother said?"

"Astrid'll watch both of our bodies."

Nadia looked at him unconvinced.

"Plus, we're in and out. Nothing else. No heroics."

"What if it doesn't work?" Nadia asked. "What if we cannot get back out?"

"It'll work."

Nadia grinned. "You're mom's gonna ground you if we get stuck,"

"Ground me?"

"You know, punish you for breaking her rules."

"Meh, maybe. But we only go if you're up for it."

"Oh, I am definitely up for it." Nadia itched to return to the Dreamworld and stick it to the Dream Killer. She was ready to get everyone out and set the place on fire.

"I believe you." Dimitri touched the corner of what Nadia knew was an unsettling smile, which caused her to soften it. "But don't get too excited. We test your ability to jump and leave." Nadia tried to move away from him, but he held her firm. "Right?"

"Okay," she sighed. "I'd just like to pay him back with a little fear of his own." Nadia tried to suppress a yawn, suddenly exhausted from the day's walk and discoveries. Ghosts, sleep sickness, evil entities lording over dreams —it was a lot, and she was still recovering from the last visit.

"Are you getting tired?"

"No," she said too quickly.

"You know, I don't need Kieran to know when you're lying." Dimitri scooted back on her bed. "Let's rest for a few minutes before the others return." He lay back, patting the area next to him. Nadia was suddenly self-conscious and a little shy. "What?"

"I'm just…" She searched for the words that wouldn't make her sound stupid or like she was fishing for compliments. "I mean, my hair is a ball of disaster. I look a wreck." Her words all ran together as she rambled. "I don't know why you, perfect, beautiful you, would want frumpy, chunky, plain me anywhere near—"

Dimitri pulled her next to him. "You do look like you lost a fight, and your hair… I don't even understand how it can get so big, but nothing about you is plain."

With her mouth slightly open, Nadia stared at him, trying hard not to catch fire or even smoke.

"You think I'm perfect and beautiful?" He asked.

Heat rose to her face, and she threw herself flat onto the bed, embarrassment rolling through her as heat rolled off of her, both competing with her constant pain. Dimitri intertwined his fingers in hers and tugged on her gently.

"Don't be embarrassed," he said as she lifted her head just enough to look at him. "You've, we've been through a lot the last few weeks. I think we are close enough now that we can comfort each other. I don't care about the blood or giant hair or the smell."

"Smell?" She shot up, grimacing through her pain. She pulled her sweatshirt up to smell it. "Do I really smell?" She definitely had a smell, but it was far more dirt and blood than armpit and feet.

"Not really," He reached out and grabbed her. "It's just easier to move you over here when you're sitting up."

"Gah," Exhaustion and pain were bringing her close to tears. "That was not okay. This is a new shirt." She smacked his chest before lying on it.

"Yeah, I borrowed it from a tribesman. Please don't

light it on fire."

She popped up again.

"I'm kidding," he said as she lay back down. "Mostly." They were silent for a few minutes while Nadia listened to Dimitri's heartbeat. "Nadia, honestly, tell me how you feel right now."

She sighed deeply, "Content." She meant it. She felt safe for the first time since arriving on Baako.

He shifted to look at her face.

"Yes, I hurt all over a little, too," she blurted out to get him to lie still. "But, at this moment, like this, I'm okay."

Warmth spread through her from Dimitri's gift, easing her aches and helping her to doze off.

Dimitri sat them both up abruptly. "You cannot sleep just yet."

She groaned. "Okay." She sat up away from the warmth and safety of Dimitri's arms. *His beautiful arms.*

Dimitri watched her. "What are you thinking about?"

"Food." Nadia said the first thing that came to her mind right as Astrid and Kieran walked back into the room.

"Good," Astrid said as Kieran eyed Nadia suspiciously. "We brought you some and a stout tea we brew for long workdays. I think you'll both need it tonight." She handed Dimitri and Nadia glasses as Kieran set a tray between them.

"Thank you," Dimitri said to Kieran. "Where's Waylon?"

"He's decided to stay among our people," Astrid

said. "He said it's too taxing to climb the stairs again tonight. I'm to give him a full report later."

Dimitri gave Astrid a brief, meaningful look that Nadia saw.

After a few bites of food and a large gulp of the strong tea, Nadia said, "Okay. Let's do this."

"I don't think it'll be that easy." Dimitri still sipped his tea. "Have you ever entered the Dreamworld without being forced into it?"

"Kind of. I mean, I knew I was going anyway, so I decided where to go."

"Yes. But I didn't go with you for the first half of that visit.

"Right." Nadia didn't think leaving Dimitri behind was a bad idea. It sucked a ton of her energy to jump both of them, and his mother was pretty adamant about him staying out. But mostly, Nadia couldn't stomach the idea of him getting stuck like Godric and losing all hope. She shook the thought from her mind. "When I jump, I think of a place, but I have left a couple of times thinking of you. To enter, I usually just fall asleep and get pulled in. Maybe if I just think of the dream castle, I can enter on purpose?" Even Nadia thought the idea sounded lame, but she felt she had to try. "Don't let go. Maybe I can pull you along."

"I think it's worth a try," Astrid said.

Dimitri intertwined his fingers with Nadia's again. "Lead on," Dimitri said, shaking their hands and closing his eyes.

Nadia closed her eyes, thinking of their intertwined fingers, then his chiseled chest, before images of him in the river entered her mind..

"Nadia?" Dimitri asked.

"Sorry," Embarrassment scorched Nadia's face. "I was distracted."

Nadia pictured the dark hallway of the dream castle they had first dropped into together. She searched for some kind of connection or urge or something. Then she felt the pull of the Dreamworld like a tie to her gift. She felt her body gasp and fall backward onto the bed.

Chapter

38

Nadia found herself standing in the dark, unused hallway again. Dimitri gripped her hand too tightly, and his eyes were still closed.

"Dimitri," she whispered, a smile evident in her voice.

Dimitri looked down at her before falling to his knees with a grunt. Nadia could just make out the large, numbered man pulling his fist back for another swing. In her panic, Nadia jumped to the bedroom, where she had been tossed like a rag doll, but jumped when another man ran at them. She landed in the hall, where Sergei had slammed his boot into her ribs. It was pitch black; the only noise was Dimitri's ragged breathing.

After a minute or two, Nadia whispered, "They knew we were coming."

"Yes, we did, my pet," a voice in the shadows answered.

Fear gripped her spine, but fury kept her mind focused. "How?" Nadia asked Sergei.

"Oh, you have your secrets, and I have mine," Sergei said in a singsong voice, clearly believing he had the upper hand, but remained in the dark.

Dimitri was still on his knees, and his hand was loosening. He must have been really hurt, and Sergei would figure it out soon.

"Time to go," she whispered in Dimitri's ear. "I,"

she hesitated. "I'll see you soon." She gripped his hand, thought about their bodies on her bed, then abruptly let go. She reached out into the darkness, still in the same hallway, and whooped. Dimitri was no longer in the Dreamworld. She had sent him back, scoring another small victory over Sergei.

"Why so happy?" Sergei had none of his usual sleaziness as he emerged from the darkness. "No guardian means no protection." His eyes were bloodshot and frightening. His hair was matted, and all of his candor gone. He looked both crazy and wild. He swung a sword at her that was too heavy for him. It clattered against the wall as Nadia realized something had changed. He adjusted his hands and swung again, aiming for her head. The amount of energy he put into the swing caused the sword to fly from his pudgy hands when he missed his mark. "End her," Sergei mumbled over and over, running at Nadia, both arms outstretched with his fist opening and closing.

The look in his eyes scared Nadia far more than the sword or fists. She ran hard, pushing her chubby body to put distance between them. She turned a corner and almost ran headlong into a numbered man.

"Finally," Sergei panted as he came around the corner. "Knock her out and strap her to the table. It's time to see what color she bleeds."

Nadia stared at Sergei. *He's lost it.*

Spittle had gathered at the edge of his manic grin. His wide eyes filled with murderous intent.

She felt truly in danger of never leaving the Dreamworld alive. With panic rising, her thoughts jumbled and crashed. *Just leave. Jump. Breathe.* The large man and

Sergei were closing in. *Run,* her mind screamed. She slammed into the door on her right, turning the handle, and falling in. She couldn't close the door fast enough before giant fingers gripped it, pushing it wide.

"Now what, my dear?" Sergei's sneer was back in place.

She was truly trapped, and Sergei planned to kill or torture her. Or both. *Leave,* her mind screamed. But Gaia's smug, beautiful face rose in her mind. *Vacation from Earthly duties...* Her rage grounded her just enough. She turned to Sergei with a wave and a wink. "Bye." She jumped without thinking about where to go. Keeping her eyes open, she watched a livid Sergei dissolve, dark halls shimmer in and out of existence, then her feet hit solid ground, and she collapsed from exhaustion in a room in the castle that looked like a small sitting room.

Nadia's temporary sanctuary had a large, ugly tapestry of a pompous-looking Duke or Earl riding a rather fat-looking pony. All the people in the tapestry were servants and peasants bowing to the man, except one. In the center of the depiction was a large man standing stock still, pointing back. He did not have the look of a grateful peasant, nor did he fit the era of the painting. She stared at the tapestry for a long time but woke, confused, with the sun high outside the window. She was groggy and felt shaky, as if she had woken suddenly and was late for work.

A door slammed nearby.

She froze. *I'm still in the castle?*

"Find her!"

Move now. Figure it out later.

Nadia's eyes fell on the tapestry again. She didn't

know why she did it, but she walked up to it and poked the pointing man. The tapestry pushed in way too far for a solid wall to be behind it. She pulled it back, and her mouth dropped open. *A secret passage in a Dream World? Why?* Nadia climbed in, letting the tapestry fall into place just before the door banged shut.

"She has to be here somewhere!" Sergei's voice was a high-pitched whine. "She cannot elude us forever. I want her found, now."

The door slammed, and Nadia let out the breath she was holding. She put a trembling hand on the wall of the secret passage. She thought about jumping out of the Dreamworld again.

"Gaia said to explore," Nadia whispered to herself, adrenaline still coursing through her and urging her to stay.

Wandering around Sergei's maze-like castle was a terrifying game for Nadia. She eluded capture more than half a dozen times by finding more secret passageways behind paintings, false walls, and through a cracked mirror. Every secret passage had something slightly weird that made it stand out. Nadia wondered more than once why an already secret place, only entered through dreams, needed secret passageways that seemed secret from its creator. Unless Sergei didn't create the Dreamworld, but Nadia didn't have the brain power to contemplate it further while dodging giant, evil minions.

With each passing minute, Nadia grew desperate to find the Prestarians. She also took vague mental notes on all the twists and turns of the castle so she could report back to Gaia like the good little soldier everyone seemed to want. Then, she stumbled into a room she recognized.

"Hello?" Nadia asked in a hoarse whisper. "Godric?"

"Nadia?" Godric said, emerging from the dark of his cell. "You came back?"

"Of course, I want to get you out of here." Nadia searched again for a lock or a way to open the cage.

"You shouldn't be here," Godric suddenly dropped his voice to a hiss. "You don't understand this place."

Nadia scoffed, thinking she understood the place better than most. "Have you tried to leave your cage?"

"What?"

"Have you tried just to tell yourself the door is open and walk out, wake up?"

He cocked his head to the side, looking at her like she was losing it.

"I can jump from place to place in here without knowing where I'm going," Nadia said impatiently. "I can leave the Dreamworld when I think of a place, or even easier, when I think of a person. Others have to be able to do that, too. Have you tried?"

"They have my body," Godric said after moments of unreadable silence. "They're keeping me alive someplace, so even if what you say is true, they would surely kill me the moment I woke."

"If you believe that, it's true." Nadia looked for a way to open the cell. "Right now, you believe you're in a cage, without freedom, without hope. So you are. Believe something else."

"Is it really that easy for you, Nadia of Earth?" The bitterness was evident in his voice. "Your guardian hasn't told you about limitations, so you have none?" He scoffed.

"You need to use your own advice and leave. Go back to your guardian and learn."

"Listen, Godric, my guardian believes as I do." She wasn't entirely sure of that and knew Dimitri would be furious when he found out she ejected him and stayed behind. Her mind flashed to an image of him on his knees, and she wondered for the hundredth time if she should have left with him. *Gaia said to gather intel,* she thought. "Without a way to open this door, there's little I can do for you out here." She stopped. She knew what she had to do, but hesitated. What if she got stuck in the cell with Godric? She had to try. "Move over."

"What?" Godric backed up against the wall. "Wait, you can't—"

Too late. Nadia had disappeared outside his cage and reappeared next to him. She stumbled, bracing herself against the wall as she caught her breath. Jumping two feet seemed to take as much energy as jumping across the castle, and her energy was nearly gone.

"I felt it," Sergei growled from the hall outside Godric's door. "She's nearby, spread out."

"So that's how they knew," Nadia said through clenched teeth, her muscles cramping.

Godric yanked her into the dark. "You need to go." His voice was barely audible. "He'll come—"

"And find you," Sergei said. He looked even more insane. The little hair he had left was greasy and sticking out at odd angles. Visible purple bags took over much of his face while his eyes were overlarge and twitchy.

Nadia reached out and gripped Godric's hand in the dark. "I don't know if this will work. But hold on."

"You can't," Sergei said in a rush. "You're exhausted and powerless." Nadia immediately crumpled to the floor, releasing Godric's hand. "It's kind of you to lock yourself up for me."

"How?" Her head swam, her words inaudible. "I'm not tired. I wasn't tired."

"Oh, but you are, my sweet," Sergei's voice was a nasal purr wrapped in apparent exhaustion.

"Get up, Nadia," Godric said from the dark.

"She can't." Sergei cooed from outside the cage.

"I can't," she repeated, half asleep.

"If you believe that, it's true," Nadia heard Godric use her own words before seeing his face swim into view. "You can leave. Think of your guardian." Dimitri's face fit smoothly over Godric's features, and Nadia knew he was right.

Sergei grabbed Godric through the cage, pulling him into the bars. "Why are you always meddling in what you shouldn't?"

"Oh, Serg," Nadia began. "Your voice makes me want to gag."

As he let Godric go, Nadia saw Sergei trembling with barely contained rage. "The first thing I'll do is cut out your tongue."

"That's so sweet." Nadia slowly rose, desperate to defy the increasingly violent Dream Killer. Her mouth fell open as Sergei walked through the bars as if they were only an illusion. "How?"

But Sergei smashed her back against the stone wall of the cage, swinging wildly at her face. "You made a fool out of me for the last time! You're nothing but a stupid girl.

You're nothing. Not needed. Not important."

Nadia was so shocked by the sudden attack that she barely got her arms up to protect her face and neck. She tried to push Sergei away, thinking of nothing but his wild swings. Then she was looking down at Godric, pinning Sergei to the ground.

"Guards," Sergei shrieked, still kicking and screaming.

"Go, Nadia!" Godric said. "Go and don't come back."

"Come with me." Nadia held out her hand to him.

"You know why I can't." He struggled to hold Sergei in place.

Several pairs of footsteps came from the hallway outside the room.

"Go!" Godric released Sergei and blended back into the dark.

"Kill her!" Sergei twisted like a turtle stuck on its back.

Kill her, her mind echoed, and she knew the game was completely over.

"If you come back here, you die," Sergei spat. "Slowly and painfully. You'll die screaming." He then smiled, and Nadia was chilled to her marrow. "See you soon, dumpling."

She jumped. She felt Dimitri's hand, smelled the herbs always present in her room, and felt all the lumps of her bed. She was back in her tiny temple room in Bedros. *He wants me dead, truly dead. All this time, he wanted me caught... What changed?*

Chapter

39

"What do you mean I can't see him?" Althea said, clenching her hands into fists. She knew she couldn't use her gifts in the Dreamworld, but she was always tempted to beat the shit out of Sergei.

"He has been a naughty prisoner, and you've not brought me the girl." Sergei's smile was alarmingly manic.

"You promised. It's part of the deal," Althea snapped back.

"The deal was broken the moment your guardian took up arms against me in my own world!" Sergei got so close to Althea that she could feel his breath on her face despite him being several inches shorter than she was. "The only reason I haven't killed both of them is because one controls you, and the other is some kind of pet to the powers that be."

"Is he okay?"

"He's alive, and that's enough. If you do not fulfill your end of the deal soon, my soldiers will do it for you, and your precious guardian will be ended." Althea opened her mouth to protest, but Sergei held up a hand. "Don't worry, I'll let you watch as I break every bone in his body. Now go." Sergei shoved Althea, and she woke only a mile from the Village of Bedros. She always stayed close to her prey, but not close enough to be seen.

"I hate that asshole!!" Althea threw three small daggers in close succession into a tree about twenty yards away. They buried themselves up to the hilt side by side. She took two deep breaths before retrieving her blades and packing her small campsite, making it invisible to everyone but the most trained trackers. *If soldiers are headed to the Village of Bedros... So am I. If she dies, he dies.*

Chapter
40

She's been in too long, Dimitri thought for the dozenth time since waking. He wanted to take her hand so if she jumped, he would be sucked in, but Astrid said no, and Dimitri hated her for it. He knew she was right. He needed to be on the outside in case Nadia sustained injuries. But he hated standing around while the woman...

I what? Love? No. I mean, I don't know...

The woman he has been tasked to protect fights for her life in there.

Nadia's head jerked to the side as she lay, otherwise, perfectly still on the bed. Dimitri hesitated momentarily before sitting next to her and taking her hand anyway. His gift told him of each injury she received, causing him to flinch every time she did. Her heart was racing, and his sped up to match.

"Fight, damn it," Dimitri growled, gripping her hand tighter.

"Owe," Nadia whispered with her eyes still closed.

"Nadia?"

"What did I do to you to deserve a broken hand?" She smiled, opening her eyes slowly.

"Are you hurt?"

"By you, no." Releasing his hand, Nadia pushed herself up to sitting.

"But you're hurt?"

"Nah, not too bad."

Dimitri pulled her into him, hugging her fiercely before asking, "Did he capture you?"

"No. Not really."

"Not really?" He watched as new cuts across her cheeks and forehead bruised. "These are new."

"Yeah, but they're no big deal."

"Why didn't you wake when I did?" He itched to heal her, but knew he was too angry to surrender anything, let alone to the peacefulness of healing.

"I stayed behind. How's your head?" She reached for his head, but he grabbed both her wrists gently.

"You. Stayed. Behind." His words fell one at a time from his mouth like weights falling through water. His rage made his face hot. *Who am I more mad at? Her for staying, the Dream Killer for existing, or me for getting hurt like an idiot?*

"I sent you out and then jumped again. I had used too much energy and basically passed out. I didn't leave when I fell asleep because, apparently, you have to choose to leave."

"And you chose to stay?"

"Dimitri, he wants me dead."

"The Dream Killer?" Dimitri went rigid as pressure started to build in his head. He took a deep breath, then another.

"Yes. He told his guards to kill me."

"You can't go back then." Dimitri stood, pacing the room again. "Never, it's not safe."

"I have to."

"No, you don't."

"There are still people trapped in there. And Gaia

said—"

"We'll think of another way." He stopped abruptly, helplessness making it hard to move. "I can't come in after you. I tried. You were gone for so long, but I couldn't do anything." He clenched and unclenched his jaw several times. "I tried everything I could think of. Astrid thinks my guardian training prevents me, or that you have some special connection to the place. But I can't sit here and watch you get…hurt."

"I'm sorry." She reached for his hands. "I'm okay."

"But what if you weren't? What could I've done? Why can you do it but no one else can?"

"I think I'm just good at dreaming. I used to love to dream. There are no rules to dreams if you know you're in one."

Dimitri ran his hand through his hair and winced slightly.

"Are you okay? You were attacked in there."

He kicked himself internally for showing a moment of weakness. "So were you." He plopped down on his bed. "It's not a bad injury."

Nadia looked around. "Where is Kieran?"

"Why?"

"Because I'm pretty sure you're lying, but he would know for sure." She grinned at Dimitri, and his tension broke. "Now, tell me the truth, or I'm off to get Kieran?"

Dimitri sighed, his trainer's voice a small whisper in his head, "Don't get comfortable."

"I was hit pretty hard," Dimitri starts. "I woke here, head wrapped and throbbing, only a few hours ago. Astrid told me we had entered the Dreamworld together, but after only a few minutes, I was ejected, and you remained. I slept for just under five hours, and have been awake for almost as long. All the while you were alone in the Dreamworld."

"Wait? Only ten hours?"

"Yeah, why?"

"It felt like I had been in there a day and a half. Weird. I wonder—"

"You ejected me?"

"Yep," Nadia simply said. "Your mom said to explore and report."

Dimitri rolled his eyes at her, fully aware she was using that as an excuse.

"And I need to save the rest of the Prestarians."

"You will, I have no doubt," Astrid said, walking in with food, saving Nadia from the lecture building in Dimitri. "But not right now." Astrid placed the food next to Nadia. "Their bodies are here, and my people are watching over them. Please eat. Then I'll show you where you can wash up and get changed."

Chapter
41

Saved by Astrid, Nadia thought as Dimitri shot a look that made it clear that the conversation was not over before leaving with Astrid.

Nadia was swallowing her last bite when Astrid walked back in with a shirt and pants for her.

"There is a small well near the south gate you can scrub down at," Astrid said. "Come, I will show you."

They moved quickly through the town until they reached the end of the village, near a mostly intact home.

"Dimitri said most Prestarians don't come into the village," Nadia said. "How did you know it was here?"

"I do not fear the dead. The living are the dangerous ones. You can wash here and dress in there." Astrid handed her a small, towel-like piece of cloth and pointed at a burned-out building with brick walls still standing.

"Thank you." Nadia set the clothing and towel near the well. A big stretch told her there was deep bruising around her ribs. But all in all, she felt like she could maybe hold her own in a fight with gifts. *Maybe,* she thought, knowing her control was laughable.

A twinge ran through her ribs as she cranked the bucket onto the edge of the well. Her fire elemental helped make the numbingly cold water feel bearable, but the penetrating cold also helped alleviate her pain. Several buckets later, she felt her hair and battered sweatshirt were as clean as water could get them. She moved into the somewhat intact house to change.

Fire. Full body... She glanced outside the door, and seeing no one, she flung the towel and her wet clothing over the wall and reached for her gift. "Fire," she said through tiny shivers. She didn't feel cold the same way, so she knew the water must have been only a couple of degrees above freezing. She waited. "Hmm, how did I do it? Last time, Dimitri saw me naked and…" Her hands lit up. "Okay, so embarrassment works." She pushed the fire over her arms, chest, and body, allowing it to cling to her like a heated blanket. Her hair blew in an unfelt wind, drying it like a blow dryer.

After a minute or two, she felt comfortably warm and completely dry. She giggled at the tickle of the flames as they fought her control. "No." Nadia gently scolded the fire. "I made you. You're part of me. So you need to learn to listen." She closed her hands, and the flames went out with a disappointed pop.

"Nadia," a small voice called only a few yards away.

"Wait, just a second. I need to get dressed." She pulled on her new shirt and pants. They were a little large, but both were soft. Her shirt was made of a material similar to cotton, and the pants were made of leather.

"Nadia, hello," a girl said as she approached.

"Hi," Nadia said, looking down at a familiar face, but couldn't place it.

"I'm Renada. I knew you were going to save us from the DreamWorld.

"Oh yes. You can see the future?"

"Kind of. I can see the finished past and possible

futures, but if the future is extremely clear, like you letting us out, then I know it'll happen one way or another. Does that make sense?"

"Yeah, I think. Do you just get images, or does something trigger your gift?"

"Both, and that's what I want to talk to you about before I bring you to training."

"Training? With whom?"

"Dimitri, but I begged some time with you first." Renada looked down, taking a few deep breaths. "Your gifts are rooted in the elements and emotions. Am I right?"

"Yes." Nadia was unsure where the conversation was going, but Renada was clearly working hard to keep her emotions in check.

"Well, you see, most people know about the four elements, but very few know of or can even use the fifth."

"Fifth?" Nadia was intrigued.

"Yes, it's a center, self, strength. It's hard to explain." Renada played with the end of her French braid. "Only those who can use it truly understand it. Well, my gift is seeing possible futures, and I think I saw you use it. I'm not sure, and not all my visions come true, thankfully so. I'm sorry, I'm rambling. It's just that if you can, you may. I mean, I don't know."

"Renada, tell me what to try, and I'll try." Nadia reached for her, but she took a small step back.

Renada's eyes were full of tears as she looked up at Nadia. "I think you just need to use your gift to understand mine."

Nadia looked at her blankly. "How?"

"Due to the nature of my gift and possibly yours,

you just need to touch my skin and be willing to try." Renada held her hands out, and Nadia took them without hesitation. "Maybe that will—"

Nadia gasped, throwing her head back just as she had done with the trees. She saw a woman looking down as she cradled and rocked her little girl. "Your mother?"

Tears streamed down Renada's face as Nadia gripped her hands, barely aware of anything but the images of Renada's childhood flashing before her.

"What do you see?" Renada whispered.

"You had a happy childhood until…" Flashes of images, men attacking a village and taking children. "Why? Why are they taking the children?"

"They're taking the gifted. They came for me, but they didn't get me. Did they kill my parents?"

"They hid you before leaving in the middle of the night. As they fled, your mother was thrown from her horse with you in her arms. She was knocked out, and you rolled down an embankment. Your father searched for you in the dark, but men were coming. He threw your mother on his horse and sobbed for the loss of his baby girl." Nadia shuddered as the images stopped. "You saw it all."

"I must have, but I've no memory of it. It must have only been a few days later, and when Braiden found me, he said I was quite injured. Astrid told me my memory of that night may return. But," Renada gulped. "But they were not killed?"

"No, they lived, but they may think you had not." Nadia wiped her own tears with trembling hands. "I'm so sorry for what you've gone through."

"Don't be. The Prestarians have been very kind, and

you've given me the gift of hope once again."

"I don't know how I did it, but I'll do it again anytime you need it." Nadia hugged the girl, careful not to touch her skin. The violence of the experience deeply shook Nadia, but she did not feel drained like she had with the trees. She took a deep breath, asking, "Now, where am I supposed to meet Dimitri?"

A few minutes and a short walk later, Nadia called to Dimitri, "What's this about training?"

"Since you cannot use your gifts in the Dreamworld, I think it is time to start hand-to-hand combat. Then maybe you'll walk away from a fight with less injuries and torture."

She pulled her hair up, aware that her face must look like a mess of bruises. "Okay, but I've had a little bit of training. I was in stage combat, where you learn to fake fight, but the concepts are the same."

Dimitri looked skeptical. "Let's see. Show me your fighter's stance." He adjusts her feet, hands, and arms, but only slightly. "Throw a punch." He held up a hand for her to hit.

Her punches were not particularly strong, and every bruise in her arms, shoulders, and ribs sang with each impact, but not loudly.

"Not bad. Now Kicks."

They worked through all the basics, and Dimitri was pleased with what she knew.

"Every day, we need to find time to work through the basics in a pattern of movements to strengthen your body and your mind. It's like moving meditation."

"Neat." Nadia remembered her last meditative

moment. "Hopefully, the movement will keep me out of trouble."

"That's the goal," Dimitri laughed as he slowly circled her. "Now, what would you do if an attacker did this?"

The heat of his body pressed into her back. He grazed her neck with his arm as if he planned to put her in a headlock, but his arms and warmth were gone before Nadia physically reacted.

"Dimitri?" she spun. "Oh my god, are you okay?"

"My bad," he said, brushing himself off twenty feet away. "I forgot what you said about your gifts and the warning you need."

Nadia covered her mouth when she saw the burns on Dimitri's arms. "I didn't mean—"

"No. I shouldn't have jumped at you. I'm training you to create control. You don't have it yet. I forgot. You're just so good at, well, everything."

She immediately thought about Godric saying, "Your guardian hasn't told you about limitation, so you have none?"

"Yeah, right." Then she noticed them. Twenty or so Prestarians were watching and applauding her. "Have they been here this whole time?"

"Probably." Dimitri cradled both of his arms. "Let's swing by Astrid's medical tent."

"I'm so sorry," Deep shame rolled through her body as she walked with him. She replayed the moment and knew she hadn't consciously used her gift. She felt a small surge of fear knowing how sensitive her neck was and then Dimitri was gone.

"Actually, your control is pretty incredible."

"I burned your arms and launched you. How's that incredible?"

"You only burnt my arms. Even your new shirt escaped unscathed, and when the wind picked me up, it didn't touch anyone else, just me, the person stupid enough to startle you." He shook his head, smiling wryly. "I need to think about how to train you without getting injured. I might need a little help."

A half-hour later, Dimitri's arms were bandaged, and Nadia was even more mortified.

"Nadia, it's not your fault," Dimitri said, taking her hand. "It seems your gifts'll always protect you, and I'm glad. We'll just have to take training a little slower so we both come out of each session in one piece, that's all."

They walked toward the sinking sun for a few minutes in comfortable silence.

"Will you tell me about this place, your home?"

He glanced around. "This place hasn't been home for a long time."

"I know, but I think I need to know the story, and I think you need to tell it."

"Why?"

"The spirit or ghost or whatever who talked through me said they have been waiting for you. Why?"

"I don't know. I was just drawn back here, and I learned long ago to trust my gut. So we came."

She squeezed his hand. "It may help."

He looked at her for a long moment. "Okay, but it's long and heartbreaking."

Chapter

42

"I was born in this village," Dimitri began after taking a deep, steadying breath. He had never told the story in its entirety. Not even to his mother. "My brother, father, mother, and I lived in a little house on the southern outskirts of town near the well. But within the large fifteen-foot wall built many years before my birth. The villagers thought a wall would keep the bad out." He looked at Nadia with what he knew was a humorless smile.

She shook their held hands, and he took strength from the small gesture.

"I was only nine when they came." He slowly looked at the burnt homes and empty streets, seeing a bright, happy village from more than a decade before. He had wonderful memories of playing with his brother and the other children, watching his father help the villagers, or the rare times his mother was home. His chest hurt as he began to tell the story of how his young life was shattered.

"My father woke my brother and me and shoved us through the small underground tunnel behind our house. He told us to run and keep running until he or my mother came for us. 'It'll be okay, my boys,' was the last thing he said to us."

His father had held Dimitri's arm for a moment longer, smiling through the tears filling his eyes. Then he pushed Dimitri through and closed off the tunnel. The tears scared Dimitri more than anything else his father had said

253

or done. His father only cried when the moment was helpless, when the patient he was trying to save was brought too late, when there was nothing he could do.

"My brother was fourteen, just a kid himself. The moment we emerged from the tunnel, we immediately hid ourselves as close to the wall as we could, never intending to run. Then, the screaming started. We did everything we could to get back into our village, to do anything, but the tunnel was blocked, and the wall entrances were locked and guarded. We climbed a tree that overlooked the city center and saw it, all of it." Dimitri's entire body shuddered, and bile rose in his throat.

"The villagers were clinging to each other on the temple's steps, surrounded by armed men, hundreds of them. My village was small, with a total population of around 300 people, comprising more children than adults. Why were hundreds of soldiers sent to our village? I didn't know more soldiers meant a slaughter. A slaughter that no one was supposed to survive."

"You don't have to keep going," Nadia said, both hands wrapped around one of Dimitri's, squeezing lightly. "If it's too much—"

"No, I'm okay." He touched Nadia's face gently before continuing. "It's good for me to get it out." He took deep breath. "My parents were not among the other villagers. My mother had been called away days before, and my father just wasn't there. We had hoped he had gotten out, but that was not my father's way. There was confusion and fear among the villagers until my neighbors were pulled to the front with their five children. Then there was silence." The hair rose on Dimitri's arm, remembering that silence. The kind of silence that cuts deep, making those unfortunate enough to hear it feel as if they had gone deaf, or maybe hoping they had. He stopped at a fork in the path to look back at the temple in the distance.

"A soldier said something that we couldn't hear, but nothing happened for a moment. He said something else before walking over to my neighbors' eighteen-year-old daughter, Lenora, and running her through with his sword like she was some kind of animal." Dimitri stopped again. His unshed grief closed his throat. After a few deep breaths, he turned to Nadia. "She watched us, my brother and I, when my parents left the village. Lenora was kind, with a soft voice, not an evil bone in her body."

Tears fell, surprising Dimitri. He had not cried for years. He wiped his eyes, scoffing at the irony. His father always allowed himself to grieve, and Dimitri never did. Dimitri always believed being a healer made his father a softer man. Guardians don't cry.

"The soldier laughed as he pulled his sword out, wiped it off on Lenora before she collapsed. The cry Lenora's mother made…" He paused and swallowed. "The soldier spoke again and again. Each time, one of the children was murdered in more and more elaborate ways. Stabbed, hanged, burned, and finally, the infant was pulled from his mother's arms and thrown at the temple doors. Their mother was beheaded, running to her baby's corpse. It was the most gruesome… until…." Bile climbed in his throat again.

He could remember it all so clearly, the scene, the smells. He knew he could never forget that day, when so many innocent people were murdered.

"Their father was tied to the back of a horse and dragged to death. It took several trips around the village for his screams to silence. We found him tied to the back gate days later, almost unrecognizable. The entire family was brutally killed in cold blood. I..." Dimitri ran a shaky hand through his hair. "I was unable to look away except to vomit. When the soldiers fell on the other villagers, attacking at will, my brother and I finally ran, even after the screaming stopped, even after the soldiers lit the village on fire, and even after both of us had cried ourselves into numbness. We ran so hard and so long that it took us two days to return to the village to tend to the dead."

Chapter

43

"You think Serg, I mean the Dream Killer ordered your village…" Nadia's voice cracked. The brutality of it shocked and sickened her. Her eyes filled with tears, and her heart broke for Dimitri and the people he had known his entire short life.

"Yes," he said, his voice pitched low, and his hand shook. "He was looking for my brother and me, but found a village full of innocent people instead."

"But why? Why was he looking for the two of you?"

"I've asked myself that over and over since that day. Was it because of my mother? Did he have a visionist, like Renada, who could see something in the future? It can't be the prophecy because my mother would've told me. I don't know, but everyone died because—"

"No." Nadia stopped Dimitri. Her tears spilled even as her voice rose. "This was not your fault. An evil, sadistic jerk somehow knew what an amazing man you'd be and wanted to get you and your brother out of the way. He's a broken man-child who wants destruction because he never understood beauty. If you feel guilt and suffer, he wins. This wasn't your fault. This was his fault, and the men stupid or horrible enough to follow him."

He reached for her face, wiped away her tears, and smiled through his pain. Nadia's breath caught, and her heart raced—her skin tingling where he touched.

He turned to the burned structure they had stopped at a few days earlier. "This was my home. I was born in this very room," he said, walking into the shell of the house that once stood there. He dropped Nadia's hand. "This is where I saw my father alive for the last time."

Nadia smothered a gasp when the ghost of Dimitri's father appeared behind him. Benicio looked devastated as he reached for his son, unable to touch him.

"Hello, Nadia," Benicio said in his wispy, calm voice. Dimitri walked right through his father's outstretched arm, unaware of his father's presence.

"I'm sure your home was beautiful," Nadia said to both men.

"It was," Dimitri said. "It was wonderful until…"

Benicio was suddenly standing directly in front of Nadia. "May I show you?" Before she could answer him, his ghostly form stepped into Nadia. Forcing her to experience an onslaught of vivid memories.

Benicio stood at Gaia's bedside as she held newborn baby Dimitri, Benicio's intense pride flowing through Nadia. Nadia saw flashes of a father's joy—first steps, playing catch, and family meals. Then he showed her the day the village was raided, feeling Benicio's fear and rage. She felt his death and knew he had died screaming.

She wanted it to stop. She tried to make Benicio stop, but he was stuck experiencing his own death to the end, allowing it to spill out through Nadia. She felt her body buckle in pain as her stomach surged, threatening to empty all over the remains of Dimitri's home. She felt hours of torture condensed into excruciating moments.

Benicio never gave up his sons, nor did he regret

one moment of the short life he shared with them. When he stepped away, Nadia's legs gave out as the phantom pain continued to roll through her body and a sob escaped her as her mind tried to comprehend the memories and emotions that were not her own.

"I'm sorry." Benicio moved further away. "I didn't know how much you would feel."

"Nadia?" Dimitri rushed to her side, but she lurched to her feet, throwing up the moment she was outside the destroyed home. "What is it?" Concern coloring his voice. Her body retched again as waves of pain, Benicio's pain, rolled through her body. She tried to stand when her body was done retching. Dimitri caught her and held her as tears continued falling. She cried for Benicio, Dimitri, and the innocent villagers as she clung to Dimitri.

"I felt," Nadia looked up, searching for Benicio. "I mean. It's just that…" Benicio was gone, replaced by other ghosts watching and moving closer. It was unnerving. "I'm okay," she said far louder than she meant to, took a few deep breaths, and tried again. "I'm okay. Please continue."

"Nadia?" Dimitri's curiosity and concern colored his voice. He pushed her back to see her face. She stepped out of his arms to wipe her tears.

"Can't a girl just overreact from time to time?" She tried to laugh, looking away from him, painfully aware of the growing ghost audience.

"Yes," Dimitri nodded. "But you're not one of those girls. You always have a good reason."

"I'll share it. But later."

"You got sick."

"I'm okay." She laid her hand on his chest. "Finish

your story, and then I'll tell you mine. I'm sorry for interrupting."

"Okay." Dimitri looked unconvinced. "I'll hold you to it."

"I know you will." She smiled up at him, and he took her hand. They started walking back toward the temple. It was a long moment before Dimitri spoke again. "Please let me know if you need me to stop."

"I will." Nadia had no intention of stopping him.

"When we arrived back at the village, the scene was terrible." He swallowed hard, visibly still affected by what he had seen. "My brother told me to wait outside, but I refused. I had to know. I had to see what happened to our father, our friends, our village. I had to." He took a deep breath. "Our house was still smoldering, as were many other homes. There was death everywhere. Bodies everywhere. Some were unrecognizable or in pieces. Every night for weeks, we were warmed by the funeral pyres of our neighbors and friends. We did not mourn openly, but I woke up screaming more than once. I turned ten among the carnage and spent the day searching for our father's body." Nadia gasped audibly despite her attempts to stay quiet. "It wasn't until we had burned all those left to rot outside that we finally entered the temple. That's when we found him. I..." He shuddered. "There are no words to describe..." His voice broke, and he swiped at tears.

"Then don't," Nadia said, dropping his hand to wrap her arm around his waist. She knew what Benicio must have looked like from the memories she had been forced to live. Dimitri's arm wrapped around Nadia, and she could feel him trembling.

"We left the next day," he said, his voice even. "For years, I was mad at my father for lying to us, sending us away, and for dying. I even hated him for letting them kill him like he had a choice." He laughed bitterly. "He was gone, and I was forced to grow up. I wonder if my father even knows."

Benicio appeared in front of them, and Nadia forced Dimitri to stop.

"What?" Dimitri searched Nadia's face.

"Tell him," Benicio said to Nadia.

Nadia took Dimitri's hands. "He knows. He's so proud of everything you've done as a child and have accomplished as a man." Nadia looked at Benicio, and he nodded. "He has no regrets about his life and never gave you up despite everything they did to him."

Dimitri stared at Nadia, shocked. "He's here?" he asked, glancing around. "He told you?"

"Yes." Tears ran down her face again.

"Thank you," whispered both father and son.

Dimitri embraced Nadia, and she felt his sobs as the grief he had held onto for all those years was finally released. Nadia cried with him, holding him tightly.

"Is he still here?"

Nadia looked around. "No, but he'll be back."

Dimitri stared at her before placing his hand on the side of her face, gently rubbing the tears away.

Nadia shivered internally, taking in every contour of his face, the tear stains on his cheeks, and the soft grey of his eyes in the setting sun. *He's beautiful.*

"What a pair we make." He chuckled softly. His voice was pitched low. "Crying in the middle of the village for anyone to see like a pair of soft-hearted babes." He wiped his tears, breaking their contact. "Come on." He retook her hand. "Let's share a meal with the Prestarians tonight. Astrid has a whole thing planned."

Chapter

44

"Right now?" Nadia asked, touching her face. "I bet I'm a puffy mess. I'm not a cute crier."

"No, you're not," Dimitri said. "I can take care of the bruising, and the low firelight may hide your puffy eyes."

"I enjoy your honesty." Nadia put as much snark into the phrase as she could, even as she leaned into his hand as he slowly healed her face. "What thing does Astrid have planned?"

"She is going to ask you how the Prestarians can repay their debt to you." Nadia's mouth fell open. "I don't know why you're shocked. I told you how they feel about you."

"Yeah, but I didn't believe you."

"Well, she's going to ask. Do you have a response?"

Nadia thought about what she needed. "Training," she said after a moment. "You can train me in combat if you're willing." She gently touched his bandaged arms.

"I am."

"But can you help me train my elemental gifts?"

Dimitri was silent for a long moment, turning his face up to the last rays of day. "No, not really," he said, taking her hand. "I can train you in meditation and control, but you're the only person I have ever heard of to have four element-based gifts."

"Potentially five."

"Five?"

"I met with Renada today." She quickly told him all that had happened. "It may have been a byproduct of Renada's gift, but I don't know."

"Five," Dimitri said in awe. "That would be, I don't even know, to be honest. But maybe we keep the fifth quiet until we know for sure."

As the chilly night air filled with music, Nadia and Dimitri walked into the Prestarian camp. The makeshift band had instruments unlike anything Nadia had seen on Earth. They sounded haunting, like wind chimes whipping in a storm, balanced against animal skin drums pounded by hand. The drums raced and rose as the chime sounds stayed fast and unbroken. Many Prestarians sang quietly to the music as they worked on dinner, but their voices only added to the eerie sound. Nadia felt her heart race as the music rose, only to relax as it ended.

"What was that song about?" Nadia asked Dimitri quietly.

"Victory and hope." Dimitri was visibly moved by the sounds surrounding them.

Nadia had hoped to blend in, but immediately knew that wouldn't happen. Every Prestarian to cross their path greeted her with a slight bow and the back of their right hand over their eyes. Dimitri got casual hellos or questions about his health.

"Why do they do that?" Nadia asked. "The hand thing, I mean."

Dimitri smiled as two kids running past stopped and stared open-mouthed at Nadia. They put their hands up and backed away slowly.

"Oh, that." Dimitri had a big grin stretching across his face. "That's a sign of respect." Nadia looked at him suspiciously. "Okay, it's the highest sign of respect often used only for great guardians of the land, like my mother. They're honoring you."

"Honor or fear?" She still eyed the boys.

"Maybe a little of both."

"That's silly. I barely did anything."

"You were right," Astrid said to Dimitri. "You said she wouldn't like it, and it appears she does not. Come, you sit next to me tonight." Nadia and Dimitri sat near the largest fire pit between Waylon and Astrid.

"Another sign of respect," Dimitri whispered to Nadia, wrapping an arm around her.

Astrid stood after most Prestarians were seated. The circle slowly became quiet.

"Nadia of Earth." Astrid used a commanding voice. "You have given the Prestarian people great gifts. The gift of freedom and the gift of hope." She paused to let the group sing out their agreement. "You did this at great peril to yourself. We ask what we can do to repay our debt."

Astrid finished, and the Prestarian camp was ringing with silence. All eyes were locked on Nadia. Even some of the ghosts were standing among the Prestarians.

Her heart was racing as she tried to think of what to say that didn't sound completely stupid. She stood. "Astrid, you and your people have already given me so much. I don't hold you in my debt." Whispers ran around the group like wind through trees. "However," Nadia silenced the crowd. "I've a favor to ask. I want to learn more about this beautiful world and train among you while we're together." Dimitri gave a slight nod of approval with a big, toothy smile. "I have, uh, special gifts. Therefore, I have special training needs. I wonder if any of you could find the time in your already busy day to fit me in." She ended a little sheepishly, no longer looking at the group.

The silence was so complete it seemed like no one was breathing, and then the clearing burst into life. People were jumping up all over camp, speaking loudly over each other. The only sound Nadia could hear clearly was Dimitri's laughter.

"What's going on?" Nadia asked, startled.

"It seems they all want to teach you," he grinned. "Even the children."

"You've bestowed another great honor on us," Astrid said, quieting the group again. "It will take some time to determine who will best suit your needs. For now, let us eat."

With that, the music started back up, and the Prestarians talked loudly over steaming plates of food.

Nadia eyed her meal suspiciously, looking at the eyes still on the spiky fish's head. "Um," Nadia said, leaning into Dimitri. "How do I eat this?"

He laughed, sliding his three-pronged fork under the skin and flipping the fish open. On the inside, Nadia discovered steamed green leaves that tasted like citrus, blending perfectly with the mild, flaky fish. Dark bread was passed around and offered to everyone. It was flatter and denser than the white bread, perfect for soaking up the juices left by the fish and greens. The bread came by twice before Nadia had to decline everything else.

When they returned to the small temple room, Nadia was stuffed and ready to sleep.

Dimitri volunteered to take the first four-hour watch.

"I'll be back before you know it," he said. "But first…" He crossed to her in two quick steps. "Before I lose my nerve." He leaned into her, and her heart started to flutter oddly. He slid his hand across her cheek to the back of her head. "You were amazing out there," he said two inches from her lips. "And, if I'm honest, I've wanted to do this from the moment we met." Their lips touched.

Nadia's eyes closed. His lips were warm and tasted of citrus. When he tried to pull away from the tender kiss, she stood on her tippy toes, wrapping both of her arms around him. She felt his smile before it relaxed into something more intimate, more urgent. He slid one hand to the small of her back, slowing the kiss.

"I have to go." He put space between them.

She was glad to see the color on his cheeks and desire in his eyes because she felt a new kind of hunger, even as awkwardness also crept in. She desperately wanted to stay in his arms, but didn't know how to make him stay. "Right," she said stupidly, resisting the urge to touch her tingling lips. "I mean, you should…" He crossed to the herb table, and she gave in to the urge, gently running a finger over her lips. *That man…* She took in his perfectly chiseled body resting a second or two too long on his sculpted butt. *That man wanted to kiss me?* Joy, confusion, desire whirled through her mind until she saw what he had.

He handed her a half-full glass that smelled awful.

"Do I have to?" She whined.

"It's only half a dose. We think it will be enough to keep you out of the Dreamworld."

"But dreamless sleep powder is seriously disgusting." Nadia plugged her nose and threw her head back as she drank the horrid liquid.

Nightmares plagued her, and more than once, Nadia woke weeping, screaming, or hyperventilating. She dreamt of Lenora, Benicio, and the other villagers being killed or dead and burning. The part of the dream that haunted Nadia the most was that the deceased would turn to her and shout something she couldn't understand. Even Lenora's youngest sibling, the infant, screamed something at Nadia before crawling over to his mother's decapitated body.

After that, Nadia decided to go for a walk. Seeing ghosts was not new for Nadia since almost dying, but opening her bedroom door to find dozens did surprise her. And they were all talking. She made it as far as the top of the stairs before she was surrounded by ghosts, loud ghosts.

"Why are you all talking to me now?" she asked the growing crowd. They still talked over each other, pushing closer. They had an urgency she didn't understand. "Wait," She held up her hands, only to be knocked back toward her room. "No touching! Please! How can I help you if you are all yelling?" Fear rose in her.

"Please," a girl Nadia's age said. "Please listen to my story."

"I would," Nadia started. "I mean, I will. I just can't hear you with all the others screaming!" She threw a nasty look over her shoulder, amazed at how irritating and intimidating the ghosts suddenly were.

The girl smiled a small, quick smile. "They all heard what happened with you and Benicio. They know you can hear them."

"Well, yeah."

"No one has heard us since…" The girl looked away, and the group started to get quiet.

"I want to help all of you," Nadia said. "What can I do?"

They all started yelling again and shoved Nadia against her bedroom door. She tumbled into her room, disoriented. When she sat on her bed, they all aggressively crowded around her again.

"You need to know," the girl whispered into Nadia's ear, making Nadia jump. "Someone needs to feel as I do."

Then the girl merged with Nadia.

Chapter

45

"Lenora," Nadia begged as all of Lenora's gruesome memories flooded Nadia's mind and body. She felt the stab of the sword, the horror of watching her family die, the despair when none of them stayed behind, and the unescapable rage and emptiness while waiting for revenge.

When the girl stepped away, another ghost replaced her. One after another, Nadia felt and saw their lives and graphic deaths. After each, she felt more and more rung out. The emotional highs and devastating lows of each ghost started to unmoor Nadia from her own mind. The ghosts all shared the same emotions at the end: rage and emptiness. They had been stuck too long.

Nadia was only vaguely aware of the room filling with sunlight before Dimitri walked in. She was still frozen, sitting on the bed, but knew very little of herself, having relived the life and death of so many. She must have looked terrified or destroyed by the way Dimitri acted.

"Nadia? Nadia?" He touched her face.

She hadn't realized she had been clenching all of her muscles for hours until he lifted one of her arms, and it ached. "Dimitri?" Her voice was harsh and worn as if she had been screaming all night. *I may have.* She wasn't sure of anything except… "Ghosts. Please make them stop."

"What are they doing?"

"Showing me, forcing me to live their lives and deaths." Her movements were twitchy, throwing her hands up as another ghost pushed forward and merged with her. "Please," she mouthed, no longer able to see past the images the ghost showed her.

When the ghost stepped away, Nadia slumped against the wall, wanting to but unable to cry. Dimitri was gone, and the next ghost was walking forward. Nadia was starting to wish for death, desperate, seeing no other way to make her turmoil stop. "Please, I can't keep living your stories."

She heard running as the ghost reached for her. Something slipped over her head, the ghost disappeared, and she collapsed into Dimitri's arms.

She didn't remember falling asleep, but she must have. When she woke, Dimitri was gone again, and a tray of bread and a pungent, but delicious juice was next to the bed. The room was blissfully quiet. Nadia remembered everything she had gone through, and there were hundreds of ghosts still in the village. After she finished the crispy crusted bread and juice, all she could think was, *find Dimitri.* She stuck her head out of her room.

Nothing and no one.

She felt something shift under her shirt and found a leather bag hanging on a string around her neck. She turned the bag in her hands, smelling it. It had a light scent of herbs and leather. Walking to the top of the stairs, she was terrified, but also wondering where all the ghosts could be and what was keeping them away. "Could this be…" Looking around again, she placed the bag back under her shirt. "Anti-ghost bag." A smile spread widely across her face as relief coursed through her blood.

"Why so happy?" A voice said.

Nadia jumped, "Gaia, geez. What are you doing here?"

"I was hoping to talk with you alone." She strode toward Nadia with a grace only the most gorgeous women could capture. "What is that? Gaia pulled the bag out and let it fall on top of Nadia's shirt.

"She is gorgeous, isn't she?" another voice spoke in Nadia's ear. Benicio stood stoically next to Nadia, seemingly drinking in the sight of his wife.

"I can see you," Nadia touched her bag. Benicio disappeared. She dropped it on her shirt, and he reappeared.

"And I can see you," Gaia said cocking her beautiful head to the side.

"No. I wasn't. It's just, never mind. What did you want to talk about?"

"I haven't seen her in many years," Benicio cut in. "And when she returns, we can't talk. She can't hear me."

"My son," Gaia was utterly unaware of Benicio.

"Really?" Nadia asked Benicio.

"Yes," Gaia said. "I wanted to check on your recovery and offer some unsolicited advice. Do not muddy the waters when it comes to my son. He's your guardian and protector, and the son of a powerful healer and a Great Guardian. You're a common Earth-born girl." Gaia paused, looking from what Nadia knew was tangled, dirty hair to the barely surviving tennis shoes Nadia had on. "Focus on training what little gifts you have, and you may live to see the end of this. But do not be a burden or distraction for my son."

Nadia's mouth fell open as heat rushed to her face. "I'm sorry, what?"

"Don't be too mad," Benicio cut in before Nadia's temper overflowed.

"Too mad?" Nadia snapped. "Your wife just insulted me in almost every way and completely unprovoked." Nadia turned to Gaia, "Did I do something to upset you, your highness?"

"Who were you just talking to?" Gaia looked around, her perfect face drained of color.

"You!"

"No, you said 'your wife.' Who were you talking to?"

"Benicio."

"You can see him? Hear him?"

"Yes, why?"

Gaia looked startled. "You see the dead?" She glanced at the bag around Nadia's neck.

"Tell her, I've seen her and have stayed with her when she visited. Tell her, nothing about that day was her fault. I knew I married an important woman and had important sons."

"He says he was with you every time you visited."

"Stop," Gaia's eyes filled with tears.

"You're not to blame for his death."

"I said stop."

"He knew he had married an important woman and had important kids."

Slap.

As Gaia's hand made contact with Nadia's cheekbone, her head snapped to the side. Nadia lost her balance, falling into the handrail of the stairs with her hip. She bent forward, holding both her side and her cheek.

Gaia bent down into Nadia's face. "I told you to stop. Learn from this mistake, or the next lesson won't be so forgiving."

Nadia stood up defiantly despite the pain. "I'm a slow learner because, ya know, I'm just some common Earth-born child and all." Gaia took a step closer to Nadia. "Go ahead, oh great guardian." Nadia's hands lit up as her rage spiked. The flames danced from hand to hand, punctuated with little pops.

"Heed my warning," Gaia said, taking a small step back. "You'll not be missed if you were disappeared."

"Threats?" Nadia was seething with anger. "I heard you great guardians are just powerful humans. Does that mean you can feel pain?" Nadia held her fire-wrapped hand out to Gaia, forcing Gaia to take another step back. "Should we put it to the test?"

"You dare threaten me?"

"You started it, your majesty."

A door opened below. Neither woman broke eye contact.

"Nadia? Mother?"

Gaia straightened and looked toward the bottom of the stairs, a winning smile on her lips.

"What is going on?" Dimitri asked, climbing the stairs.

"Just a misunderstanding, sweetie."

"Can you stay a bit, mother?"

"How I wish I could, but I must away." Gaia dragged Dimitri a few steps away. Speaking loud enough for all to hear. "You need to teach your Earth charge some manners, or I will be forced to do so."

"What? Why?" Dimitri asked as Nadia scoffed, still playing with her handful of fire.

"We'll talk soon, my baby boy." She gave Nadia a wide smile before disappearing once more.

Dimitri turned to Nadia. "What's going on?"

"Your mother hit me." She extinguished her fire, placing the warm hand on her aching cheek.

"What did you do?"

"What did I do? You're kidding, right?"

"Nadia, why would my mother hit you?"

"Because she didn't want me to tell her what your father wanted me to tell her."

"Where did she hit you?"

"Here." Nadia could feel her face swelling and knew Gaia had left a mark.

"Ouch. Next time, listen to her." He reached for her face.

She moved away. "Did you not hear me?"

"My mother's a great guardian and deserves your respect. If she doesn't want to hear something, then she shouldn't have to."

"Something? It was your father."

"But if she asked—"

"You can't be serious. Your mother hit me because she was throwing a fit. Then she threatened me."

"To do what?"

"To make me disappear."

"I don't believe that."

Nadia's mouth dropped open, and she felt the first signs of angry tears. "Your great guardian mother is a bully."

"You're being childish."

"I'm what?"

"She's my mother and the guardian of death and rebirth. She has her reasons for all of her actions, and I respect her decisions."

"Her decisions to insult me or hit me?"

"She asked you to stop."

"She hit me."

"You're being unreasonable. You won't have an interaction like that with her again if you just watch yourself around her."

"I suppose you think I am muddying your waters, too?"

"Muddy my what?"

"Your asshole mother—"

"There's no point continuing this conversation when you're like this." Dimitri turned to leave.

"What?"

"Learn from your mistakes," Dimitri said over his shoulder.

Nadia stood at the top of the stairs as her guardian left without turning back. She crossed to her room and shut the door, allowing her tears to spill. She was furious at Gaia, Dimitri, Benicio, and all the other stupid ghosts. Tears fell freely down her face. She felt foolish and childish and wanted nothing more than to leave Baako for good.

"I'm sorry," a voice said from the door.

Jumping, Nadia backed toward her window.

"Lenora?"

"Yes, and I'm sorry. I tried to tell you all day, but you couldn't see me."

"Why now?" Nadia felt her neck and realized her pouch was missing. "Gaia." She growled, rage and fear competing in her mind.

"I'm here to warn you."

"About what?" Nadia sighed deeply.

"More ghosts are waiting to show you their stories?"

"Well, that's a hard pass." Nadia knew she couldn't handle more merging without losing herself completely. "I can't…"

"It seems it doesn't work if you can't see us."

"Great. Now would be a great time to have a guardian." Nadia bitterly searched through the herbs, thinking about what else might work. "I wish I had opened that freaking bag. Wait, maybe salt." Salt represented the purity of Earth, but on Baako, would it repel ghosts? She was amazed that she even needed to figure out how to repel ghosts. She also knew she'd rather face Gaia at her most pissed again than face a ghost that wanted to share anything. She grabbed a handful of salt. *I wanted a stupid adventure and landed in this hellscape.* She thought about Dimitri, his dismissal of her and his kiss while he held her. She touched her lips and then her swelling cheek. *Assholes.*

She took a deep breath and left her room as if she couldn't see anything but the stairs. Half wishing Dimitri was there and half glad he wasn't, she brushed away her tears and adjusted her ponytail like ghosts weren't screaming at her as she crossed to the stairs.

"Hey, girl. Can you see us?"

"She can. I know she can."

Nadia reached the top of the stairs before a ghost

stepped into her path. She flinched.

"She saw me," the older male ghost yelled in her face, and she looked right at him. "You see me."

"Yes," she said. "Yes, I can see you, but I'm late for training."

"Yeah, well, I'm dead." The ghost shoved Nadia, and she stumbled back. His ghostly face split into a wicked smile.

Nadia took a step back. "Listen," she said. "I'll try to help all of you, but I cannot be shown any more of your lives. Please. I'm begging you to just, just leave me alone."

"Or," the ghost man said. "I can just control you and take my revenge."

"Can he do that?" Nadia asked Lenora. She only shrugged. Trying to hide the tremble in her hands, Nadia gripped the salt tighter. "Not happening. You don't have my permission to enter my body." She tried to push past him. He shoved her harder, and she fell to the floor. She pinched her eyes shut, expecting blow after blow or another terrible story, but nothing came.

"You can't stay there forever," the ghost said.

He can't touch me if I don't see him, but I can still hear him, so now what? "You're right." Nadia stood slowly with her eyes closed. She inched toward the stairs despite the ghosts screaming profanities at her. "Super mature, dude." She reached out with one foot, then the other.

"Nadia?" a voice Nadia didn't know called from the bottom of the stairs. "What are you doing?"

Nadia opened her eyes, surprised. She saw a living man for only half a second before the ghost was in front of her again. He ran at her, hitting head first into her chest and the hand still gripping the salt. Nadia became weightless long enough to hate Gaia absolutely before slamming into the railing of the second-floor landing.

Chapter

46

Air blasted from her lungs, and painful stars danced behind her eyelids.

"Why didn't that work?" the idiot ghost screamed somewhere near her.

She kept her grip on the salt and her eyes closed even as she was lifted into someone's arms.

"Are you okay?" the living man asked. "Let's get you out of here."

"I don't need rescuing," Nadia said repeatedly, letting the new man carry her away from the raging ghost.

"I didn't think you did," the man said, a smile clear in his voice. "What happened?"

"A dead jerk," Nadia said, her breathing finally normal. "He tried to merge with me."

"Merge?"

"It's a long story."

"Sounds like a fascinating one," the man said. "I'd love for you to tell me sometime, Nadia of Earth."

Her lids were hit by the afternoon sun. "I can walk." She blinked a few times as she was gently set onto her feet. She took a few steps forward like a baby deer learning to walk before she fell over. The man scooped her back up and practically ran to the medical tent.

"I think you have a concussion," the man said. "My mother'll fix you up in no time. Tell me about yourself, Nadia."

"How do you know my name?"

"Everyone here knows you, and I keep tabs on my tribe."

"Who are you?"

"Oh," he smiled down at her. "Where are my manners? I'm Braiden, Astrid's oldest child. I have been away, scouting and spreading your story."

Braiden had a handsome boy next door face with hazel eyes and a quick smile. He was bonier than Dimitri, and she guessed, shorter too. He strained a little to keep his pace and hold her. She felt self-conscious about her weight even as she traced the lines of the handsome newcomer's face.

"What happened?" Dimitri called out as they got closer to the tent.

"Get out of my way, guardian." Braiden had a sharp edge to his voice.

"Answer me."

Braiden pushed past Dimitri into Astrid's medical tent. "Mother," he placed Nadia on a cot. "She was thrown ten or fifteen feet into the landing railing. Her head and body cracked the wood and bent the metal, and she hit it so hard I thought she was going to go through it."

"How?" Astrid asked, immediately tending to Nadia.

"Ghost," Nadia said. The spinning of the room made her want to vomit.

"Where's your pouch?" Astrid asked.

"Gaia took it." Nadia looked anywhere but at Dimitri until the spinning became too much. Then she closed her eyes and placed her head in her hands.

"Where were you, guardian?" Braiden asked.

"What?" Dimitri's voice was deep and threatening.

"Where were you when Nadia was being attacked?"

"I was… She and I had… It's really none of your business, tracker."

"It's everyone's business," Braiden said. "This woman and her safety are everyone's business."

"Get out of my face." Dimitri's quiet tone made Nadia look up. Braiden and Dimitri were toe to toe, making their height difference clear. Braiden was a good five inches shorter and significantly less muscular. But his smile showed he wasn't intimidated by the differences.

"Stop it," Astrid said. "This is a medical tent, and this woman is injured."

"This woman is critical to our survival. She's the only person who can enter and leave the Dreamworld, and she nearly died on your watch, or lack of, again." Braiden shoved Dimitri.

Dimitri took one step back and rocked forward, pushing Braiden back.

"Are you kidding me?" Nadia asked. Her head and back were throbbing.

Both men continued to stare at each other.

"You're not enough for her," Braiden said.

Nadia was shocked when Dimitri's fist swung at Braiden's head. Braiden was too fast, ramming Dimitri in the stomach. Dimitri grabbed Braiden around the throat and slammed him on top of a small table in the middle of the room, shattering it.

Nadia stumbled between the two men, unaware she even chose to stand.

"Nadia." Dimitri reached for her.

"Don't touch me." She held out one flaming hand toward each man. "I don't know of any woman who would appreciate the show of ego you're both playing with." She swayed wildly as her head pulsed. Both men moved toward her, and her hands flared, causing them to jump back. "If you both don't leave, I'll not be responsible when my gifts flare out of control."

"Nadia, I can help," Dimitri said calmly.

"I don't want your help." She was on the verge of tears, looking at no one. "I just want to be left alone. No prophecy, no injuries, no goddess, no men. Please!" She closed her eyes, hoping that would help her head, but kept her hands lit.

Nadia swayed wildly again, and Braiden said, "Let's go, guardian. My mother'll help her, but if you need help—"

"We'll be fine." Astrid said to the men. After a few moments of silence, she said, "They're gone."

Nadia's body and rage collapsed.

"Let me help you to bed. You shouldn't have used so much of your gift while injured. That was risky."

"Did you want them to go to blows over some stupid damsel in distress version of me?" Nadia lay in bed on her stomach. Her face still hurt, but it felt like a tiny pinch compared to the deep ache in her back and head.

"Yes, but Dimitri could have healed you with a touch." Astrid wrapped an herb-soaked bandage around Nadia's head.

"Not if he was busy beating your son."

"Herbal healing will take longer, possibly a day or

two."

"Can I stay here?"

"Yes."

"Without visitors?"

"That I cannot promise. May I see your other injuries?"

As Astrid gently lifted Nadia's shirt, her breath caught. "Great Guardians," she said like a prayer.

"I'm pretty sure they won't help." Nadia smiled with no humor.

"You need healing both inside and out."

Astrid created an herbal dreamless sleep shot and a dozen herbal wraps. After she helped Nadia drink the terrible concoction, Nadia was deeply asleep before any wrap touched her skin, but woke suddenly and on edge. She found Dimitri sitting in the dark on the cot next to hers.

"Sorry." Dimitri half rose.

"For what?" Nadia clenched her eyes shut as her head pounded and her stomach flipped like she was going to vomit.

"For startling you." He paused, and Nadia let the awkward silence stretch on, unwilling to speak. "I brought you stew and more of the bread you liked," Dimitri said after a few minutes.

"Thank you." Nadia opened her eyes and winced as she adjusted her position. "But I'm not hungry." She watched Dimitri reach for her before letting his hand drop to his lap. "You don't need to trouble yourself, Dimitri. I'm okay." The lie was clear to her even before she finished.

"Nadia, I owe you an apology."

"For what?"

"For my behavior with Braiden."

"And."

"And what?"

"Your mother hit me, told me I'm not good enough for you, and stole my ghost protector thingy."

"Oh."

"And you walked away."

"She's my—"

"You walked away after you accused me of deserving to be hit."

"Yes, but—"

"Your mother's a bully, and you're supposed to be my guardian against bullies."

"Nadia," Dimitri jumped to his feet. "She's my mother and a great guardian."

"What's your point?" Nadia watched Dimitri's outline pace the dark room. "She's still a jerk."

"Great guardians are above reproach. They don't make mistakes or bully or hit people for no reason."

"Or steal their ghost protector, putting them in immediate danger?"

"Exactly, wait—"

"Okay. Then maybe you should take your mother's advice."

"What advice?"

"Get me trained and keep your distance."

"Nadia, you're being a child."

"Get out," Nadia's voice broke. Rage and exhaustion filled her eyes with tears.

"What?"

"You heard her." Braiden walked into the medical

tent with a lit candle. "She said, get out, mama's boy."

"You have a death wish, don't you?" Dimitri sounded as stupid as his comeback suggested.

"Stop." Nadia rose. Braiden brought the candlelight closer, and both men gasped. "What?"

"Your face is swollen and bruised," Braiden said.

"Oh, that must be the no-reason injury I received earlier from someone above reproach."

"What?" Braiden asked, holding the light higher.

"Nothing," Nadia turned away from both of them. "I don't mean to be rude, gentlemen, but I am not good company right now."

"You do need to rest." Braiden set the candle on the table beside her bed. "I just came in to tell you trainers have been chosen, and you can start training the moment you feel up to it."

"Who chose them?" Nadia didn't look up.

"I did," Dimitri said, and Braiden cleared his throat. "With the help of Astrid."

"Thank you," Nadia said. "I look forward to meeting them tomorrow."

"Tomorrow?" Dimitri questioned.

"Yes," Nadia said. "Tomorrow. I'll be up for it."

"My mother also asked that I replace your wraps."

"I'll help," Dimitri said.

"Dimitri, thank you for bringing dinner, but I do not need it." Nadia tried to make the dismissal both obvious and gentle. "Braiden can handle the wraps without help."

"I'll make the sleepless dream powder then," Dimitri crossed to the herb table.

"No, thank you. I already had some a few hours ago

and will not take any more tonight. My head hurts enough that the Dream World sounds like a welcome relief." She flinched the moment she realized how much she meant what she had said.

Dimitri must have heard it as well because he waited until Nadia looked at him before giving a slight bow. "Sleep well, Nadia of Earth. Please remain safe. Your training will begin tomorrow."

Nadia turned her head away, allowing tears to fall gently.

Ten or so minutes later, just as Nadia was drifting off, Braiden asked, "Are you asleep?"

"No."

"I need to lift your shirt to replace the wraps. Do you want me to get my mother?"

"Don't be silly. Here." She lifted her shirt, and Braiden hissed. "Yeah, your mom reacted that way, too, but I've had worse."

"I'm sorry."

"For what?"

"Your stay here has not been enjoyable."

Nadia winced at his touch but giggled at his words. "Enjoyable was never part of the plan."

"Maybe not, but when you're done saving us all, I'd love to show you Baako as it was and how it could be again."

"Tell me about it," Nadia said, needing a distraction.

"Okay, sure, but please try to sleep." He paused gently laying another wrap on her back. "When I was a kid, the Prestarian tribe was more of a village by the sea. We used to swim in crystal-clear water and catch these huge fish that my mom could turn into a pull-apart feast. My mouth is watering just thinking about it."

He spoke fondly of his childhood, learning his gifts, and tracking in relative safety. He spoke as if the deadly changes came slowly, like a creeping army, unseen until they were all around.

Nadia listened to all he was saying, becoming more and more depressed and angry. She had nearly lost her life, gained and then lost her guardian, and had incredible abilities but little control. She was hunted by the living and dead while awake and asleep. *I hate this place.*

Chapter

47

Nadia fell asleep mad. So when she woke in the Dreamworld, a wicked smile spread widely across her face.

"Let's see who the damsel is now," she said quietly, taking a few steps before she thought of her last visit and Sergei's determination to kill her. She hesitated only for a moment before her anger won out. She had a single-minded focus: get the Prestarians and get out.

She ran through the empty hallway for five minutes before she heard someone humming. Nadia immediately knew it was a Prestarian and a trap. She also knew her recklessness would get her killed someday, but she ran straight for the sound anyway. Nadia slowly opened the door to reveal a circular room with a dozen or so women and girls in a small circular cage.

"You shouldn't be here," the woman said. "It's a trap."

"I know," Nadia searched the cage. It had no door, just like the cage Godric was in. "How did you get in there?"

"We don't know," a teenage girl said. "We all just woke up in here after you left."

"Then the Dream Killer told one of us to hum nonstop no matter what," the first woman said.

"Sounds a little desperate. Stand back against the wall, please." Nadia watched as they all pressed against the far side of the cage. She closed her eyes and popped into the center of the small cell, just missing the occupants. "Okay, we're going to try something new. I think I can pull you out in groups."

"How?" one of the teenagers asked.

"I force your sleeping self to wake. I've done it with Dimitri a few times. Does that make sense?"

"Not really," an older woman said. "But we trust you."

The occupants all nodded.

"Um, alright. Then let's do this. You and you, grab my hands. When I let go, you wake."

"Quickly. We don't have a ton of time."

"You have no time," Sergei said as he sauntered into the circular room. "Oh, I have missed you, my plump, little rump roast."

"Trust me," Nadia whispered to the two women gripping her hand. "Reach out and grab another hand." The four women gripped tightly. "Hey Serg," Nadia concentrated on Astrid's medical tent, the broken table, the wraps on her head and back. She jumped and gasped after releasing the women from the Dreamworld. "Suck on that, you dream villain."

"What did you…" Sergei trailed off as his face slowly turned puce with rage. "How dare you! Guards!"

"Serg, please throw a fit. It's such a great story to tell when I leave this crappy fun house."

Sergei stepped through the bars as if they were not there and punched Nadia across the face, exactly where Gaia had hit her.

Her sleeping and Dreamworld head snapped back. She dropped into fighter's stance, and Sergei jumped out of the cage. She ran at the bars, fighting the solid metal. "I'll figure your trick out, you weasel. But do you know *my* trick?" Nadia smiled through her pain. She grabbed two girls' hands, and they were gone.

"Stop it!" Sergei jumped up and down outside the cage.

"Come in and make me, old man."

"Old man? I am not old."

"Could've fooled me?" Nadia grabbed two more hands and released both girls to the outside. Sweat was pouring down her face, and the weakness the jumps were causing was becoming more pronounced.

"Go ahead, release the stupid pests," Sergei said. "You'll have no energy left but to fall into my arms."

"Don't do it if it is too much," an older woman whispered to Nadia.

"Everyone take hands and don't let go," Nadia told the woman. "Serg, you silly balding beast, I'd have to be dead to fall into your stubby arms."

"Funny joke from a caged child," he sneered.

"If you liked that, you'll love my next joke." Nadia grabbed the hands of the women closest and jumped.

She heard Sergei scream, "You can't leave."

She thought about Dimitri and Astrid's tent, but also Sergei's face. She felt his sausage fingers wrap around her leg. She released all the captives as she was being yanked back.

Shit, she thought, terrified for the first time since entering the Dreamworld. *I am not going back. He'll kill me.* She felt his fingers rake her leg, then she slammed onto the floor of the empty cage.

"Back so soon?" Sergei stood over her. "Take her!"

Nadia was picked up off her feet, one numbered man holding each arm. "I can walk, idiots." She was even angrier than when she entered the Dreamworld. They set her between them but did not let go. "So what treats am I headed to now?"

"Very few get the pleasure of what you are about to experience, and even fewer live to talk about it," Sergei's glee saturated his voice and his walk as he led the way. "I bet you will be a very submissive little servant after this, or dead. Either way, I win."

There was a noticeable difference in him. He was far less manic, and Nadia's terror grew with every gleeful step Sergei took. If he was that happy, then she was in big trouble. She thought about trying to jump with both numbered men, but knew she had blown her energy, and her fury was waning. *Stay mad*, she told herself. *Mad makes you strong. Stay mad.*

They descended one staircase and then another, taking Nadia deeper into the castle. They saw no other people as the air became damp and musty. They were underground, and she knew she would not find her way out of this area on foot.

Her heart thudded in her chest as they stopped outside a thick wooden door with metal bracing.

"We're here," Sergei said. "Oooh, this is going to be so much fun. You. Go get me a chair so I can listen to the sounds of a petulant little girl being broken." He laughed and clapped lightly as one of the numbered men ran off. Sergei grabbed Nadia's shoulders from behind. "Open the door." The other numbered man let go of Nadia to swing open the massive door.

Now, Nadia's mind screamed. She spun around in Sergei's arms to face him, jabbing with one fist and throwing a punch with the other. Both were weak and sloppy, but they were enough. Sergei squealed, falling back and grabbing his face. Nadia turned and ran hard. *Not today,* she thought, until she slammed into the large, numbered man returning with Sergei's chair. She bounced off and hit the ground. Her head bounced, and her eyes blurred. *Concussion number two.* She tried to scramble away. The large man brought his massive foot down on her knee, and she cried out in pain. *Leave, damn it. Jump!* The large man picked up his foot to slam her knee again. She screamed and jumped with the last of her energy.

Chapter
48

Nadia sat up in the medical tent, surrounded by so many people that she thought she was about to be attacked by more ghosts. Then she realized they were the women she had just saved from the Dreamworld, and they were applauding. Nadia struggled to focus on each face, smiling through her pain.

"They refused to leave when they saw you did not wake with them," a gentle, masculine voice said in her ear. She turned to Braiden, and his smile melted. "You're in pain." She nodded once. "Ladies, Nadia is now out of the Dreamworld, but she needs rest just as all of you need food and company."

Each woman took Nadia's hand and brought it to their forehead before leaving the tent. When they were all gone, Nadia sucked in a pained breath, trying to keep from writhing. "He slammed my knee," she said to Braiden. "A giant man smashed my knee, and it hurts a lot."

"Do you want me to get my mother?"

"I just want it to stop hurting." Nadia held her knee, her eyes closed against the pain and dizziness.

Braiden lifted Nadia's pant leg. "Your knee is unseated. I can reseat it, but it'll hurt."

"Do it." Nadia felt an internal pop, and the pain lessened, but it still ached.

"What are you doing?" Dimitri stood in the tent entrance. "Get your hands off of her."

"Guardians are meant to guard, so be a good little guardian and stop talking. I'm working," Braiden rubbed something into Nadia's knee.

Nadia was gripping both sides of the bed, glancing back and forth between Dimitri and Braiden, but unable to see either clearly.

"My head," she said. "I hit it again."

"Okay," Braiden said. "I can make a wrap for that. Guardian, we need my mother and a food tray. This is going to take a while."

"It doesn't have to," Dimitri sat on Nadia's other side. "I can heal her."

"Making her weaker in the long run," Braiden scoffed. "I don't think so. You run along and master your little gifts while I nurse Nadia back to health."

"You're starting to piss me off, tracker," Dimitri leaned over Nadia into Braiden's face.

"Back off, guardian." Braiden didn't stop his treatment.

"I would love to see you try and make me." Dimitri took Nadia's hand.

Nadia felt a moment of heat pass from Dimitri's gift into her hand before her bed was knocked over, sending her sprawling. Her swollen knee and face slammed into the dirt floor.

"What the hell?"She spat out dirt. Both men stood sheepishly near where the bed had been.

"Nadia, can I—" Braiden started.

"Here, let me—" Dimitri cut in.

"Get out," Nadia said, still on the ground.

"You need treatment," Braiden said.

"I can heal you," Dimitri said.

"I'd rather be in pain than deal with the two of you acting like I'm some toy to fight over. Get out." Fire danced on her skin and through her hair. "Don't come back in here until you understand. I'm no toy, no damsel, no game. Now, go before I lose control!" Flames were jumping off her hands in the men's direction.

"I would leave, gentlemen," a new voice said. A woman with fire-red hair stood at the tent's entrance with Astrid. "We fire wielders do not ask twice without consequences." The men left before the woman said, "Nadia of Earth, I am Falleen, your new fire trainer."

While Astrid worked to get all of Nadia's injuries dressed, Falleen talked to Nadia about her control, the fire elemental, and what Nadia had already done with fire. They discussed how the fire gift makes the user more hot-headed and volatile. Then they set up a time to train even while she was still healing.

"Baby steps," Falleen told Astrid after the healer protested. "She can work with this gift because it's more than a gift. It's part of her since the blending. Even sick or hurt, she has more control than most, and it's far more dangerous to delay her training."

The moment Falleen had left, Astrid asked, "Do you want to tell me what happened?"

"In the Dreamworld?" Nadia was trying to find a comfortable position on the bed she was starting to loathe.

"No, with my son and Dimitri."

"Same as last time," Nadia felt too tired to talk about idiotic men. "I'm some shiny, new toy for the boys to fight over. I hate it, and I don't want to see either of them until they grow up."

"But you are shiny and new, Nadia of Earth." Astrid smiled. "You're unlike anyone they have ever met, with powerful gifts, a hero's heart, and a sharp tongue."

"All of that's ridiculous, and none of that's reason enough to fight over me, especially to the point where I get injured in the process. I don't accept the 'boys will be boys' mentality. So they will either learn that, or I'll travel alone in this world and any other."

Nadia woke early and was blessedly alone. She checked in with her body. Arms, they could be worse. Legs, one was good, the other was trash. Back, it could be a lot better. She stood to see if her knee could take her weight. It could, but barely. All in all, she felt up for a slow walk and still needed to retrieve her sweatshirt from the well near the south wall.

She left the tent deep in thought. *Men are stupid—all of them. Sergei's a dangerous man-child. Braiden is, I don't even know. He's adorable, but what's his game? And Dimitri...* She shook her head as a deep sadness settled in her chest. *It doesn't matter. I need to accomplish my Dreamworld spying and go home.*

She was blissfully alone as she limped to the well.

"Nadia," a male voice called moments later.

Her fists clenched. *Damnit. Breathe. It's fine.* She turned around to greet her guest.

Braiden walked up, carrying a large tray of breakfast foods. "Good morning," he said with a winning smile.

"How did you find me?" Nadia tried to keep her

pain and annoyance out of her voice.

"That's my gift," Braiden said, setting the tray on the well's edge before spreading out a blanket he had flung over his shoulder. "Will you join me for a picnic?" He set the tray on the blanket and offered to help Nadia sit down.

"I'm okay," Nadia lied. "How did you use your gift to find me?"

"I see through the person I'm tracking." He poured steaming tea. "I can see through your eyes to see what is around you. I can also feel through them, but I try not to if finding the person is my priority. Emotions get in the way of tracking. I saw the well and knew right where you were. These must be yours." He stood and handed Nadia her sweatshirt and the tattered shirt she had borrowed from Dimitri.

"Thanks." Nadia hugged the sweatshirt to her chest. "I'm not comfortable with your gift. It feels, well, intrusive, invasive."

"Ouch," Braiden said. "Intrusive and invasive? I can see through your eyes, but I don't hang out in your head or see your thoughts."

"But you feel my feelings?"

"Yes, but only if I choose to. I didn't with you. I was in and out. You were missing, and I got nervous. So I just peeked."

Nadia gave him what she hoped was a deep, unbelieving frown.

"I swear." He leaned forward. "Peek. Oh, the well. Out. I swear." He held both of his arms up.

Nadia leaned against the well, looking at Braiden.

"What if I promise not to do it again?" He smiled,

and Nadia felt herself relax.

"Fine," She was trying not to like the stupid boy. "But I'm still mad at you."

"Why?"

"You fought with Dimitri again."

"Yeah, I—"

"Stupidly and hurt me while showing off your manliness."

"It wasn't—"

"I'm not going to put up with your, I don't know, stupidness anymore. Next time, you'll both leave with burns."

"Okay," he said. Arms up again. "I'm sorry. You're right, and we're both stupid. I'll not let the guardian antagonize me anymore."

Nadia rolled her eyes and looked away.

"I'm sorry. I'll not behave like that again." He took one of her hands, and she looked at him. "I promise. Please eat with me. You must be hungry."

Nadia gently pulled her hand away. "You're lucky."

"Why?"

"Because I'm starving."

They ate silently for a few minutes before Braiden reached out to Nadia's sweatshirt and said, "Did that come from Earth?"

"Yes. It's the last piece I have from Earth except for my beat-up shoes." She wiggled the foot on her good leg to draw attention to her tennis shoes. "Everything else got burned."

"Is that the only reason you are out here all alone?" Braiden sipped his tea.

"No." Nadia crumbled bread in her hand. "I wanted to be alone, and most Prestarians do not venture into the village."

"How thoughtless of me." Braiden jumped up. "Do you want me to leave?"

"Really?" Nadia asked. "No fuss, no weird formality?"

"Really. I understand wanting peace and silence. That's why I'm so grateful I'm a tracker. It's me and nature most of the time. Silence, well, when I'm not looking through someone. Do you want me to go?"

Nadia thought about it and realized she didn't. She found Braiden interesting, and his company felt comfortable. "No, please stay and eat."

"Okay." Braiden plopped back down.

They talked until all the food was gone, and the tea grew cold. Nadia was amazed at how easy it felt. She liked Braiden's charming smile and laid-back demeanor. He made her feel seen. She laughed.

"What's so funny?" Braiden asked, interrupting her musing.

Nadia blushed deeply, "I was just thinking about how being with you makes me feel seen, and then realized that's your gift. As a tracker, seeing and finding people is what you do."

"I can't imagine a time or place where you wouldn't be seen, Nadia of Earth." Braiden leaned closer to her. "You're fascinating, genuine, and possess an enviable strength." He pulled her hand up to his mouth and kissed it gently.

"Stop it, you giant flirt." She took her hand back.

"Guilty, but I wasn't lying about you. You really are amazing."

Nadia blushed deeply again, torn by the feelings coursing through her. She was actually enjoying the silly boy's flirtations. She sighed, "This was a great moment of peace, but now I need to get back to reality. Can I ask you for a favor?"

"Sure," Braiden said. "Well, within reason."

"May I use you as a human crutch to return to the tent?"

"Oh, yes, that I can do."

"What did you think I was going to ask for?" She giggled.

"One of our moons." He cleaned up the blanket and flung it over his shoulder. "Which I would have done my best to give you."

"Stop flirting with me," Nadia said as embarrassed heat poured off her.

"But I love watching you turn red." Braiden picked up the tray. "Here, hold this, and I'll hold you."

"I can walk." Nadia tried to stand. She fell into the side of the well when her leg would not support her weight after sitting for so long. Braiden looked at her with one eyebrow raised. "Fine." She took the tray, and Braiden swung her into his arms.

Chapter

49

When Braiden and Nadia got close to Astrid's tent, they were laughing again.

"Oh, hello, guardian," Braiden said as they entered the tent. "Have you been waiting long?"

"No, not really," Dimitri said through clenched teeth. "What's so funny?"

"Just a story you missed." Braiden gently set Nadia onto her usual cot.

"I'm sure it was wonderful," Dimitri said. "But if you could be so kind, please leave."

"Can't," Braiden said. "I have to make a wrap for Nadia's knee." He shot Nadia one of his winning smiles, and she couldn't help but smile back.

"I've also been trained in herbal remedies, and I can heal her with my gift. So thanks, but run along."

Braiden paused while making the wrap, then turned to Nadia. "What would you like?"

"Braiden, thank you for the offer," she started. "But Dimitri and I should talk."

"You got it, my lady." Braiden did an exaggerated bow before taking Nadia's hand and kissing it again.

"Stop, you goof." Nadia smiled widely. "Thank you for breakfast and your company."

"I'll be around if you want more of it." Braiden swept from the tent.

Dimitri walked over to the wraps Braiden had been

making. "How are you?" He asked without looking up.

"I'm, I guess, I'm alright." She was unsure how to answer. "I'm training with Falleen today."

"She told me. I think it's a good idea."

"I'm glad you think so." Nadia was surprised at the raging emotions bubbling up. "Why are you here, Dimitri?"

He looked up at her, confusion written across his face, "I'm your guardian. It's my duty."

"I think," she began, her voice cracking. "I think we should talk about that."

"What?"

"Your mother doesn't like me."

"No, it's just—"

"Let me finish, please. She doesn't like me for whatever reason and wants you to keep your distance from a girl child from Earth. Train me, yes, but stay away. So I think it's only right I give you a choice. It's just, I, um, I would understand if you didn't want to be my guardian anymore."

"Because of my mother?"

"I mean, I know it's probably unorthodox or whatever. I could train with you, but adventure on my own, kind of like when you stay here while I wander around the Dreamworld."

"I never. She was wrong—"

"You won't be put at risk, and your mother won't be unhappy with either of us. I just ask that you decide in the next few days, so I can make whatever plans I need to move forward." She stared at her hands when she finished, willing herself not to cry. Her throat was tight, and she was sure Dimitri could see her heartbeat as it pounded at hyperspeed.

He sat on the bed next to her with her wrap in hand and his face unreadable. "You want to release me from my guardianship?"

"I won't come between a mother and a son." Her voice broke. She took a deep breath. "I also never said I want to release you, but I will if it's the right thing to do." Nadia didn't want him to stay out of some obligation, putting them both at risk because of his awful mother. She was shocked to realize how much she wanted him to stay, wanted him to want to be her guardian, wanted him to want her as much as she wanted him even now. Heat rose to her cheeks, and she fought tears.

Dimitri reached out a hand and gently placed it on her aching knee.

She felt the warmth of healing spread from his hand, and her pain eased, but her heart broke. *Is he healing me so I'm whole when he walks away?* She tensed as Dimitri stood and, without a word, left the medical tent.

Nadia stared at the tent flap, tears filling her eyes. She was afraid to move, afraid to breathe. If anything about the moment changed, she'd unravel.

When Astrid entered from the same tent flap moments later, Nadia's eyes spilled over, and sobs raked her body. She was gasping for air while twisting and untwisting the blanket in her hands.

"Nadia?" Astrid said. "What's wrong?" She pulled Nadia into her arms.

"Dimitri left," Nadia sobbed. "He doesn't want to be my guardian because his mother hates me because I'm clumsy, fat, and awful. He just healed my knee and left without a word."

"Nadia. What's all this talk? Dimitri hasn't left you. He's your guardian."

"I released him. I told him he didn't have to be my guardian if it meant driving a wedge between him and his mother. She hates me, Astrid. Why does she hate me so much? She healed me, too, and then turned on me."

"Sh sh sh," Astrid said. "This'll all get sorted out. You just need to finish healing, and you will see. He'll come around."

Nadia only gave herself ten minutes to wallow before she washed her face and retied her hair. She was puffy-faced, but armed with a new ghost bag and a lot of rage. The training session with Falleen took place near the well with a water wielder on standby if needed.

"This was not my idea." Falleen eyed the younger woman standing next to the well with contempt. "I'd have no issue controlling the fire you create."

"The counsel said—" the woman began before Falleen turned to glare. "It wasn't my idea either…" The woman jumped up on the side of the well, looking away.

"I've heard," Falleen turned her attention to Nadia. "That you are capable of lighting your entire body aflame."

Nadia felt her face heat with embarrassment, remembering the first time it happened. She nodded to Falleen.

"Show me."

"Oh no," Nadia shifted uncomfortably, rather fond of the clothing she wore. "Last time I did it, it was a mistake, and nothing I wore survived it. I mean, the elemental blending destroyed my clothing, but a full body of fire would do it too." She stopped abruptly. Falleen had her hands on her hips. "Sorry."

"You can cover your skin and clothing in fire without destroying either. However, out of an overabundance of caution." She threw another look at the water wielder. "We can start with your hands. Light them."

Nadia held her hands out, also glancing at the water wielder. The woman was staring at Nadia with a mix of fear and excitement. "Um, sure." *Fire.* Nothing. *Light up.* Nothing.

"Whenever you're ready," Falleen said impatiently.

"You don't have to be—"

"Very good."

Nadia's hands were both lit up with dancing flames. The little spike of annoyance she felt at Falleen's tone had been the trick.

"Put them out and do it again."

Falleen pushed Nadia to light her hands over and over, until it happened immediately without the need to summon any emotions. Then she taught Nadia how to manipulate the fire into a ball that could be thrown. Nadia struggled to keep the ball together at first, but by the time the training was over, the two women were playing catch with fire.

Nadia smiled broadly despite her sore back. "This was great. When do we train again?"

Nadia skipped dinner, opting for avoidance and pain management before sleep. Despite having her ghost bag, she also stayed in the medical tent.

Astrid brought Nadia some bread and cheese before she redressed Nadia's back injury. "Are you willing to take a little dreamless sleep powder?" Astrid asked, gently placing the last wrap on Nadia's back.

Nadia's face twisted. "Fine, but I hate it."

Astrid smiled widely. "I'll make it the way I used to make it for my sons."

A few minutes later, Nadia had a steaming mug of honey and lavender tea with only a hint of fresh-cut grass mixed with cough medicine and an old penny. It was palatable. She sipped slowly and fell to sleep more normally rather than suddenly.

Then a small quake jolted her awake, shaking her back and forth, until she opened her eyes and realized it wasn't a dream. Nor was it a quake.

"What the heck? Stop."

A hand covered Nadia's mouth, and her first reaction was to bite down hard.

"Owe," someone whispered.

"Who are you?" Nadia tried to jump up.

"Nadia, it's me." Althea hissed in the dark, physically holding Nadia in place. "Stay quiet."

"Why are you here? Where've you been?"

"I can explain later. Right now, we need to go."

"No." Nadia sat up. "Explain now. What's going on?"

"The village isn't safe," another voice spoke from the dark.

"Who's that?" Nadia said.

"Who's who?" Althea armed herself and looked around.

"There are monks and soldiers here," Lenora said in her ghostly whisper.

Nadia immediately reached for her ghost bag. It was on the outside of her shirt, no longer touching her skin. She glanced at Lenora again, seeing her terror. "Are you okay?"

"Who are you talking to?" Althea rounded on Nadia. "Do you see—"

"No," Lenora said, drowning out Althea. "They've tied up the people. They're going to kill them all. They'll die like before. You have to stop them. You have to. It can't happen again. I can't watch them all die again."

"Tell me where the Prestarians and Dimitri are." Nadia crossed the tent, trying to take Lenora's shoulders, but passing right through her.

"On the temple steps, but unconscious." Lenora trembled, going almost completely translucent. "They were eating and just fell asleep. The soldiers are looking for you, searching the tents, tearing up their camp."

"Asleep on the Temple steps?" Nadia questioned Althea.

"Yes, or dead," Althea said. "We have to get you to safety, and then send help."

"You're kidding, right?" Nadia shot a look at

Althea. Nadia took stock of her body. Arms were good. Legs were much better. Back was still iffy, but her gift felt full and ready despite training or maybe because of it. Nadia realized she was itching for a fight.

"What are you doing?" Althea stopped Nadia from exiting the tent.

"Fighting back." Nadia twitched her fingers, trying to call her gift of fire to them.

Nothing.

"Hmmm," Nadia said.

"You can't fight back." Althea was inches from her face. "You're leaving with me, one way or another."

Nadia heard the threat, and her wind gift reacted, causing Althea to stumble back.

"Thanks, that helps." Nadia played with the fire between her fingers. She thought about Dimitri walking out, and the fire spiked as wind picked up in the little tent.

"Stop," Althea said. "We'll be seen."

"Good," Nadia said. "Seen is exactly what I want."

"They're coming," Lenora's scream ripped through the air.

"Please," Althea said. "Please, come with me."

"I don't run from a fight," Nadia said. "It's one of my many charms." She shot Althea a smile before extinguishing her hands and leaving the tent.

Nadia felt rather than saw the low-burning embers of the fire pits throughout camp, bringing them all to a roaring blaze long enough to take in the scene around her. Tents destroyed, food trays and plates strewn all around, drag marks in the dirt, and the Prestarians propped up on the temple's stairs, tied together by their arms and feet.

Lenora came up next to Nadia, and her ghostly form vibrated.

"Are they…" Nadia started to ask.

"They're breathing."

"They can't be in the Dreamworld." Nadia tried to convince herself. "Dimitri has too much training to get sucked in." Dimitri was lying slightly in front of the Prestarians at the far end.

"What'll you do?" Lenora asked.

"Whatever I have to." Nadia had no idea what to do next.

"Girl!" A soldier in mail and helmet yelled at Nadia. "Stop." He drew his sword, and two other soldiers followed suit. "Are you Nadia of Earth?"

"Yep." Nadia continued forward. "And I don't remember inviting you to our campout."

"You did, though," another man called. "Just by being here."

Nadia knew his voice. "You?" She asked the monk she had sent flying the last time he tangled with her. "What could you possibly want?"

"You're an impertinent curr."

"And you're a medieval potato sack," Nadia shot back.

She deliberately looked past the monk at the unconscious people, looking for faces she knew. Braiden, Astrid, Keiran, and some of the women she had saved the day before all tied together and lay in heaps like discarded laundry. It infuriated Nadia.

Another scream ripped through the air as three other girls Nadia had just rescued from the Dreamworld were being dragged toward the temple. The soldiers threw one of the girls in front of the other Prestarians at the feet of the monk. She was sobbing, bruised, and terrified.

"Give yourself up," the monk said to Nadia. "And no one has to get hurt."

"It seems she's already hurt."

Three soldiers ran at Nadia, and she reacted exactly as she always did when someone ran at her, throwing the men. The men landed thirty feet away while the other soldiers stepped back. Nadia buzzed with the energy of her gifts.

"Juvenile display," the monk said, pulling the sobbing girl up by her hair. He placed a dagger at her throat, and Lenora screamed, startling Nadia.

"What do you want?" She asked the monk, almost afraid to hear the answer.

"You," he said, pointing the dagger at Nadia and then back to the girl's throat. "Only you."

Nadia took in the scene again before making eye contact with teh girl. She was maybe 13 and terrified. "Let the girl go. And you have a deal."

The monk smirked. "First, lie flat on the ground."

"You're kidding, right?" Nadia's fear was palpable, even as she kept her features as neutral or snarky as she could. "I like these clothes and they're clean."

"Now. Or I'll kill this one and move on to the next." The girl in his grasp whimpered as the knife pressed into her throat.

"Fine." Nadia slowly lay flat on her belly, still looking at the monk. "Done. Now what?"

"Take her," the monk said to a handful of soldiers,

who immediately tied Nadia's hands behind her back and wrapped the rope around her waist and throat.

She was desperately searching her gift, her mind, her memories for a plan or a way to be the savior all the Prestarians believed her to be and save the girl.

Soldiers pulled her to her feet, shoving her forward. She stumbled until another soldier caught her by the elbow.

"Get ready to fight," a voice Nadia wasn't expecting whispered.

Chapter
51

"Althea?" Nadia questioned quietly.

"I can hold the soldiers for a few minutes,"Althea said before a blade bit into Nadia's wrist as Althea cut the ropes. "But I can't stop the monks. Can you handle them?"

Nadia dropped her head ever so slightly to show she could even though she had no idea how. *Think.* Butterflies filled her stomach as she realized how many lives were in her hands.

"You boy?" The monk yelled. "What are you doing?"

Althea ripped off her soldier helmet, stepping out from behind Nadia. The soldiers around Nadia took a shuddering step before freezing in place.

It was unnerving. Only their eyes could move. Nadia shuddered.

"Fight!" Althea screamed, straining to keep hold of the soldiers' minds.

"Right." Nadia raised her hands, yelling, "Run!" at the girls as she threw fireballs into the monk's face. He dropped the knife to protect himself. "There." Nadia pointed at the temple. "All of you, go." The doors blew open, and the three girls sprinted inside before the doors slammed shut with another gust.

"Your grasp of your gifts is impressive," the monk said. "You'll be an adequate vessel."

"Stop. I don't care about the ravings of another

madman." She reached for her gift, preparing to send the monk flying again, mostly out of spite.

"Nadia!" Althea screamed. Three more monks were running at her, and two more at Nadia.

"Oh, good." Nadia crossed to Althea. "I was hoping to invite more of your poorly dressed friends to the party." Nadia held out her lit hands, daring the monks to get closer. "Let's see if I can try something new."

Thunder rolled loudly.

"You can't stop our combined powers," one monk said. "A little rain will do nothing but help the ground soak up your friends' blood."

"Why are you all so dramatic?" Nadia was trying to focus her gift. *I have one shot at this.* "Don't run," Nadia said to Althea. *Please work.*

"No problem." Sweat was rolling down Althea's face as she spoke through clenched teeth. "But whatever you're going to do, you better do it damn quick."

Nadia allowed her rage and fear to overtake her control, focusing them into her gifts, her need to act, and her desire to save them all. "Release the soldiers," Nadia said as the wind picked up. Althea looked at Nadia, confusion all over her face. "Do it!"

The sky opened up the moment the soldiers started to move. At first, the soldiers looked up just as confused as Althea, then began to scream and run for cover as fire-laced raindrops left welts on their skin and burned holes in their uniforms.

Nadia smiled, even as the first inkling of exhaustion crept through her gift.

"The monks," Althea yelled over the sound of the

storm hitting all around them.

The monks stood among the unconscious forms of the Prestarians, protected from Nadia's storm.

"Cowards!" Nadia ended the rainstorm but kept her hands lit.

"Take hands and do not release them at any cost," the first monk yelled. He was the clear leader of the group. "We'll outlast her."

He was not wrong. If she kept up the giant displays of power, she would burn out. *Think.* She turned her focus to the main monk. Throwing baseball-sized fireball after fireball, Nadia could slowly close the gap between her and the monk. But each one sizzled and died on an unseen wall a foot in front of the monk's grinning face. Rage surged within her, causing her fireballs to grow while also making them tighter and more dangerous. She threw one after another until the monk on the far end dropped to his knees. Nadia watched his skin turn gray. He released his neighbor's hand, falling away from the rest. He was dead before he hit the ground.

Nadia hesitated, her hands extinguished. *That's what Dimitri meant when he said others died from overusing their gift.*

"Nadia," Althea pulled her behind one of the burned-out structures.

One magical dagger after another plunged into the wall that was barely big enough to protect Nadia. Nadia heard the thud of another monk falling.

"You're coming with me, even if I have to bring you in pieces," he yelled at her.

"He's using their gifts?" Nadia asked Althea, but

Althea was gone. "Perfect."

The shock of seeing the dead monk clung to her like a spider web she could feel but not remove. The strain on her gifts and her body from the display of power was starting to roll through her, even as a creeping numbness in her right hand and arm grew. Her wrist still bled sluggishly where the ropes had been cut. However, none of her pains mattered the moment the monk started another assault of daggers. Nadia ran hard for the next burned-out house just east of the temple.

"Sir," she heard one of the monks yell. "You're killing us."

"Keep moving," was the main monk's only reply.

Nadia ventured a small peek and saw another monk fall dead. Four remained, and they were all a little gray around the edges.

Tha's right, follow me this way and away from the Prestarians and Dimitri, she thought, grateful for a small victory even though she was starting to feel as bad as the monks looked.

"Sir, please," a monk said.

"Shut up," the main monk yelled back. "We will give everything for the one we worship. Do not be ungrateful for the opportunity."

Nadia stood up and bolted to the next house, trying to pull the monks even further from the temple steps. Diving behind rubble, a dagger grazed her side without cutting the skin.

Too close, she thought, her panic rising. She was exhausted and wasn't sure how much unleashing she could do, but she knew she had to try.

"Come out, girl," the monk said.

Nadia popped up but dropped immediately. He was only ten feet from her and still flinging daggers. She belly crawled to a broken, charred tabletop. Holding it against her back, she ran full out to the side of the temple, stopping only when one of the daggers pierced through the table and into her right shoulder blade. Stumbling, she dropped the table, dislodging the blade and catching herself on her arms before sprawling on the dirt. She lay still, expecting more daggers, but none came.

Getting up slowly, fear crept up her throat even as her determination grew. She brushed herself off as the monk slowly approached, with only three other monks remaining.

"Okay." Nadia was grateful her adrenaline was keeping the pain from the dagger wound at bay. "You got me. Now what?"

"Now, you come with us." The monk had a big, toothy grin, a dagger gripped in his hand. "True believers always win. We'll be rewarded greatly, my friends."

"What are you rambling about?"

"The one we worship, your destiny."

Nadia laughed. "You're cracked if you think I'm going back to the orange-eyed freak."

"You will, but he'll no longer be needed."

"Wait, what?"

"No more talking, girl child. It's not for you to know. It's only for you to follow and do as you're told, as all females must." He threw the dagger, but it was flung away as gale-force winds whipped through the small clearing.

"We females must do what now?" Her voice was calm even as her gifts burned with the rage she felt. She could see his mouth moving, but the wind drowned out any stupid statement he was trying to say.

Nadia slowly spun in a circle, dragging the wind with her even as it pulled on the last of her gift. She twirled it into a tight tube and sent it at the remaining monks.

Their eyes were huge as they took in the small, forty-foot twister. One tried to turn and run, but the other's held him in place, hands still gripping each other. They must have believed their shield would protect them, but Nadia's creation ripped their hands apart before picking up each of them and ejecting them violently by slamming them against the ground, rubble, or the temple walls.

Her body was taut as a bow string as she worked to keep the twister in place, waiting for the next attack. When nothing happened, she took a deep breath. *It's over.*

The wind tube burst, and Nadia dropped to a knee, panting, as her head spun and her shoulder ached. Her stomach flipped as her eyesight shimmered, dancing with stars, and blackness crept in from the edges. She felt used up, empty, and terrified thinking about the monks dropping dead from using too much of their abilities. *I'm okay. Just tired. It's over.*

"Nadia?" A beautiful male voice called as he rounded the corner of the temple.

Dimitri. It's over.

Nadia struggled to her feet, her hands trembling so much that it was difficult to push off the ground. She looked down to gather herself before trying to walk, the memories of the day threatening to crash over her, deafening her, drowning her. *Stay mad,* she thought, desperate to cling to something. *Dimitri left you twice and fought Braiden like a child.*

She heard noises and looked up at the second floor of the temple. The girls she had saved from the Dreamworld were leaning out the window, applauding.

Nadia smiled up at them, "Come down. It's safe."

Then she saw him, and the roaring in her head started again.

The main monk had slammed into the side of the temple. It was clear from the angle of his body and the blood droplets hitting his face with each struggling breath that he was broken, but somehow still alive.

"You cannot fight your destiny, Nadia of Earth and Baako." His teeth were covered in blood, and his body was rigid as he fought to speak. "You will succumb."

"What?" Nadia crossed to the dying man, exasperated that he would waste breath on spewing nonsense.

"You'll soon find out." He shuddered, and his body relaxed into a slump. Even as his eyes faded, they remained locked on Nadia's.

She stood in roaring silence, trying to feel nothing for the evil man dead at her feet, dead by her gifts. Tears sprang up, exhaustion permeated her body, and bile rose. *I killed this man,* she thought. *He was a terrible person. But I killed him.* She trembled all over, fighting not to throw up, but was grateful for her repulsion. It showed she would never be the power-hungry, sycophantic fanatic the monk had been.

Chapter

52

"Nadia?" Dimitri said, reaching for her.

She brushed him off, not taking her eyes off the dead monk's face. "We should go to the Prestarians to make sure they're all okay," she said but made no effort to move.

As she started to walk, Dimitri grabbed her arm. "Nadia. I'm so sorry."

"Later." Nadia tried to pull her arm back, turning away from the monks body. "Please."

Dimitri held it, looking at her wounded wrist. "Are you okay?"

"I got cut being freed from some ropes." Nadia glanced back at the monk. "I'm fine."

"You're not fine. Your shoulder—"

"I'm fine for now." She jerked free of Dimitri. "Please, I need to make sure everyone's okay. I need to keep moving." She looked up at Dimitri with tears in her eyes. She stumbled, exhaustion washing through her as the realization of how many she had killed was clawing its way into her mind. She didn't mean to… "Please."

"Okay." He wrapped his arm around her waist. "We'll check on the Prestarians, then you can rest someplace safe."

"Someplace safe," Nadia repeated, looking at the monk's body until he was blocked from view.

Dimitri gently directed her with a hand resting on her lower back, but Nadia was barely aware of him as she fought the memories of the fight trying to overwhelm her. Her adrenaline was giving way to shock and hysteria.

Breathe, she told herself every time her chest seized or her body shuddered.

Dimitri glanced down at her every few steps. Nadia never returned his look, choosing instead to stay focused on anything else. She named every Prestarian she knew as they walked through the village. She counted steps, anything to keep her focused in the moment, or she would fall apart.

"Nadia," Astrid called from among a crowd of smiling Prestarians. "You're truly among the greatest. You've saved all my people from the Dreamworld and the monk's soldiers."

"Everyone is out, then?" Nadia asked.

"Everyone," Astrid had tears still on her cheeks. She put both of her hands palms out on her forehead and bent at the waist. All of the Prestarians followed.

"What is happening?" Nadia whispered to Dimitri before realizing he, too, was bowing to her.

"They're honoring you," Benicio said as he appeared beside his son. "This honor is often only given to the great guardians, Nadia of Earth, but you've truly earned it."

"Thank you," Nadia said to the living and the dead. "But they came for me."

"As they had for my sons," Benicio said. "You're exhausted, but I have another favor to ask. The dead wish to talk to the living. Will you be our voice?"

Nadia nodded, hoping the talk would be quick because her knees were beginning to shake. "Astrid, the dead would like me to convey a message." Benicio spoke, and Nadia told the onlookers, "Due to the bravery and respect shown today and since you've arrived, most of the dead can leave this place and join those already crossed over. Those that stay say all the Prestarians will be welcome in the Village of Bedros for as long as it stands."

"Thank you," Astrid said to the space around her, visibly surprised. "We're honored by your gesture of friendship and wish those of you leaving safe travels to the other side."

With that, the Prestarians began to disperse, speaking in low voices. Dimitri touched Nadia's shoulder, smiling down at her before crossing to talk with Astrid.

"Nadia," Benicio said. "This is Maddox, and he has something to ask you."

"Hello, Maddox." Nadia smiled at the young teenage ghost, swaying a little. "What can I do for you?"

"Uh, call me Max, and it's nothing, really," Max started. "I just wondered. I mean, I plan to tag along with you for a while if that's okay?"

Nadia glanced at Benicio, "Sure. Why not?"

"I figured I'm a better travel companion than that lump of a babysitter you have over there." He nodded at Dimitri.

"You have no idea," Nadia said as the numbness in her arm began to tingle.

"Okay, Max," Benicio cut in. "I need to talk to Nadia. Go make mischief somewhere else for a little bit."

"You got it, old man," Max said before moving off. "Hey, before I go," he said to Benicio. "Thanks for letting me tag along with you even though you didn't know it until you died."

Benecio shook his head. "He has been around longer than the rest of us, but he can be valuable to someone who can see and hear him."

Realization hit Nadia. "Was he the boy from the story Dimitri told about you and the village?"

"Yes."

"Wow, okay."

"I will also cross, but first I must know that you will save my boy."

"Dimitri?" Nadia asked. "I'm not even sure he wants to be around me anymore."

"Don't speak like that," Benicio said, standing before her until Nadia looked up into his ghostly face. "My son's better when he's around you."

"That's sweet." Nadia gave him a weak smile that didn't reach her eyes. Her body was starting to ache, and her mind to wander. "But your son has walked away twice. I think he has made his choice."

"He's stubborn, but you'll see, he'll come around. He knows you are his present and future."

"What?" Nadia was starting to get lightheaded.

"You'll see, but Dimitri is not the son I was talking about," Benicio said. "It's Dimitri's older brother, Godric."

"What?" The sunken face of Sergei's prisoner flashed before Nadia's eyes. "Your son is Godric? He's a prisoner in the Dreamworld."

"I feared as much. Though I'm relieved to hear he's alive. He's a guardian, and I've seen his charge without him. The one thing that could keep my son from his duties is death or imprisonment."

"He's a prisoner of the Dream Killer, both asleep

and awake. Godric said they are holding his body, so I can't save him like I did the Prestarians."

"I know I'm asking a lot, but please try."

"I will." Guilt spread through Nadia like a toxin, adding to the nausea she was beginning to feel. She had left Benicio's son behind, left Dimitri's brother locked in a cell, wasting away. "I promise."

"Who are you talking to?" Dimitri asked.

"Your dad."

"Don't tell him about Godric," Benicio cut in. "It'll be a distraction he doesn't need."

"Hello, Father." Dimitri looked around.

"Give him another chance." Benicio appeared next to his youngest son.

"He wants you to know he loves you," Nadia said, not responding to Benicio.

"I'm not bound to this place any longer." Benicio reached for his son, but stopped before his hand passed right through. "I'm going to crossover."

"He's no longer bound to this place," Nadia said, choking up. "He's going to leave, but he wanted to say goodbye and apologize for dying when you were so young," Nadia repeated Benicio's words to Dimitri.

"No, Father," Dimitri said, wiping at his sudden tears. "You have no reason to apologize. You saved me and Godric. I'm," he cleared his throat when his words got stuck. "I'm so glad you're no longer stuck here. I love you."

"I love you, too, my boy," Benicio said before disappearing.

"He's gone." Nadia had tears streaming down her

face while she swayed on her feet. "But he said, I love you, too, my boy, before going."

"Thank you," Dimitri said. "Thank you for… Nadia? Are you okay?"

"Oh." The world was spinning. She grabbed her head, taking deep, slow breaths.

Dimitri grabbed both of her wrists, causing her to flinch, a sharp pain ripping into the cut. It was deep and bleeding still.

"I," Nadia tried to say. "Look. I. Some. Cut. Blood."

Dimitri said something, but she could only hear rushing water and unrecognizable noises all around her, causing her to look around. Dimitri took her wrist, and she focused on him smelling her cut. The color drained from his face as she started to float. Not float, was carried into Astrid's medical tent.

"What?" She said as Dimitri's voice penetrated her foggy mind. "What, Dimitri?"

"Stay awake," he said.

"Put me down." Motion sickness was creeping up her throat. "Please, I'm going to puke."

"Astrid," Dimitri said. "I need you."

"What is it?" Braiden's voice said from behind them. "What's happened?"

"I need your mother, not you," Dimitri replied.

"Dimitri, please," Nadia said, though her words were slurred.

Astrid's face floated into view, but the world's sounds came in shattered waves. Astrid took Nadia's arm and smelled her wrist.

"How?" Astrid said before Nadia heard nothing but

rapid heartbeats.

"I can't," Nadia wiggled in Dimitri's arms. "What are you saying? I hear too much. It's too loud. Put me down. I need to stand." She fought. "Put me down." Her ears were roaring. The harder she fought, the tighter Dimitri held her and the faster he moved. Nadia's vision faded to black with only splotches of color and sparks.

"Nadia, stay awake." Dimitri shook her gently as all the sounds around her burst into life, overwhelming her senses.

She gasped, grabbing at her ears. "It's so loud." The sound overwhelmed her, causing an immediate panic attack. Fear closed her throat and forced her to move. She flopped out of Dimitri's arms landing on her butt.

"Nadia," Dimitri dove for her.

Nadia started to run before she had decided to. She had to get away. She slammed into Braiden and past Astrid. She had to get away from him, them, from the noise, from the nightmare of the monk's dead eyes. The moment she was alone, the roaring quieted.

She made it to the temple steps before the rushing in her ears returned. She grasped her ears, doubling over.

"Stop. Please stop," she repeated over and over. Gasping when she felt a hand grasp her uninjured wrist, she breathed in the familiar, disgusting taste of dreamless sleep powder before collapsing.

"Nadia," a gentle voice spoke from above her, outside her. "Nadia, it's time to go."

"Where?" She asked without opening her eyes.

"To a village, a few days' ride from here," the voice

continued.

She knew the voice. Her aunt? A friend?

A few days' ride? She sat bolt upright. Baako, Dimitri, the Dream Killer all came slamming back. Astrid was sitting on the foot of Nadia's cot in the medical tent. Sweat sprang to Nadia's forehead, and she felt the color drain from her face before she dove for the empty water bucket and vomited everything she had ever eaten and more. Astrid handed Nadia a wet cloth as they sat back on the bed.

"That might've been from the dreamless sleep powder," Astrid said.

"I really do hate that stuff." Nadia wiped her mouth.

"How are you feeling now?"

"Shaky and a little bit terrible." Nadia noticed her wrist was wrapped, but wasn't sure why. "What happened? Did I get injured?"

"You don't remember?" Dimitri said from the door.

"I remember the monks and the ghosts leaving, but then it's all a little blurry."

"Nadia." Astrid took Nadia's uninjured hand. "This may be difficult, but tell us about what happened with the monks."

Nadia took a deep breath. "Althea woke me up," she began.

"Althea?" Dimitri asked, looking at Astrid.

"Yeah," Nadia was annoyed by the look they shared. "She wanted me to leave with her, but I couldn't leave you all to die. I thought Althea had left, but she came back dressed as a soldier. I had been caught and tied up, and Althea cut my ropes." She looked down at her bandaged wrist. "And my wrist."

"That piece of shit." Dimitri slammed both fists on a cot.

"We had suspected she was a traitor," Astrid said. "But this is treachery beyond what I thought her capable."

"What are you two talking about?" Nadia was feeling the beginnings of a headache as the emotions of the fight came flooding back. "Althea saved me and then helped me fight."

"She poisoned you," Dimitri knelt in front of Nadia. "She poisoned you with an incredibly dangerous mixture. That's why we need to leave."

"All arrangements are made," Astrid said, rising. "There are two horses for you, picked from a group left by the soldiers. You'll travel north for a few days, and we'll follow a day or so behind you. Braiden will track you through his gift."

"What poison?" Nadia asked, hearing little else. Her stomach flipped as she replayed the moment Althea cut her. "She helped me." She couldn't imagine Althea would poison her or how she could. If she wanted Nadia dead, she could have left Nadia to be killed by the monks. *But the monks didn't want me dead...*

"We must go," Dimitri said, also rising. "We can talk on the road."

"No," Nadia blinked, trying to clear her head. "We talk now."

Dimitri and Astrid exchanged looks.

"She has a right to know," Astrid said. "She can help to slow the effects."

Dimitri sighed. "The poison Althea used is a

combination of toxins and a very potent sleeping draught that'll slowly put the body to sleep, one or more systems at a time. You'll lose your hearing, sight, ability to walk, taste, and even your ability to breathe before the poison runs its course. It'll put you into a catatonic state and then… and then nothing because we'll get to the village and the ingredients needed for the antidote."

Nadia sat open-mouthed, gently rubbing the bandage on her wrist. "Why'd she do this?" She asked, staring at the floor, unable to look at Dimitri. *Why is he even coming? Out of guilt?*

"We don't know," Astrid said.

"The reason is unimportant," Dimitri said. "What's important is keeping you calm."

"Keeping me calm?" Nadia's confusion grew.

"The more worked up you get, the faster the poison spreads," he said.

"You cannot use your gifts," Astrid said.

Nadia looked at her sharply. "What? Why not?"

"Your gifts activate certain ingredients in the poison. It'll achieve the effect of speeding you toward your death."

"I've already used my gifts, like all of them, to fight the monks." Nadia rubbed her temples.

"Are you okay?" Dimitri asked.

"No," Nadia was trying to hold back tears. "How could I be? I freaking fell asleep in my safe bedroom not that long ago and woke up here. In this stupid world, with its stupid villains, and now some stupid woman is trying to kill me, slowly. No one knows why. I have killed, like, I don't even know how many people, which is terrible."

Tears were streaming down her face. "And I see ghosts because apparently, I've already died once, but sure, give me poison. Maybe when I die this time, I'll be able to see fairies or Santa Claus." She took a shuddering breath. "Oh, and your stupid mom, who is obnoxiously pretty, hates me."

"Nadia," Dimitri reached for her. "She doesn't hate you."

Nadia moved away from him. "She hit me, and you took her side despite everything that you and I, that we… You walked out. Twice. Twice Dimitri! I, you, we. I hate it here."

"Dimitri." Astrid wrapped her arms around Nadia. "She'll meet you outside in a few minutes."

Nadia pressed into Astrid's shoulder and openly sobbed.

"He left. Tell me what's going on."

Nadia told Astrid about the fight and Gaia's coldness. She told Astrid how terrible it had been when Nadia believed for a split second they'd all been killed and how mad she was at herself for feeling so deeply for a guy she barely knew. She even told her how she offered to release Dimitri from his guardian duties and the monk's dying words. Astrid let Nadia talk and sob without interrupting.

"You've been thrown into a situation that no one wants or envies, but everyone expects you to succeed at all costs, and you have made it look easy. I can't imagine what you've been through and what you'll face. Dimitri's a guardian, but he's also a man and human. All little boys love their mothers, and all humans are flawed, but he'll always fight for you when you truly need him to. Don't doubt him, and don't doubt yourself. You must go, Nadia, and we'll follow."

Chapter

53

Hours into the slow ride north, Nadia was getting sore. She had never ridden a horse before, and her butt hurt from the saddle, her back hurt from the fight, and her wrist hurt from stupid Althea's cut. She was brooding and silent most of the time, though she often took comfort in petting her new horse. Nadia named her Betsy because her coloring reminded her of a dairy cow, but that's where the resemblance ended. Betsy was a well-trained war horse that took to Nadia right away.

Maddox suddenly appeared in front of Nadia and Betsy. "I'm so bored, and you're so boring!"

"Max!" Nadia calmed Betsy after she sidestepped the ghost. "She may not be able to see you, but she can feel you. Animals are smart and loyal and wonderful," Nadia cooed, petting Betsy again.

"Who's Max?" Dimitri brought his giant war horse closer.

"A bored teenage ghost tagging along with us for a while unless he scares my beauty again."

"Eww." Max floated next to Nadia. "You treat that horse better than, well, your babysitter."

Nadia glanced at Dimitri, meeting his eyes before immediately looking away. "She deserves it. Don't you, my beauty."

"He's pouting again." Max got closer to Dimitri's face. "He's been doing it all day. Look at you, pout, hear your voice, pout. He's kind of a giant baby."

Nadia giggled, "You're not wrong."

"What are you two talking about?" Dimitri asked, overly casual.

"You," Max said into Dimitri's face.

"Max." Nadia raised an eyebrow.

"We should stop," Dimitri rode closer to Nadia.

"Why?" She asked.

"Lunch, and I bet you're getting sore." He jumped off his horse before grabbing Betsy's reins. "Do you want help getting down?"

"Nah, I got it." She didn't really, but she gently swung her leg over Betsy, letting both legs dangle, before she promptly fell off, landing on both knees. She caught herself before her face hit the ground.

"Smooth," Max said, laughing so hard Nadia was sure the living could hear him.

"Shut up, Max." Nadia's face was boiling with embarrassment.

"Are you okay?" Dimitri extended a hand.

Nadia ignored it. "I'm fine, just clumsy per usual."

"Nadia—"

"Dimitri, I'm fine."

"No, I mean, I'm glad, it's just, what I wanted to say, I'm sorry."

"Bahaha," Max laughed as loud as his wispy ghost form would allow. Nadia shot him a look, and Dimitri followed her gaze.

"Ghost? I mean, Max?" Dimitri asked.

"Yes. He's being a child."

"Forever and ever," Max said.

"You know, Max, you're the only ghost I've met that floats," Nadia said. "The rest sort of shuffled around."

"Stupid, right? I mean, we're dead. Why walk?"

Nadia shook her head, smiling. "Sorry, what were you saying?"

Dimitri had started a small fire and prepped the usual stew. "It can wait."

"No, really. Max is quieter and promises to stay that way while we talk, or so help me, I'll figure out how to cross you over."

Max stuck his tongue out at Nadia and disappeared.

"He's gone. Go ahead."

"Wait? Gone, gone?"

"Oh no, Max seems more advanced than the other ghosts. He disappears, floats, and does tricks. He's a kid, so he acts like one as a ghost, too."

"Got it," Dimitri didn't look up. "So he'll be with us for a while."

"Yep," a voice responded, but Max didn't appear.

Nadia laughed. "Yes, I think so. He seems to be enjoying himself."

Nadia watched Dimitri silently stir the food for a few minutes. She was in no hurry to talk with him, and he seemed to be in no hurry to speak.

When he finally handed her a bowl of food, he said, "How are you? I mean, how are you feeling after the fight and—"

"Which one?" Nadia asked before taking a big bite of stew. She usually loved his stew, the flavors bursting in her mouth, the perfect tenderness of the meat and veggies. It was magical, but she swallowed the bite, confused at how dull and lifeless it was.

"The fight between the monks."

"So not our fight." She took another bite, thinking her rage was ruining an amazingly flavorful meal. The second bite tasted just as empty, like nothing. She could feel the warmth and texture, just no amazing flavors.

"I deserve that," Dimitri said. "Nadia, when you said you were releasing me from my guardianship, I thought, I mean, I didn't think." He set his bowl down. "I care for you too much, and I thought, I knew that could be, could cause issues. What if we're attacked, and I take my focus off the fight because I care, no, what I'm trying to say? Why am I so bad at this?"

Nadia watched Dimitri's eyes fill with tears. He ran his hands through his hair before abruptly standing.

"Do you know what I'm trying to say?" he asked.

"No." Nadia was a little concerned that Dimitri had snapped. "Are you okay?"

"I love you, or I was falling in love with you," he blurted, landing on his knees in front of her. "And it scared me so much, then you almost died in the river, and I broke. I vowed to distance myself. I can't be your guardian and break whenever you're hurt or in danger. I mean, you're a proven risk. How many times have you been at death's door? No, I, it's not important, that's not what I'm trying to say."

Nadia's mouth was hanging open while tears filled her eyes, too. "You what?" she asked when Dimitri took a breath.

"See, see, even you're shocked, so when my mother, when she was cruel," he took a shuddering breath.

"I took the coward's way out to protect myself. Then you said, you suggested I should or could leave, and I left, oh Nadia, it was the biggest mistake of my life. I got to the temple and realized how foolish I was being. I love you, and I walked away. Who does that? I tried to go back, but I heard you sobbing, and I couldn't face you. I couldn't face the pain I had caused you after everything you had been through, everything I contributed to." He took her free hand. "I'm so sorry. I, please, please, forgive me for everything." He laid his head on her hand.

Nadia's heart was racing while her breath came in short bursts.

"Nadia?" Dimitri asked, looking up at her.

Tears were streaming down her face. "I don't understand. You love me? The chubby, Earth-child your mother hates. Me, the clumsy, accident-prone girl with volatile, untrained gifts who may or may not be on death's door again?"

"Yes." His face was full of expectation.

"Dimitri, what? This doesn't make any sense. You left; I was so sure you wanted to leave, but you're saying you didn't. What?"

"I love you, Nadia of Earth." Dimitri took both of her hands. "I think I have from the moment you tried to fight me in the woods the day you got here."

"What?" Nadia said, still crying.

"You don't have to say it back." He let her hand go. "I know what I did—"

"This is too much. You left. I thought you were leaving forever. It hurt so much."

"I know."

Nadia looked anywhere but at Dimitri, trying to figure out how she felt. *He left you, walked out,* part of her mind was saying calmly and rationally, while the other part was doing somersaults and cartwheels. *Love! Me, he loves me.*

She looked down. "Did you do something different with the stew?"

"Um," from the look on his face, he was not expecting her to talk about the food. "No, it's one from the same batch as before. Why?"

"I can't taste it." Realization dawning on her. Holding it up to her face, she sniffed. Nothing.

"You can't," the color drained from Dimitri's face.

Max appeared behind Dimitri. "Tell him we need to go. Now. The village can't be that far, right?"

"Max thinks we should go," Nadia said without inflection. The poison took two senses in one shot. Nadia's two favorite senses. What's the point of eating if the flavors are dead and empty?

"Finish eating," Dimitri jumped up. "Then we can go."

"I'm done," Nadia said, holding her bowl out to Dimitri. The words hung in the air. "We should go."

Chapter

54

"Do you want to talk about it?" Dimitri asked as they slowly rode.

"Talk about what?" Nadia asked as she spiraled into a dark place.

"Whatever you want," Dimitri said. "Whatever'll help you get out of your dark mood. You're even starting to freak out your horse."

"Her name is Betsy." Nadia scratched Betsy behind the ear.

"My apologies." Dimitri bowed slightly in his saddle to Betsy. "This is Dragon."

"Dragon?"

"Yeah. When picking out our horses, this one blew snot all over me." Dimitri shrugged. "It made me laugh, so I named him Dragon."

"Gross. But it's nice to meet you, Dragon." Dragon snorted, and Nadia laughed. "Okay, yeah, I get it."

"We should stop soon. No reason to risk the horses in the dark."

"Except Nadia's been poisoned," Max said, suddenly appearing.

"Max," Nadia almost fell out of the saddle. "You scared me."

"I mean, you can hang with me if you do die. I'm just not sure Earth people stay or get sucked back to their weirdo planet or whatever."

"Thanks for the offer."

"Offer?" Dimitri asked.

"If I die, I can run with him."

"She's not going to die." Dimitri slowed the horses before jumping off. "She'll be fine and alive, and you can hang out with her while she's alive. No dead, I mean death or ghost running. May I help you down?"

Nadia thought about her near faceplant last time. "Sure." She swung her leg over and reached out her hands to Dimitri. He lowered her gently, holding her longer than needed when her feet hit the ground. "Thank you. I, um, we should—"

Nadia's breath caught as Dimitri leaned in. The whole world seemed to vibrate, but before his lips touched hers, she realized the world was vibrating, and it was wrong.

"What's that?" Nadia asked, breaking the embrace.

"I'm sorry," Dimitri said. "You just, I thought we could—"

"No," Nadia placed a hand on his chest to quiet him. "Do you feel the ground? It feels like—" She gasped as the ground rolled violently.

Two massive, old trees near them were uprooted as they bent and broke, screaming in pain and despair.

Nadia grabbed her ears as Dimitri pushed her out of their path.

"They're screaming," she said. "It's terrible. The trees are saying it isn't natural. It's a gift. Is that a thing? A ground-shaking gift?"

"It's a thing," Dimitri said. "Rare, but a thing. We should go. Can you disconnect from the trees?"

"No." Nadia tried to pull away from him. "We need to stop this before more trees die." Nadia was yelling because her mind was pounded by hundreds of tree voices crying out in pain and for justice. "The trees." She buckled at the pain in her head. "The trees."

"Disconnect." Dimitri wrapped his arm around Nadia's waist to keep her from falling further. "Close off your gift. Remember the poison. Disconnect."

"I can't," She started running in the direction she knew the quake had to have come from.

"Nadia, no," Dimitri yelled.

"Stop," Nadia screamed aloud. "I'll help you, but where's the ground shaker?" The trees directed her to a clearing a hundred yards from the road. "Please quiet down so I can think."

She scrambled through the thick brush, unaware that her borrowed clothing was getting snagged and ripped. At the edge of the clearing, a hand snaked out around her waist. She swung, and Dimitri caught her wrist.

"Wait." Dimitri pulled her back. "You don't know who you're running toward, and you need self-preservation. But," he said, cutting Nadia off before she could protest. "If you're going to do it anyway, let me help."

"We need to hurry." Nausea rolled through her. "The trees... I think another quake is coming."

"Okay," Dimitri said. "Let me think."

"I'll look." Max appeared next to them. "Wait, here." Before Nadia could tell Dimitri what Max was doing, he returned. "It's a little girl, like little maybe eleven or twelve and raggedy and dirty. She's tiny for such a big gift, but why flatten the forest?"

"Max says it's a little girl." Nadia's nausea grew. "We're out of time." The land was shifting, and the trees were screaming again.

"Nadia." Dimitri stood in front of her. "Don't use your gift. The poison, stay calm."

Max was also saying, "Stay here. You can't do anything. Let the babysitter go."

The trees were screaming in fear, screaming for her to act, and the land was creaking and bracing before it broke.

"STOP!!" Nadia screamed aloud and through her gift.

For a moment, everything quieted.

"I heard you." Dimitri's shock was clear on his face.

"I'm sorry." Nadia rubbed her temples. "I didn't mean to scream."

"No," he said. "I heard you in my head and with my ears."

Nadia looked to the clearing. "The ground has calmed. Maybe she heard me, too."

"I don't understand." Dimitri took one of Nadia's hands. "How'd you do that?"

"No idea." Nausea was creeping up again. "Let's work it out later. I'll be right back."

"No, wait," Dimitri said, but Nadia was already running directly for the gift she could inexplicably feel.

"Wait," Nadia was yelling with her mind to the little girl. "I'm here to help you. Please wait. My name is Nadia. Please don't shake the ground." Nadia saw the little girl right before she heard the bow's twang. Slamming into the girl, Nadia pinned her to the ground as Nadia lit the night up with the element always so close to the surface. The arrows disintegrated in the fire, and Nadia's head spun. *Deep breath. You're fine. Get up. Get her to safety.* "We have to move. Are you okay to run?"

The girl nodded her filthy, matted head, her eyes wide with shock, her face gaunt. "They's gonna be mad if I leave," the girl said. "They say I'm their property and nothing else."

"Not anymore," Nadia said gently, even as her rage rose. She grabbed the girl's hand and stood slowly as the world spun slightly, but they ran as fast as they could.

When they reached the tree line, Nadia stopped behind a large tree, panting. "I'm so sorry to drag you. Who was shooting at us? Who's mad you left?"

"Soldiers," the girl said, her eyes still giant white and brown orbs. "You really Nadia of Earth? They's trying to kill you and now me, I'm sure."

"I am, and they won't succeed," Nadia said between breaths. "What's your name, sweetie?"

"I don't have one," The girl hung her head. "I's always told I'm nothing, and nothing gets no name."

Nadia immediately felt her rage rise and had to close her eyes to avoid lighting any part of herself on fire.

"I'm sorry." The girl flinched away from Nadia. "I shouldn't of said that."

"Oh, no." Nadia took the girl's dirt-covered hands. "I'm not mad at you. I'm mad at those men who made you feel like you were less than the beautiful and powerful little girl you are. I don't have as much control over my gifts as you do, so I had to calm down, that's all."

"You thinks I'm beautiful. Even, even looking, like, I mean, covered in yuck?"

"Of course," Nadia said. "No dirt can cover who you are, but now we need to meet up with my friend and our horses to get out of here." Nadia noticed the girl was only wearing a sack as a dress and no shoes. Her feet were already pretty beat up, with fresh blood on the toes of one and the top of the other. "Can you ride on my back?"

"Really?" The girl smiled. "Okay. Fun."

"Allow me," a voice said.

The girl screamed as Nadia said, "No, shh. This is Dimitri. We're safe now. He's my guardian and won't let anything happen to you. Plus, he has to carry me all the time."

"Really? Okay, if you say he's safe." The girl looked at Nadia with pure trust, and Nadia knew she would die for that filthy little creature to keep her safe.

They heard dozens of horses.

"Time to go," Dimitri scooped the girl into his arms. "The horses are this way."

They picked through the woods toward the road. Dimitri led the way, and Nadia followed, her adrenaline burning through her system.

"How much further?" Nadia said through harsh breaths.

They almost fell onto the road as another group of twangs sounded, then another, and another.

"Go," Nadia hissed as Dimitri hesitated. "I got this."

"No, Nadia," Dimitri yelled.

Nadia turned and held both hands out. Fireshot from

her hands like fire hoses spraying at a burning home, disintegrating the first round of arrows, but the second round of arrows made it a couple of feet closer. The third was only a single arrow and punched through her fire into her left hand. The hand went out even as her right hand kept up the spray for a few more seconds. She felt nothing, no pain even as her legs gave out. She shook her head slowly, sitting in the dirt, not sure what she felt. Her gift was right under the surface, ready to be used, but she couldn't quite reach it. Her body and mind felt sluggish.

"Don't move, honey," Nadia heard Dimitri say to the girl. Then Nadia was lifted off the ground like she had so many other times. "Can you ride?"

Nadia nodded even though she wasn't sure. Dimitri put her on her horse behind the girl.

"Nadia is going to hold the reins, but I need you to hold them too," Dimitri told the girl. Then he took Nadia's hand. "What happened?"

"An arrow," Nadia slurred. "I'll wrap it while we ride."

"Okay," Dimitri said. Then, turning to the girl, he said, "If you think you or Nadia is going to fall off, let me know first, okay?"

"Fall off?" the girl asked. "Is this horse good or mean?"

"Her name is Betsy, and she is very gentle." Nadia finally got her arms to do what she wanted. She wrapped the girl tightly, head still spinning, and nodded to Dimitri. "We got this. Lead on."

Chapter

55

"Dimitri," Nadia said in little more than a whisper, a few hours after they fled the soldiers. "I need to stop."

"We can't," Dimitri said back.

"Betsy, stop." Her horse obeyed. "Stay put, sweetie." Nadia slid off the back of the horse.

"Nadia," Dimitri's voice was somewhere above her. "We have to keep going. The soldiers—" He abruptly stopped talking when Nadia's convulsions started.

The first one was fast but happened before Nadia could reach the ground. She had felt for some time that something was wrong with her body.

"I knew," she said to Dimitri when her body's convulsions slowed, and she could speak again. Exhaustion seeped into her words. "I knew something was wrong, probably an hour ago."

"Why didn't you say anything?"

She didn't respond as fear saturated her body.

"Nadia?" He came closer. "Look at me."

Nadia turned away from his voice, "I can't."

"When? When did you lose your sight?"

Nadia felt a tear roll down her cheek. "Around the same time, I realized something wasn't right in here." She pointed to her chest. "Around the same time, I realized this was more poison." She held up her sloppily wrapped hand.

Dimitri took it, and from what Nadia heard, he sniffed it. "I need to clean it and rewrap it."

"The arrow made it through my fire," Nadia said while Dimitri tended her hand. "The person knew. They knew what I would do. It had to be Althea, right? But why? Why's she trying to kill me?"

"Kill?" the little girl asked. Nadia heard a light thud before the little girl took her other hand. "You sick? Someone hurt you?" Nadia nodded. "How can I help? You have to get better. You saved me, so I save you."

"You know what would really help?" Nadia stared at their held hands, but seeing only the blackness she had seen for the last hour. "If you pick a name, so I can properly introduce my friend to you."

"Okay, let me think," the little girl said.

"I'm sorry if this hurts," Dimitri said to Nadia. "We have to hurry. I don't think we lost the soldiers or Althea."

"I don't feel any pain. I barely feel you wrapping it." Dimitri hesitated in his movements, and Nadia could imagine the exact look of worry that crossed his face. "I know it's bad, but I have a feeling not hurting will be a blessing very soon. If nothing else, I still have my voice and my hearing." Nadia paused. Her body stiffened out of her control. She felt the tiny hand leave hers before she fell back. She heard more than felt her body flail and kick. *The seizures must be another side effect,* she thought, while her body did whatever it wanted. *I must think of a pleasant way to pay Althea back.*

"Nadia," she heard Dimitri say as she felt her body jostling around. "Nadia, wake up, please."

Nadia was confused. Every bump, every hiccup that ran through her body made her mind start over. *Where am*

I? Horseback?

"Dimitri?" she asked. "Where's the girl and Betsy?"

"What? Not worried about me?" Max said from somewhere nearby.

"Of course, but you can't be hurt," Nadia said.

"That's funny," Max said. "You not asking about me hurt a little."

Nadia tried to giggle but wasn't sure it worked.

"Dimitri, what happened?" She asked.

"You started to convulse and passed out," Dimitri said.

"How long ago?"

"Yesterday," came a small voice when Dimitri didn't answer. "Don't look at me like that, big man," the girl said. "You said I deserve the truth, so she do too."

"Big man?" Nadia heard the smile in her own voice.

"You saw'ed him. He's pretty huge."

"Did you pick a name?" Nadia asked.

"Yep, Enid," the girl said. "I hear'ed it when I was little. Mayhaps it was my mama's name. But I always liked it."

"It's beautiful. Just like you."

"You right, big man," Enid giggled. "She lose her sight, alright. Ain't nothing beautiful about me."

"Oh, I don't know," Dimitri said. "I think you're pretty adorable."

Enid giggled again. "Where we going? My butt's starten to ache."

"There's a village another half day's ride from here," Dimitri said.

"Half day?" Enid said. "This big pony is nice and

all, but that don't make my butt or her back any happier."

"I like her," Max said nearby.

"Me too," Nadia said.

"What?" Dimitri asked.

"Max likes Enid, but she's right. You both can't ride all night, and we'll go faster in the daylight."

"The soldiers—" Dimitri started.

"Have you heard them at all?"

"No," both Max and Enid said.

"No," Dimitri followed.

"Enid," Nadia started. "Your gift is with shaking the land, right?"

"Yeah. But I can also feel the ground, like movement of heavy beasts and water."

"So if a rider was coming, you could feel them?"

"Yep. If it's real quiet and I'm real still, I can feel people walking too. Some just feels heavier."

"Dimitri, you can pick the place, hide our tracks, and then everyone rests for a few hours." Nadia tried to reach out and touch him, realizing she had lost all control of her limbs. She took in a shuddering breath as fear crashed through her. *What will be next?*

"What's the matter?" Dimitri asked.

"I'm just tired," Nadia lied. "And I'm grateful to be stopping for a bit."

They rode on for another half hour, and Nadia struggled to stay awake while hiding her inability to move.

"Dimitri," Nadia said quietly as he brought Dragon to a stop. "I need you to get me down. I can't move on my own anymore."

"I know." He slid Nadia off Dragon.

He cradled her to his chest. She was grateful to hear his steady heartbeat.

"I'll be right back." He leaned Nadia against what she believed to be a fallen tree.

Moments later, she heard the quiet steps of Enid.

"Dimitri said he's going to check the perimniter—"

"Perimeter." Nadia gently corrected her.

"Yeah, and tie up the horses." Enid half-sat on Nadia. "Sorry."

"No need to be sorry. It's been a bit of a long and terrible day for you."

"I mean, kind of," Enid said on Nadia's right. "You saved me from awful men. That's pretty great."

"You're right," Nadia said, dozing off. "Are you able to sleep?"

"Maybe."

"Shhh," Max said from Nadia's other side. "Someone's coming. A woman."

"Where's Dimitri?" Nadia said to Max.

"I'll find him," Max said as Enid said, "I don't know, but someone is coming." Fear in her voice.

"A woman," Nadia said. "An evil woman."

"She walks heavy."

"Nadia," an easily recognizable voice said from a way off.

"Althea," Nadia's anger boiled up. She tried to stand, bawl her fists, anything, but her body refused to respond. She reached for her gift, and her head started to spin. "Can't wait any longer for your poison to kill me, so you've come to slit my throat?"

"No," Althea sounded closer. "I'm sorry, I didn't mean to. I mean, I had to—"

"Why are you here?" Nadia asked. "Why did you do this?"

"I have to take you to the antidote and him," Althea was right next to Nadia.

"Him?" Nadia asked. "Him who?"

"You can't take her," Enid said, and Nadia felt Enid leave her side.

"No, Enid," Nadia was desperate to use her arms or gifts. She felt her hands warm, but her ears filled with the sound of raging water. Nadia's chest constricted, and she struggled to breathe. When she got herself back under control, there were sounds of a scuffle, and she felt completely helpless again.

"Althea." Nadia was trapped inside her body. "I'll go. Just leave her and Dimitri alone. Please."

"It's the only way to save you," Althea said. "Stop squirming, you little brat."

"Enid." Nadia tried to guess where they were. "She needs me alive. That means she has to reverse the poison. I'll be okay as long as I know you're okay."

"Fine," Enid said. "But where's you going?"

"I'll tell you," Althea said. "But you won't be able to share it until you wake."

"Wake?" Enid asked.

"There's a large house due west of the village Dimitri is taking you to," Althea said. "That's where the Dream Killer lives and works. Not a castle, just an old, big house."

"What?" Enid asked.

"Oh, and tell Dimitri not to drink or eat anything offered to him when he arrives and to trust no one." Althea paused. "Can you remember all that little girl?"

"Yes. I'm not stupid."

"Great."

Then Nadia heard blowing and smelled the faint scent of dreamless sleep powder. "Did you just drug Enid?" Nadia's voice shook with rage.

"Dreamless sleep is the safest place for her. However, you aren't so lucky."

"What the hell does that mean?"

Chapter

56

The lights she could suddenly see were blinding for only a moment before she realized what was going on.

"Shit."

"Language," came the voice Nadia absolutely loathed.

"Why am I here?" She asked, seething as she stood. "How am I here?"

"None of that matters anymore, my dear," Sergei said with his usual gleeful sneer. "You won't be here much longer."

Nadia immediately tensed. She was in a small, dungeon-like room. There was only one small slit of a window too high up for Nadia to see out of and a grimy table with shackles dangling off the sides.

"You finally decided to kill me?" Nadia shook out her limbs, running through her options for escape.

"No. I don't need to. You failed, and you're being sent back."

Nadia's head cocked to the side, "what are you talking about?"

"You failed, you pathetic twit, and now you leave."

"Leave to where?"

"I imagine whatever hole you crawled out of." Sergei flicked a hand at Nadia. "The best part is, you leave with the knowledge that all those you have met here will be killed to put this world rightfully and firmly back under my control.”

“No. You can’t.”

“Yes. You gave these idiots hope for all of what, weeks? And now you leave them here to rot on this antiquated world. Isn’t that great?”

“No.” She stepped toward Sergei. “You won’t. I haven’t failed. I destroyed your monks. I escaped this place so many times.” An image of Dimitri dead, the color drained from his lifeless face, wounds visible all over his beautiful body, appeared in her mind. “No. This is just one of your stupid games.”

“No games and no more talk. Enjoy Earth. Bye-bye, dumpling.”

Nadia sat up, the image of Dimitri’s dead body still seared into her eyes. She reached out and pulled her covers up to her face, breathing slowly and deeply. Fabric softener and vanilla floated into her senses, calming her.

Fabric softener?

Jumping up, her heart knocked with an irregular rhythm in her chest. Her breath came in gasps as she spun before collapsing in on herself, feeling everything and nothing.

She was home. Earth. Arizona. Her cozy room with way too many pillows on the bed. The queen-sized bed she missed every time she slept on dirt. Plants surrounded her on every surface near the two windows. It looked exactly as she had left it weeks ago.

Then, she heard them. Her mom and sisters were talking in the kitchen. Pancakes, butter, and syrup wafted into her room. She really was home.

Nadia stood frozen with indecision. Part of her wanted to run to them. Hug them and never let go. Tell them why she had been gone for so long. Make them believe it wasn't her fault. She never wanted to leave them. But another part of her, the treacherous part, longed for Baako and Dimitri. She couldn't just leave Enid and Prestarians behind to fight and die. She had to return, even if it meant leaving her family again, right?

"One thing at a time," she told herself as she ran from her room.

She stopped on the threshold of the kitchen. Her mom was at the stove in her pajamas, and her sisters were chatting at the kitchen table with their bedhead and long nightshirts. Little Hazel was ten, and Cassandra was fourteen, both excitedly talking about something on Cassandra's phone.

"Good morning, Nadia," her mother said.

"Mom," Nadia mouthed, running to her and embracing her. "I'm so sorry. I didn't mean to leave. I was taken. I mean, I woke up there, and this evil dude tried to kill me a lot."

"Honey, woah," Nadia's mother said. "What do you mean you left?"

"I've been gone for weeks."

Her sisters laughed.

"Bad dream, sis?" Cassandra asked.

"What? No." Nadia looked from face to face. "You thought I died. I saw it." Their smiles began to slip. "You were standing right here, holding my urn while I was stuck on Baako."

Nadia's mother reached for her. "You've been

home, sleeping in your room. You had school yesterday. You haven't been gone at all, let alone weeks. It was just a dream."

"A dream?" Nadia pulled away from her mother. "It couldn't be."

"Mom?" Cassandra asked. "Is she having one of those, uh, moments? You know," she dropped her voice. "Moment of mental crisis, the shrink talked about."

"No, no," their mother said. "You're not, right, Nadia?"

"Moment of crisis?" Nadia asked.

"You remember, hon," Nadia's mother said. "When your dreams seem like reality and reality seems like a dream. The psychologist called it a moment of paranoid psychosis. You're okay, though, right?"

Nadia stared at her open-mouthed, confusion scrambling through her head. *This is real, and Baako was real? Was Baako a dream? Dimitri, a dream?*

"Why don't you go and do what the psychologist suggests?" Nadia's mom reached for Nadia again. "You know, take a hot shower and feel every moment of it: the water, the soap, the shampoo. Then get dressed, and we can talk through your latest dream. If you hurry, breakfast will still be warm." Nadia's mom gently turned Nadia around and pushed her toward her room.

Walking slowly and numbly, Nadia stopped in the hall, leaning against the wall, taking deep, steady breaths. *It can't be fake. It wasn't a dream.*

"Mom, this is like the fourth time this happened," Cassandra said in the kitchen. "The shrink said she could get dangerous."

"Hush," their mother said. "She's harmless, but I'll give her the rescue meds with breakfast."

"Will that be enough?"

Nadia crossed to her bedroom before she could hear anything else. None of it made sense. She didn't have psychosis. Baako wasn't a dream. *It couldn't have been.*

She took her shower, running through all the reasons Baako was real. When she entered the kitchen again, she was clean and ready to talk. Nadia had to convince them she wasn't crazy, but how? Tell them the truth about her visit to Baako, or pretend the last few weeks were a crazy dream?

"You look nice and comfy," Nadia's mother said, gesturing to the large plate of food beside her. Cassandra and Hazel were outside playing. "I'm not sure it'll be cool enough for a sweatshirt.

Nadia glanced at her clothing. She wore her favorite blue jeans, t-shirt, tennis shoes, and sweatshirt. All of them had traveled with her to Baako and were either burned to nothing or ripped up.

"Oh my god." She took a shuddering breath. "It was a dream."

"Why don't you tell me about it?" her mom said.

"No, I think I'll just go lie down. I'm feeling a bit off." Nadia turned and ran from the kitchen, locking her bedroom door before throwing herself onto the bed. Her heart raced, and her breath came in gasps. She was on the edge of a panic attack. *Check-in,* she thought. *Arms: fine, great, no issues. Legs: good, no injuries, no lasting effects. Back: um, a little twinge, but good.*

That was evidence enough. She felt great. Every

part of her felt healthy, rested, and whole. "But I never told him I love him," Nadia said into her pillow. "I love him, and he wasn't real? No, he's real, just gone. I don't know." She gave in to her overwhelming emotions, allowing body-racking sobs to roll through her, using her pillows to muffle the agony spilling from her entire being.

Chapter
57

It was all so normal, so boring. Nadia woke to her irritating alarm, dressed, and attended her morning classes. She had forgotten about her English assignment, but her professor gave her an extension to turn it in. She headed to her tedious bank job from school for a five-hour shift. She got home after everyone else was getting ready for bed. She found a note on the counter from her mom about dinner in the microwave. Nadia tried to eat it, but it tasted so bland, so Earthly—nothing like the spectacular food on Baako.

She went to sleep and repeated the same routine for the rest of the week: school, work, a cold, bland dinner, and sleep. When Saturday came along, she woke to her sisters and mom waiting for her in the kitchen.

"Nadia," her mom started. "We want to talk with you."

"Yeah, you've been kind of a bummer all week," Cassandra said.

"Cassandra," Nadia's mother gently scolded. "What she means is we're worried you may be depressed."

"What?" Nadia asked. "You haven't even seen me all week."

"That's kind of the point," Hazel said. "You used to come upstairs and tell us about your day or dumb dad jokes or whatever."

"Yeah," Cassandra said. "You used to make it a point to see us off to school and try to pick us up whenever you had a chance."

"You haven't been eating either," their mother said. "Don't think I haven't noticed."

"First off," Nadia said. "I never used to do all that before I left for Baako. I mean, I picked you up from time to time, but my schedule has apparently changed. Second, and no offense, but your food is not awesome. It tastes like store-bought, bland Earth food. Dimitri used to make this amazing stew. It had these carrots—"

"Nadia!" Their mother snapped. "Stop it. That was a dream, and you're scaring your sister."

Hazel did look scared, but Cassandra looked mad. Nadia had no idea why. She hadn't done or said anything. She just lived each day until the next came, not bothering anyone.

"Baako or whatever you're calling your dream is not real," their mother said. "Dimitri's a fictitious man you invented to make yourself, I don't know, more important. It's part of the psychosis, the doctor said."

"I don't have psychosis." Nadia pushed back from the table. "I went there. It was real. This isn't. You aren't. You mourned my death. I died in your world. You just can't remember."

"I think I would remember mourning one of my children." Their mother rose from the table. "Nadia, I need you to take your medicine. It'll help, dear, and then we can talk."

"No, I'm fine," Nadia looked from face to face. They all looked startled. "I'm fine. I won't talk about it anymore. It's fine. I'm just going to lie back down. I'm fine, really."

"Nadia, wait." Their mother pushed a pill into her hand. "Please." Tears were in her mother's eyes.

"I'm fine." Nadia lost all conviction. Whenever her mother cried, Nadia would always break down too.

"Please," Nadia's mother said, handing her a glass of water.

Nadia popped the pill in her mouth and drank.

What felt like minutes later, she woke to her alarm going off. She was disoriented, sitting in the middle of the kitchen. Her hands and clothing were sticky, but the room was too dark to see. The smell, a smell she knew, coppery and dead. She stumbled to the light switch, gripping the wall long enough to allow her head to stop spinning. Slowly turning, she started screaming.

Her sister, Cassandra, was in pieces around where Nadia had woken. Bite marks and slashes all over her remaining flesh. Hazel's little body curled on the couch with apparent head wounds and defensive marks. Nadia stared, tears running down her face as Enid lay dead with an arrow wound. No, Hazel, with a head wound. Her little sack of a nightgown was soaked in blood. No, she wore shorts and a shirt. Nadia blinked and shook her head.

"Mom!" Nadia yelled. "Mom, please." She was relieved and heartbroken when she found Astrid on the other side of the island. Wait, no, Astrid isn't on Earth. It was her mother. Stabbed repeatedly. Nadia ran to the sink and threw up. Wiping her mouth on the back of her hand, she saw it.

Blood. Blood on her hands and her mouth. A bloody knife and baseball bat were near where she woke. She started to tremble as she reached for the phone.

"911, what's your emergency?" the voice on the line asked.

"I think I killed my family." Nadia dropped the phone and crossed to the front door. She sat on the front steps and waited.

Red and blue lights were blaring outside her home in seconds, and she was in the back of a squad car.

"You have the right to remain silent," the monk rattled off.

"You're dead." Nadia looked hard at the man.

"Are you threatening me?" the monk asked. No, the cop. In blue, with a badge.

"No." Tears fell down her face. "What's happening to me?"

"You're being arrested for the murder of your mother and sisters," the cop said, in his brown robe with the large orange eye on the front. "Pretty gruesome, too. How could someone your size… That's for homicide to figure out." The monk walked away in his blue cop outfit.

The days blurred, making Nadia lose all track of time. She was booked, cleaned, and put in a cell by herself, deemed too big a risk to be around others. She had a state-appointed lawyer, and due to the sensation of the murders, she would be tried immediately. Shuffling into the courtroom, she was shackled and dressed in orange. Dimitri sat behind the defendant's table, dressed in a suit and looking slightly disheveled.

"You're—" Nadia started.

"Late," he cut in. "I'm sorry about that." His smile faded as he looked her over. "You already found trouble, I see." He pointed at her shackles. "You should sit before you fall."

"But, this can't be real." Nadia sat beside her lawyer in his animal skin coat and pants.

"I assure you, it is. And we have a serious uphill climb in this case. But I'll do my best to protect you."

"That'll never happen," the prosecutor said. "You're out of your league with this case."

Nadia looked into the beautiful, smug face of Gaia in maiden form. "Wait, you're the prosecutor?"

The woman's face lost all its daunting beauty as she nodded. "Yes." She leaned into Nadia's face. "And I'm asking for the death penalty."

"But, you're his mom," Nadia said, rubbing her eyes.

"Is that some kind of joke?" the woman asked as the defense attorney chuckled.

"All rise," someone yelled, and Nadia was forced to her feet.

"You!" Nadia yelled. "You did all this?"

"Keep your client in check," Sergei said, dressed in all black. "Or I'll have her removed."

"You can't. This isn't real!"

"Please calm down," Dimitri said. No, the attorney said, no Dimitri.

Nadia shook her head, grabbing it with both hands. "Stop! Stop! STOP!"

"She can't use this to plead insanity," Gaia told Sergei. "She was tested and deemed competent."

"You aren't real," Nadia screamed at the woman. "He's doing this!" Nadia ran at Sergei. "Stop it!" Then she felt a lightning surge as a taser dug into her back.

"Get her out." The judge stood. Then he burst into laughter as the room faded. "I'm sorry, it was too good—her shaking and screaming. I couldn't keep character. Next time, I promise." Sergei was standing over Nadia's prone form. "What was that, dear?"

"I hate you." Nadia still trembled. Everything had been so real. Turning her hands over, she checked for blood, the blood of her family members. The smell of death clung to her. It was nothing like she had experienced in the Dreamworld before. "How'd you do it?"

"I bet you want to know." Sergei was grinning like an idiot.

"I asked, didn't I?" Nadia said, sitting up, pushing herself into a corner of the dungeon-like room.

"That's the little surprise I've been dying to introduce you to," Sergei said. "Behold, the nightmare creature." He paused for some dramatic effect, but nothing happened. "Do you get it? I'm the Dream Killer, but my little pet is the nightmare creature." He waited again. Nadia glanced around but saw and heard nothing. "Well, I think it's clever."

"Have you lost your mind?" Nadia was still unable to stand. Her muscles were cramping, and she was trembling. The dead faces of her sisters and mother kept floating in front of her eyes. She thought she had killed them. She knew she had killed them. She shuddered, and an involuntary noise of agony came out of her.

Sergei started to laugh again, but was interrupted by a soft knock on the door. "What could you possibly want?"

"The guardian's coming," the man at the door said. "Your mother saw him coming up the road."

"Is she ready?" Sergei asked.

"Yes," the man said.

"Good. Leave the Dreamworld," Sergei pushed the door closed. "And don't bother me while I'm working."

Nadia tried to reach out to her real body, but she couldn't feel it. She tried to think of Dimitri's face.

"Hello, Nadia," a voice said from within and around her. It made her skin crawl, and goosebumps covered her body. It felt like a void far too easy to fall into, a space between life and death, an impossible choice.

"Who?" Nadia started, all thoughts of anything else drained from her mind. "What was that?"

"My friend," Sergei said. "He's here to teach you what happens to stupid little girls that won't learn their place."

"I am not a tool for your amusement," the voice said throughout the space, and Sergei backed into the door.

Nadia would've laughed if the voice hadn't filled her with such dread.

Sergei didn't control whatever monster he was hiding.

"Nadia of Earth and Baako," the voice said. "If you are prepared, we will begin."

58

Dimitri had been running since leaving Enid in the village inn. He had paid for a week, left her with all his gear and food, and promised to return. When he had handed her all of his money and a simple, drawn map of where the guardian training camp was, he knew from the look on her face and the tears in her eyes, she was terrified he was abandoning her.

"What if Althea was lying?" Enid had asked for the fifth time.

"I asked around," Dimitri had told her. "The innkeeper confirmed her story, though he had no idea what the house was used for. He said a girl and her very sick sister had passed through here only a day ago. I have to go get Nadia. If I'm not back in a week and the Prestarians don't arrive, go here." He had pointed at the map. "They'll take care of you and will want to know where the house is."

"But I can't—"

"Enid, I'm counting on you." He had given her a quick squeeze as someone knocked on the door. Dimitri had pushed Enid behind him before opening it.

"Sorry to bother you, sir," the innkeeper's wife had said. "Althea, your friend, had this commissioned while she was here and asked that it be delivered to you when it was finished."

"What is it?"

"She said it would help her sick sister."

Dimitri had stared at the tiny bottle in shock. "Thank you."

"Also, sir, we've a bath for the little one and a hot meal on its way."

"Thank you. I am expecting some friends in a day or two. They'll take charge of Enid. Until then, I am trusting you and your husband with her and anything that she may need. I already commissioned some clothing that should be delivered later today. Please treat her like a daughter, or I'll know why."

"Understood, sir," the innkeeper's wife had said. "We wish you good travels, and we'll watch the little one."

Enid could defend herself with her gift, but he trusted the innkeeper and his wife to care for her.

His thoughts were interrupted when the house came into view. He had been seen and didn't care. Speed, not stealth, was his goal. Nadia was quickly running out of time, and he had the antidote in his pocket.

An older woman was sitting at a small table with two chairs, tea, and cookies, waving to him as he walked up.

"Hello there." She had a grandmotherly smile. "What brings you to my home?"

"Hi, ma'am." Dimitri bowed, not removing his eyes from her. "I do not mean to interrupt your afternoon tea, but I am looking for two women who may have passed by here in the last day. One is very sick and I need to get to her before she dies."

"Two women, you say." The woman leaned back before shaking her head. "No, I do not think, yeah, I don't remember two women."

Dimitri saw she was lying, but kept his expression neutral.

"But if you want to sit with me for a few minutes, I can ask the staff to see if they saw anyone."

"I don't have the time." Dimitri walked toward the woman.

"I must insist." Her smile slipped. "I mean, you look dead on your feet. Please sit. One cup and a cookie, and you can be on your way."

Dimitri sat with no intention of drinking or eating anything. He took in his surroundings, trying to figure out a way in and out of the giant house. He counted the windows on the three-story home, calculating potential size.

"You have a lovely home," Dimitri said as the woman poured him a glass of steaming tea. "Do you manage this place on your own?"

"Oh no." She held up the cookie plate, and Dimitri took one, setting it by his glass. "My son is here with me." She paused. "Eat, dear. Those cookies are my favorite."

Dimitri brought the cookie to his mouth, taking a deep, subtle breath before shoving the whole cookie into his mouth. He took another one before swallowing the first. Took a large sip of tea. "The grounds are huge." He gestured. "How far back does your property go?"

The woman turned in her seat, and Dimitri shifted both the new cookie and the one he pretended to eat into one hand before dumping as much of the tea as he could onto the soft treats, soaking them.

"Yes, it is a lot." She looked out. "But we do have a household staff that works hard to keep it beautiful."

Dimitri chucked the cookies into the nearby bushes,

set down his mostly empty tea glass a little louder than he intended. "Sorry." He swayed gently in his chair. "I am suddenly quite tired and a little dizzy."

"Maybe some water will help?" The woman rang a small bell, and Dimitri slipped from his chair.

"This doesn't feel normal." He looked at the older woman. "Did you…" He allowed his words to slur.

"Guardians are so stupid," the woman said with a vicious smile. "But now my son has two he can play with."

"Another guardian?"

"You don't know?" She laughed. "Your brother has been our guest for quite some time now."

Shock broke through Dimitri's facade. "What?"

"My son is going to love this! He always wondered why you didn't come sooner. But you never knew. How great!"

"Why are you doing this?" Dimitri asked, remembering to act drugged as he fell forward onto his stomach. *She's lying. She has to be.*

The woman rolled him over onto his back. "Because you're in the way." A large man opened the front door as she was speaking. "Take this idiot and throw him into the front room with Sergei's little spy. I'm sure that'll be a fun reunion." She laughed through her teeth like a snake. "Oh, and your little girlfriend is probably already dead. If she isn't, she'll be soon. No one survives him."

Chapter
59

"Ready to begin what?" Nadia asked the bodiless voice Sergei seemed to keep as a pet.

"Oh goody," Sergei said.

"Deep breath," the voice said, then claws were digging into Nadia's head.

She screamed. Her head felt like it ripped open from temple to temple. She could feel spiky tendrils moving through her mind like it was a filing cabinet. Searching one memory and then another. Oily fingers left stains on her life as it flipped through the last few weeks, then months, then years.

"Stop!" The pain receded until she only had a slight pounding behind her eyes.

"What just happened?" Sergei was clearly angry. "You didn't finish your task."

"She pushed me out," the voice said with no change in inflection.

"Pushed you out? How's that possible? You're the freaking Nightmare Creature. Grab onto a memory and turn it into a painful adventure!"

"Or what?" the formless voice said. No inflection was needed to hear the warning.

Nadia flinched slightly, but Sergei cowered.

"You're right," Sergei bowed.

Another knock on the door.

"Sir," the man said. "You need to come."

"I'm busy in here."

"Sir," the man trembled. "It's important that you come now."

Nadia gasped. The room faded in and out. She couldn't take a deep breath.

Sergei looked at her and back at the man. "I'm coming."

"We will meet again, Nadia," the voice said.

Not if I die first. She finally felt her body as it struggled to take a breath. Everything went black in both worlds.

Chapter
60

"Dimitri, damn it, I told that girl to tell you not to eat the food," Althea said the moment Dimitri was tossed like a rag doll onto the floor and the door was shut.

He immediately sprang to life, slamming Althea against the wall and pinning her with his forearm to her throat. "My brother's in the Dreamworld?"

Althea nodded awkwardly as tears sprang to her eyes.

Dimitri felt nothing but loathing toward her. "How long?"

She said nothing.

He pressed harder, shaking her slightly. "How long?"

"Two years."

"And. You. Never. Told. Me?"

"He would've killed him."

"Nadia's dying because of you. Why shouldn't I crush your throat right now?" Dimitri was shaking with rage.

"I," Althea tried to choke out past Dimitri's forearm. "I was trying to save Godric." Dimitri pulled his arm back a little so she could talk more clearly. "Two years ago, we were ambushed, and Godric was taken. I either worked for the weaselly little psychopath, or Godric would be killed. I had no choice."

"There's always a choice!"

"Shhh. They'll hear you."

"Where is she?"

"I don't know."

Dimitri pressed on her throat again.

"I mean it," she struggled out. "The deal was to bring her here. She was supposed to be given to someone else, but now he wants her dead."

Dimitri punched the wall right next to Althea's head.

Althea turned away from his fist. "I'm so sorry. He's going to kill them both."

"If he does, you'll be next. How do we get out of this room? I have to get the antidote to Nadia. At least, I am assuming that is what this is."

"The innkeeper gave it to you?" Althea rubbed her throat the moment Dimitri released her.

Dimitri nodded.

"Then yes. I had it made for you."

"Where is Nadia being held?"

"I don't know. Her mind was in the Dreamworld and they may have moved her, so I'm not sure."

Dimitri's rage ignited again as he looked at the woman he had hated for many years. "In the Dreamworld because of you." Dimitri's voice was quiet and even, but a small amount of joy flashed in his eyes as he watched Althea shrink away from him. "It doesn't matter right now. Nadia's all that matters. How long does she have?"

Althea crossed to the door without looking at Dimitri or saying anything.

"How long, Althea?"

"Honestly, the knife cut and the power she used

should've brought her down. The arrow strike should've made her comatose a day ago and dead soon after."

"If she's dead—"

"When she got here, she was alive and fighting."

The door swung open suddenly.

An enormous man stood in the doorway.

Dimitri reached for his gift, crouching low, but struggled to feel it fully.

Althea grabbed his arm. "Wait."

Dimitri looked at the sweat on her brow and the blank look in the man's eyes. "Your gift?"

She nodded. "There are magical guards on the building, but they've not been refreshed for weeks. I've been trying to use my gifts for hours. I don't know where she is, but he does. Our cover is that he was asked to move the prisoners. So you lead, and he'll shove you around if anyone is coming.

The man grabbed Dimitri, shoving him out the door.

"Hey," Dimitri said low and pissed.

"Sorry." Althea had a smile clear in her voice. "He got overzealous. Nadia's unguarded because this idiot is her guard."

Dimitri tried to keep his face neutral and allow the giant of a man to push him around, but they saw no one in the halls. Entering the room, Dimitri could see how pale Nadia was, and his stomach dropped. "Nadia?" She was cold when he pulled her into his arms. He sat on the bed to balance her weight while pulling the stopper out of the tiny antidote bottle with his teeth. He leaned her head back and dumped the liquid into her mouth, and waited.

Nothing happened.

"Nadia?" Dimitri held her face with one hand. "Please, Nadia. Please." His voice broke as his heart shattered. *She's dead*, the logical side of his mind said, but his voice kept saying, "No, please, no. No. Wake up, Nadia. No, please, no."

"I'm so sorry." Althea was still near the open door. "Your brother, I had no choice."

"There's always a choice, my dear," Sergei said, pushing the guard aside. "You chose to kill this girl, and now I choose to kill your guardian."

Althea launched herself at Sergei but was stopped by the guard she had been controlling. Dimitri watched as he picked her up and threw her across the room. He felt nothing as she slammed into the wall, slid down, and began weeping.

"You failed, guardian." Sergei turned to Dimitri. "You killed your charge with your idiocy and lack of experience. Then walked right into my open arms so I could kill you and your brother simultaneously, like my moron soldiers should've all those years ago. Mommy dearest will be so happy."

Dimitri looked at Sergei through his tear-filled eyes. He felt like he was unraveling, unmooring from his own body while being held together by a thin layer of skin. He thought he would explode with grief and hopelessness. *I did this.* He gently pulled Nadia to his chest, unwilling to let her go. *I failed.*

"You're a monster," Althea said from the floor.

"No, you are," Sergei said. "You killed this girl and still failed to get your love out of my grasp." He took a deep breath. "But to prove I'm not the monster here, I'll give the guardian a few moments to mourn his charge while I figure out where to burn the body. Be back in a couple of minutes, dearies." He left, shutting the door behind him. They heard him screaming at the guard for a minute before stomping down the hall.

"I'm so sorry, Dimitri. I wouldn't blame you if you did kill me."

Dimitri hadn't realized he had started rocking Nadia in his arms. Tears spilled freely down his cheeks and onto her pale, still face. He wiped them away and buried his face in her tangled hair. "Please, Nadia." He took her hand, remembering all the times the small gesture brought him solace and comfort. Her hand dwarfed in his, her small fingers lacing through his larger ones. He froze.

"I love you," a rasping voice said, and Dimitri's breath caught. "I didn't tell you before, and I should have." Dimitri sat up so quickly, he jarred Nadia's body and pulled their hands apart.

Her eyes were open, and she had a slight smile on her lips.

"You're alive!" He kissed her. Relief washed through him as he felt her warm lips. His desperation drove his need to touch her, taste her mouth again. He wrapped his hand through her messy hair as he pressed their bodies together. He held her tight, even as he leaned back to make sure he wasn't dreaming. Her skin was flushed. "You're so beautiful," he whispered as he kissed her again, more gently, relief and love flooding his body.

Chapter

61

"Enough kissy face," Max said with a clear ick in his voice. "How do we get out of here without getting you killed again?"

Nadia smiled and pulled away from Dimitri. "I'm alive. No idea how, but I am." Dimitri leaned in to kiss her again, but she reluctantly stopped him. "We have to find a way to rescue your brother and get out of this place, and I think I have an idea. Max, can you keep watch for a minute?"

"You got it, boss," Max fell into a sweeping bow before shooting from the room.

"Dimitri," Nadia said. "For this to work, you have to leave me here. Convince them I'm still dead. Convince Sergei specifically, and I think he'll bring you to Godric's body."

"You've seen it?" Althea asked.

"Not his body. I met Godric in the Dreamworld a couple of times."

"You met him?" Dimitri asked, still holding Nadia.

"Yes, and I'll tell you all about it when we get out of here." Nadia gently pushed Dimitri's chest to help herself sit up. *Arms. Surprisingly alright. My hand hurts.* She glanced at Althea, then pointedly looked at her wrapped hand, flexing it gently.

"Are you okay? Physically?" Dimitri asked.

Legs. Good actually. Sleep, even evil Dreamworld

sleep, helps. "Yeah, I think so." Then her family's dead faces flashed in her mind, and she gasped.

"What?" Dimitri asked, reaching for her. "What is it? Where do you hurt?"

"I don't." Focusing on his beautiful face, she placed a hand over his heart, knowing the steady beats would calm her. "I'll explain more later. Now, I need to die again, and you need to convince them that I am."

"I'm not leaving you here," Dimitri grabbed her hands. "I just got you back."

"You have to. I'll have Max, and I feel pretty good. Nothing like dying again to cleanse the system."

Dimitri searched her face, not smiling at her morbid joke. "There has to be another way."

"If you come up with one in the next minute, let me know," Nadia said. "Althea, I owe you a beating or two, but I need you to play along."

Althea nodded from the floor, "Anything to save Godric."

"Yeah," Nadia filled her voice with as much sarcasm as she could. "I know, literally anything or anyone."

"They're coming," Max said, sticking his face back in the room. "The short, fat guy and two big guys. They're huge."

"Sergei's on his way back with two huge henchmen," Nadia said. "Don't fight them unless you absolutely have to. If they're as big as they appear in the Dreamworld, they pack a punch."

"I hate this," Dimitri said. "I don't even know your part of the plan."

"I hate this, too, but it has to happen." Nadia grabbed Dimitri, pulling him close and kissing him one more time just in case. "Remember, I'm dead."

As the door opened, she was limp again, trying hard not to breathe while Dimitri was draped over her body on the bed.

"Stay alive," Dimitri whispered. "I love you," he said louder.

"Ah, that's heartbreaking, if I had a heart to break." Sergei laughed. "Times up. She goes to the fire, but first, you two reunite with a long lost brother and lover." Sergei made a kissing noise. "Get them."

There was a scuffle before Nadia's body was shoved out of Dimitri's arms so hard she almost rolled off the small bed.

Dimitri must've fought back a little because Sergei laughed when he left, saying, "Stupid guardians. You never know when to call it quits."

Then silence.

"They're gone," Max whispered.

"Why are you whispering?" Nadia whispered back. "No one can hear you but me."

"You're not wrong. But pretending they can makes it all more exciting."

"Okay," Nadia smiled. "Then we whisper and tiptoe."

"We also try to keep you alive, while I save the day as usual."

"Can you find where Dimitri was taken and check the halls?" Nadia asked after she carefully stood up for the first time in a few days. She was glad her body was willing, and she wasn't stiff.

"Yeah," Max said. "What are you going to do?"

"Light this place on fire."

"Wait, really?" A grin spread across Max's ghostly face.

"Yep. The only way to cleanse evil is to burn it. Meet me back here in a few?"

Max nodded before passing through the door.

Nadia turned to the bed she had been lying on and lit her hand on fire, pressing it to the sheets. "Eat slowly," she said before releasing the flame to devour everything in the room. "Don't eat anything innocent of this place and burn with as little smoke as possible." She hoped the fire understood.

Max floated back in moments later. "That squat, old guy is so loud, it was easy to find them. They're two floors below us. There's another guy's body in there, and Althea is whining in a really annoying way, tears and all."

"Was anyone in the hall?"

"Nope."

"Great," Nadia opened the door and shut it, hiding the fire until it burned through the room. "I need to get close to them, then jump into the Dreamworld."

"You're going back in?"

"I have to."

When they reached the bottom of the second staircase, Max asked, "Is this a good idea?"

"Probably not," Nadia cringed, thinking about facing the nightmare creature again. "But I have to release Godric." She sat down against an alcove wall near the stairs before allowing the Dreamworld's pull to yank her in. "Godric?" Nadia whispered, hoping he had not been moved.

"Nadia?" Godric looked absolutely destroyed—bruises, cuts, and so, so thin.

"Yes, and today you're leaving with me whether you want to or not." Nadia reached for his arm.

"You know I can't." Godric stood just out of reach.

"Dimitri and Althea are with your body right now."

"What? No. How?"

"No time to explain." Nadia was finally able to grab his arm. "When you wake, don't move, don't react, and try to breathe as normally as you can. They're not alone, but they will be."

"I don't understand."

"You don't need to." Nadia took both of his hands.

"Wait," Godric started, but Nadia had already begun to jump. She released Godric and jumped into the nightmare creature's room. It was almost too easy to do both. She was just learning how to master this place and had a little twinge of regret in her plan to destroy it. Then she remembered Godric's beaten body and knew it had to go.

"I told you we would meet again," it said. "I did not

think it would be so soon, though."

"Are you a captive?" Nadia asked.

There was ringing silence, and Nadia felt an oily tendril reach for her mind.

"No," She mentally slammed it away. "Don't do that. I'm trying to help both of us and my friends. Are you a captive?"

Another ringing silence, and then the creature said, "Yes."

"Great." Fear ran through her. "Do you have a physical form?"

"No. I use the form of others."

"Wait, like possession?"

"Something like that," the creature said.

"Yikes. Can you hold Sergei in here?"

"Not for long."

"Hold him for as long as you can, and I'll be back."

The door of the dungeon room flew open, and Sergei stood flanked by two giant men. He smiled, and Nadia smiled back.

"You're alive?" he asked, not looking surprised. "So many tricks."

"You're gonna love the next one." Nadia popped out of the Dreamworld.

"Here," Max yelled from down the hall. "They're in here."

Nadia ran to the locked door. Grabbing the doorknob, she cranked her fire element up to a ten, melting the entire mechanism off the door.

"Time to go," she said to the stunned room. "Godric, you up for an escape?"

"Godric isn't," Althea started.

"I am." Godric sat up slowly. He looked just as awful in the real world as in the Dreamworld.

"Are you sure you're up for this, brother?" Dimitri took one of Godric's elbows to help steady him.

Althea's shock melted from her face before she threw herself at Godric.

"Uff." Godric gave a small laugh. "Careful. I'm a little beaten up."

Nadia interrupted the moment. "Dimitri, I need you to carry me."

"Are you hurt?" Dimitri asked.

"No, not at all. I just need to keep Sergei busy in the Dreamworld."

"You can't go back," Dimitri started to argue.

"I can, and must. I'll be fine."

"I'd listen to her," Godric said. "I've seen her in action in the Dreamworld. Plus, she has that look. You know?"

"Yeah," Dimitri frowned. "I do."

He scooped her up, and Nadia immediately jumped back into the Nightmare Creature's room, landing in front of a frozen Sergei. "Let go!"

Sergei blinked, and Nadia punched him in the face before jumping to the hallway outside the room. She landed between the two men who were flanking Sergei and ran with both in hot pursuit. She took stock of her energy and how many times she could jump again. She felt okay. Two of three solid jumps before she got tired. Five or six before she passed out.

Keep distracting and get a little revenge.

She jumped back to the hall outside the creature's room, appearing in front of Sergei. He flinched, throwing his arms up. Kneeing him squarely in the crotch, Nadia smiled widely until Sergei pulled her down as he fell forward. She ripped at his depleted hair, kicking wildly to escape him. Once untangled, they both stood up, panting. Nadia swung at his face and jabbed at his throat, but neither made contact. He was moving in weird twitches. She swung again and again, hitting nothing but air. Winded from the effort, her breath came in short gasps.

"Too slow, Nadia," Sergei's voice sounded pinched, but victorious. He punched her solidly across the cheek, causing Nadia's head to fly sideways and her mind to jump, but only partially.

She was seeing both Dimitri's tight jawline and Sergei's pudgy face, straddling both worlds.

"Uh oh," Sergei said. "Is someone losing their grasp on my world?" He shoved her, smashing her head against the Dreamworld wall.

Chapter

63

Nadia completely popped out of the Dreamworld with a jolt.

Her head throbbed and swam as Dimitri set her on her feet.

"Are you okay?" He asked.

"Yeah." Nadia rubbed the back of her head. "I think so."

"Did you start the fire?" Dimitri asked.

"Fire?" Nadia looked around the large room. Flames were creeping up one wall, devouring every ugly piece of tapestry and ancient wallpaper. "Oh yeah, that was me."

"Nice touch," Dimitri half smiled. "But now what?"

"We fight," Godric said.

A handful of large guards and a dozen or so soldiers were blocking their way out of the house.

"I'm up for it." Althea took Godric's hand. "I would love to lay waste to this place."

Nadia could see Althea's love for Godric every time they looked at each other, but Nadia still didn't trust Althea and never would.

A hysterical scream ripped through the large room, drawing everyone's attention. Sergei, disheveled and manic, ran in.

"What have you done, you, you raging… you piece of… you horrible girl!" He moved further into the room even as the fire pulled down large sections of the house behind him.

Nadia smiled broadly.

"He seems mad." Max appeared next to Nadia. "Do you think it was your redecorating that upset him?" He laughed loudly.

"I told you I'd kill you." Sergei walked toward her, flanked by his two giant bodyguards.

"I remember." Nadia still grinned.

"Don't interrupt!" Sergei jumped up and down, throwing a toddler-style fit.

"Is he always like this?" Dimitri asked.

"Most of the time," Nadia said. "To be honest, this is him being pleasant."

"Do we need to be concerned about the fire?" Godric asked.

"Yes." Nadia watched the fire eat its way across the ceiling. "I've never tried to stop a fire, and this one is burning through this horrible place really quickly. We should probably go sooner than later."

"Don't let them leave! Kill them all! But leave me her." Sergei pointed his pudgy finger at Nadia.

"I'm flattered," she said as the room erupted into movement and noise.

Dimitri stood next to Nadia, watching a handful of soldiers go after Althea and Godric while Sergei's other men stalked toward Dimitri and Nadia. The remaining men guarded the large front door, many holding large swords or small crossbows.

"How are your gifts?" Dimitri asked. "Are you good to fight?"

"I am." Nadia rolled a small fireball between the fingers of her right hand.

"I have to shift, so I won't—"

"Fight like I'm not here, or you'll get yourself killed. I can take this overgrown man-child."

Dimitri touched her face before dropping into his panther form and jumping into the fray.

Nadia watched him briefly before turning her attention back to the villain who had stolen her dreams and tortured her for weeks.

Sergei's fists were clenched so hard his knuckles were white, and his face drooped in a scowl.

"So you're going to fight me in the real world?" Nadia was genuinely surprised. "You couldn't even fight me in your made-up psycholand where I had no real gifts."

"Your cockiness'll be your undoing."

"Actually," Nadia lit both of her hands. "My cockiness may be well earned, but let's play and find out."

"Go get her, fools." Both Sergei's henchmen slowly walk toward Nadia, armed with large swords.

"Still too much of a chicken to fight me yourself, I see."

Nadia moved with the men, her fear growing as she frantically tried to remember how to throw wind. She dodged the first lunging man, but only missed the second sword by dropping onto her back. One lumbering giant swung his sword at her head, causing her to roll as fast and far as she could. The man followed, hacking at her, chipping the ground closer and closer to her head. When she hit the far wall, she was panting with fear and effort. She scrambled up, but it was too late.

The man raised his sword to finish her.

The need Nadia recognized as her gifts pushed her to defend herself by any means necessary. She threw fire into the man's face, aiming for his eyes.

He yelped, dropping the sword to protect his now blistered face, a look of pure hate washing over his features. He reached for her neck, and her wind lifted off his feet, throwing him right into the sword of the second man. Both men smashed onto the ground, the blade sticking out of the thrown man's chest.

Nadia watched in horror. She never intended to kill him. She had never meant to kill anyone.

The smashed man was unconscious even as the man with the sword through his chest fought to get the blade out. He grabbed it with both hands and tried to tug it, never looking at Nadia as he cut and recut his hands, trying in vain to remove the weapon that had already killed him.

When his body finally gave out, Nadia had tears in her eyes. Logically, she knew he would have killed her, but…

"I guess it wasn't your cockiness," Sergei said behind her. "It's your pointless empathy that's your undoing."

Nadia glanced over her shoulder at the sword held above Sergei's head. Mind blank as she stared into the victorious face of the short, sadistic man.

"I win." Sergei pulled the sword back clumsily.

Nadia's empathy broke.

Memories of how Sergei had tortured her for amusement deafened his screams when she started punching him in the chest with flaming fists. She heard every insult, felt every touch, bruise, broken bone, smell of his breath, and saw her own blood caked in her hair as she punched him in the face, head, throat, body. She hit over and over for the images of her dead family, the death of the monks, the capture and torture of the Prestarians, Dimitri's village, and all of her haunted nightmares. She just kept hitting him.

Chapter

64

"Nadia?" Dimitri broke through her rage.

She stood over a semi-conscious, bloody Sergei. He was weeping softly as he clutched his head.

"Nadia," Dimitri touched her blood-splattered arm. "He won't hurt you anymore."

Nadia was panting. Her chest was tight with unspent tears at all she had endured. She looked down on the man who wanted her dead and saw nothing but a broken little boy trapped in a worthless man's body.

"He won't hurt anyone anymore."

"Are you sure?" She asked Dimitri as tears cleansed her face of Sergei's blood.

"We need to go." Dimitri pointed as the fire brought down part of the far entrance.

"You're coming too," Nadia told Sergei as he tried to sit up. "The people you tormented can decide your fate."

A woman in her mid-to-late sixties, with a well-fed look about her, ran from the smoke-filled hallway, screaming, "No! He's our son," at another older man.

The man looked familiar, with shabby gray robes and wrinkled hands. He had been in the torture chamber during her first visit and had just sat there.

"That, that boy," the shabby man turned to Sergei's mother, his face contorted with rage. "Is an abomination and no son of mine. He did this." The man gestured wildly around, his wrinkled hands opening and closing. "His stupid games and ludicrous followers burned my family home and destroyed my Dreamworld. He had one job." He pointed at Nadia. "And couldn't accomplish that. Failures do not exist in my family."

Dimitri pulled Sergei to his feet, keeping Sergei in front of him. "Nadia, we have to go. The whole place is going to crumble."

The flames burned everything in sight. The heat didn't bother Nadia, but she felt it in her chest whenever something large fell in the room. Even surrounded by danger, she couldn't look away from the shabby man and woman who birthed a monster.

"What are you going to do?" Sergei's mother screamed, lunging for the man.

"What I should've done years ago," the man said.

"No!" Sergei's mother pulled out a dagger and tried to stab the man. The move was clumsy and put her off balance.

The man grabbed her dagger hand, twisted it, and stabbed Sergei's mother in the chest so fast Nadia didn't have time to react before the knife was removed and thrown in her direction.

As if in slow motion, she watched it fly past her and stick firmly in Sergei's chest as Dimitri held him up. Despite the noise of the fire and fighting all around them, she heard the thump of the dagger finding its mark. Dimitri immediately released Sergei and ran past Nadia toward the shabby man. But Nadia was frozen, watching the man who created and occupied her nightmares look down at his bleeding chest, before dropping to his pudgy knees, and falling forward onto the knife. She watched as blood began to pool around his partially propped-up body, and the color faded from his usually over-red face.

Her nightmare was over. Sergei was dead, but only numbness spread through Nadia.

Then the ground bulged and exploded into the room, throwing everyone several feet. She felt her small connection to the Dreamworld shatter as "thank you" reverberated through her body. She could feel the ground heave again and knew a much larger explosion was coming.

"Dimitri!" She screamed. "Dimitri, the house is going to explode. Dimitri!"

A hand shot out of the smoke, wrapping tightly around her arm. She lit her arms on fire.

"It's me. It's only me." Dimitri had a cut over his eye and was covered in ash and dirt. "We have to go."

"Althea? Godric?"

"The first explosion sent everyone else running." Dimitri grabbed her hand and started running toward the exit. His hand tightened as the ground began to shake.

"We will meet again, Nadia of Earth and Baako," the voice Nadia only knew as the Nightmare creature said before both Nadia and Dimitri were launched off their feet as the house exploded. They hit the softer ground outside the house causing the breath to fly from Nadia momentarily.

"What happened?" Godric dragged Dimitri away from the house as it began to fall in on itself, crumbling deep into the dungeons of the second basement.

Nadia didn't scramble back. She just watched the house disappear in smoke and flame. "My fire didn't do that," she said to no one. *I hope no innocent was still in there.*

"Then what did?" Dimitri helped Nadia stand.

"The nightmare creature." She continued watching the house burn.

"He's out?" Godric asked, horror on his face.

"Yes," Nadia said. "An older man in gray robes killed Sergei, and the first explosion happened moments later. I heard it."

"The explosion?" Dimitri asked.

"No," Nadia shook her head slowly. "The creature. Then the second explosion happened, and it said it would see me again. What is it?"

"Something unimaginable," Dimitri said.

"Something made of pure evil," said Godric. "Sergei was bad, but the nightmare creature makes Sergei look like a saint. That's why the monks followed it and died for it. Pure power and pure evil."

"Wait, the monks follow that thing?" Nadia asked.

"Yes," Godric and Althea said at the same time.

"Nadia!" A scream of joy and happiness ripped through the air. "Nadia, you're okay!" Enid was running down the open road, followed by Astrid and Braiden. They were all grins. Enid slammed into Nadia without stopping, knocking them both into Dimitri before they all fell to the ground.

"Why are you crying, sweetling?" Nadia asked as Enid sobbed into her. Enid was clean and well-dressed in a soft fabric shirt and pants. Nadia was amazed at how adorable she was under all the dirt and pain.

"I thought you were," Enid started through her little

sobs. "You saved me, and I couldn't, I mean, I don't ever want to be left again." She glared at Dimitri through puffy, wet eyes. "Never again. Got it, Big Guy!"

"Okay, okay." Dimitri was half lying on the ground. He put up both hands in surrender. "You win."

"You can stay with us for as long as you want," Nadia said into Enid's hair as she gripped the little girl. "But I must warn you, I'm clumsy and constantly finding trouble everywhere."

"That just sounds like adventures to me," Enid said.

"Me too," Max said. "Where to next?"

To be continued in

Of Traitors and Roots

Be the first to hear about upcoming books,
events, and more!

Acknowledgements

I feel truly blessed to have such a fantastic group of women who have had my back through all the ups and downs of being a writer. I would be remiss if I didn't start with my mother. She raised me to be strong, but always answers the phone (even if it is three or four times a day) when I need to chat, vent, or cry it out. She has also been my most significant and loudest supporter.

My youngest sister, Amy, has had the pleasure or displeasure of reading every version of my book even before I had any idea how to actually write. She hates talking on the phone, never watches my reels, and answers texts in 1-2 business days. But I know she would go to war for me.

My younger sister, Amanda, has not been subject to reading my book at every step, but has inspired me regardless. She's living the dream with her three beautiful kids and all their insane sports and events. She has a gorgeous house that she has made a home (and redesigns said home quite a bit).

Both of my sisters work in the medical field and would be my first pick if we were to face a zombie apocalypse. There would be a lot of screaming, panic, and possibly dying, but it would be so entertaining until then. Come on, sisters, we could still be a hilarious ghost-hunting crew!

Writing is often a hard and solitary craft, so you need to surround yourself with a community of other brilliant writers. I found my community while getting my MFA at the University of Nebraska, Omaha. AD Uhlar, Kristin Ganoung, and Tachney Perry have put up with my shenanigans for a few years now, and it was absolutely time well spent. They are so generous with their time and critiques. We all genuinely want each other to succeed. Sometimes that means tough love and ego-busting critiques, but both are critical in raising each other up. Despite living so far apart, we laugh and share in each other's lives.

Speaking of UNOmaha's MFA program, do it! If you are considering doing this writing thing as full-time as possible, but have a career, a family, or just can't stop your life to start an MFA program, consider a low-residency program. The experience was incredible, even though most of it was during COVID. Mentors like Kevin Clouther, Jessica Hendry Nelson, Patricia Lear, and so many more made the experience one of a kind.

I never called myself a writer despite having written for years. Then I went through the UNOmaha program, learned everything I didn't know, tightened my craft, and created worlds every semester. I got feedback from authors, mentors, and fellow students, which taught me to take criticism and choose what I wanted to use and disregard. I met lifelong friends and spent ten days every summer and winter surrounded by the energy of writers at all levels of learning and success!

This thing we call writing is filled with challenges, but the adventures, joys, creations, and accomplishments win out! Everyone should write and read. All good writers do read a lot, and all good readers are here to support writers! Without the support of other readers and writers, I would not be part of the tiny percentage of people who start a novel and see it through to publishing!

THANK YOU!

About the Author

Patti E. Jones is a writer, designer, traveler, and observer. She still believes in magic, chooses joy, loves to laugh, and adores her fur babies. She collects degrees like others collect art. She has an MA in English and a second MA in Communication from Arizona State University. She also has an MFA in Creative Writing from the University of Nebraska, Omaha, and is pursuing a PhD in English with a Literary and Cultural emphasis from Old Dominion University starting in the fall of 2025.

She has taught English for higher education since 2021 and volunteers at the local library to teach creative writing. She encourages everyone to pursue a craft like art, writing, dance, and anything else that makes their heart sing. She has also created an artist and writer conference and a creative arts literary magazine, both of which can be seen on her website at writingwithfurbabies.com.

She has traveled to a dozen countries and most of the United States, but she currently lives and has adventures in the Pacific Northwest. She intends to keep traveling with her co-pilot fur babies and devour all the audiobooks as she zigzags across the country.

Her classroom is filled with laughter, snacks, and encouragement, because she believes no one is a bad writer. Most people only think they are bad at writing because someone told them that, crushing their confidence. The more you write, the better the writing. If you believe you're bad, then you are right. So make mistakes, do the work, laugh at yourself, but keep writing and believing in yourselves!